MAGIC WORDS

Julius Meyer and Standing Bear in an undated photograph.

MAGIC WORDS

GERALD KOLPAN

PEGASUS BOOKS
NEW YORK

MAGIC WORDS

Pegasus Books LLC
80 Broad Street, 5th Floor
New York, NY 10004

Copyright © 2012 Gerald Kolpan

First Pegasus Books edition 2012

Interior design by Maria Fernandez

Photograph of Julius Meyer and Standing Bear courtesy of the Douglas County
(Nebraska) Historical Society

Library of Congress Cataloging-in-Publication Data is available.

ISBN: 978-1-60598-369-1

10 9 8 7 6 5 4 3 2 1

Printed in the United States of America
Distributed by W. W. Norton & Company

For Kate and Ned

R YLAND NORCROSS KNEW THAT IF HE WAS LATE AGAIN FOR the midday meal, his father would have his hide.

The week before, he had been tardy due to a post-school game of mumblety-peg and Daddy had taken a stick to him. It was a half-hearted beating; performed mostly for the benefit of his mother, who held all family gatherings to be sacred, particularly the noon meal. "A chicken," she always said, "is an impatient bird. She gets angry if you keep her waiting, especially if I've dressed her up."

As Ryland flew through Hanscom Park he calculated the interval between the first toll of the bell at the Third Congregationalist Church and the sound of his initial footstep on his front steps. He shuddered at the sum.

The boy poured it on. He jumped to the seat of a bench, clambered over the top of its backrest and landed hard on the park's cinder path. He cut across lawns and swung around trees and raced through the central gazebo where, a mere ten days before, he had heard the great Sousa band. Through a stand of dogwood only just begun to bud, he could see the twin gables of Jimmy Withers's house and his own chimney well beyond it. His only hope now was that the oven had been slow on the biscuits, or his father's late arrival due to a transaction at the feed store or a chance encounter with a crony.

The Third Congregationalist had reached its fifth peal as Ryland's right foot caught something too soft for stone, but too hard for earth. He fell to the ground midway between where the ashes of the path met the scissored edge of the greensward. His shoulder hit first, then his left hand. The impact knocked out most of his wind.

The sight of a staring brown eye, open and dead level with his own, took the rest.

Ryland scrambled to his feet and doubled over, fighting for breath. He knew this eye and the body to which it belonged. He had seen them nearly every day of his twelve years.

In life, they had belonged to a man who sold his family their piano and had seen to its safe delivery; a kind man who would playfully pull Rylands' hat down over his eyes and give him penny candy for free; a storyteller who had regaled him with tales of Sitting Bull and Spotted Tail from back in the days when such men were still nightmares on horseback.

Ryland crouched down and shook the man twice.

"Mr. Julius? Mr. Julius, wake up!"

Mr. Julius remained still. Standing again, the boy began to stagger toward home. As the wind returned to his lungs, he ran even faster than before.

His father would know what to do. Daddy had known the dead man ever since he was eight and Julius not more than thirteen; he had always referred to him respectfully as a "white Jew," someone who could be trusted around your money or your wife without cheating you out of either. He loved to recount how Mr. Julius cheerfully put up with his boyhood shenanigans—letting him browse the dime novels even when he was certain he hadn't so much as a penny. After he married, wasn't it Julius who extended him credit even though his brother had refused? And when it was discovered that the "guaranteed" fireback he had received from Boston was of inferior iron, hadn't he refunded every cent to Daddy? Mr. Julius wasn't old; he had never seemed sick. In fact, he was known for an electric energy that ran from morning until night. How could he be dead in the middle of the day?

When the boy reached home, he bounded up the steps two at a time. His father listened carefully as he explained the cause of his lateness.

"All right, son," Lemuel Norcross said, "you've had a fright, for sure. Lie down on the daybed here until you get your breath back. I'll fetch the proper authority."

Lemuel mounted his horse and went in search of Constable E. Seymour Palmer. At the police station, the deputy informed him that the boss was across the street at Gaita's in the process of a haircut. Lemuel walked to the shop and repeated the grisly tale between strokes of Gaita's straight razor.

"Well, then," the constable said, as the barber dusted his fat neck, "we'll go have a look-see. But this better not be another prank. I still got glue in my gun from the last one."

Lemuel and Palmer left the shop and crossed the square into the park. As they rounded one of the new street lamps, they could clearly see both the body and Ryland, who had returned, as he said, "to guard the remains." Soon they were all standing over what had been in life Mr. Julius Meyer: late of the Indian Wigwam Trading Post and the Meyer furniture and cigar stores, agent for the Provident Life Assurance Company, founding member of the Standard Club and Temple Beth Israel, and friend to red and white, Jew and Gentile, Negro and Chinaman.

Palmer squatted down beside the body.

It had fallen on its left side, the arm tucked under the torso. Beneath the head lay a circle of crimson that had soaked into the path cinders, forming a sort of halo. Even in such an unusual posture, the clothing looked amazingly unrumpled, but this was typical of the spirit now departed. Nobody knew Mr. Julius Meyer to ever have a crease where he didn't want one; at least not when he was dressed as a white man.

"Looks like he's been shot," Lemuel said.

"I reckon," said the constable.

Palmer pulled at the curly hair. The side of the head closest to the ground now lay exposed for detective work.

"Bullet in the temple. Shirt's red, too. Help me turn him over."

Palmer and Lemuel took hold of Julius's striped gabardine jacket and pulled. It struck the constable that he had never felt a fabric so smooth or fine. Not on a man, anyway. As the body rolled to the right, they saw the Colt revolver gripped in its left hand.

"Yep. He's been blasted here, too: one to the chest. You ever know Julius to go armed?"

"Not since the Wigwam days. I don't understand it. Sure, there's kike-haters here, but most of them is cowards, inbred to a double row of teeth. If any of them have the gumption to kill Julius, they don't have enough to do it in broad daylight. And I don't care if he had his Sunday clothes on. He'd have fought. Ask any old Indian."

Palmer rose from his crouch and spat away from the corpse and the wind.

"Well, we better work fast," Palmer said. "Jews'll want him planted by tomorrow-day after, latest. Ryland!"

The boy jumped.

"Ryland, I want you to run like hell for Doctor Ball. If he's not there, look for him. Check Marty's or The Smiling Irishman. *Don't get Watkins.* Last time we had a case like this he charged the county a hundred dollars and I caught hell. Just find Doc Ball and tell him we got a situation here." Ryland nodded quickly and took off.

When the *Evening World-Herald* reported on the incident two days later, many of Omaha's citizens concluded that Ball must have been even more drunk than usual at the time of his investigation. The headline read:

JULIUS MEYER ENDS HIS OWN LIFE BY PISTOL ROUTE
Lying beside a bench in Hanscom Park, a bullet hole in his left temple and another in his left breast, a revolver clenched in his left hand, the body of Julius Meyer, president of the Metropolitan Club and a resident of Omaha for over forty years, was found at 11:58 Monday forenoon.

The story went on to detail Julius's recent bout of depression, brought on by a battle with ptomaine poisoning. It speculated on the state of his finances now that he had closed the various businesses he had run with his older brother, Max. It even hypothesized that perhaps his lifelong bachelorhood had left him with the kind of emptiness reserved only for those unblessed by children.

Still, years went by before the chatter finally abated. Why would the man whom the children of the city called "Uncle" want for the attentions of the young? How ill could he have been, having just taken a brisk walk that ended two miles from his door?

And considering that the report stated that either wound could have been fatal, how could Julius Meyer have killed himself twice: a mean feat for any man, even if one accepted as gospel the witchcraft of the Jews.

1

FROM THE COLD FOREDECK OF THE *Balaclava*, ALEXANDER Herrmann observed that it would take a magician of stellar reputation to escape the humanity strangling the Philadelphia Lazaretto.

He had been told there were such crowds at the processing station at Castle Garden. But that was in New York; anywhere one went, the landscape was choked with people. They packed the theatres, filled the parks, and lived eight and ten to a room. At the old fort where the immigrants were processed, queues were so long and quarters so close that fisticuffs would originate among husbands and fathers angered at the proximity of strange men to their wives and daughters.

He had expected Philadelphia's immigrant entry point to be different than this, and in some ways it was. Rather than a forbidding old military installation, the Lazaretto was bucolic—a series of structures in the colonial style set in hundreds of acres of farmland and decorated with manicured lawns. Its site on the Delaware River spoke more of a country estate than a quarantine station; its weathervanes and cupolas would not have been out of place at a university in the Old Dominion.

Alexander began counting the ships. There were two in front of the *Balaclava* and eight behind, each one dutifully waiting its turn for a chance at a rickety berth. At the starboard dock, a giant iron-hulled barquentine disgorged hundreds of steerage passengers chattering in a dozen languages. The varieties of speech aside, Alexander was amazed at how much each immigrant resembled another: the same frayed dark suits and bowler hats, the same wrinkled notes pinned to each coat, scrawled with the name of a relative or local committeeman. The women and children came wrapped in whatever would serve against the late November chill, their long skirts and trousers encircled at the hems with filth from below decks. Even the dead were indistinguishable. From a hatch on the far port side, he could see men in stained white coats removing linen-wrapped bodies from the hold; the freedom they had sought in America would now have to be provided by God, not Lincoln.

Alexander had just turned from the sights of the shoreline when the arguing began.

He didn't understand the words, but he knew they were in Russian. At first, two voices seemed involved, then three, then the shouting blended with the general cacophony of the Lazaretto—a few more foreign souls attempting to make a point at the tops of their lungs. As he rushed toward the din, Alexander began to recognize one of the voices. It was thin and young, but with a fierce tone and a sarcastic edge that

2

he could well discern through the chatter. Gaining the quarterdeck, Alexander pushed his way through a small crowd that had gathered around three quarrelling boys. Two of them were steerage rats from Moscow or Rostov or Odessa.

The third was his younger cousin.

He was smaller than his two antagonists and as dark as they were fair; but to listen to their raised cries was to believe that they had all grown up in the same town, perhaps even in the same street. His vowels were their vowels, his consonants identical. He was guttural where they were; and when they squeezed the letter "y" in the manner of the steppes, he choked it harder, bringing an arrogance to the dispute that required no translation.

Alexander stepped forward and stood beside his cousin. He raised his walking stick.

"What are they on about?" he asked in their native German.

"They saw my curly hair and the pretty clothes you bought me and called me a Jew. They threatened to pull down my britches to prove it."

"They're putting the gangway down, Julius. Let's just get out of here."

"No! No, leave me alone, Alex. You'll ruin everything. I've got them confused. I've told them I'm Russian, too."

"I don't care. Your brother told me to bring you to this country alive."

Perhaps it was the hurried *Deutsch*, or the sweat on Alexander's brow, but the larger Russian, the one with red eyes, smiled and called out to Julius. He reached into a drooping pocket and produced a short fish blade, tossing it from hand to hand.

"What is he saying?" Alex asked.

"He says if I'm not circumcised now, I soon will be."

Laughing, the Russian waved the blade in the direction of the smaller boy's groin as his companion circled toward Alexander's back.

3

"Julius," cried Alexander, "tell them they are right. Tell them we are Jews."

Julius opened his mouth to protest but his cousin cuffed him on the ear.

"Tell them!"

The curly-headed boy did as ordered. To Alexander's ears, his Russian seemed even more perfect than before.

"Now tell them what they've always heard is true. That we are all of us demons, and if they don't leave us alone, we will bring hell down upon them."

"What?"

"God damn you, tell them!"

The boy obeyed, which enraged Red Eyes even more. His lieutenant, whose grin revealed teeth more green than the river, moved to grasp Alexander from behind. Julius leaped up on a barrel, sidestepping the knife and taunting the Russian about the uncertainty of his origins.

Alexander feinted in time to avoid Green Teeth's arms and grabbed the boy by his wretched coat. Spinning around twice, he flung him to the deck. With a bellow of rage, the Russian jumped to his feet in time to see Alexander reach into his breast pocket as if to retrieve a weapon.

As Green Teeth charged him, Alexander crossed his elbows to form an inverted "V," and knit his fingers together. Then he spread them apart, fanning them wide like a deck of cards.

His hands burst into flame.

The fire was blue at its base and smelled of lamp oil. The light March wind bent the fire forward over Alexander's fingers and into the face of Green Teeth. The boy recoiled with an oath and ran for the nearest hatch. Alexander turned, whirling on one foot toward his enemy's companion. Red Eyes collapsed to the deck in terror, begging mercy from the demon in the fine suit. With a sleek flourish, Alexander raised both arms above his head as if to administer the *coup de grace*, but instead rotated each wrist with a snap, instantly extinguishing the flames.

Through his smoking hands, Alexander stared down at the frightened Russian and pointed toward the gangway. He uttered a single word in English. He had learned it from cowboy novels.

"Git."

The boy ran for the quarterdeck, hot on the heels of Green Teeth, who now stood remonstrating with a Lazaretto official. The Russian pantomimed fire and put his fingers to his forehead to indicate the horns of Lucifer. By the time his friend reached him, two large sailors had taken Red Eyes into custody. As if he were on fire, Green Teeth made for the *Balaclava's* starboard bulwark and hurled himself over her side. He bounced off one of the ship's newly tied lines, nearly crushing a rat using it as his road ashore. He plunged beneath the river's surface and bobbed back up with a repeated cry that sounded to Alexander like "choff."

"Russian for 'devil,'" Julius said.

He snorted into his nose and made for the foredeck. With a sigh, Alexander followed him through a forward hatch, around a course of deck chairs and past a line of customs inspectors holding pencils and tablets. He turned right at the Captain's Mess and bowed his head to avoid scraping it on the ceiling of the dank passageway. When he arrived at the small stateroom they had shared, he grabbed his cousin by the shoulders.

"This is madness," Alexander said, slamming the door behind them with his foot. "Just because you can speak like they do is no reason to goad them. The next time I might not be close by—and then some other pigs will slice your throat and count you as another victory for Jesus and the Czar."

Julius glared at his cousin. He shook off Alexander's hands and walked toward his narrow, unmade bunk.

"But you are *always* close by, Alex—ever-present, like God. *Guttenu*, the way you hover about me, He's your only competition. Except God doesn't get his miracles by mail order, does he? 'The Hands of Mephistopheles,' I believe the trick is called. Two pounds, ten plus post from Mr. Cantor's in London."

Alexander grabbed a brush and comb from the overhead cupboard and angrily stuffed them into his suitcase.

"If it weren't for that two pounds, ten, they would be picking a fish blade out of your ribcage. It's bad enough I've spent the past ten days watching you argue with Russians in Russian, Serbs in Serbian and with every German on board. Believe it or not, dear cousin, baby-sitting you isn't my primary mission in life."

"No, Alex, your primary mission in life is to play lackey for your brother. Rabbits from hats! Sawing women in half! Artists at work, God save you."

Alexander turned away from his cousin. He reached into a small chest of drawers and began to remove his shirts and collars. He gently placed each one in a leather suitcase plastered with travel labels: New York, Paris, Istanbul.

"Julius, this word game you play with people—it squanders your gift."

The younger boy smiled. As if to mock Alexander, he switched from German to English: perfect, unaccented, and sufficiently sprinkled with the sort of idiomatic phrases that only one born in its homeland could know.

"Don't lecture me about gifts, Alex. You and that charlatan brother of yours sell lies for a living. You wave your wands and scare the yokels—and they swallow it like flies eating shit."

"That's what they pay for," Alexander said, closing the suitcase. "We agree to lie well and they agree to believe us. But Julius, when you deny that you're a Jew . . ."

"Did anyone in your America ever grab you by your earlocks? Did anyone ever pull your prayer shawl down or throw your black hat into the gutter? In your America you looked like everyone else. In Bromberg being a Jew never got me anything but a beating. No more, Alex. No more *yeshiva bocher* taking the back alleys to avoid the krauts and polacks. I'm in your America now. I'll tell them I'm a *schwartze* if it keeps me in one piece—and I'll do it in any language."

Alexander locked his case just as the deep whistle of the *Balaclava* sounded debarkation. He could hear sailors shouting that the time had come to go ashore.

Julius grabbed his carpetbag and flew through the stateroom door. Alexander watched him disappear down the grimy hall, running hard until he encountered the ancient British steward who had seen to their needs during the long crossing. Julius stopped to smile and pump the old man's hand. As he had throughout the voyage, the boy greeted him as a countryman, his accent a perfect reflection of the cockney's own. He spoke in rhyming slang, referred to the old man as "ducks," and finally departed down the corridor with a jaunty "t'ra."

Alexander glanced after Julius and then paused in the hall. When the steward reached him at the door, he cheerfully blocked the old man's passage.

"Thank you for your fine service," he said. "I shall miss it when we leave the ship."

The steward bowed. "It was nothing, young gentleman."

"Ah, but even nothing deserves the proper something."

Alexander crossed his hands in the air, his fingers fluttering like the wings of a dove. Then he reached behind the steward's ear, produced a silver dollar, and placed it in the old man's palm.

⊰◇⊱

It was a journey of nearly two hours from the *Balaclava* dock to the City of Philadelphia. From the Lazaretto's home village of Tinicum to the Belgian block streets over which their cart now jangled, the cousins had seen mostly marshland and grass, punctuated here and there by a shack or dilapidated barn. Buffeted by the hard roads, they were hungry and exhausted when at last the Walnut Street Theatre came into view.

Julius was less than impressed.

By European standards, the Walnut was hardly grand. It had been built in the old Philadelphia style—its face nearly unadorned but for six Doric columns and some ungenerous sprays of filigree—reflecting the philosophy of the old town in which it was built. The Quakers, founders of the city, had fought the commonwealth for years to ban the wickedness of public performance, relegating all such foolishness to the far side of South Street, the town's original border. With such sentiments in mind, the architects had probably been right to choose austerity over splendor. The Walnut was, after all, not a dime museum or a tent circus but a palace of culture in which the likes of Forrest and Booth portrayed Hamlet the Dane and Othello the Black for the edification of a grateful public.

The cart stopped at the corner of Ninth and Walnut. Alexander paid the driver, and the cousins jumped from the rough seat. The man handed down their trunk and bags, made a clicking sound to his two filthy bays, and left with neither good-bye nor thanks.

Alexander straightened his jacket and began to pick up his trunk; it was then that he noticed the tall posters lined up against the Walnut's columns.

What he saw filled him with dread.

FRIDAY EVENING, NOVEMBER 17, 1866. LAST PERFORMANCE BUT TWO!

BENEFIT OF

PROFESSOR CARL HERRMANN

THE GREATEST MAGICIAN OF AMERICA!

HE OF THE AMAZING VANISHING SPARROW,

HOUSE OF BEWITCHED CARDS, ETC.

NOW OFFERS THE PUBLIC HIS GREATEST ILLUSION! THE ONE

AND ONLY ORIGINAL TO HIM AND SINGULAR

BULLET CATCH!

THE AMAZING TRICK WHICH HAS CAUSED THE UNFORTUNATE

DEATH OF OVER 50 FINE PRACTIONERS OF THE MYSTIC ARTS!

FOR THIS

ONE NIGHT ONLY

THE GREAT HERRMANN WILL PERFORM THIS MOST

DEATH DEFYING OF ACTS USING, UNLIKE IMITATORS,

A GENUINE REVOLVER BULLET

OF LEAD WHICH SHALL BE SUBJECT TO METICULOUS INSPECTION

BY MEMBERS OF THE AUDIENCE AND

QUALIFIED MEMBERS OF THE LOCAL CONSTABULARY!

THIS SHALL BE CAUGHT IN THE TEETH OF THE ARTIST!

Alex took hold of his cousin's ear and, ignoring the astonished box office clerk, dragged Julius into the Walnut's lobby. From the antechamber, he could hear his elder brother's voice reverberate, screaming and swearing in two languages: English for the understanding of stagehands and assistants, German to articulate profanities for which only German would suffice.

The cousins hurried into the auditorium. It was a large, sweeping arc with a double balcony and a proscenium more highly decorated than the Walnut's austere face might indicate. Below the gilded seraphim and the two-faced god of the drama, the stage was cluttered with large cases and sundry machines. The equipment was painted in lurid shades of black and orange, and festooned with question marks and Chinese characters.

At stage center stood a tall and slender man in shirtsleeves. His silver waistcoat was unbuttoned, and his black hair fell in rings over his forehead. In his left hand, he held a silver revolver, while his right gestured grandly toward the chandelier. At the sight of him, Julius gasped in recognition: the burning eyes, the pointed eyebrows and waxed mustaches above the long, pointed goatee. It was if Mephistopheles had left Hell for the day to entertain Philadelphia's damned souls.

The demon stared out into the rows of seats, finally fixing Alexander in his gaze.

"Well, little Alex. I thought it was me who did the disappearing. You were supposed to be coming from Prussia, not Mars."

"Put the gun down, Compars," Alex said. "We've spoken of this before. You can't do the Catch with a live bullet."

The magician paused for a moment, stared at his brother and then, with a grin, fired three rounds into the upper flies. The chief stagehand ran out a back door. Julius was so quick to leap behind one of the orchestra seats that his hat met his foot on his way down.

"I see," Compars said, spitting on the stage. "Of all of mother's sixteen children, you are the one God has sent to provide me with sage advice. And why not? You are only twenty-nine years my junior. Why *wouldn't* I listen to such an experienced expert on what can and cannot be accomplished on a stage? Perhaps I should simply turn over this franchise to you now. You are after all, nearing twenty-one."

"Compars . . ."

"I remind you we are in the United States!" the magician shouted in English. "You will refer to me at all times in public as Carl or Herr Docktor or perhaps, as you should, dear brother."

He fired another round into the ceiling, loosening a chunk of plaster the size of a hog's head.

"And now, since you appear to be in the mood to tell me things, pray tell me this: where is the brat you were sent to fetch for that fool, Max?"

"Like everyone else here, 'dear brother,' he is in hiding for his life. I beg you. Put down the pistol and take away the posters. To carry out your plan, you need a confederate. None of your other aides knows how the mechanisms of this trick work. That leaves me alone to pull the trigger—and I refuse."

From his hiding place on the theatre's floor, Julius peeked from between two seats at the figure onstage. As Compars turned red, he looked to the boy even more like the devil. The magician raised the pistol once more toward the ceiling but received only a hollow click for his efforts. He looked up at the silver gun and threw it to the stage. Compars kicked the weapon into a footlight, clenched his fists at his sides and stomped toward his dressing room.

Alexander scurried toward the orchestra pit and leaped onto the stage. He picked up the revolver from the floor and put it in his over-coat pocket. Steadying himself against a huge papier-mâché playing card, he motioned for Julius to rise from his hiding place and called for the stage manager. Presently, a short, fat man emerged from the stage-right flies. He was pale and perspiring freely.

"Sir," Alexander said, "please allow me to apologize for my brother's behavior. He is an *artiste* and, as you must know better than anyone, such men are sometimes given to temperament. I expect he shall be fine directly. In the meantime, I ask that you please have your men remove any and all posters that contain mention of this bullet catch. The Great Herrmann's show will go on, I promise, but without that particular feature."

The stage manager nodded and proceeded down the steps toward the lobby. Julius emerged from his sanctuary and walked down the aisle toward his cousin.

"Now I see why you say he treats you like a slave," Julius said. "It's because you defy him."

Alexander brushed his hair from his eyes. "This isn't the first time I have saved him from himself," he said, his breath still short. "Two years ago in Chicago, he insisted on placing himself upside down in a tank of water with a large window at its front, padlocking it, and then trying to escape. We told him the trick wasn't nearly ready, but he would have none of it. I had to take an axe to the window in front of a thousand people. For months afterward his reputation was as shattered as that glass. It has taken until now for him to regain his rightful place in the show business. Since I was your age, it has been my place to keep him from committing suicide for his art. He's no good to the audience dead."

Julius picked up a black wooden wand that was lying on a box beside him. He waved it tauntingly in the air before a burly prop man grasped it from his hand and disappeared into the wings.

"He is the Great Herrmann, Alex, not you. He is your older brother: old enough to be your father. My brother is a great man, too. He's smarter than anyone. He is making lots of money in the West. When I get there I won't be stupid, I'll listen to him. I'll do everything he says and be rich."

Alexander smiled slightly. "Well, while you're getting rich, make sure you don't let him kill himself, even if he asks you to. C'mon, let's see if we can find the great sorcerer."

That evening, The Great Herrmann presented his act, the very same performance that had delighted the Walnut for the previous two weeks. There were, as the new posters proclaimed, "thrills for the gentlemen and refined amusements for the ladies." Compars, suave and self-possessed in his black tailcoat, disappeared through a trap-door onstage and materialized in the balcony; he burned Alexander alive and then conversed with his ghostly form as it hovered above his ashes; cards came to life in his hands; doves transformed from feathers to silk.

For this performance and the two that would follow, a dozen Philadelphia police constables had been engaged. They were there to maintain order among those who had seen the posters promising the catching of a genuine revolver bullet in the mouth of the artist. As anticipated, there were members of the audience who objected loudly to not witnessing the feat for which they had bought their tickets. Confronted by such a ruckus, an officer would immediately escort the malcontent to the street, applying force commensurate to the degree of resistance. One polite man asked for and received his money back; another was given a season pass. The story ended somewhat worse for a Mr. Simon R. Tracey of Brewerytown. He had stood up in the second tier and hollered, "Coward! Where's the Catch, then?" Tracey spent the weekend in Central Holding, where he was surrounded by inebriates and petty thieves and accosted by a procurer who insisted that the sodomite he represented was a real woman.

It fell to Alex to pay the policemen: ten dollars each and an equal share in a case of good Irish: the going rate for security in The City of Brotherly Love. Yes, it was expensive, but his brother's hard-earned reputation hung in the balance. Besides, Captain Riordan of the Third District (who was in for ten percent) assured him he was getting a bargain. It would have cost even more had his cops been off duty.

Julius had watched as the officers received their money and smiled through their mustaches. America was just as his brother had described it: filled with small men looking for small money, hicks easy to outsmart and drunkards not paying attention. Perhaps when they spoke of "the land of opportunity" this is what they meant: a society of limitless marks waiting to be taken; where it wasn't even necessary to cheat them to make their treasure your own.

2

I N 1866, OMAHA, NEBRASKA WAS A CITY NOT YET A CITY IN A state not yet a state.

It was later said that if the place had gained any success, it was literally taken out of some poor animal's hide. Bear, buffalo, muskrat and beaver were all abundant and there for the trapping, waiting to be cut into coats and stoles and blocked into hats. Early in the century, competition was so great among the fur trappers that they seemed only too glad to skin each other along with the varmints. Men were shot over a few pelts or had their goods stolen en route to market. Relative peace was established after the War of 1812, when, with the cooperation of the government, John Jacob Astor took control of the trade. With his monopoly forcing lower prices per pelt, anyone who now wanted to make a decent dollar left the wilderness and took a job with the approaching railroad or helped supply those who did. The men swinging the hammers would need flour and coffee in the daytime and whiskey and women after dark; and those who could provision them stood a good chance of leaving this life a good deal richer than they had entered it.

Max Meyer had seen the need and brought tobacco to Omaha: first as a greenhorn fresh from Europe, a canvas bag lashed to his back, later as a merchant, greeting carloads of Virginia and Latakia leaf. When the business began, his mixtures filled crude pipes made of mud or clay; but before a year was out, Max would be displaying briers and meerschaums of cherry and fruitwood and blending his plants in secret concoctions rare and aromatic. He sold cigars and cigarettes and the papers in which to roll them. In time, he followed his smoking products with other luxuries: thick, black chew; newspapers and periodicals from New York, Philadelphia, and Boston; soap; hair tonic, and the kind of jewelry that a roughneck might buy in a town whose female population consisted chiefly of prostitutes.

Max looked through his window at Farnam Street and watched his customers as they dug train beds for the railroad that would connect Des Moines to Omaha and Omaha to California. The men worked quickly, fighting the deadline the government had placed on the Cedar Rapids & Missouri and the cold that nature had laid upon their bare eyes and hands. There was more than enough work in Omaha, regardless of race, religion, or past criminalities. Despite the Civil War, the government had proceeded with the provisions of the Pacific Railroad Act of 1862, which vowed to unite the land by rail. With the unpleasantries concluded, it would probably be only a year or two until the locomotives (now stopped over a hundred miles away in Iowa) would begin to arrive in town, their cars laden with all the good things of Eastern industry. Max had already made the necessary deals with his suppliers for the items he would need in the amounts required. His small business had already made him comfortable; he looked forward to being rich.

Max fixed his eyes on a giant Negro whose head was wrapped in a stained cloth. All morning long he had swung his sledge like a piston, not stopping for rest or water, perhaps afraid that even a moment's pause would freeze him solid. As Max watched the huge man lift and strike, his reverie was interrupted by a voice he had come to dread ever since its small owner had first been allowed to walk abroad alone.

"The Union forever!"

On the boardwalk that fronted the Nickel & Dime Saloon, Lemuel Norcross began his daily adventure. He swung under a hitching rail, jumped to a horse trough, and skidded the length of its frozen surface. He twisted in the air, gave a strangled shout, and landed hard on the ground, his tiny boots cracking the surface of the frozen mud. He whirled once more, whinnied like a stallion, and stooped to pick up a dry, white branch unearthed by the rail gang.

"Springfield Percussion rifle!"

In the boy's hands, the stick spat fire, single-handedly holding off the gray hordes of the Confederacy.

"Liberty and union! Long live Mr. Lincoln!"

Max frowned at the noise. He turned on his heel, hurried to the news rack at the rear of the store, and turned to face the door. If the boy were to enter his shop today, the large rack of dime novels would be his goal. He would skip in with a loud and cheery hello, run to the little paper-books, and pick up copy after copy in his grubby hands. He would ask Max a thousand questions—why wasn't there a Mrs. Max; why did Mr. Max talk so funny; was Mr. Max sad about the president? In his hoarse and chirping voice, the boy would announce each title aloud: *The Romance of the Squatter Wife*, *The Shawnee Scout*, *The Disagreeable Death of Dangerous Dan*. With the noon whistle about to blow, the rail workers would soon be crowding the shop in search of Weyman's Long Cut or the latest *Police Gazette*. The fact that the boy could read at the age of seven might have made him a credit to his mother, but in the world of men, Lemuel Norcross was a marked deterrent to the vital transactions that took place amid conversation unfit for children.

His eyes now fixed on the street, Max watched the little figure's every move. Lemuel jumped from a rain barrel to an apple box, slid down in a drift of snow, and began to run in the direction of the store. Max braced himself for the boy's onslaught of chatter when he saw the boy stop dead center in the street. Max abandoned the periodicals, walked back to the shop window, and looked east.

With the winter sun at their backs, the riders appeared as thin silhouettes against a burst of yellow. At first, Max was blinded by the contrast, the black shapes persisting in his retinas and blocking his vision. But as the men rode into the shade, the glare in his eyes dissolved to reveal a quartet of warriors, hard in their expressions and Ponca by their dress. They were prepared for the cold as no newcomer could be, each man's face encircled in stiff fur caps still bearing the heads of three raccoons. The headdress on the tallest rider was faceless and black, its texture like shag tobacco, huge horns springing from its temples. Thick buffalo robes tumbled to their boots. Two were colored a rough, soft brown; the others were as pale as a church girl's flesh. At the edges of each garment could be seen an inch or two of the wooly hair that formed its lining—the exterior of the bison pressed to the outside of the man. As they rode closer, Max could see the stick-like paintings adorning the robes: a deer hunt in reds and blues; a war victory in purples and greens; and on all four robes, men. Some were posed horseback, pulling strong on their bows; others were foot soldiers, giving flight to arrows that would send their rivals to the unknowable.

The braves halted before the door of Max's shop. With a single motion, the tall rider dismounted and tapped his pony's nose to keep him still. As he paused to pull his robe tighter, he noticed Lemuel Norcross standing like a statue in the middle of the street. He raised his hand to the boy and smiled.

Max stomped from the shop, a Chesterfield overcoat still hanging from his left shoulder. He patted the breast pocket of his suit coat. The short-barreled .45 was still there.

"*Nein*," he shouted at the tall man. "No. No. I tell you before. No Indian here. No Indian."

The tall brave turned away from Lemuel. Frowning, he plunged his hand into a small pouch at his belt and produced a newly minted territorial dollar. He held it up to Max like a mayor presenting the city's keys.

"Tobacco," said the brave.

Max's face reddened as he buttoned the Chesterfield to the neck. "*Nein*. Tobacco you want? In the saloon there is tobacco. *They* only will let in an Indian. Not shopkeepers. Maybe you should grow tobacco. I tell again like I have told you from long. No Indian in the stores. No Indian. Go."

The brave looked down at Max and then at the dollar. It glinted in the winter light as he held it higher and scowled at the white man.

"Tobacco," he repeated, "for Standing Bear."

Max felt a chill from within, a coldness left over from the old country.

These savages had been ordered here by a king; in Prussia he had seen the lengths to which kings would go to get what they wanted and the things that could happen to their underlings when those wants were thwarted: titles stripped, ranks reduced, lands taken. He knew that reasoning with the Indian was of no use. Besides, reason depended on language. The Indian spoke no German and

Max no Ponca; and neither party's English was equal to such delicate negotiations.

Max cursed in Yiddish and looked at the brave. "You," he said, motioning to the man. He pointed at the three other riders and shook his head back and forth. "Not them." The tall brave signaled to his lieutenants, wrapped his robe tighter, and followed Max into the shop, shaking the snow from his boots.

For the better part of an hour he inspected the various wares, picking things up, holding them to the light, sniffing them. At last, he pointed to a glass jar filled with light-colored burley and held up the dollar. Max weighed the correct amount and placed it in a cotton sack. He took the coin, and returned a silver ten-cent piece to the Indian.

The tall brave bit into the dime, then took the package with a grunt. Turning toward the door, he noticed the small white boy from the street. He was standing at the magazine rack, looking up from the latest edition of *Colonel Custis' Weekly*.

The Indian walked slowly toward the boy and put his left hand on his shoulder. With his right, he plucked the book from the boy's grasp. He began to page through it, grinning at the engravings depicting chapter six of *Dick Lightheart Encounters Injun Joe*, but frowning at the profusion of little black marks that only served to turn the paper gray.

Lemuel Norcross watched as the Indian returned the dime novel to his hands. The brave strode back to the counter, retrieved the dime from his pocket and placed it carefully to the right of the cash box.

"For boy," he said, and walked through the door.

Lemuel looked hard at the shopkeeper.

"Is it mine, Mr. Max?" the boy asked.

Max looked down at the dime. "Yes, yes," he said. "Take and go. It's soon lunch whistle. The men will need their tobacco. Go. Read. By me, you'll not come back."

Lemuel paused for a moment and then ran from the store at top speed, stuffing the book into his coat.

Max put the dime in the cash box and walked to the window again. The Indians had fallen into the shadows, the clacking of their horses' hooves echoing across the ice. Lemuel Norcross raced after them, shouting and whooping like a red man born.

"Hooray!" Lemuel Norcross called from the street. "Long live Chased By Owls!"

Max Meyer shook his head. Perhaps once his younger brother arrived, he could begin to make sense of this land. What kind of country raises a little boy to cry out the name of a sworn enemy of his race? Surely, only in America could a savage receive such gratitude for the purchase of a lurid tale printed on cheap paper for the entertainment of children and fools.

3

As Julius Meyer stepped from the last train heading west, he squinted his eyes against the whiteness of Boone, Iowa's world. All within his vision appeared solid; variations created by hillside or ravine turned into one endless sheet of paper. In the past hundred miles, the only contrast he had noted was the slate-gray ribbon of the Des Moines River, sad and frozen in place. Julius wiped his nose on his sleeve and pulled his cap low over his ears. All he wanted was a fire and a bowl of soup.

Fifty feet from the face of the steaming locomotive, the railroad ended. Just as in Omaha, a mass of humanity in all sizes and colors was swinging sledges and clanging down sections of new track. The bosses hollered orders at the men and the workers translated the shouts into their native tongues as the town's few merchants prepared for the noon rush.

Picking up his bags, Julius heard a melody; a surprisingly jaunty tune more suited for summer sunshine then the prevailing chill. Coming closer to the tracks, the voices of the blacks cut like ice axes through the cold. The whites and even some of the Chinese joined in for the chorus:

> *Take this hammer,*
> *Carry it to the captain.*
> *Take this hammer,*
> *Carry it to the captain.*
> *Take this hammer,*
> *Take it to the captain.*
> *Tell him gone, oh lord,*
> *Yes, I'm gone.*

Shivering, the boy turned from the singing and searched his coat pocket for the transfer providing passage to Omaha. Guessing that they might know where to go next, Julius followed a group of about a dozen passengers toward a large canvas tent. Beside it stood a wooden post topped by a worn sign:

STAGE

The scrawl held no meaning for Julius. His genius lay not in reading languages, but speaking them; still, the letters on the sign matched those on his transfer and he entered through a flap made ragged by the wind. Inside, a sickly-looking woman approached him.

"Take a number," she said and handed him a piece of worn cardboard.

The tent's interior was warm, the heat provided by an old Franklin stove and the bodies of the travelers. Each one held a card marked with their number, entitling the holder to a turn at remonstrating with an official seated at a low table. The man wore a cap in the style of a train conductor, the word "agent" inscribed in brass above the brim. As he drew closer, Julius could hear a strange, ringing splat and slivers of anguished conversation. Set before the agent's fingers was a small sign with a name burned into its surface:

MR. HARRIS T. BOGARDUS
OVERLAND STAGE COMPANY
BOONE, IOWA

When his turn finally came, Julius handed the number and transfer to the man.

"Well, what is it? Hurry up, boy," Bogardus said.

"Yes. When will the coach be leaving?

Bogardus paused and spat a rich mixture of saliva and tobacco into a nearby spittoon. It rang like a dinner bell.

"Not today, son. Pro'ly not tomorrow, either."

"But why, please?

"Too cold. Temperature's got to get to forty. Any less, freeze to death: driver, horse, and fare."

"Please. My brother is expecting me."

A wooden stamp came down on Julius's transfer like the judgment of the Lord.

"He's expectin' you not dead. Take this, turn left outside."

Bogardus returned the transfer to Julius, accompanied by a skeletonic key from which hung a large wooden tag reading *No. #8*. Julius made his way through the crowd and stopped to wrap his scarf twice around his head. Turning left as instructed, he could see what looked like tarpaper shacks set in three long rows, moaning in the wind. Some sang high, the holes in their walls whistling like fifes; others intoned lower scales. Their bass and timpani was banging shutters.

Number Eight was in the center of the first row. From behind its door, loud enough to be heard over the wind, Julius could hear snoring. He climbed the single step and jiggled the key into the lock.

As the door rattled open, he was nearly knocked back outside by the force of an ungodly stench. It was a smell that carried within it all solids and fluids the human can produce. It seeped from overflowing chamber pots; wafted from a mess that was once a good night's liquor and rose from two sleeping bodies laid out on straw long unreplaced. Fighting a wave of nausea, the boy raised his handkerchief to his nose and closed the door behind him. His head swam; but it wouldn't do to faint now, considering what he might land in.

"Hey, boy. That door ain't shut all the way."

The voice came from the far left corner of the shack. At first, Julius couldn't see to whom it belonged, but a second shout revealed a grizzled head, its hat still on, rising from beneath a soiled blanket.

"I said, shut the fucking door, boy!"

Julius turned toward the door and shoved it hard. With this last source of fresh air eliminated, Julius stumbled toward a half-filled bucket and gave in to his revulsion.

"That's all right, lad. Let it out. Ain't one of us come into this hell hole without first we served it our dinner."

When he finally was able to lift his head, Julius could see that the man beneath the blanket was now sitting up. His hat was worn and stained with sweat, and his buckskins had seen their best days years ago. Although it was winter, the man's complexion had the ruddy cast of a farmer. His beard was gray except at the mustache and the swath beneath the lower lip where some black fought to remain. Julius could feel his own cheeks turn from green to red at the sound of the man's laughter.

"Nothing to be ashamed of, boy. When I first come in here, four days ago, I think I gave up dirt I'd et as a child. And believe me—this is the goddamn Ritz compared to some burrows they got here. 'Course, it's probably a little worse 'cause of old Jim Riley over there."

The man pointed to a series of lumps beneath two horse blankets. The covers had been pulled over the figure's head so that only his boots were exposed. Julius realized that the snoring he had heard upon entering the shack was now silent.

"Is he sick?" he asked the gray man.

"He's dead, buddy," the gray man said, chuckling. "Dead three nights. I've been meaning to bring him outside, pack him in snow. But the wind whipped up last night so's you couldn't walk abroad and he ain't begun to stink yet, so I went back to sleep and left it for today. Guess that little stove makes it warmer in here than I thought. That's him in the air all right, so into the drifts he goes. They'll keep him fresh 'til the ground's soft enough to bury him. Probably April."

The boy looked on in horror as a broad, gapped grin spread across the gray man's face.

"You know," he said. "Planting season."

The shack rang with laughter. The gray man slapped his thighs beneath the blanket and shook his head back and forth. When he was finished, he rose from beneath his bedding and approached Julius.

"Well, what do you want? The head or the feet?"

Julius didn't answer but moved instinctively away from the face of the corpse. As they lifted him from the floor, the blanket fell away from Jim Riley's shoulders. His eyes and mouth were open. They carried the body through the door and dropped it in a drift at the side of Number Eight. Wiping the snow from his hands, the gray man knelt down, shot his cuffs, and pulled the boots from the dead man's feet.

"Waste not, want not, my sainted mother always said."

The task completed, the two kicked up enough snow to cover Jim Riley and hurried back inside. Perhaps it had been the open door or the absence of a rotting man in their midst, but Julius found the air in Number Eight not quite so foul as before. The gray man reached into a pouch at his belt and pulled out something that looked like a sliver of wood. He looked at it for a moment, then bit into it and began to chew. With a look of satisfaction, he held it up to Julius.

"Jerky?"

The boy held up his hand and murmured a polite decline. He might be getting used to the shack, but not so much that he could eat in it.

"All right, boy, suit yourself. Better get some rest, though. My bones tell me we'll be on our way day after tomorrow and you better hope it heats up enough to travel but not much more. Standing Bear—ol' *Ma-chu-na-zha*—and his boys have been known to venture this far east this time of year, but with weather like this I think they'd just as soon sit warm in the wigwam, so to say."

"This Standing Bear is an Indian?"

"An Indian? He's *the* Indian, son."

The gray man sat down on the floor and removed his moccasins. He reached for Jim Riley's boots and slipped them over his worn stockings. Satisfied that they fit, he slipped beneath the blanket again. Julius found a spot near the window seemingly unfouled by human liquids or dirty clothing.

"What's your name, boy?"

"Julius Meyer, sir."

"John Nathan McGarrigle, at your service. But my friends and enemies call me Prophet John."

"I'm sorry," Julius said, "but I am European. In English this word can mean more than one thing. 'Profit' as in money, or 'prophet' as in one who sees the future. Which are you, please?"

The gray man stared at Julius for a moment and burst once again into laughter. He pointed at the bewildered boy as if he were a zoo exhibit and coughed and choked until he could speak again.

"You going to Omaha?"

"Yes, sir."

"You'll find out," he said, and collapsed into the straw, helpless.

⊰◇⊱

The next morning was colder than the last, and true to the gray man's prediction, the required temperature wasn't reached until the day following. This was determined by Mr. Harris T. Bogardus of the Overland Stage Company walking into the Lament, the shack that served as the village saloon, taking a shot of whiskey, walking outside for a few minutes, and walking back in. If Mr. Bogardus instructed the drivers to harness the horses, those bound for points west could proceed. If he ordered another shot, they would remain trapped in Boone until the weather deigned to cooperate.

At the instant Bogardus set down his glass and called for his men, the travelers ran to their shacks, gathered their trunks and carpetbags, and piled into four waiting stagecoaches. Julius shared his with a married couple from Ohio, a laborer seeking railroad work, Prophet John McGarrigle, and a prostitute whose perfume helped to mask the aroma of the other passengers.

When the coach arrived in Omaha some ten hours later, Julius's brother greeted him with a cup of strong tea, a silent nod, and a brown paper voucher. It read:

BRUNO'S NEAPOLITAN BARBER SHOP
SIGNORE B. GAITA, PROP.

THIS COUPON ENTITLES THE BEARER TO ONE (1) BATH
INCLUDING HOT WATER, SOAP AND LAUNDERED TOWEL.
REMITTED: 25 CENTS. 35 CENTS SATURDAYS.

Max pointed toward the barber's red and white pole and went back inside his shop. The boy, still carrying his suitcase, walked across Farnum Street, dodging piles of frozen horse manure and patches of black ice.

As he walked into the shop, Julius saw four women waiting for their turn at the warm water and soap, the whore from the stagecoach first. Doing quick calculations in his head, the boy estimated that, with their ablutions and powder and dressing, his wait would be something close to an hour per woman.

Leaving his suitcase to hold his place in line, Julius walked across the room to a dark man carefully stropping a razor on a long leather belt.

"*Buon Giorno, Signore,*" he said.

Ten minutes later, Julius was luxuriating in a copper tub. Following their short conversation, Signore Bruno had told the whore that, for his health, this young man must precede her. Escorting his charge through the bathroom door, the barber personally supervised the heating of Julius's water and, with a flourish, threw in some special scented salts, usually five cents extra. He instructed his attendant that there would be no rushing of this bath; and that he was to accept no gratuity, as this young man was his *ospite*—his guest.

Leaving the boy to undress, Signore Bruno returned to his strop. *He would get to the bottom of this.* It was simply impossible that this dark *bambino* could be German and even more impossible that he could be related in any way to such a man as Max Meyer, a sour and disagreeable sort and a Christ-killer to boot. No, this boy was *Italiano*: and by his speech, from very near his own village on the *Costiera Amalfitana.*

4

ONSIDERING ITS LOCATION IN THE WORLD AND THE TIME period it occupied in history, the food served at the Nickel & Dime should have been a lot worse. As it was, its cuisine had made the saloon the class of Omaha. This was entirely due to the fastidiousness of its cook, an enormous black man who called himself Doris.

It was said in Omaha that he had run away from a plantation in Albemarle, North Carolina, bringing with him every secret of Southern cuisine. He produced biscuits as light as butterfly wings; fried chicken encrusted with bread and herbs; and ham and gravy that had once caused two fur trappers to fight it out over an evening's last portion. The battle only ended when Doris himself emerged from the kitchen with two platters, having split the order in two and augmented it with some chicken-fried steak *gratis*. He cracked the plates down on the table, threw a dishtowel over his shoulder as if it was a feather boa, and barked at the two combatants:

"Now you girls eat."

The fight probably would have continued, but the trappers weren't willing to risk the chef's wrath, which was as much a local legend as his victuals. They had both been present the night Packy Girard had complained that his steak was tough and had watched in amazement as Doris bum's-rushed him into the street, where he landed under a horse that, at that very second, proceeded to relieve itself. With this image in their heads, they disentangled, rose from the floor, and tucked into their meals as ordered, neither of them wishing to live with the stigma of having had their behinds whupped by a sodomite. Such a fate had befallen Packy—forcing him to leave town for points east, no longer able to abide the new nickname his fellow rail workers had awarded him: "Pansy" Girard.

Doris, however, liked to say that he was very much like most of the wildlife back home in Stanley County: dangerous only when provoked. The rest of the time, he would go to great lengths to please a customer, especially one he considered a friend. And so, as he did every morning except Saturday, he gathered up the special meal he had so carefully prepared and entered the Dime's dining room.

To the unknowing eye, the big breakfast looked the same as any other: eggs, steak, cornpone johnnycake, and biscuits. But instead of frying the eggs in bacon grease, Doris had swirled them in butter. Rather than fry the steak in a pan that was also home to pork and crawfish, he cooked it in a fine Dutch oven that was used for no other purpose. Neither the biscuits nor the johnnycake contained even a teaspoon of lard, but were made instead with heavy, clotted cream.

The tray held high above his head, Doris swept toward the table by the window, the one he reserved for Mr. Eli Gershonson every day.

"Here you are, Mr. Eli," Doris said, "and there's not so much as a pig's whistle in it."

Eli Gershonson saluted with his coffee cup and looked down at the enormous breakfast. "But Doris, this is too much. How can you expect one man to eat all this?"

Doris gave a girlish laugh. "Oh, Mr. Eli, you say that every morning, and every morning we ain't got to wash the plate because you make it so clean. Anyway, she'll want to pick at it. She don't help much, but she help."

Gershonson and the chef both laughed. At each breakfast, as the lady and Mr. Eli would converse, she would dip a fork into his eggs or break off a piece of johnnycake the size of a thimble and make it last an hour. Doris liked to believe she couldn't resist; that hungry or full, his food could tempt even an iron will or a starvation diet.

Doris gave Eli a wave and walked back into the kitchen. Gershonson looked down at his eggs and reached for his pocket watch.

Two minutes to eleven. She would be on time. She always was.

He straightened his tie and wondered how long he would be able to afford this luxury.

After all, the hour he spent with her each morning was prime for business. There were customers waiting on farms and at mining claims and in outlaw redoubts. They needed what he sold: the pots and pans, the tea and coffee pots, the yarn and needles and bolts of cotton and gingham. And yet here he sat, a perfectly respectable businessman of marriageable age, dressed in his finest suit and waiting to receive a whore as though she were a duchess.

She descended the stairs at exactly eleven.

Eli had seen this costume before and was pleased, as it was one of his favorites. The full, billowing skirt was of wine-colored silk brocade in a rose-and-vine pattern. Every step down the balustrade caused it to catch the light in a different place so that its flowers would by turns appear either a deep scarlet or a milky pink. Above it, she wore a short jacket in iridescent blue satin with pagoda sleeves double-piped in white. From beneath this peeked a modest shirtwaist, gathered at the throat and topped with Irish lace, its whiteness only serving to highlight the deep red of her skin and the blackness of her eyes. The whole was in perfect taste for the time of day. Only the color and amount of paint applied to her high cheekbones and wide mouth gave any hint of her chosen career.

Eli Gershonson rose from the table. "Miss Lady-Jane," he said with a bow.

"Mr. Eli. Hello. You're looking especially handsome this morning."

She greeted him in this way (or with the equivalent compliment) every morning. Even so, her words made him blush; and he was grateful to hide his red face by stepping behind her to pull out her chair. When they were both seated, Eli placed his napkin in his lap and began to eat.

"So, my darling," Lady-Jane said, "how is your business?"

This first bit of small talk was always hard for him. Even though they had been meeting like this for a year, he still needed the first few minutes just to drink her in. This morning, for instance, he delighted to see that she had dressed her hair away from her face; it lay against her proud head flat and tight, terminating in a coal-black *chignon*. Her eyes were large and sloped up slightly at the corners. Unlike some black eyes whose beauty depended on mystery, hers could be read easily: mirth, doubt, pleasure, and worry were as plain as a Sunday headline. Perhaps it was because her mouth gave them so much help that he could see so well in their darkness.

"Well, I can't complain. After four years in this wilderness, it seems I've built a little clientele. They tell me they trust me. They tell me to come back. They ask me to bring things they need. So? What else can a peddler ask for besides a healthy horse?"

Lady-Jane picked up the coffee pot and refilled his cup. She took a morsel of johnnycake from his plate and popped it in her mouth.

"I'm only glad that you're doing well enough to continue our mornings," she said. "I really do look forward to them. And my offer still stands. After all, you're paying me enough to buy all of my services."

Eli blushed again, this time in her full view.

"You know it isn't personal, my darling. But my faith frowns upon such things."

Lady-Jane quoted the verse to herself: "Thou shall not offer the hire of a strumpet . . . nor the wages of a dog." Not very flattering; but her job was to make him feel good, not remorseful; and such a sensitive soul as his needed no more guilt upon it. Still, there was no harm in teasing him; that was very much within the parameters of their arrangement.

"I notice it hasn't kept other gentlemen of your religion from a good time. And I like you much better than any of them."

Eli's smile tightened. "So, if you like me so much, you couldn't eat something? I suppose it wouldn't make any difference if I asked you for the millionth time to take a roll and butter?"

She poured herself a cup of coffee and added three lumps of sugar. "I never have an appetite in the morning, my dear. You know that. Now. What adventure are you off on today?"

With a shift in posture and that single question, she was no longer the whore forbidden by the Torah, but a creature beloved of God: the Dutiful Wife, buttering a biscuit for him and enquiring after his most mundane of goals. Such questions were as much a part of her tool kit as her lip rouge and tightly cinched corset. *Did you take a scarf? Are your horses due for shoes? Do you have a clean handkerchief?*

"My nephew arrives from the East today," Eli said, his mouth filled with yellow egg. "He is only a little younger than you. Three or four years. He is coming to help out at the tobacco store. His name is Julius. Mr. Max is his brother, my sister's husband, may she rest in peace."

Lady-Jane's mouth turned down.

"I wish him the best of luck," she said. "Of course I won't be able to do it at the store. My kind's not welcome in there."

"Be patient with him, my darling. I know he is not a nice man. There are only a handful of us Hebrews in this place, and even me he treats like a stranger. But in keeping you out, he isn't different from anyone else in this town. The treaty isn't going well. The Sioux are attacking the Ponca from the east and people are getting caught in the middle. The man is only doing as his neighbors do."

Lady-Jane reached for his cup and filled it again. "And I suppose they think that if I walk in to buy a bar of soap or drink a cup of tea, I'll walk out with a scalp? Trust me, dear Eli; my schedule is a little too full for me to spend time spying for Standing Bear. Those upright merchants should know that. They're the ones keeping me busy."

Eli blushed from his neck to his bald pate. This time Lady-Jane knew she had embarrassed him, crossing the line that separated her reality from his fantasy. Perhaps it was only because he had earned her trust that she had allowed her anger to appear; but that was not what he was paying for. She took his hand and smiled into his face. He brightened and his color returned to its usual paleness. He squeezed her hand and then dabbed his mouth with his napkin.

"If it was up to me, my darling, you could walk everywhere in this world with respect. But I only sell people pots and pans and tea kettles, not new brains."

The remainder of the conversation was happier: gossip, weather, the finer points of the winter fashions. Finally, Eli Gershonson set his napkin neatly to the right of his empty plate and rose. It was part of their understanding that she remain seated until after their closing pleasantries. She handed him his rough wool scarf as he put on his coat.

"Miss Lady-Jane, I sometimes think this breakfast is what keeps me alive in this wilderness. I thank you so much for sharing it with me. In my mother's tongue we would call this a *mechayah . . .* a pleasure."

She offered her hand. "The pleasure is mine. And I don't think it will surprise you to learn that other ladies of my acquaintance are envious that I get to spend my early hours with such a gentleman. Until tomorrow, Mr. Gershonson."

"Tomorrow," he replied with a bow and then walked toward the double doors and out into the cold.

Once Eli was out of sight, Lady-Jane called for Kevin Flatley, the busted gold miner who sometimes served as the Dime's maitre d'. She ordered a rare steak and a shot of Scotch whiskey and asked for that morning's newspaper. Kevin nodded as if the motion would imbed her words in his brain and headed toward the kitchen, shouting for Doris.

Lady-Jane placed her napkin in her lap and lifted her plate. There, as it did every day, lay a ten-dollar gold piece. She appreciated such subtlety, counting it yet another measure of her client's respect. After all, there were certain things even a whore shouldn't let her john see her do. Tucking into an enormous breakfast was one; accepting payment in her palm was another.

Lady-Jane took the coin from the tablecloth and placed it carefully inside her bodice between whalebone and breast, shivering at its temperature. *Cold cash,* she laughed to herself. *Enough of these, and age eighteen will see me off my back and on my feet.*

5

COMPARS HERRMANN WAS ALWAYS FOND OF SAYING HE WAS happy he had built in the City of Brooklyn.

Manhattan, just across the river, was so filthy and congested, it had become nearly impossible to walk the streets without fear of approach. Costermongers sold everything: toys, periodicals, books. One had even offered up a skull he insisted belonged to William Dorsey Pender, the rebel general mortally wounded at Gettysburg. Beggars were even more numerous. Most were veterans, some still in their bedraggled uniforms, begging alms while pointing to missing limbs and holes where eyes had been. With the rise of the moon, men of every station screamed in drunkenness or lay prostrate in the gutter from laudanum. After ten, whoremasters ruled the streets, offering the services of sisters, wives, even mothers. In the past year, it had gotten so even a Vanderbilt or a Van Den Heuvel couldn't walk abroad without a bodyguard or at least a strapping footman.

Compars had visited Brooklyn many times to perform. In its hills and farms he saw his longed-for Prussia; and its row homes and sleek ferries recalled his beloved Vienna and London. In 1862, he recruited every workingman not at war and began construction of a great house situated on the bluffs overlooking the East River. Built to his specifications, it contained all things dear to him. The halls and foyers held his collection of diaries, posters, and handbills, meticulously documenting every engagement of his long career. The vast parlor was dedicated solely to the display and preservation of over two hundred portraits of the magician, rendered in all media from charcoal to oil, plus photographs. A great library dominated the ground floor. It held not only a huge compendium of tomes on every subject, but also his prized collection of miniatures: over a hundred tiny painted images detailing the highlights of his life from birth through his first triumphs in magic. Below the street, an entire wing had been constructed for the fabrication of new illusions. Here, using the newest steam-powered machinery, the magician and three assistants labored day and night over the complex and delicate apparati by which the Great Herrmann presented new thrills to his public.

It had not been easy for Alexander to persuade his brother to allow him to work in the shop. Compars had told him that there was no need. His assistants maintained his equipment—and once he retired to Austria in a few years' time, all of the miracles of his brilliant career would become the boy's inheritance, making any of Alex's own inventions unnecessary. In order to persuade the great man, Alex presented a set of detailed diagrams illustrating an illusion he was preparing. The drawings indicated such elements as where a trapdoor would be, how it would operate, and how large a sack would be required for his assistant. Compars finally agreed to let Alexander take the northwestern corner of what he always called his "laboratory"; and even this only became possible when an insubordinate ironworker was dismissed for failing to address the Great Herrmann without the required honorific, "Herr Docktor."

Yet within a month, Alexander's joy at a place to work turned to frustration, and the device he had taken weeks to build became a mocking Frankenstein.

From the outside, it looked like a normal high-class steamer trunk of brown morocco, with customary straps and hardware in brass. On this rainy afternoon, he had crouched inside it four times, pushing out the false panel at its rear. On the first attempt, the trap made too much noise, enough for an audience to hear over the orchestra. His second and third attempts were simply too slow, indicating that he had made the panel too heavy.

Now, as he again rolled through the trapdoor he watched as, instead of swinging shut, it followed him toward the floor. Looking up, Alex could see it hanging from a single hinge, the other one broken by the speed of his exit. His eyes filling with tears, he stood up, snatched the door from its twisted bolts and hurled it across the room.

"Crying is for women and children."

Alexander turned toward the cellar doorway. Compars stood on the last step in shirtsleeves, a slight smile visible beneath his devil's handlebar.

"Of all our sainted mother's sixteen children you, my dear Alex, are the most stubborn. Perhaps because you are the youngest, nature waited until you were born to forge a will into iron. But I tell you once again—our mission here is to do the undoable, not the impossible."

Alexander wiped his eyes with his sleeve. His face burned with shame.

"It will work," he said.

Compars walked from the stairway into the cluttered shop. He picked up the trap door from the spot where it had landed and examined it.

"Let me see if I understand. A trunk is carried onstage. You have an assistant—a female, no less!—deposit you into a great canvas bag and padlock it. You get in the trunk, she straps it shut and then stands atop it—a position so unladylike that half your audience will bolt. She is then concealed to her neck by a cloth screen. She drops behind it and begins counting. In what—ten seconds?—the screen falls to reveal not her, but *you* atop the trunk. You jump to the stage, unlock the trunk, a figure inside the bag stands up, the padlock is removed, and the woman is inside."

Alex nodded, his expression now changed from humiliation to defiance.

"Poor Alex. I tell you once again that this trick, even if you can make it work, will do little for our reputation. Such a simple substitution will be seen by the public for what it is—the work of a mere apprentice. And this plan to use a woman assistant dressed like a harlot will offend the very people you hope to entertain."

"She will not be dressed as a harlot, Compars."

"What else will the ladies in the parquet circle call a girl clad only in tights and slippers: an acrobat?"

Alexander took the broken hinge from his brother's hands. Carrying it to a nearby workbench, he picked up a hammer and began banging at the mangled brass. He wondered if his motive was to repair the hinge or drown out his brother's words. Compars came up behind the boy and put a hand on his shoulder.

"In only a few years' time, I will retire and return to the civilization of Europe. I will personally name you as my successor and my secrets will become yours. Alexander! Successor to the Great Herrmann! Through you, I will never be forgotten. The public that adored me will flock to see you do all the great things I have done. In this way you will have a good life—and the audience that has been so good to us for so long will not be cheated of the artistry they have come to expect."

Alexander's eyes filled with rage. "And would you *be* the Great Herrmann if you had only performed the act that our father left you? Silks and doves and rabbits from hats? You, who left medical school for magic? You, who invented The Suspension by Ether? You, who even now, God help us, wish to perform the Bullet Catch with a real slug? You have never stopped creating. Why do you deny this tradition to me?"

Compars sighed and turned on his heel toward the doorway. He stopped at the entranceway and looked back into the vast room. His brother looked small in the corner.

"There is an old saying, boy: when a woman does not love you, she will not accept your gifts. I have lived now forty-six years; and I am not boastful when I say that many women have performed miracles greater than my own simply to be in my company. But even so, I have found that, with a woman of real character, the adage holds true. No bauble, diamond, or ruby will move her once her affection is gone."

He paused on the second stair and turned down the gas lamp at its landing.

"So, I believe it is with *all* love, my Alex. Those who do not love you spurn the good you have to offer. But you are young. Therefore, I will grant you the time to do what the whole world has done—fall in love with the Great Herrmann. Only then will you know the wonders that await you when you become the Great Herrmann yourself."

6

FIVE DAYS BEFORE HIS DEATH, ROBERT INGRAM CAME INTO Omaha on what he called "a refreshment run." At the behest of General George Crook, he had been scouting the Indian territories all of May and June, trying to keep an eye on Standing Bear while avoiding the soldiers of Chased By Owls.

With three months' pay in his pocket, he hit the city like a red-headed cyclone. He ate and drank his fill of Doris's chicken-fried steak and collards, gave up forty dollars to a cardsharp named Jameson, throttled him for cheating, and then spent the night with Lotus Chu, the Nickel & Dime's "exotic" Chinese courtesan. Second only to Lady-Jane Little Feather in sheer expense, Lotus was renowned throughout the territory for her famous "hanging basket" mechanism and her oriental philosophy of providing value for money.

Prophet John McGarrigle also visited the town that night, although hardly in such plush accommodations. It cost him twenty-five cents to stay at the Corner Pocket, a building little more than a large lean-to and the city's cheapest brothel. The nightly tariff was normally fifty cents, but John had chosen Lil Wilson for his companion and so received a discount. Once a prime attraction of the Pocket, Lil was no longer allowed to provide complete carnal services to visitors, owing to an advanced case of gonorrhea. Made blind by the disease, the strong massage and the sweet embrace had replaced her former specialties. Such an arrangement was fine with John, his primary interest being the half of her bed she wasn't using.

The following morning, McGarrigle awoke, put a territorial quarter on Lil's pillow, dressed, and walked out onto Farnam Street. Halfway up the block, he noticed young Julius Meyer placing black shag tobacco in the window of his brother's shop. The gray man waved to him, and Julius returned the salute. In the aftermath of their winter adventure, the boy had gotten to know the prophet. He often came into the store for plug and was never without an anecdote or funny story. The boy enjoyed consulting John about atmospheric conditions, amazed by his accuracy and the detail of his forecasts. Not once had the prophet been wrong, even predicting to the hour when the first thunderstorm of June would turn to hail.

"It's a gift," he would say, "until it's a curse."

Julius smiled and waved back as the gray man walked through the Nickel & Dime's double doors.

A few minutes later, the first scream cut the air.

The hair on the boy's neck rose, each strand sending a chill down his back. The sound seemed at once low and high, its top almost womanly, its bottom froggy and strangled. This was as he always imagined a *dybbuk* might sound, howling as it emerged from hell to possess a human body. Alarmed, Julius locked the shop and ran across Farnum Street and into the Dime. The few men who were in the saloon at that hour had ducked beneath the gambling tables or hidden behind the bar. One even lay down on the stairs that led to the rooms of the girls, flattening his body against the steps as if to pass through them to safety.

At the center of the room, John McGarrigle stood moaning like a soul denied heaven. His body, bent nearly double, shook and vibrated, different parts at different speeds. His beard stood away from his face and his eyes were rolled up in his head. Pale as a hanging prisoner, he raised his arms to shoulder height and pointed both index fingers at Robert Ingram.

"Don't leave here, Bob," he thundered at the terrified scout. "Go back to Fort Kearney and you'll be as dead as Lincoln!"

The prophet screamed again. He shook the index fingers at Ingram like a disapproving schoolmaster. Julius looked down at the boots of the late Jim Riley and saw that they had begun to dance. John's pupils returned to their sockets and were now huge and staring.

"If you go back to Kearney, Bob, we'll bury you hairless! Tell the brass to go to hell or that's where you'll be by next full moon! Don't leave here, Bob. Don't leave . . ."

Prophet John strangled on the word. With a gurgle, he spun around once and hit the floorboards as if touched by the finger of God.

No one in the saloon moved. It was as though McGarrigle's performance had created a magic circle around him, an invisible barrier no patron dared cross. One of the prostitutes, a thick blond girl from Indianapolis called Polack Jenny, crossed herself with the expertise of a Mother Superior.

Robert Ingram sat frozen, his face ashen and his breakfast untouched. After what seemed an hour, he rose from his chair and threw a dollar bill on the table. Without a word, he ran from the saloon and into the street. Julius could hear his horse's hooves on the ground. The sound headed west and out of town.

With no one coming to his aid, Julius stepped toward the fallen McGarrigle. Of course, Max would have said such *knarishkeit* was none of his business; that the crazy *goyim* should be left to their self-induced suffering. But was it not one of the six hundred thirteen *mitzvos* to offer aid to an afflicted friend?

As the boy bent to examine the prophet, he felt someone clutch his shoulder. The grip was not hard, but he could feel the pressure of sharp nails through his coat. Julius reached up to release the hand and was amazed at its softness. Every hand he had shaken here had been rough and calloused with labor. The fingers of the railroad workers some-times felt like the stones they had been breaking. Even the hands of the delicate Chinese women had been swollen into hardened gloves.

The soft hand spun him gently around.

"Leave him alone, Jew boy," the woman said. "When he's like this, it's best to let him be. Wake him and it's like stirring a sleepwalker. Only he's armed—and you wouldn't want your throat slit trying to do a good turn for a madman who won't remember it later."

Julius had seen the dark woman before, walking in the streets and passing in and out of the Dime. Max had called her a *kurva*, Yiddish for whore. In his first days in Nebraska, such talk had shocked Julius, but soon, to hear a woman referred to as a "whore" became like hearing a man called a "miner" or a "cowboy." In fact, most of Omaha's female population had been involved in the trade at one time or another, owing to the huge majority of males to females and a singular lack of discernment on the part of the men.

Lady-Jane Little Feather smiled into Julius's eyes and let her hand drop gently from his shoulder. He felt a small ache where her hand had been.

"I knew a boy in Europe who had such seizures," Julius said. "We used to have to put a stick in his mouth and hold him until the doctor came."

Her smile broadened. "No doctor needed here, boy—which is good, since there's not one for a hundred miles. No, this is just John's little present from the Lord above. I reckon sometimes when He gives you one, he doesn't wrap it up in ribbon and paper. Anyways, he'll be up in an hour, we'll buy him some rotgut, and he'll be right as rain. Only don't touch him now if you want to live."

The boy nodded. "That man he was pointing at. He seemed very frightened."

"As well he should be. He's as good as dead, and he knows it."

Julius looked past her at the body on the floor. It had begun to twitch like a napping dog. She took his elbow and walked him to a table facing the door.

"This only happens a few times a year," she said, sitting the boy down. "But when it does, the subject of his advice better listen. Back last spring, Darryl Pangborn was supposed to put a roof on his house. Him and the prophet were shooting the breeze in front of Seaford's store when the fit took John. He told him to stay close to ground until fall. Darryl didn't listen and he fell ten feet off the roof and another twenty down a well. They brought him up in pieces."

Julius put his hand to his head and wiped a bead of sweat from his cheek. Lady-Jane held up two fingers to a passing waiter.

"The year before it only happened once, but that was worse. General Charlie Hardy had come from Washington to inspect some troops and asked John to scout him to Kearney. John got a visit from God or the Devil or whoever this comes from and told him to stay put. Well, the General got to the fort, all right, just not the way he expected. Chased By Owls sent him and his guards back to Kearney in twelve leather pouches—each one had their ashes inside plus their rank patches.

Charlie's bag had a little something extra. His mustache. They cut it off his face."

Lady-Jane produced a black ebony holder and a box of matches from her small beaded bag. She placed a cigarette in the holder, lighted it, and took a long pull.

"You'd better scat, boy. If Max knew you were in here talking to me, he'd skin us both. And don't worry about the prophet there. By tonight you'll probably see his ass thrown out of here for fighting or cheating at cards or some other activity that proves he's a healthy white man of the plains."

The waiter brought two double shots of whiskey to the table. Lady-Jane handed one to Julius and raised the other in a toast.

"C'mon, boy," she said, like a mother offering milk. "It'll steady you up. And as far as I know, it's kosher."

⊷◈⊶

Close to midnight, Julius was awakened by a commotion in the street. Buzzing with fatigue, the boy rose from his bed and walked to the window.

Below, he could see the lights of the Nickel & Dime and hear its laughter and music. Julius cocked his head and listened as if such gaiety could force the prophet's fit from his mind. As he turned back toward his bed, a commotion arose in the saloon's front window. Through it, he could see the figure of Mack Swain, the Dime's nightside bartender. Larger even than Doris but far less affable, Swain was known for a short fuse easily lit and a limited tolerance for property damage. Only the week before, he had split the skull of a miner who had missed a spittoon and hit a damask tablecloth. It was said around town that Swain would rather see three of his girls busted up than one of his mirrors.

A knot of men had formed around the saloon's entrance, some encouraging the ruckus, others attempting to restore what passed for order at the Dime on a Saturday night. But both factions parted like the Red Sea when Swain's big back burst through the door like a well-dressed block of granite. As the bartender twisted around to face the street, Julius could see that he was dragging a smaller man along with him; he was bearded and dressed in filthy buckskins.

Red-faced and panting, Swain tossed the man into the air. At the apogee of his flight, he seemed to hang suspended, the fringes of the buckskins forming a series of arcs that fluttered like waving wheat. Lady-Jane had been right. Prophet John McGarrigle had recovered enough to get himself in trouble and now lay sprawled and smiling in the dirt.

Julius took comfort at the sight.

As for Robert Ingram, he ignored the prophet's alarm. Ingram had never been superstitious; to give credence to a lunatic would have gone counter to the habits of a lifetime and sullied his reputation with his Army employers. In the event, his common sense earned him a hail of Indian arrows, the fatal ones piercing his left ear and right eye. By the time Chased By Owls was finished with Ingram and his party, all twenty of its members were dead and bald. The bodies were left half naked to the buzzards, the braves having stripped the soldiers of their uniform tunics and Robert Ingram of his brown buffalo coat. From then on, any white man seeing the warriors would know that their garments had been earned by the deaths of their enemies—and that all the power of the brave bluecoats now resided on *their* backs.

7

AFTER TWENTY YEARS IN THE SHOW BUSINESS, COMPARS Herrmann knew it took more than talent or the simple working of miracles to draw the attention of the press.

He had tried minor bribery, but it couldn't always be counted upon to work. A few tickets here and there might attract a reporter with children to entertain. A box of cigars (bearing his likeness) could arouse the interest of an editor too broke to buy his own. But the better-paid journalists would often refuse his largesse, lecturing him on the purity of the fourth estate; or even worse, accepting his gifts while writing nothing about his engagement.

In the end, the solution proved as simple as human hunger.

On an October evening in 1845, Compars asked one Billy Glenn, a reporter for the Cincinnati *Enquirer,* to join him for dinner. Glenn readily accepted and over the course of several hours tore through turtle soup, a sole filet, duck *a la Rouennaise* and a Princesse Bombe Glacée.' He washed each course down with the appropriate wine and finished off the meal with most of a bottle of Benedictine. In between dishes, Compars managed to relate the amazing components of his latest engagement. When the evening was over, Glenn let fly with a belch like a bullfrog in season, thanked his host, and left the restaurant having made no promises of coverage.

The next evening, the *Enquirer* carried a five-inch story with a headline that read:

GREAT HERRMANN ASTONISHES CITY!
Magician's latest exhibition a milestone in the prestidigitational arts!

The article couldn't have been more laudatory or detailed if Compars had written it himself. It chronicled every trick, previewed every joke and witticism. The audience's astonished reactions were described as if the reporter had actually attended; and the entire performance schedule was included so that no citizen of the great metropolis would be so unfortunate as to miss "this most spectacular of magical triumphs."

From that day forward, all of Compars's engagements were preceded by an elaborate buffet for the local newspapermen. No matter how small the city or how large the press corps, no expense was spared to provide reporters with the sustenance necessary for them to defend a free society.

Included might be clams on ice; hand-sliced beef roasts *au jus*; carrots glazed in butter and sugar; and a variety of cheeses accompanied by fresh-baked breads. Local actresses (or women who claimed to be) would circulate about the room serving *petit fours* and tiny sherbets; and of course, the bar would be as open as the heart of the great magician himself.

It was just such a spread that now greeted the gentlemen of the press. The chef had outdone himself, producing a unique set of food-stuffs tempting to the palate and pleasing to the eye, even sculpting Compars's head and shoulders in blue ice surrounded with fruit and roses.

Once the newsmen had eaten and drunk their fill and the personalized cigars were distributed, Compars leapt up onto a small platform. He reached into the air with his right hand and produced a panatela of his own. In his left appeared a match, already lighted. He ignited the cigar and took a few amused puffs.

"Gentlemen, I hope you have all enjoyed your luncheon. I believe I will not be contradicted when I say that Lovejoy's is New York's finest hotel and that Chef Denys is a magician in his own right!"

The newsmen applauded and grunted various "hear hear's" and "bravos," punctuated by loud and appreciative burps.

"As you are all my friends, you know that although I live in this greatest of all nations, I was not privileged to be born an American. Therefore, the countries where I made my reputation are constantly clamoring for my presence. I do not think I am immodest when I say that my European public has been too long deprived of my presence on the stage."

"Oh no, that's not immodest!" cried out Murphy of the *World*.

"Humble to a fault!" said Miller of the *Post*.

Compars joined in the drunken laughter and took a long pull on his cigar.

"But gentlemen, I must admit a problem. Every time I attempt to leave these shores, imitators rush in to fill the void left by the Great Herrmann! Shameless, they attempt 'The Floating Boy,' the 'Bird's Head Restoration,' etcetera. These inferiors endeavor to re-create my unique artistry while taking the very bread from my mouth."

"I got a roll right here!" hollered Collins of the *Mirror*, holding up a seeded Kaiser.

"Let 'em eat cake!" shouted Spalding of the *Eagle*.

"So how then to satiate the hunger for my abilities across the sea while protecting my interests here at home? How to preserve the magical legacy I have taken decades to build while warding off these copycats and mountebanks?"

"Monty Banks?" yelled Smith of the *Sun*. "Don't he work for the *Herald?*"

Compars once again joined in the mirth and then held up his hands for order.

"Still, for the Great Herrmann every problem has a solution, gentlemen! Therefore, indulge me while I direct your attention to the cabinet now being wheeled onstage . . ."

The laughter died down as a young assistant appeared. He was large and muscular with hair the color of a pumpkin, and was dressed in a black monk's robe. He wheeled an immense lacquered box to the center of the platform and whirled it about twice. The cabinet was painted a deep mandarin and was covered with Chinese characters and question marks. The redhead positioned the box at center stage and opened its front door.

"As you can see, my friends, an ordinary empty cabinet—nothing within her but thin air. And now, professor, if you please."

The magician gestured toward a pianist seated at a huge black grand. He struck up a lively waltz, causing some of the more inebriated newsmen to begin dancing with each other. Compars closed the cabinet and shot his cuffs, producing a huge black silk that he and the redhead proceeded to drape over the box. When it was completely obscured, the assistant pulled the hood of the monk's robe over his head. Folding his arms, he turned his back to the audience.

Compars reached into the air again and produced a small percussion pistol. He displayed it to his audience and shot once into the air. Then he quickly grabbed the black silk and pulled.

Where the largest question mark had been there was now an exclamation point of equal size. The magician turned toward the astonished newsmen.

"And now," he said, "I shall introduce you to the personage who shall represent the legacy of Herrmann in this greatest of all republics. The only man who is fit to amaze and astound America in my great tradition. Gentlemen, I give you . . ."

Compars leapt at the box and threw open the door to reveal a space as empty as before.

At first the journalists were silent; but when the Great Herrmann turned toward them and shrugged sheepishly, cigars flew from mouths and men dribbled beer and whiskey on their vests. They laughed and applauded in mock appreciation until Compars raised his hands to quiet them once more.

"My good friends, I simply don't know what to say. I had hoped that in my Cabinet of Wonders I would find my successor; but it has brought me only embarrassment and defeat before you, my honored guests. But wait! Perhaps my redheaded friend will know where my replacement has gone. Besides, it is very rude for him to stand here all this time with his back to you. I shall make him mind his manners."

Compars turned to the hooded figure and snapped his fingers imperiously.

"I say, young man! I, the Great Herrmann, command you to remove that absurd hood and turn and face my guests."

At first, the robed figure hesitated. Then he slowly reached up, grabbed the two sides of his hood, snapped it back, and turned toward his audience.

The reporters gasped.

Where the big redhead had stood was a completely different man; a satanic figure who looked for all the world like a younger version of The Great Herrmann himself. He possessed the same penetrating blue eyes and raven hair; the identical spade-shaped beard and wax-tipped mustache. He bowed to the newsmen with a flourish of both arms, his graceful hands completing the gesture like a pair of landing birds.

"Holy shit!" cried Knoblauch of the *Whip*.

The younger Compars unknotted his rope belt and swiftly removed the monk's robe. He was as thin as a marsh reed and dressed in a swallow-tailed coat and double-breasted vest of silver brocade. His patent leather boots shone beneath gray spats.

"Gentlemen," Compars said, clapping his twin on the shoulder, "allow me to introduce you to the only man on God's green Earth capable of accurately reproducing the marvels my audience has come to demand! He has, these past two years, often traveled the smaller provinces with an act that is nearly a perfect duplication of all my genius has produced. His resemblance to your humble servant is far from accidental as he is in fact, my own beloved youngest brother. And so, gentlemen, it is my distinct pleasure to present to you my singular and only designated successor . . ."

And here, the "professor" began a fanfare that started at the lower keys and ended at the highest.

". . . Alexander!"

The younger man bowed again and immediately launched into a series of small miracles. He produced cards from his mouth and eyes; he released a white rabbit from his bare hands; he materialized a fully lighted birthday cake from a seemingly empty hat. With each new illusion, the reporters applauded louder and scribbled harder. Even the chef was enlisted for the occasion. At the sound of a whistle from Compars, M. Denys made his way through the gathering with a large covered silver dish. Stepping to the platform, he removed the cover with a courtly bow.

"*Voilà!*"

On the platter sat a whole roast duck, surrounded by potatoes and tiny green peas. The young magician studied the bird for a moment, took a white silk from his pocket, and passed it over the steaming dish. When he snapped the cloth away, the meal was gone, replaced by a live mallard, quacking in terror at the sudden transition.

Finally, the two brothers moved to opposite sides of the platform and produced twin revolvers. They fired them in perfect unison and as they did, a gigantic poster unfurled from the ceiling. It was a portrait of Alexander in full color, his splendid head encased in a leaf-encrusted oval. All about the likeness were scenes from Compars's career: his appearances before royalty, the classic tricks he had listed for the reporters; and at the bottom, in fine hand lettering surrounded by flames, read the legend:

ALEXANDER THE GREAT
Brother & Sole Successor to the Great Herrmann

The journalists applauded thunderously and raised their glasses in tribute. With a grin, Compars reached into the air and plucked from it an elaborate German *bierstein*. He lifted its pewter lid, placed the stein to his lips and took a long draft.

"Drinks for everybody!"

The assembled press cheered again and made for the bar. On the way, two of them mounted the makeshift stage and linked arms with Compars, dragging him from the platform.

Alexander stood in front of the cabinet, alone, the playing cards and black robe in a pile at his feet. Looking toward the bar, he saw the reporters clapping his brother on the back and toasting his health. One of the "actresses" was handing out cards printed with Compars's biography on one side and his own on the other. Finally, a group of liveried waiters accompanied a huge cake—a real one this time—on its journey from the kitchen. On its top stood a profile of his brother in spun sugar and paste; its lowest layer was encircled with the words, "Farewell, Prof. Herrmann, *Illusioniste Extraordinaire!*"

Alex threw the revolver to the floor. Without looking back, he walked through the black backdrop and exited the ballroom through a door at the rear. In the deserted corridor, he found the redheaded assistant busily packing his master's equipment.

"What're ya doin' back here, Mr. Alex?" he asked. "Plenty a' good drink still in there and the the press boys will be wantin' yer comments."

Alex smiled at the young Irishman. From the banquet room, he could hear the "professor" strike up *Auld Lang Syne,* quickly followed by drunken voices mangling its lyrics.

"It's Mr. Dowie, am I right?"

"Yessir," the Irishman said. "Yessir, Seamus Dowie, sir, at your service."

"I expect you haven't eaten, Seamus. Neither have I. Here."

Alex reached into his fine morning coat and produced the perfectly roasted leg and thigh of a Long Island duckling. He handed it to Dowie.

"Just an *hors d'oeuvre,* my friend. Let's to Delmonico's for some beefsteak and beer. As to sticking here for *Herr Docktor* and these ink-stained dolts, never have I seen a better occasion for a magician to vanish."

8

LEMUEL NORCROSS ENJOYED HIS NEW JOB. IT WAS EXCITING and grown-up and it paid better than any other work a ten-year-old could find in Omaha.

His duties were specific and unchanging. He would arrive at the Corner Pocket around seven in the evening and rake the rat pit until the surface was flat and even. About an hour later, the handlers appeared with their dogs, each a different breed of terrier: Cairns, Westies, Norwiches, Lakelands, and a few mixes. They were little—the largest not much more than twenty pounds—and the boy loved to assist their masters in petting and massaging them.

At ten o'clock, the audience began to arrive and the wagering began. Lemuel was entrusted to hold the money and keep the odds, no one expecting a mere baby to possess either the guile or the courage to indulge in any dishonesty. As the money changed hands, the boy watched as, one by one, the dogs were weighed and the rats counted out. The number of rats placed in the pit equaled the weight of each dog: ten pounds, ten rats; twenty pounds, twenty rats and so on. The bets were based on the amount of time it took a given dog to kill every rodent in the ring. Lemuel received no money for his services, but tips were generous, and there were nights when he placed as much as ten dollars in his mother's apron.

The first animal up this evening was called Handsome Harry: a champion Cairn owned by a railroad brakeman named Adolph Karns. The crowd stomped and cheered as the terrier was placed into the pit and began pacing in anticipation. Sherdlu, one of the Pocket's rat catchers, hefted a pulsating bag over the ring and turned it over. Fifteen rats—the number corresponding to Harry's weight—poured into the ring.

Almost before they hit the ground, Harry was on them, lifting and shaking them, sometimes two at a time. Once one was killed, the dog moved immediately to the next. When all the rats were dead, a bell sounded to indicate the time.

As the bloodied dog was lifted from the pit, Lemuel Norcross looked at the numbers written on his slips: one minute; fifty seconds; seventy seconds. It wasn't until he saw the sixth slip that he found the number he sought, accompanied by the name of the winner.

"We have a victor, gentlemen!"

Basking in the attention, Lemuel raised the yellow slip above his head. The ring announcer shouted above the din.

"A winner here and one winner only. At seventy-six seconds, the exact time for the mighty Harry, the proceeds of this evening's first bout benefit one of our most charming citizens, the one and only Red Rose of Omaha, Miss Lady-Jane Little Feather!"

The crowd roared its approval as Lemuel raced to the center of the tiered benches. As he reached Lady-Jane, she stood to acknowledge the applause and whistles and accepted her winnings from the boy. Smiling into his flushed face, she peeled off a dollar from her roll and handed it to him. Lemuel whooped in gratitude, bowed to his benefactress, and hurried back to take the next round of wagers.

Lady-Jane returned to her seat, placing the winnings discreetly into her bodice. Her companion took a long drag on his cigar and wrote the number thirty below his name, his bet on the next dog.

"As usual, you are lucky," he said, "and prudent."

"If by that you've guessed that I'm not going to bet again tonight, then you're right. This is a bird in the hand, Calhern: and if I'm ever to stop screwing cowboys, I'll need a cage full."

Adrian Calhern handed his marker down the aisle. As it made its way hand over hand to his right, a drunken Hunk Marston approached from his left. He saluted Calhern in the manner of an Army veteran and offered him congratulations on his girl's good fortune.

Calhern removed his hat and stood to face Marston, his cold stare quickly removing the good nature from the young man's face.

"Never mind that, bucko. You have a balance due at the Dime. A bar tab of fifteen dollars, and eighteen dollars for the use of my women."

"Gosh, Mr. Calhern. As much as that?"

"Yes, Hunk, as much as that."

The second dog, a nineteen-pound Skye named Jock, was lowered into the pit. The dog was known to be quick and vicious. In honor of that reputation, the men cheered louder at his mere appearance than they had for Harry's triumph.

Marston put his hand to his chin. "Well, gee, Mr. Calhern—how long do I have to pay it back?"

It was only the crowd's own noise that kept them from hearing the howl as Calhern snatched Marston's hand and bent it straight back at the wrist. When Hunk tried to free his hand, the pimp head-butted him. Hunk reeled amid stars and planets.

"This, bucko, is what I call the quality of mercy."

Calhern bent the hand back a little more. The crowd cheered louder as the rats were released from the bag.

"One fraction of one more inch and this wrist breaks like a swampy cattail," Calhern said. "Breaks so it don't get better. Breaks permanent."

The roar was deafening as Jock lit into the rats. One attempted to scratch his eye and was bitten nearly in half.

"But if I break it, Hunkie, you don't work. You don't work, you don't pay, savvy? So now—right now—you'll leave this place. You won't drink, you won't gamble. You'll live the pure life, and all of your wages from the livery will go to me until we're square. They don't, your wife meets the ladies that have serviced you so well and I break this hand and then the other."

Jock crushed the largest and last rat against the pit wall. His official time was announced as one minute flat: slower than usual.

Calhern released the hand from his grip and sat back down. He took a lace handkerchief from his pocket and wiped his hands as if to remove any essence of his victim. Finally, he looked up at Marston and, raising his hand, waved him off as if instructing a child to run along and play.

"Go," he said, "and sin no more."

Hunk Marston made his way through the cheering throng and out a side entrance. Calhern put his cigar back in his mouth and began to study the yellow sheet bearing the names and weights of the remaining contenders.

Lady-Jane stared straight ahead.

"If you performed that little song and dance for my benefit, you needn't have bothered."

Calhern didn't look up from the dog roster. "At this late date, my dear, you should know that your benefit is all that matters to me in this world."

"That's good, Calhern—because on July thirteenth, I turn eighteen. The vault opens, I walk in and collect every penny I've earned since I started in the profession."

Calhern again wrote his name on the slip and whistled for Lemuel Norcross. As the boy came running, he rose to pass his bet down the line. No money changed hands. His credit was always good at the Pocket.

The crowd screamed as the next bout began.

"You don't have to present me with a sum, my darling. I know how much I owe you. I believe that God himself sent me by the Indian school that day. That he meant me to find you. The soldiers killed every other child in that school, burned it, brave and buck, but they left you alive for me to love."

Lady-Jane was a scarred veteran of such grand speeches. They had worked well four years ago when Calhern had found her waist-deep in ashes, starving and alone. Back then, his kindness had seemed genuine, and, by the lights of a man in his business, it probably had been. He fed and bathed her. He bought her clothes from the East and jewelry from Max Meyer. He beat her only when she deserved it. And when she fell in love with him, he trained her in the art of what a man likes and the sacrifices that must be made to achieve a degree of marketable skill.

When he first offered her to another man, Lady-Jane wanted to run or refuse; but she owed him for everything, from her shoes to her life. He told her it would only be for this one time. The client was neither old nor ugly but a boy not much older than herself, brought to the Dime by his father for some "experience."

She weighed disgust against fear and fear against gratitude, and her career began. By 1867, when ten dollars bought flour for a year or rent for a month, it was also the amount that bought the Red Rose for a night. Half of the fee, Calhern had told her, would be put aside; and when she reached her majority she would receive the funds to which she was entitled. Lady-Jane had kept strict accounts. The number stood at over twelve thousand dollars.

The dog in the pit was let loose. He was a small, scrappy mutt with a patch of brown over one eye. Calhern fell silent and reached into his vest for his watch. He snapped open its case and began to time the match. For the first time, Lady-Jane noticed that the little portrait opposite the clock face was his own.

He swore into the watch. The dog was slower than it had been all year. Calhern sighed and turned toward his companion, his eyes filled with regret.

"As sure as the Lord made you beautiful, I know that I should repay you double. Which is why it's doubly hard to tell you that I can't pay you at all."

Lady-Jane was still. She had rehearsed this reckoning in her mind many times in recent days; how he would balk and bargain, the charm he would use to dispute her numbers. But her brain had never defaulted to what he had just said: *I can't pay you; I can't pay you at all.*

Calhern checked off the next name on the roster. "Of course, that don't mean I'll never. I just can't right now. These dogs and the cards have been mean to me of late—and I've had to give that bastard Swain twenty percent more of the Dime's pleasure business. Add to that Addie Jackson dying of the syph and Peggy Bradley running off, well, you see how it is."

Lady-Jane didn't move. She thought for a moment of the tintypes of famous chiefs that adorned the upstairs parlor of the Dime; how the inscrutable faces exposed to the indignity of the camera betrayed nothing before the white destroyer. She forced her face into the same stillness.

The pimp's face brightened. "But see, if we work together we can make this right. One more year, maybe two, and I'll pay you back with interest—everything you've made up to now and everything you will make. We'll raise your fee from ten dollars to eleven and that extra dollar will be yours to keep."

He began to laugh.

"Just don't tell Lotus. She'd skin me alive and eat me for chop suey."

Lady-Jane shook her head as if she understood his problem. He clapped her on the back for a good sport and sighed over his losses as the final match ended with a rout by a sixteen-pound Lakeland bitch named Jenny. This time, Calhern had been off by over twenty seconds.

The crowd rose and parted to allow the pit's only woman to pass. Soon they were outside. The night was soft with spring.

"It's been a bad bargain for me tonight, my love. I guess I left more markers in this place than them dogs did rats. Still there's always more to be made in the big world. No one knows that better than you."

Calhern stepped in front of Lady-Jane and with fingers as deft as a pickpocket's, plucked the night's winnings from her bodice.

"See? There's money everywhere."

He smiled, touched the rim of his hat, and walked in the direction of the Pink Lady.

She waited until he was out of sight and then strode quickly through the town until she reached the Dime. She unlocked the private entrance and ascended the winding stairs. There was a time when such a cavalier betrayal would have caused her to weep, but tears had long since deserted Lady-Jane. Peggy Bradley, the girl who had run away, had told her this would happen; that one day she would receive the final scar on a hardened heart.

"Cherish it, girl," Peggy had told her. "It's your armor. Without it, they'll own all of you. And then you may as well jump from the top of First Baptist."

Removing her hat and shawl, Lady-Jane sat down at an antique partner's desk. She plucked two sheets of fine white notepaper from a cubby above the blotter and began to write two identical notes. They would go to two people she hoped to spare her hatred—the last warm emotion in a soul turned to ice.

⊰◇⊱

As he did at seven every morning, Julius descended the stairs from the apartment he shared with Max to the sales floor of the M. Meyer Tobacco Company.

He would usually be alone at that hour—having awakened to his brother's bed neatly made and his brother not in it.

But on this morning, he found Max already seated in the center of the shop, fully dressed and shaved, and surrounded by brown cardboard boxes.

"Come here," Max said.

Julius wasn't used to seeing his brother much before ten. By that time, he had swept the shop, restocked the shelves, culled the unsold periodicals and opened the door for the eight o'clock rush. By nine, he had waited on dozens of Omaha's citizens stocking up on black shag or enough cigars or plug to last them the day. Once the commotion died down, he checked the inventory; then he tallied the invoices and composed the order telegrams to be sent to the suppliers back East—all this before his brother so much as drew a breath by the pipe racks.

Once Max did arrive, he invariably spent his first working hour negating everything the boy had done.

In their native German, he would upbraid Julius for his numerous errors in commercial judgment. *Nein! The chew plugs should be placed bottom label out so that ladies buying for their men can see them better. Nein! Nein! You call this writing clear? I can't tell if this says three dollars or five dollars the way you write! Nein! Nein! NEIN! Who allows a widow with four children to buy quarter candy and writing paper on credit? Are you mischigah or only stupid?*

Not that any of these retail disasters ever encouraged Max to arrive any earlier. He always claimed that his pre-dawn absence was prompted by his need for prayer and reflection and the holy maintenance of his body. But in a town the size of Omaha, secrets were like teakettles: no one could see the water but everyone could hear the whistle. Julius had long known that if his brother's body was in for maintenance, the mechanic was likely Lady-Jane Little Feather or, in a down month, someone less expensive.

Peering over the boxes, Max didn't bother to greet him, which surprised his brother not at all. As Julius had not yet begun his day's work, there was no reason to criticize him—and since there was no reason to criticize him, there was therefore no reason for Max to say anything to him at all.

The boy knew better than to inquire as to the contents of the cardboard boxes, but noted that each one bore the name of a printer from Des Moines. As his brother's buck knife cut through paste and panel, Julius smelled fresh ink and wondered what could have made his brother indulge in such an extravagance.

Max reached into the first box and removed a stack of cream-colored papers. Each was folded twice and covered with type and pictures. Without a word, Max peeled off one of the papers and handed it to Julius. The cover read:

M. MEYER TOBACCO CO.
Omaha, Nebraska. Since 1864.

The company name had been hand-drawn with great skill, every letter like a carving in ivory, festooned with oak leaves and filigree. But even more startling was the fine engraving just below the elegant trademark. It depicted an Indian chief in full headdress. He wore a beautiful buffalo robe, and his wrists were adorned with jewelry. The face wore a grave but contented look and he appeared to contemplate the very essence of the primitive as he enjoyed a long-feathered pipe. The artist had rendered the smoke so that it rose from the bowl and billowed about the old brave's head in curlicues. When the smoke finally reached the top of the page, it gracefully surrounded the words *your satisfaction guaranteed.*

Julius unfolded the brochure. Inside, there were more fine illustrations: wild Indians in full battle array and demure red-skinned maidens, their hands and necks laden with fine stones and gems. In one corner, there was a detailed drawing of a beaded purse, in the other a striped blanket with a pattern of running horses. The copy read:

> We of The M. Meyer Tobacco Company, Omaha, have long prided ourselves on supplying our clientele with the finest in tobacco products as well as fancy gifts from around the globe.
>
> Now, we are happy to announce that Meyer can offer even more!
>
> In addition to the fine items for which we are justly renowned, our customers may now also avail themselves of the beautiful craftwork created by the Indian peoples with whom God has allowed us to share this great land! Savages though they may be, we submit that no other

people on Earth have yet attained the appreciation of nature or the matchless craftsmanship evinced by these wild tribes.

From their red hands, we now offer exquisite blankets, belts, robes and hats as well as jewelry in silver and gold. These items have been attained at considerable danger to our staff, as there are still those among these untamed peoples who would seek to make war on their white betters. But thanks to the courage and shrewdness of our traders, we are now able to offer these unique items at the cheapest possible price, for the personal delectation of the most discerning ladies and gentlemen.

The boy handed the pamphlet back to his brother.

Julius turned to Max. "The courage and shrewdness of *what* traders?"

Max still said nothing. Laying down his knife, he pointed toward the door.

Prophet John McGarrigle was as silent as Max Meyer, but for a different reason: he was asleep. The activities of the previous evening—which had included the sampling of some freshly distilled white lightning at Pat's Pair o' Dice—had apparently overcome his usual alertness. Upon his arrival only a few minutes before, he had made the mistake of leaning against the shop's door jamb for what he thought would be a moment's rest and went out like a light. Julius looked down to see Jim Riley's boots crossed one over the other in a jaunty manner, as if McGarrigle were a city swell reclining on a lamppost, the better to observe the ladies.

"*Shiker!*" Max cried at the scout, using the Yiddish word for drunkard. "Wake up. You have to today take mein brother to the Indians."

The Prophet awoke with a start but began to smile almost immediately at the sight of his former roommate. He held up an index finger as if to beg a moment's forbearance, then stuck his head out the doorway. He spat a part of last night onto the rough wooden boardwalk and turned back to face his hosts.

"Nice to see you, Mr. Max. Young Jules."

"*Ach*," Max said. "Are you ready to leave? It will only take mein brother a few minutes to gather from what he has and then you and him will go by the Indians."

"The wagon's loaded," Prophet John said. "Just got to water the mules. Everything I need is on my person and everything they need is on theirs."

"Good." Max turned to Julius. "You'll now go and get ready clothes and from what you need for two months maybe and you'll go with the McGorgle."

"Go?" Julius asked. "Go where?"

"By the Indians. Your uncle, the Gershonson, says that now he is from them buying what they make. Trinkets, belts, blankets, and all *chazarei* what is made by them. All of a sudden, right away they want such things in the East. The women in Manhattan want they should look like savages. The men wear buffalo robes to Wall Street. Who would believe such nonsense? But they buy, so we sell. So the McGorgle will take you and you'll trade."

"So the courageous, shrewd trader is *me*—the one who faces the considerable danger?"

"Only advertising, young Jules," John said. "Tales exaggerated for the Eastern Seaboard. Be of good cheer, for you are in good hands. I've faced down Chased By Owls and still I eat and breathe; smoked pipe with Standing Bear himself and I trod God's earth. Your brother hired me to lead you around the shit piles, so to say; and bring you back with plenty pretty merchandise and them black curls intact."

Julius looked from the gray man to his brother and shook his head. Max's eyes popped wide.

"You won't do it? And who it was what brought you from Europe, you shouldn't starve? Who took you from that *yeshiva* orphan house and away from those fanaticals? It wasn't for me you would be begging already in the street with a beard and earlocks or be fifteen and married to some two-headed girl you first laid your eyes on under the *chuppah*."

"Your brother makes a point," said the Prophet, helping himself to a piece of Helm chew. "Share the riches, share the risk, I always say."

Max grabbed the tobacco from the scout's hand and turned on Julius in a cold fury.

"So maybe you don't like being an American boy," Max said in German. "Maybe you'd like to go back to the old country, eh? I'll write to the Governor and put your papers in. I'll tell him my brother prefers Prussia with the fucking Polacks and the Germans and the goddamn *frum* Jews to America with the *goyim* and the Indians. I'll get you a ticket and before you scratch your dick you'll be back from where I took you. There, nobody will ask you to do anything except beg them for a bowl of soup or lie still while they beat you."

Julius stood still between the two men, his eyes like coals, his fists clenched at his sides. Damn the danger. Could the hatchets of Indians be more humiliating than his brother's condescension? Could a hail of arrows be much worse than the gray man's string of inanities?

Julius threw the pamphlet down and stomped through the rear of the shop and up the stairs. Max and Prophet John could hear the banging of a suitcase and the rapid clatter of boots. A few minutes later, Julius came back down, his suitcase in his hand and his hat on his head. He walked past his brother as if he were another display of meerschaums and into the street.

When he had walked a few yards, he felt the rough hand of Prophet John on his elbow. He cursed and shrugged the gray man off, walking hard toward the livery where Max had boarded the mules.

"I understand, young Julius," the prophet said. "Big brothers like things their way. I had one myself, name of Carter. Wouldn't give you a canteen if he owned the Great Lakes. Every time he got his hands on a dollar bill, he would smell it like a flower. Get four or five, and it was like his boyfriend sent him a bouquet. Believe me, young Jules, he made your Max look like a philanthropist. I guess that's what comes of having the birthright. What's mine is mine and if I figure yours is mine, then that's mine, too."

Julius thought his head would explode from McGarrigle's gibberish. At the corner by the Dime, the stable came into view.

"And don't worry for your life, young Jules. Remember, there's only so dead you can get. I've been charged with the protection of many in my life, and my survival rate, roughly calculated, is above seventy percent. And while some ended up dead, I'm proud to say that none was dead aplenty."

Julius stopped in his tracks. His head buzzed like a swarm of bees.

"What the hell is that supposed to mean?"

McGarrigle snorted into his nose. "See, in my years as a scout I've been caught in some fights here and there; some of them what was with me joined the upstairs chorus, and that's a fact. Soldiers looking for Indians—pilgrims trying to bed down a wagon train. Some got killed by arrows. *Woooshhh!* Through the heart or ear, nice and clean. Some got shot by pistols. *Bang!* Done for. And I reckon it was little comfort to their kin that they were dead. But dead aplenty, well, that's something else."

"What's the difference?" Julius said. "When you're dead, you're dead."

Prophet John chuckled and shook his head. "Oh no, young Jules, nothing like it. When a foe puts a bullet in your brain or a road agent cuts your throat, you're dead. When you get the influenza and they pull up the sheet and read over you, you're dead. But when say, you fall seventy feet from a cliff and land with your eyes on two rocks, or you crawl ten miles through the Mexican desert with a gila monster hanging from your ear, or Chased By Owls makes you watch while he slices your gut and throws your entrails to the dogs, well, son, then you're dead aplenty."

Julius glared at the gray man and began to walk toward the stables again. The prophet took his arm.

"It's all right, young Jules. John McGarrigle is here to care for his baby. We'll come back weighed way down with wampum and you and your brother will be rich enough to leave these wilds and return to where they pray in your native tongue and wait for the Jew messiah. Besides, I'm something of a celebrity among the Poncas."

Julius whirled on his boot heel and shouted into the scout's face. "I suppose you're going to tell them about tomorrow's weather. Or maybe fall to the ground and howl and convulse and give Standing Bear a great premonition."

McGarrigle looked into the boy's earnest face and coughed deeply. Then he burst into laughter.

"No, no, my boy," Prophet John said, shaking his head back and forth. "I'm not due, not yet. And anyway, when it comes to the big chief of the Poncas, he's no different from anyone else. I've only got so many fits in me. They each comes with a single warning. And I only hand out one per customer per lifetime."

9

J O ANN McGREEVY HAD SPENT A GOOD PART OF THE DAY with a rag in her hand.

In the rest of the house, she might entrust such work to the maid, or enlist her lazy son Richard for some tasks. But in this room, only the landlady herself handled the chores, thus ensuring that the cleanliness of the home matched the quality of the tenant. If she was forced to take in boarders, at least she had found one who was what her late husband always called a "Christian gentleman." And even if the gentleman wasn't actually a Christian, he maintained all the qualities of the breed; and it wouldn't do to have him return from his business to the kind of filth Omaha produced as routine.

Mrs. McGreevy had just finished straightening the last doily when she heard the bells on his wagon. She hurried downstairs to the kitchen and hung her apron on its hook. Making for the front entrance, she shouted for her son and then took up a position to the left of the door.

Even without being able to see inside it, Mrs. McGreevy could tell that the wagon was far lighter than when it had left nearly three weeks before. Back then, its oblong body had sat mere inches from its springs, so laden was it with worldly goods. Its exterior had been so completely covered with merchandise that its mustard-yellow paint could only be seen through the tiny spaces between the items. Now Mrs. McGreevy smiled to see the big, fancy letters that adorned the side panels in black and green. They read: E. GERSHONSON. A SQUARE DEAL.

Approaching the house, the peddler shouted something to his mules that was likely the Yiddish equivalent of "whoa." The animals stopped at the garden fence and bent their necks to a trough of water placed there in advance of their arrival. The driver let go of the reins and gave a small wave in the direction of his landlady.

Mrs. McGreevy called for Richard again. From the rear of the house loped a gangly youth of about sixteen.

"Take Mr. Eli's bag down from the wagon and get his rig to the livery," she shouted. "Make sure they see to his team proper."

Richard shook hands with the peddler as Eli Gershonson clapped him on the back, causing the dust to rise from his own sleeve. The landlady saw her son's sullen expression change in an instant and knew that Gershonson had slipped a reward into his palm.

Eli picked up his one small carpetbag. Mrs. McGreevy descended the front steps and met him at the center of the path.

"Oh, Mr. Eli, I am so glad you are home safe. I trust your trip was a profitable one?"

"Thank you very much, Mrs. McGreevy," Eli said. "Yes, somehow the highwaymen missed me and the Indians left me alone again. Maybe I lead a charmed life, or maybe it's because the Holy One, blessed be he, took my hair before they could."

Both of them had heard this joke many times before and laughed at its welcome return.

"As to profit, I won't know until the sums have been done, but as you can see, all has been sold. Praise God."

"Praise God," she said. "I've prepared all your favorites, Mr. Eli. Tonight there's brisket of beef."

"Mrs. McGreevy, how often have I told you not to go to any special trouble for me? If you make a ham for your boarders, I'm not offended. A few eggs and your bread and butter and I'm a happy man."

She raised her eyebrows and waved him away. "They'll eat brisket of beef and like it. With potatoes and root beets, who wouldn't? Now, give me that dusty coat before you bring the entire wilderness in the house with you. There are muffins on the table—no lard, Mr. Eli."

Mrs. McGreevy helped him off with his coat and vest. Quickly surveying his back and shoulders, she could immediately see how much weight he had lost in his weeks away. He removed his hat and followed her into the vestibule. She paused at the chest beneath the mirror and picked up a white envelope. She handed it to him and took the hat in exchange.

"This came for you this morning. The rest of your mail is in your room. I'll brush your hat and by the time you've freshened up, your tea will be ready."

"In a glass, like I like it?

"In a glass, Mr. Eli. One cube of sugar."

Gershonson nodded and climbed the stairs. His room was spotless; even the lace curtains had been taken down and laundered. On his pillow was a voucher good for a bath and shave at Bruno's Neapolitan.

A single white rose from the vine by the front door stood in a bud vase on the dressing table.

Eli put down his grip and sat heavily on the bed. Only now, in this clean environment, did he notice his own smell: a mixture of road and mule and man. As he opened the white envelope, he noticed that his hands had become tight and dry, the skin cracked near the fingernails.

The note was written in a small careful hand, as if the correspondent had learned just enough of the alphabet to live in the world of adults. Eli drew his bent spectacles from his vest pocket and began to read:

> *My friend—*
> *If you valu your life, I beg you do not go to the nickle + dime*
> *this Friday. Do not go in the morning nor at noon nor at nite.*
> *Do not go for biznis. Do not go for work nor eat nor drink.*
> *Of this letter tell no one.*

There was no signature: not even an X or a set of initials. Eli read the letter again, this time more slowly. What could be so dangerous beyond the fights and shootings that routinely took place at the Dime? Surely, this warning wasn't about misunderstandings over cards or women; every man knew which tables had the potential for trouble and how to avoid them; and he was never known to frequent the Dime except in the mornings when most villains were asleep. Perhaps it was a prank; or maybe it was a way of frightening him away from Omaha; one less Jew to cheat good Americans on the price of an iron stockpot.

Gershonson placed the letter on the dresser and walked to the calendar that hung by the north window. He noted where he had circled his departure date of May 12, 1869 and counted forward seventeen days. When his hand came to rest on the twenty-eighth, he quickly realized that today was the Friday of which the letter had warned. Eli opened his pocket watch and saw that it was a bit before five. After a change of linen and Mrs. McGreevy's brisket of beef, he would say the prayers he had neglected in the wild and retire to observe the Sabbath. Regardless of the note's admonition, the next night he would discuss the mysterious letter with the sheriff, as any law-abiding citizen would.

At dinner, none of the boarders complained about the brisket of beef (or any other of Mrs. McGreevy's dishes), and they were suitably entertained by Eli's recounting of his adventures in frontier retailing: there was the rancher who insisted on being present the entire time his wife was inspecting his wares, lest she be led into temptation; the little boy who inspected one of his funnels and, using it as a top, persuaded his mother to buy it for him as such. Finally, he related how a man near Lake Platte had attempted to pickpocket him. Experience had taught Eli never to carry anything in his trousers or coat. When the man came up empty, the peddler asked what he needed besides his money. Embarrassed, the pickpocket replied that he could use a good penknife. Asking the robber to wait a moment, Eli brought out a flat case containing a dazzling assortment and sold him one. By the time this last story was told, Mrs. Emmanuel Wilson, the wife of the town's assistant druggist, was laughing so hard that she begged to excuse herself and ran for the privy.

The sun now nearly down, Gershonson rose from the table, offered the widow his compliments for the delicious meal, and bade his friends good night. By now they knew that it was time for Mr. Eli to begin his religious observance. His fellow boarders had long gotten used to the idea that he would not so much as read a newspaper or light an oil lamp from now until the following evening; and while there were a few among them who worried about the ultimate fate of his immortal soul, as people of faith, they respected his practices. One and all, they wished him a good day of rest.

Eli made his way to his room and opened the top dresser drawer. Inside was a purple velvet bag embroidered with Hebrew characters. Pulling on the drawstring, he removed a *yarmulke* and a black and white silk prayer shawl and put them on. Picking up his prayer book, he stepped to the window and began his lonely keeping of *shabbos*.

As he rocked back and forth over the verses, Eli noticed that there was far more light than usual for the time of year. Normally in May, he raced to reach the *aleinu*, hoping it wouldn't become too dim to finish the service. But as his finger glided down the lines of text, the world got brighter, until he could feel the light penetrating even through his closed eyes.

On the final word of the *adon olum*, Eli Gershonson said amen. He placed his prayer book back on the dresser and looked down at Omaha.

Below, men and boys rushed about, some bearing buckets of water, others shouting in panic. Women fainted in the street or screamed, frozen in place. An acrid smell filled Eli's nose, like charcoal and coal oil. He heard a small explosion, than another, and at last, saw the great lantern that had allowed him to so clearly read the word of God.

The Nickel & Dime was ablaze.

Fire poured from every room. Those windows left closed exploded into the evening, showering glass on the would-be firefighters; those left open fed air to the flames, igniting the floors above them. The overhang had collapsed onto the ground, spreading the inferno to the adjacent buildings. As the timbers fell, their fires consumed the boardwalk like a hungry dog. Men stumbled through the smoke coughing, others vomited from the fumes. Eli was horrified to see two bartenders stagger from the blaze, impaled by copper coils from the saloon's whiskey still.

From his window, Eli saw six men attempting to restrain Mack Swain, who had somehow survived the conflagration and was trying to reenter the building. As the big man tried to tear himself from their grip, a figure emerged from the smoke and nearly ran into his arms. Her face was like the coals in a stove and her long gown and hair a mass of flame. Unable to recognize her, Mack called out the names of several of his prostitutes. Attempts were made to capture her; but she zigzagged through the town center, too engulfed for anyone to approach. Overcome with horror, Swain fell to his knees and foamed at the mouth. What had been Hannah Miller collided with a hitching post, ignited it, and was still.

Eli threw off his *tallis* and skullcap and ran downstairs. The other boarders had already reached the street. Mrs. McGreevy and Mrs. Wilson held each other and wept. "Those poor girls," he heard Mrs. Wilson say. "To be used like they were in life, and now to die like this."

Eli thought of manning the bucket brigades; but when the southern wall of the building crashed to earth, he knew saving either humans or structure was hopeless. By now, all who would die were dead or would wish to be.

Emmanuel Wilson supported his wife as she fainted. Mrs. McGreevy hurried to the kitchen for water to revive her. Alice Worzchowski, the schoolteacher who lived in 2B, crossed herself and collapsed onto the shoulder of Harry Birch, the livestock auctioneer.

Eli Gershonson, too shocked to weep, closed his eyes and began to pray *kaddish* for strangers and whores. But the words, usually so automatic, had turned as dry as the black cinders that floated everywhere, and the ancient chant strangled in his throat.

He had been warned; and he knew who had warned him.

⬥

The spring went quickly and so far, Prophet John had been right. As their journey progressed, neither Julius nor McGarrigle had received so much as a scratch.

Over nearly sixty days of travel, they had encountered only those who wished to exchange goods, not gunfire. The Indians had been more than happy to trade for their work, and the level of their craft was indeed equal to some of the finest guilds of France or Germany. Their hospitality, while primitive, was offered with an open heart, and Julius learned to navigate their arcane rituals of visitation and dining. Only once did he risk offending his hosts. During a meal with the Otoe, the two men were offered the tribe's finest delicacy: boiled dog. As the pale meat made its way around the party, Julius looked up for any sign of help from Prophet John but received only an amused grin. Making the sign for thanks, the old scout took a piece and bit into it with relish, rubbing his stomach as his eyes closed in beatific satisfaction. Only when the dish was set before Julius did John intercede, his fingers pointing at the miserable boy and tracing shapes in the air. The assembled elders smiled knowingly and the chief gestured to a woman nearby. She ran from the lodge and returned in moments with a tray of boiled turkey eggs.

"Take one and eat it," John said. "I've explained to our friends here that you're an 'egg eater.' That's how the red man calls the Hebrew. They know that there are certain items that your gods won't allow you to eat on pain of no admission to the Jew paradise—things like Fido here—so they've brung out the old hen fruit. Too bad, boy—you don't know what you're missin'. After a meal like this, I could bark all night."

As fine as their luck had been, Julius made no secret of the fact that he would have been far happier back in Omaha or even, God forgive him, the Old Country. There, every Jew was used to handling local threats like brutal Cossacks and Jew-baiting cops. But how did one deal with the mindlessness of nature—the coyotes that howled through the night or the venomous serpents that waited for a man to put a foot wrong? What was the polite way to tell an ignorant Sac or Fox chief that one's teeth were not up to the task of masticating his prized buffalo jerky?

John McGarrigle quickly tired of such complaints. If something rattled in the brush, the prophet simply listened to the sound, ascertained its point of origin, and then informed Julius of the presence of "brother snake" and what good eating he made when grilled. More than once, Julius had seen him place his rifle on the ground and raise his hands to the sky before a well-armed tribe of hunters, a gesture of peace that was always accepted. Perhaps the prophet was brave, perhaps a fool, but his techniques were effective and the ensuing barter lucrative. The pair collected moccasins, dolls, headdresses, and robes. They exchanged tobacco for fine bows and traded cash for carved statues and pottery.

Now, with fall approaching, their wagon and pack mules were heavy with goods. In a week or ten days, they would be back in Omaha. Julius imagined walking through the shop door and searching his brother's face for signs of approval. Finding none, he would then rent Bruno Gaita's bathtub for a full hour and dissolve the months of grime and fear.

He smiled as he cinched one of the saddlebags closed.

"John, if I believed in God, I'd suppose we'd been blessed."

"I was born that way," the prophet said. "My dear mother used to tell me that on Christmas Eve, 1820, the night she birthed me, some of the other whores saw a bright light in the east. With the railroad bigwigs all over the territory these days, you meet an awful lot of people who act like they're Jesus Christ. Shit. They ought to meet someone with a real claim."

"Seriously, John, I didn't expect to make it back alive when we started out. And after a few weeks of staring down savages, I was even more convinced. But here we are, going home—going home rich."

"*Kina hora*," John said.

Julius stared at the prophet, not certain of what he had heard. For the first time since their journey began, the boy saw the scout's face betray irritation.

"That's right, young Jules. *Kina hora*—your own people's word in the original Jew. Don't be surprised, boy. I know every phrase the world says to ward off the Evil Eye. The eye-talians call it the *mallocio*, the Mexicans *mal de ojo*. I can't pronounce the Chinese word, but I've learned to spit over my shoulder like they do."

John demonstrated the technique.

"And it's a good thing, too. Because with you temptin' fate by talkin' about how we ain't got ourselves killed and bitching the rest of the time, I'll probably need to learn it in the ancient Greek. Now take that coffee cup and turn it over."

"What?"

"Goddamnit, turn that coffee cup upside down, put it on the ground lip first, and leave it there. And you call yourself a Jew."

Julius saw the old man was in earnest. He took the cup from its place by the fire and inverted it. When he looked up again, he saw the cloud of a wagon approaching their camp. It was a fine vehicle, lacquered in black and pulled by a fine team of matched grays. As it emerged from the dust, Julius could see it was accompanied by a small contingent of cavalry, six men, their uniforms barely worn, their weapons still shiny and sleek with bluing. They could not have been more than a day out from home.

The wagon came to a stop before the prophet. A beefy sergeant, his face already red with travel, gestured to a private, who leaped from his horse and pulled the vehicle's door open. Out stepped a man of medium height sporting blonde mutton chops and a fine black suit. He wore rimless pince-nez and carried a clipboard thick with papers. He made no effort to shake hands or exchange pleasantries.

"Freytag," he said, as if the name held the same greeting value as hello. "Raiload siting superintendent. Central Pacific."

The prophet nodded. "John McGarrigle. This here's my young employer, Mr. Julius Meyer. Can we offer you all some coffee?"

"No, thanks. We're just out here inspecting this pass of ground to see if there's a best place to lay tracks without we disturb some redskin ghosts and get the natives up in arms. Been out here long?"

"Close on three months. Out of Omaha."

Freytag's taciturn demeanor changed in an instant. He raised his eyebrows and whistled.

"Omaha, eh? Guess you missed the murder-fire."

"Murder-fire?" said Julius. "What's a murder-fire?"

"That's a murder, son, where somebody uses a fire like somebody else might use a gun. They think they know who did it, but I can tell you, whoever it was was plenty mad."

"What did they burn and who was it they murdered?"

"It wasn't a who, son," Freytag said. "It was a them. You'll be familiar with the Nickel & Dime Saloon, then?"

Julius's heartbeat skipped and he felt his stomach tighten. There were few people he cared about, but those few were apt to visit the Dime at least once in a day.

"Burned to the ground—sunset, two month ago. Nothing left but ashes and chimneys. Whoever did it set the fires in little piles all around the building so that even if you got one place under control, another coupla flames would be eating the place somewheres else. About twelve of the whores went up in smoke. Another two of them was burned so bad, the sheriff has to guard them day and night to keep citizens from killing them out of mercy. All told, about twenty dead. But the worst was that pimp, the one called Calhern. I think I will take that cup of coffee."

Julius turned the cup back over and filled it from the pot. Freytag took a sip and frowned.

"Whoever it was did this wanted him found—closed all the doors to his room to give it a better chance of not burning when the rest did. He was bound with leather at the ankles and wrists and tied to his bedposts—like an Indian stretches someone over an anthill—took the mattress out from under him so that he was lying on just them metal springs. Well, sir, she lit a fire under them springs and cooked him, like you'd grill a chicken. When they finally came to lift him off the springs, what was left of his body went with them, but his hands and feet stayed tied to the posts."

Now it was Julius's turn to whistle.

"Dead aplenty," he said softly.

"What's that?"

Prophet John stroked his beard. "You said you think they know who did it?"

"Well, after it was all over, everybody started looking for their friends or their favorite whores or their kin. They was mostly able to figure who was who by something on the body, like some jewelry or a scar. Even a girl burned to the skull is still gonna have a gold tooth or a tattoo somewhere. They say that Swain, the bartender, went insane and they're sending him to a nuthouse in Denver. Doc says he'll probably never recover."

Freytag took another sip of coffee, then dumped the dregs on the ground.

"After they was done weepin', and wailin', people began to notice that the place's top girl, this Indian name of Lady-Jane, weren't among the dead or the survivors. No one saw any red skin fall off a bone and not so much as a hair comb of hers was found in the rubble. People looked up and down for her, but no dice. Yes sir—she'd disappeared like snow after rain."

Prophet John stroked his beard. "Word was that she was about to leave the life. Why torch the place if she had a foot out?"

"Don't ask me to figure the Indian," Freytag said. "They can live among us for years, learn our ways, even sleep with our men like she did. But I guess you just never know when that bloodthirsty nature will come back out. Made that way, I guess. The government and the holy rollers are trying to civilize them. You ask me, they're best civilized dead."

Freytag took a step forward and then stopped. He seemed to stand suspended in place for a moment, almost as if he had paused to step back or suddenly forgotten how to move. Julius heard what sounded like a thump hit the man's back and then watched as Freytag stiffly dragged his left leg up to meet his right. He stood that way for what may have been a second, and then his mouth dropped open. From it poured what looked to Julius like all the blood a man needed to stay alive.

Freytag's eyes opened wide as if seeking the answer to how his life could drain from him so quickly. Then, almost like a dancer performing a pirouette, he twisted around once and fell. The two arrows in his back were in almost perfect alignment, each positioned perfectly to pierce a lung.

Prophet John flew through the air and hit Julius hard. At the instant of impact, he reached out and plucked a Henry rifle from its spot by the fire. Three arrows sliced through the air Julius had just occupied. More took their place: from right and left, from ground level and from above.

"It's the death rain, boy," the prophet said. "Get down and stay down."

John had tackled Julius so as to place them between two large boulders. Peering over the larger one, the boy could see a big sergeant attempt to escape from a screaming brave armed with a Sharps buffalo rifle, a gun made to kill a sixteen-hundred-pound beast at four hundred yards. From a distance of ten feet, the Indian drew a bead on the soldier and fired. The sergeant disintegrated.

Before they could draw their guns or pull swords from their scabbards, the bluecoats were cut down like ducks in a sideshow. Once the men were separated from their horses, the braves unsheathed their knives and dismounted, seeking the hair of the living and the dead. Julius saw one warrior strip a dead corporal of his tunic and put it on. Whatever power its owner had possessed in life would now be transferred to his enemy.

Prophet John dodged and weaved; standing to fire, then taking cover between the rocks. The Henry picked off one, then two, then three of the braves. Bullets ricocheted off its gun barrel and arrows missed by the length of a honeybee. To Julius, the prophet seemed utterly changed: no longer the affable barfly dispensing cornpone wisdom and wild predictions, but the kind of fierce fighter that young Lemuel Norcross loved to read about; a dime-novel hero, jaw set tight against the foe.

As he watched the soldiers fall, the superstitions of Europe and the mumbo-jumbo of eastern deserts came flooding back to Julius. He could hear the *kaddish* in his head and his mind recited the *sh'ma*: the final prayer of the people Israel declaring the oneness of God.

Then a sharp grunt, half said, half sung, cut through the internal words. It was uttered low and in a strange language; spoken by a voice born to command.

"Stand up, boy," John McGarrigle said.

Julius slowly rose from his place between the rocks. Prophet John stood where he had fought, his rifle now empty. Above him, seated upon a magnificent pinto, sat a tall brave. He was somewhat older than his surviving troops, and his buckskins were adorned with the history of his victories. From his moccasins to his knees, he was soaked with blood.

During the attack, Julius had hardly known fear. The arrows had flown too swift; the gunfire had cracked too loud. But now, seeing the Indian above him, he became truly frightened. He had seen the face on posters above amounts of reward money; a photograph in the newspaper office window warned of his atrocities.

It was one thing to be quickly massacred; it was another to become the prisoner of Chased By Owls.

10

ALEXANDER HERRMANN HADN'T SO MUCH AS PALMED THE Queen of Hearts as he strode from the wings and onto the stage; yet the applause was more fitting for the end of a performance than the beginning. As he bowed to the audience, the sound came toward him in waves. It felt, he said later, like the ocean at the height of summer but it smelled not of salt, but of money. For the past two hundred nights, every seat—and all the places to stand—had sold to someone. Men cheered, women fainted, and louts screamed "fake" from the nosebleed seats while being treated to "Cutting Off The Bird's Head," "The Goldfish Bowl From Thin Air," and "The Original Floating Boy."

At first, the sages of London's press dismissed this "Alexander the Great" as a colonial interloper, someone who could teach the great magicians of Britain exactly nothing. But before his tenth performance had ended, Fleet Street had changed its mind. The papers hailed him as "a genius," a "rival for Robert-Houdin," and "a modern-day Merlin." The *Times* wrote, "he has brought the ingenuity of America to the hoary old world of stage magic." *The Illustrated London News* went so far as to credit the supernatural:

> "Professor Herrmann's prestidigitations are so calculated to amaze that it fair makes one wonder if some arrangement has not been made with the spirit world or even a bargain concluded for the mountebank's soul."

Alexander wished it had been that easy.

Almost from the moment they had combined their efforts, Compars and Alexander had begun piling up money. In a matter of months, enough had rolled in to allow the elder Herrmann to purchase a small castle in Austria. With his brother now comfortably ensconced near Vienna, Alex had received permission to leave America, the better to mine the plentiful pesetas, marks, pounds sterling, and lire of the old land.

To this end, Alexander had now toured Europe for over a year with barely a stop for pleasure or rest. When he had first arrived in Spain, the houses had been nearly empty; by the time he departed, there were fistfights over tickets. Still, this made little difference in Germany, and he had been obliged to start again, this time in a theatre in Hamburg so small that to load in his equipment, he had to cut a hole in the roof. Before a month was out, crowds were queuing up and Alex found it necessary to move to the Friedrich-Wilhelm-Städtisches Theater in Berlin where, on opening night, he pulled a banana from the trousers of Frederick I, Grand Duke of Baden.

Nothing, however, equaled his reception in England. From the moment of his first appearance, Londoners both high and humble vied for whatever seats they could afford. It was rumored that the ninth Viscount Arbuthnott had offered to fight a duel with a fellow peer over the royal box. During a matinée, an East Londoner named Richard Little had been dangled from the third balcony by a man who demanded to take his place on the bench.

Despite the chaos, Alex was grateful for the warm reception and determined to give his all for the public—some of whom had gone without luncheon or dinner to save the few shillings needed to see him. By the end of each performance, he was soaked through with perspiration, his voice hoarse, his fingertips bleeding from the sharp edges of cards.

But in spite of these efforts, he also knew that part of what had made London a unique success could be credited not only to *what* the show was but *where* it was. If ever a theatre had been designed to make its patrons believe the unbelievable it was the magnificent old pile in Piccadilly known as the Egyptian Hall.

Its façade, five stories tall, could have been the passage to the tomb of Isis and Osiris, both of whom stood fifteen feet high above its entrance. Its sand-colored frontage had been molded to resemble the stones from a pharaoh's resting place. Mighty columns framed the stepped doorway; and just above the two statues sat a pair of golden lions, back to back, topped by a woman with a face like Cleopatra and the wings of a desert eagle.

Inside, the Egyptian Hall was no less impressive. Throughout its many rooms, history unfolded as mythology and architecture over-whelmed the senses. Giant pilasters lined the walls, their capitals in styles from palm frond to elephant. Every floor and ceiling seemed populated by a race of human-animals. There was Bast, part cat, part woman; Set, with the head of an aardvark; and Khonsu, who carried the moon in the beak of a falcon.

Before every performance, Alexander would wander the great rooms enjoying the attention of their puzzled attendees. Even in Victorian London, known for its dandies and eccentrics, there were few figures more remarkable than Alexander the Great. Now six feet tall, Alex had grown lean and muscular. His hair, center-parted, was trained into curls and dyed jet-black, as was his devil's beard. A high white collar offset an inky velvet opera cloak lined not with the usual white silk, but a blood-red satin that faded to purple in the shadows. Just above its brocade fasteners rode rows of gold medals, each a gift from a king or queen. The whole was crowned by a shining silk hat, concave to the top, its grosgrain band a perfect match for the cape's scarlet interior.

Alexander held up his hands to both acknowledge and quiet the applause.

"Thank you, thank you, gentlemen and ladies. The generosity of the London public continues to amaze and astound even one whose livelihood it is to amaze and astound. And so, I welcome you to this, my two-hundredth performance in your great city. Two hundred performances at which, I am happy to say, no seat has gone unfilled."

The crowd exploded again, their applause muffled by gloves in the orchestra and amplified by shouts above the mezzanine.

"In fact, my good friends, I am so happy to have your company here tonight that I have decided to prepare a small sweetmeat for your pleasure. But first, I will need the assistance of a gentleman in the audience who might still be in possession of his hat."

Immediately, a well-dressed man near the front of the house stood and raised his black beaver stovepipe.

"Ah! I see we have an admirer of the late President Lincoln with us tonight—and now, if you please."

The stovepipe was passed over the heads of the patrons until it reached the apron of the stage. With the grace of a practiced juggler, Alexander rolled it from his right hand, down his arm, behind his neck, across his left arm and into his left hand. The audience laughed and cheered.

"A very fine but otherwise ordinary beaver topper," Alexander said, throwing the hat in the air and catching it behind his back. "We know it is not a trick hat because that would involve an unthinkable deception on the part of the young Duke Alfred of Saxe-Coburg-Gotha, whom I thank tonight for his assistance."

As the Duke stood and the crowd applauded, Seamus Dowie wheeled a table onto the stage. It held four oversized containers, each marked in huge letters: FLOUR, SUGAR, MILK, and EGGS. Beside these sat an equally large china bowl, a wooden spoon the size of a small oar and a tall candle, already burning. Seamus helped Alexander off with his cloak and coat.

"Maestro, if you would be so kind?"

To the tune of a cheerful waltz, Alexander plucked the big spoon from the table and began to mix the ingredients in the big bowl: the flour into the sugar; the sugar into the eggs; the milk to blend in all together. He kept up a steady patter, sometimes imitating a French *chef de cuisine*, other times becoming an old English grandmother, "maikin' a dessert fer the wee ones."

"Very good! We now have the perfect mixture for a cake." He dipped his finger into the white concoction and put it to his lips. "And if I say so, a right good one. Now all that remains is to bake it. But wait!"

Alexander looked around the stage in mock dismay. "It seems my assistants have tripped me up again. They have neglected to include an oven here on the Egyptian stage. Oh, well . . . no matter."

The audience gasped as Alexander slowly poured the entire contents of the giant bowl into Duke Alfred's hat and gave it a few shakes.

"And now, for the baking."

Alexander took the hat in his left hand and, whistling a merry tune, held it over the flaming candle, keeping it close enough to appear to do the job but not so close as to singe the stovepipe.

"Voilà!"

With a flourish, Alexander reached inside and, with a sudden tug, produced a lovely pink and white three-layer cake, properly decorated and iced. On its surface were nine lighted candles.

He placed the cake on the table and tilted the Duke's hat toward the audience, revealing that it was not only undamaged, but also as dry and free of foodstuffs as when first surrendered. Alexander then tipped the hat to the patrons and passed it back to the properly grateful Alfred, who rose to his feet and applauded with such enthusiasm that his young wife lifted her silk fan to hide her embarrassment. After the proper number of bows, Alexander again held up his hands for silence.

"Thank you, gentlemen and ladies. And now, if I may, I would like to call to the stage one Master Sidney Lydon."

As more applause rained down, a beaming youngster in his Sunday best nervously approached the proscenium and joined Alexander onstage. The wizard picked up the cake and held it high, placing his remaining hand on the boy's shoulder.

"Now, Sidney . . . have we ever met?"

"No, sir, never," the boy said, even these few words betraying his Cockney heritage.

"And am I perhaps acquainted with your mother or father?"

"Oh, no, sir."

"And yet, Sidney, there is something I know about you. In fact, I know that today is indeed your birthday! And how old are you today, Sidney?"

"Nine, sir. If you please."

"Nine! And would you be so kind, Sidney, as to count the number of candles on my little cake?"

Sidney shyly raised his index finger and slowly counted each burning head.

"Nine, sir."

"Very fine. Now, can you read, Sidney?"

"Oh, yes, sir."

"Good! Then, Sidney, I am going to lower the cake down so that you can see its top. When I do, would you be so kind as to read to me and all of our friends what is written there?"

The drums played a roll. Alexander lowered the cake slowly, building as much suspense as possible, until he again laid it on the table.

"Come, come, Sidney. What does the miracle cake, mixed by Alexander the Great and baked in the hat of a nobleman, say?"

Sidney peered over the top of the cake. His eyes widened in disbelief.

"It says . . . Happy Birthday, Master Sidney Lydon."

From nowhere, Alexander whipped out an oversized hand mirror. He held it above the top of the cake so that the nearby audience could read the amazing greeting in its reflection.

Now the crowd was on its feet, clapping and stamping, crying out "bravo!" and "well done, yank!" Even the various inebriates in the theatre's upper reaches managed to applaud as the magician presented the cake to the boy and Seamus Dowie escorted him back to his tearful mother.

When the demonstration at last subsided, Alexander bowed again.

"Please don't be disappointed, gentlemen and ladies. I promised you a sweetmeat, and a sweetmeat you shall enjoy. At the conclusion of this performance, you are invited to our theatre's foyer, there to partake of London's biggest birthday cake. A cake inscribed with the names of all those under twelve in tonight's audience celebrating their nativities tonight!"

For the next hour, Alexander built wonder upon wonder. He caused a lemon to give up a six-foot silk; produced a bowl of live goldfish from the ether; burned the Lord Mayor's handkerchief, then restored it to him; "killed" Seamus Dowie with a knife throw to the chest and brought him back to life. With each illusion, the gasps became longer and the applause louder. It was only after an encore that included the famous "floating boy" that he was finally permitted to leave the stage.

The man in the brown checked suit had watched the entire presentation from the wings, his brow taut with concentration, his hands moving in nearly exact unison with those of the performer. When Alexander would pick up a wand, the man's hands would pantomime the gesture; when the magician would stretch a long silk, so would the man, his bald head bobbing in exact time to the music.

"I'll be askin' ya ta refrain, sir."

The bald man turned at the sound of the Derry brogue and was met with a right to the nose. When he regained consciousness, he found himself sprawled on a watered silk divan in an ornate dressing room and facing Seamus Dowie; his red hair had fallen over his forehead and he was gingerly rubbing his knuckles.

"Don't expect no apologies, mister," Dowie said. "I don't know how ya got in here but yer not the first to be tryin' an steal the boss's business. Yez are all alike: jackals what wants to be eatin' off the lion once he's made the kill. Well, soon's he's done with the public, we'll be after findin' out what ya know, and then we'll be callin' in the police and press boys ta expose ya fer what ya are."

The big Irishman rose from his chair and opened the door. Just beyond it, he could see Alex signing his final autograph of the evening and taking the card of a particularly attractive young woman. Seamus gestured to him from the doorway. Alex blew a few kisses to the backstage stragglers and, swirling his cape behind him, strode into the dressing room. The bald man sat up straight on the divan.

"What's all this, then?"

"Found 'im stage right flies makin' head notes on our whole play. T'ink he's been here before. Knows yer patter like he wrote it. Knows yer music like his mother's lullabies. I've already fisted 'im. Figured to give ya a turn before we put 'im out a' business, permanent."

Alexander stared at the bald man but made no move to strike him. Instead, he moved forward and, reaching out slowly, took the fabric of his lapel between his thumb and forefinger.

"Very nice," he said. "Ravenscroft?"

"No," the man said. "Actually, a new fellow. A co-religionist named Landau in New York."

Alex nodded. "Well, the suit looks just fine, but you, dear brother . . . you look like hell."

The man ran his hand over his clean pate and smiled.

"It is amazing how attractive a bit of hair and beard makes a man and how hideous he can be when all that's left is the face beneath."

Compars Herrmann turned his gaze toward the stunned Seamus. The redhead quickly bowed to his old master and began to murmur an apology.

"Don't be remorseful, Mr. Dowie," Compars said, massaging his jaw. "You did your job. And that roundhouse of yours left me more convinced than ever that my successor is in the most capable of hands."

Alex laughed and again pointed to his brother's pate. "I assume this great sacrifice has a purpose?"

Compars picked up an open bottle of champagne and poured three glasses.

"Yes, dear boy. I did it for you: the same reason I have made so many sacrifices. Considering the current state of your skills, it is likely that you may inhabit this theatre for five, six, even seven hundred performances. But if it were known that the original—*me*—was here in Europe, the spotlight would fall off of the copy—*you*. That, we cannot have." He placed the bottle back in its bucket and passed the glasses to Alex and Seamus. He clicked his heels, saluted, and took a deep draught.

It had been over two years since Alexander had seen his brother; but Compars's condescension still rankled. In that time, Alex had become used to being his own man, making his own decisions, even changing small features of the act to suit himself. Tonight, as hairless as a moth larva, his brother had returned, making his usual dramatic entrance, attempting to upstage him even if the audience consisted only of a single mystified Irishman.

"I suppose I can only be grateful that my big brother has seen fit to visit me—and in such an unbecoming state. But somehow, I have the feeling that this is more than a social call. What? Have you come to inspect the paint on the Spirit Cabinet? Or maybe you're just concerned about the overall health of the doves."

Compars gave a slight smile and walked to a desk by the door. As he poured himself a second glass, he noticed a large paper diagram in the center of the blotter.

The blue-lined schematic was almost a work of art in itself. It depicted a large steamer trunk, surrounded by arcane mechanisms and various sliding panels. The renderings were exquisite in their clarity and simplicity, obviously the work of a master draughtsman;

but their beauty was marred by dozens of notations and corrections scribbled across their surface. "NO!" read one, "DAMN FOOL!" another. The big paper looked as if it had been crumpled into a tiny ball and then unfolded again. In a rectangle at the right-hand corner the title read:

SUBSTITUTION TRUNK: DESIGN NO. 17.

Compars took another sip of champagne and set his glass on the desk, carefully avoiding the large sheet of beige vellum.

"You are as perceptive as you are adroit, brother. Yes, I am here for reasons other than the social or the exhibition of my new nakedness, so I'll make this brief. As the newspapers will report tomorrow, yours truly, Compars . . . known as Carl in America and everywhere as the master of the mysterious, showman unique and magician extraordinary . . . has officially retired—which for you only means that 'Alexander the Great' no longer exists. As of this moment, little *Sasha*, you are the Great Herrmann."

11

WITH A SHOUT, LEMUEL NORCROSS TURNED LEFT OUT of McCullough's alley and onto Farnam Street. He performed two expert cartwheels and landed on the boardwalk in front of the M. Meyer Tobacco Company.

Planting his feet, Lemuel reached into his pocket to make sure he hadn't shaken loose his treasure.

They were still there: two ten-cent pieces, the full purchase price for places unknown, women chaste and beautiful, and heroes as unflawed as they were unbowed. Mr. Max Meyer would have no cause to throw him out today. When he approached him and said, "what, you think maybe this is a library," Lemuel would reveal his hard-earned money and assure Mr. Max that his browsing was merely the necessary preamble to the purchase of not one, but two works of literature.

Peering through the wavy glass, Lemuel saw that Mr. Max wasn't in either of his usual places—sitting by the cash box or refilling the tobacco jars. Instead, he was pacing back and forth across the shop's worn wood floor, shouting at a young man in a magnificent uniform.

The officer couldn't have been older than twenty-five, but the insignia on his shoulders was embroidered with the eagle of a full colonel, the yellow field surrounding the bird indicating cavalry. On his head sat an immaculate blue slouch girdled with the special braid that pegged the wearer as an Indian fighter, and from his thick belt hung a sword fit for a knight. Its scabbard and handle were of a black so shining that they seemed dipped in water, and its brasses so polished they shimmered like true gold. It was raiment designed to command respect; but Max Meyer seemed unaffected by it, dressing the colonel down as if he were an employee caught at theft.

"It is already thirty days mein brother is missing," Lemuel heard Max say. "You send men out, you bring men back, but still no boy you bring and I am out my outfit and all that I have traded with the savages. A fortune this is!"

Lemuel watched and listened as Mr. Max excoriated the young colonel. He berated him for laziness; accused him of collusion with rival merchants; even intimated that perhaps he had struck some sort of arrangement with Standing Bear or another of the thieving primitives.

"What, maybe Red Cloud lets your men have his squaws at night? Or maybe you think these animals should mix in. Be with us, with houses and in our schools and in church with you and Jesus Christ. Let me tell you, Colonel Miles, you look very nice in your suit. You hurt my eyes from your shining buttons. But maybe you should a little get that uniform dirty looking for my goods?"

Colonel Nelson Appleton Miles stood straight as if a superior had called him to attention. If he betrayed any indication of insult, it was only a slight reddening of his complexion that began at his brown-blond mustache and extended to his eyes. Lemuel Norcross imagined the colonel was waiting for Mr. Max to exhaust himself, run out of names to call him and his army; and at length, this is what appeared to happen. Max's words shortened and slowed, then finally stopped. He went to the stool behind the cash box and sat down heavily, plucking a cigar from a wooden box and glaring at the young soldier.

"Mr. Meyer," the colonel said, "I wonder if you might be finished?"

Max cast his eyes down in disgust and said nothing.

"Sir, I do not wish to add to your burden. But I tell you now that if your brother and his guide have fallen in with a hostile tribe, then I beg you, for your own sake, to give up hope now, so that any good news may come to you as a boon."

Max nodded. He placed a dime into the cash box as payment for the cigar and lighted it.

"So you are saying they are dead."

"I am stating only the facts, Mr. Meyer. The bodies of Mr. Freytag, the railroad site superintendent, and those of a six-man party of our cavalry, were found some two hundred-odd miles from here in the Niobrara, near the Dakota line. They were filled with arrows and shot, and some had been scalped. With them was the wagon containing what little remained of the goods your party had traded. We found neither your brother nor Mr. McGarrigle, dead or alive. This could mean that they escaped; it could also mean that they have been taken captive. If this is the case, I fear it would be better for them had they joined my dead compatriots."

Max inhaled deeply. "What is done is done. Who is dead is dead. Mein brother, he knew the risk. The Prophet John is one less drunk.

But mein stock cannot die. Mein investment cannot be tortured or made a slave. Those goods are mine; and I tell you, Colonel, you must get them back. This is a business. And who can do business without what to sell?"

For Lemuel Norcross, there was now no mistaking the change in Miles' face: it was the same expression that his mother gave him when he returned from the rat baitings, covered in sawdust and blood. But there was an element other than mere disgust in the young officer's face, a weariness. Miles stepped closer to Max Meyer, drew himself up yet again, and put his right hand on the hilt of his saber. For the first time, the boy heard anger in his voice.

"Mr. Meyer, not very long ago, it was my duty to preserve the union. I fought and watched my soldiers die to end the bondage of the black man. I had the honor to serve at Antietam and was shot twice at Chancellorsville."

Colonel Miles walked toward the counter. He stopped as close to Max Meyer as the glass top between them would allow and then leaned forward. Max put his cigar down. The respect that had been missing in his face seemed to arrive all at once.

"Since then, my duty has become quite different. I have gone from freeing one inferior race to eliminating another. I've killed more of those 'animals,' as you call them, than I care to count. I have shot them from their horses and ordered their wikiups and lodges burned. I have seen their children legally kidnapped and sent to schools charged with turning them white as sow bellies. I have seen treaties signed and then become the instrument to break them. Once an officer and a gentleman, I am now a garbage man—charged with dispatching any and all refuse that might collect upon the railroad tracks of the Central Pacific Railroad. This refuse consists mostly of Indians. Braves, yes, but also the females and the children and the old and sick. My orders are to take my big blue broom and sweep them from the earth."

Lemuel Norcross watched as Miles stepped back from Max Meyer, his eyes blazing as he struggled to regain his composure.

"And so, Mr. Meyer, if in the course of my next garbage run, I should run across some of your precious items, I shall do my best to return them. And should we, by some miracle, find your brother alive, I shall also facilitate his safe homecoming, although, having now met you, I am sure you will feel far more joy at the return of the former than the latter. Good day to you, sir."

Colonel Nelson Miles turned smartly on his heel and left the shop. Lemuel could hear the sharp clank of his sword and spurs as he passed him at the doorway and strode onto the street. Miles mounted his horse—a big chestnut with a white blaze—and kicked him hard enough to make the animal cry out. It reared for a moment and then galloped hard in the direction of Fort Kearney.

Lemuel Norcross looked after the horse and rider until they disappeared in the dust. He hesitated a moment and then stepped into the store. He hurried to the rack, picked up the latest *Colonel Custis' Weekly* and *Dixon Hawke's Case Book* and brought them to the counter.

Max Meyer did not seem to see the boy as Lemuel plunked the two dimes onto the glass surface. He waited for some acknowledgement of his payment, but all the shopkeeper could manage was a grunt toward the window. He turned away from the boy and disappeared into a back room.

Lemuel Norcross looked after him for a moment and then, stuffing his prizes in his shirt, ran from the shop. He vaulted over a horse rail and turned twice in the air over a salt lick. He imagined himself in the uniform of Colonel Nelson Miles, shooting down Confederates, Old Glory high above his head. The brasses of his uniform shone even brighter than the colonel's own, his sword brightest of all. He could almost feel it penetrate the neck of Robert E. Lee or Standing Bear or all foes foolish enough to risk his steel.

Chased By Owls had never understood his chief's patience for the white man.

To the tall brave, they were no different from the plagues of mosquitoes in summer or the rattlesnakes that emerged from their holes in spring. All were messengers of evil, sent by That Which Cannot Be Known to test the resolve of the human being. There was no offense in dispatching the snake and the mosquito; they had long ago proven themselves wicked. So it was with the white man, a fool who respected nothing. He squandered all that was given to him and blasphemed as a way of life.

Like all demons, the whites practiced invisibility. Yes, the Brulé Sioux might try to push you west or east, take your water or enslave your women; but their chiefs met you face to face, leading their soldiers and painted for war.

The Ponca never saw the white chiefs. They sat in Washington and sent agents to do their stealing; mercenaries dressed in blue and paid in gold. With the stroke of a pen, they took a hunting ground. With fire and sword, they stole a sacred altar or a tract of soil the buffalo had enriched for a million years.

Now they sought to take the Niobrara. Chased By Owls spat in disgust when he recalled the sordid history of this greatest of thefts.

In the white year 1858, the Ponca had signed yet another treaty with the devils. In return for their lands—ninety-six thousand acres of good earth and water—the tribe was to receive thirty years of their enemy's money, a school, grain and timber mills, and instructors to teach them how they all worked. The tribe, who had been warriors since the Creator scooped the earth from the claws of a turtle, would now become farmers and herdsman living on a strip of land between the Niobrara and Ponca rivers. The paper promised that all of this would serve to "colonize and domesticate" the tribe: a fitting fate for Whip and Strong Walker and Heavy Cloud, the spineless jackals who had sold them out.

As a boy, Chased By Owls had watched as the Ponca tried to become farmers. He saw men who had once brought down beasts that could feed the tribe all winter holding rakes and hoes. The *Wakanda*, angered at such an unnatural display, set the very earth against them. In the first year of planting, locusts descended on their corn and wheat; in the next, drought and flood. And even when the tribe managed to bring in a meager harvest, the Dakota and Brulé raided their villages, taking the food from their mouths. Hemmed in by hostile tribes, the Ponca hunted buffalo only at the greatest risk. Soon, some could be seen begging on the docks of the Missouri River, their gums bleeding from scurvy.

This was bad enough. But in the last year of the white men's war with each other, the treaty was amended and the chiefs, afraid to fight, agreed to a new indignity. The thieves would now move the Ponca from the miserable tract of land remaining to them to another sliver farther east. The pact claimed this action was necessary to return the tribe's burial grounds and move them out of range of the Dakota Sioux, who were attacking them from the west. By 1868, however, even this insulting fiction was altered by the so-called "Fort Laramie" agreement. The government now said that the Ponca were to be moved once more, this time to a place called Oklahoma, the current dumping ground for all the yellowbellies and turncoats who had spent too much time with their enemy and now valued life more than freedom.

In view of such history, it had been especially irksome for Chased By Owls to spare the two devils now stumbling behind his horse.

Had it been his decision, he would have buried them alive near an anthill or roasted them like fresh elk. Such methods had been useful in keeping the whites away back when the Ponca had had the courage to use them. But he was a soldier, not a politician:

and tribe policy stated that, regardless of color, there was to be no killing of any holy man or his familiars. Still, there was nothing in this code that obligated Chased By Owls to provide comfort to the shaman in question. If the captive's wrists bled from the pressure of the rope or their legs had trouble keeping pace with his horse, this was not his fault. If the whites fell and were dragged for some distance, this was regrettable, but he had a schedule to keep; and the convenience of two demons was far less important than making camp before nightfall.

The sun had not yet burst the horizon when the party reached the village. At the sight of the victors, the houses emptied of their inhabitants. Laughing and dancing, the Ponca poured onto the dirt common, delighted to see their warriors dressed in the coats of their enemy, fresh hair dangling from their belts and spears. Fists raised high, the people descended upon Julius and the prophet. The women and children pushed them. The old men pelted them with stones.

Chased By Owls was in no hurry to effect a rescue. It was a good thing for the most powerless of a powerless tribe to vent their frustrations on the prisoners. Besides, a little pause would allow him to hear his people call his name and sing his praises. He would wait until the moment blood was drawn, then order them away. The tribe would be satisfied with their small revenge and he would be seen as not only strong but just. Combining slaughter with mercy was a quality required of a leader.

Made slow by his journey, Julius was the first to bleed, a sharp stick drawing a line of red over his left eye. The boy had attempted to defend himself against the villagers; but with his hands bound he could do little more than raise them to his head, defending his brain and eyes from hands and rocks. He understood nothing the Indians said; but he knew well their gesture and expression. In their savage smiles, he saw the Germans and Poles who had beaten him back in Prussia. In their grunts and groans, he heard the same mocking and derision.

Chased By Owls could see the terror rise from Julius like fog from a lake. On the journey from the site of battle, he had considered a quick death for the boy. But for such a weakling, death must be a lesson: and lessons take time.

The brave thought differently about the old man.

Chased By Owls smiled with respect as McGarrigle lashed out in every direction. Deprived of his fists, he struck with his feet, kicking high into the faces of men and women alike. Every salvo of spit was met in kind and doubled; and every Ponca curse was answered in that very language, plus English.

Soon a spot of blood appeared on the prophet's neck. It was little more than a scratch, probably from some old grandmother's nails. Satisfied, Chased By Owls called out to the village to end their assault.

"I did not spare this waste of humanity out of compassion," he told the crowd. "None other of their party survived. We took their battle dress and now wear it ourselves. We carry their hair and will soon burn it in a fire of derision. We attacked them by stealth and none of our party died. We left their bodies as food for brother vulture, may he cover their bones in his excrement."

The tall brave now walked toward the prophet. McGarrigle lunged at him but was restrained by three warriors.

"These were left breathing because our chief seems to think this one has magic. We have seen him before and witnessed how gods work through him. But I tell you, Chased By Owls gives this no weight. The whites have long fornicated with demons; and any medicine that comes from them must be of the devil.

"Still, magic or not, the status of the old man does not absolve this stripling. The Unknown willing, that magnificent head of curly hair will soon become a wig for our children's play. See how without honor he is! He has even lost control of himself. The yellow pool sits by his boot. I think now I will make him a slave. It is what the coward deserves more than death.

"Cowards may also live if I wish it."

The man emerging from the lodge was small. His face was high-cheekboned and deeply creased from mouth to nose. The eyes were set deep in the brow and slanted slightly downward, their pupils a color between agate and amber. Around his shoulders he wore a huge chain of bear claws, and his neck was girdled with the teeth of his rivals.

"Look alive," McGarrigle whispered to Julius.

The small man stopped to smile at his people and then strode across the compound. He nodded to John McGarrigle and, walking past him to Julius, placed a brown hand on his shoulder.

Something broke inside the boy and he began to weep. Standing Bear turned toward Chased By Owls, the amber eyes daring him to laugh. The tall warrior remained as silent as everyone else.

Through his tears, Julius saw hope. Perhaps he would enjoy a death quick and merciful. Soon the breath returned to his lungs; and the sorrow that had blinded him ceased flowing long enough for him to see a woman emerge from the lodge of the chief.

Her dress was a strange mixture of the savage and the civilized. Her short jacket was of stiff green corduroy, its lapels piped in white and its cuffs encircled with silk-covered buttons. At her neck were two pieces of jewelry: one, a gold-plated locket of the kind sold from his brother's jewelry case; the other, a choker with its beads in a blue, red, and yellow ziggurat pattern. Below this, she wore a long skirt of buffalo hide, painted with flowers and animals. Her black hair was down and set in braids reaching to her waist. The huge disc earrings of the Ponca framed her beautiful red face.

Julius Meyer fainted with her name on his lips.

◈

The boy looked thinner than she remembered, and, with the kind of beard that travel creates, older. Almost before he struck the earth, she and two slaves were ordered to carry him into the main lodge and provide him rest and water. Voice Like A Drum, the old medicine man, ran for his herbs and salts.

She cared little for the boy's welfare; to her, he was just another of the whites lucky enough not to be at the Dime when she torched it. She saw in his face the features of his hated brother and Adrian Calhern and every other man who had robbed her and held her in bondage. She followed the order to tend him as she did every other command; when told to raise his arms, she obliged; when instructed to apply a stinking paste to his chest, she complied.

It was a far cry from her life as the Red Rose of Omaha.

When she had first appeared in camp, hungry and exhausted, Standing Bear had immediately recognized the beauty common to the clan of his brother's third wife. Satisfied that the girl was not a white decoy or some Brulé spy, the chief honored his obligation to receive her. Whore or not, she was Ponca. She was given food and water and, after what seemed hours of public discussion, made to stand under a linden tree at the rear of the main lodge. Shivering in the night air, she watched perhaps a dozen men enter the building, all carrying long ceremonial pipes and pouches of Indian smoke. From inside, she could hear them grunt and moan. After so many years away, her native tongue should have been as mysterious as Sanskrit; but she caught many more words than she would have thought possible, once again hearing men make her the subject of a bargain. Only this time, the men were red.

"This corruption may not be entirely her fault," Standing Bear said, lighting his pipe with a cinder. "From what she tells me, she was taken from her school and forced into slavery by one of the whites she killed. We must also remember that she is the niece of Buffalo Bull and from a respectable family. We also can't forget that the whites have powerful medicine. After all this time, who knows what witchcraft they have performed on her? A race that worships a dead body nailed to a tree is capable of anything."

Smoke Maker opened his pouch and filled his bowl. "All of this is true. But there is still no changing the fact that she has been the white man's slut. She could have chosen death before the magic you mention had a chance to take effect. Any Ponca woman worth the name would have slit her own throat rather than be traded like a horse among the whites."

The discussion went on through nightfall, with many solutions and compromises offered. It was suggested that she be allowed to stay, but only as a slave; that she be given as a daughter to Sun Seen By All, whose own child had died the month before; that she be cleansed and rehabilitated through prayer and fasting.

At last, Chased By Owls raised his pipe.

"This woman is Ponca and not only by name," he said. "I know this because in the end, she behaved as a warrior woman should. She burned the house of her shame with many white devils inside. I'm told there are white whores left alive who still scream from their burns. Good! Let every cry be a reminder to the whites that even an Indian with whom they sleep may seek her freedom in their deaths! I see the burning of the wicked house as a purification of her spirit. And any woman who can kill that many demons in a single evening can live in my village and welcome."

Standing Bear surveyed the faces of the council. "This is uncharted territory for us. I cannot dishonor my house by taking her as my daughter, and my wives would make my life hell if I made her one of them. She could be a slave, of course, but we have agreed that she is Ponca, and such a fate is fitting only for scum like the Pawnee."

"It is truly a problem," said Big Elk, rubbing his eyes against the smoke. "But perhaps there is some other way for this woman to live here that has not yet been revealed to us? I suggest we give her a place to sleep and then put her among our people and see what the spirits decide. Who knows? She could turn out to be a lot less trouble than some of the women around here."

The men of the council nodded. With the affair resolved, Standing Bear emerged from the lodge. He walked to the center of the village and gestured to two young braves to bring Half Horse to him.

As a boy, Half Horse had been shanghaied into a white school and had learned about enough English to get slapped in a saloon before he escaped with the left ear of the school superintendent and a copy of an English dictionary. He was highly esteemed for staying up late at night reading the big book, but in fact, he only looked at the pictures, translating the names of the things he recognized into Ponca. He used the ear as a bookmark.

Half Horse listened closely as Standing Bear explained the situation and then left the lodge to translate it for Lady-Jane. Seeing the lack of comprehension in her face, he repeated his speech perhaps a half dozen times. When at last she nodded her understanding, he smiled at his accomplishment. *He needn't be so prideful,* Lady-Jane thought, *it's not that my Ponca is so bad but that his English is far worse.*

The decision of the council meant that she would be safe, at least for the moment. With the peace between the government and the nations so fragile, she knew the blue coats would not look for her. It would not be worth the political fallout for them to invade a village over a burned-down cathouse. Besides, Lady-Jane had never told anyone in Omaha that she was Ponca; and even if she had, it was unlikely they would have remembered such an insignificant detail in the life of a red slut, no matter how expensive.

But even with her life spared for now, she wondered what kind of life it could be. Plains Indian society had as rigid a social structure as the castes of India. Among the Ponca, a daughter of her age would normally be chaperoned by her family, her father or brothers constant guardians of her virtue until she was betrothed. But Lady-Jane had come to the tribe with no virtue to protect; and so no brave would be chosen for her. And while even a slave might bear a warrior children, the council had decided that no man was to touch the newcomer, lest he be contaminated by whatever the whites had left inside her.

⊰❖⊱

Once they had decided not to kill him, the Ponca debated several days over Julius Meyer.

Buffalo Bull suggested he be made the personal servant to a deserving family; Voice Like A Drum asked that he undergo a complete religious conversion so that he might eventually become a respectable member of the tribe. Chased By Owls, thwarted in his vote for death, urged that he be cut behind one knee and live out his days without either the honor of escape nor the dignity of work.

In due course, it was decided that the boy be made a woman.

This humiliation seemed to satisfy the council members hesitant to anger the prophet's gods, as well as those eager to exact punishment. The boy would gather herbs and fruits, sew clothing and footwear, and care for children. He would kill and skin dogs and prepare meals for the warriors. Unlike the rest of the women, the egg eater would not provide the men sexual pleasure, lest the council be accused of promoting pederasty. When his lighter labors were completed, the boy would tan hides.

Julius soon wondered if he would not have preferred death.

Tanning bison was a backbreaking and nauseating process. It began with removing the buffalo's brain from its skull, mashing it into a paste, and then spreading the mixture over the animal's skin. Added to this then were proportions of bone marrow, liver, soapweed, and the grease of an elk or bear. As the mixture soaked into the flesh, Julius and the women took hold of opposite portions of the skin, stretching and pulling in an attempt to sufficiently thin the hide so that it might be used for a robe or *wikiup*. This done, they would then beat the hide with rocks and branches, the better to break down its cells and reveal its softness.

After tanning, the boy's arms were covered with a thick, stinking white slime. By the end of a day, his clothing was covered with grime and fine dust that seeped beneath his eyelids and turned his finger and toe nails black. When the women anointed their hands or went to the river to bathe, he was allowed only enough water to sustain his life; any more was considered a luxury unfit for one without a role among the Ponca.

As much as the hunger and more than the exhaustion, Julius despised this desecration of his body. Back in Bromberg, a bath was not only desirable, but commanded for any proper Jew. Prior to the Sabbath, the men and women would queue up at the synagogue *mikveh*, the ritual bath located just beyond the ark. The water removed not only a congregant's ordinary sins, but a good portion of the week's uncleanness—the manure of the ghetto's horses, the droppings of its mice and rats, the grease of its kitchens. As he did all *yiddisher* ritual, Julius rebelled against the forced immersion. Fed by an underground spring, the *mikveh* was freezing cold and he was always embarrassed to appear naked before the other men; the rite completed, he would emerge into the early evening, his hair and earlocks still damp, and shiver in the Prussian winter. Now, his hands black and his body smelling of buffalo, he longed for that bath; for the shock of immersion and the chill that crept beneath his hat and absolved him of wrong.

The Ponca women with whom he worked didn't seem to mind his filth or smell; that would have required them to take notice of him. In the days he had been among them, none of the women had said a word to him; and when he tried to speak to them, they turned away. The silence left him to learn his new skills through observation only; there was no instruction either by word or example. Because of this, Julius often made mistakes and was beaten for them by the group's *grand dame*, an unreconstructed battleaxe named One Who Runs. If he made too many errors in one day, she would turn him over to her son—a squat brave with a gray streak through his hair. He wouldn't stop until he had drawn blood.

The only exception among the women was a girl of perhaps sixteen. When he had first seen her, Julius had been too miserable to notice much, except that she seemed less filthy than the others. But as time went on, he noted that the girl always greeted the women with the same smile she had for everyone. Nothing seemed to disturb her serenity. If a stitch was dropped or a hide patch wasted, she would laugh; if a pair of moccasins consisted of two lefts, she would laugh harder. In her presence, the other women would miraculously take on these traits, behaving like work was play and as if Julius was actually something above a dog—deserving respect for perhaps no other reason but that he walked upright. Julius soon learned the reason for such deference: the young woman was Prairie Flower—the daughter of Standing Bear and his first wife, dead since the whites' Great War.

When he had been in the village long enough for the moon to cycle, Julius began to itch. In that time, only his lips had touched water and he wondered if his condition stemmed from some parasite or just his own sickness with himself. Soon, the scratching manifested itself as a rash across his face and arms. The people of the village recoiled in mock horror at the sight of him, or teased him that the red bumps would spread further and were likely fatal. Only Standing Bear's daughter looked at him differently. Though she remained as silent as the others, her eyes bespoke sympathy.

On the day Julius sighted her by the river, he could only remember the words the prophet had quoted so often: *fortune*, he always said, *favors the bold*. He waited until One Who Runs lay down for a short nap following the midday meal. With the other women following suit, he slipped away from the circle and made for the river.

She stood on a stone outcropping, which jutted out over the water. In her hands was a large earthen jug painted with elk and warhorses. From his shelter behind a tree, Julius noted for the first time the delicacy of her neck and the wideness of her eyes. Summoning his courage, he stepped into the open and began to walk toward her, bowing every few feet until he was close enough to speak.

He pointed toward his wrist, black with dirt and scaled with red patches.

"Please, princess," he said, in the Ponca he had managed to learn, "might I please have some water for my hands?"

Prairie Flower looked at him and smiled. Her face filled with a kindness he had not seen since his mother had died in his arms. Julius bowed again and turned his face toward the ground. He could hear the shifting of the water in the jug as the girl raised it to her shoulders.

In a blast of white light, his head and neck became a band of pain. Before it could subside, he took another blow, this time feeling the crunch of wood against the forearm he had raised in defense. He fell on his face, and earth filled his mouth. The cudgel came down again, this time on his unprotected flank, and he thought he felt a breaking in his ribs. Then his eyes filled with red; and just before it faded to black, he glimpsed something beautiful: an ivory-colored band of bear claws that clattered against each other, making a high and hollow sound like a skeleton deep in dance.

12

I F THERE WAS SAFETY IN NUMBERS, THEN THE PONCA HAD TO be the most endangered people on the Plains.

The legends said the tribe once included more than two thousand souls, happy and rich with land and game; but this was before the grandfather of Standing Bear broke away from the Omaha for reasons no one could remember. Years of conflict followed with the loathsome Dakota, followed by the white man, who brought gunpowder and diphtheria and smallpox to further reduce the population; and as the Ponca dwindled, so did their land. They had once occupied a large tract north of the Niobrara River. Later, the so-called United States had moved them east. Now the whites were demanding they move again, this time a ride of many days south.

Standing Bear would have understood this request if the whites had simply committed their usual treachery and broken the treaty of 1868 as they had so many others. But this time the agreement had been breached not because of the usual avarice, but because of what the whites called an "oversight." Someone in an office somewhere had simply *not remembered* what the parties had previously agreed to. Had his people been the size of the Sioux, an official apology would have been drafted and the mistake quickly rectified; the last thing the government wanted was seven tribes and ten thousand fighters painted for war. But the Ponca were fobbed off with a few written regrets and then told that the results of the "mistake" would stand. The Sioux would now own the tract they had long lived on. It had taken most of what was within Standing Bear to endure such an insult. The arrival in the new land had taken the rest.

And now, with all of this on his shoulders, he was faced with the unpardonable sin of the boy.

Had he been a farmer or stray cowboy, the decision would have been simple; so simple that Chased By Owls would have already made it. But the tall brave had also captured a shaman: and where the fate of a shaman was concerned, there were the spirits to consider.

It was a point not lost on John McGarrigle. And he behaved accordingly.

As Julius watched from a place along a wall, the prophet stalked the center of the main lodge, spewing a mixture of Ponca, Spanish, and English words. His fingers flew around his body, signing in every shape from great arcs to small circles. Not even the boy's facility for language could decipher the exact meaning of the old man's oration, but it didn't take an interpreter to understand that he was pleading for Julius' life.

"No use to smoke a pipe with all those old ones, Chief, not about this. We both know that ol' Chased here would love to see my young friend roasted until the face exploded off his skull. You can let him do it. Go ahead! But we both know that if he does, it'll bring a shitstorm of ghosts down on your heads. I'll call on every shaman in this world and the next—and you won't see a buffalo or a stalk of corn between now and the return of Jesus."

McGarrigle spat on the lodge floor. The boy had understood a few of his words: "pipe," "spirit," "face," and "ghost": but he could not for a moment fathom why John had pointed to him and invoked the Son of God.

John knelt beside Julius, still speaking and signing.

"Three seasons ago you saw my ghost dance and heard me speak the future. So if you think all this gyratin' and hollerin' is just a bad case of gas, then go on and kill this boy. But if you do, you'll have to deal with my God *plus* the Jehovah of the egg eaters. And I promise you they'll both be goddamned mad."

Standing Bear knew there was no choice but to take such threats seriously. Three years before, he had indeed witnessed the medicine of the gray man with his own eyes; and the terrible result of ignoring his warning.

The occasion had been yet another treaty meeting between the Ponca and General George Crook, the great chief who commanded all the territory's bluecoats. The prophet had been present at the gathering, having contracted to guide Crook's soldiers safely through the Indian lands and back. The negotiations had been both grueling and tedious, and the whites' interpreter, a typically traitorous Pawnee, took forever to translate each sentence. When McGarrigle became possessed, Standing Bear was standing next to his horse, a big gray whose color became steadily darker toward his hindquarters and turned white again at the tail. He never forgot this detail because, at the time, it seemed to him the animal was the exact same color as the man.

The scream that split that day would have been worthy of any of his braves in battle. The prophet's hands shot into the air as if trying to take hold of the empty atmosphere. With a choked rasp, he fell shaking into the dust, and for a moment it looked as though he would burrow through the earth. Finally, with a howl like brother coyote, he staggered to his feet and pointed a shaking finger at a tall young brave named Big Rain. He spoke and signed and shrieked at the hapless interpreter, ordering him to translate his words.

"Your raid on the Lakota tribe will fail and you'll die," he shouted at the astonished brave. "Their camp is not where you think it is. It will take you long to reach them and you will arrive weak and exhausted. They have many guards around their women and horses. If you go, they will bury you in pieces, jewels in your jaw . . . jewels in your jaw . . . jewels in your jaw . . ."

Standing Bear remembered how McGarrigle had punched at the air and then fallen to the ground. Three of the bluecoats rushed to his side and dragged him beyond the shadow of the lodges. At the next day's round of talks, the chief inquired as to the health of the old scout. General Crook informed the chief that Mr. McGarrigle had not awakened; he would not for two more days.

By that time, Big Rain had left to raid the Lakota. When the party didn't return, Standing Bear ordered a search.

A day's ride from their camp, Chased By Owls located what little remained.

The skull had been placed on a pike by the main trail, an agate bracelet hanging from its mouth. Chased By Owls remembered that Rain's wife had given him the trinket upon the birth of their first son, and since that day he had never seen him without it. The heads of the remainder of the party lay at the pike's base, stacked in a jaunty pyramid, their various personal effects placed where eyes or ears or teeth had been. Their flesh had long become food for vultures.

Standing Bear nodded again and turned toward the prophet.

"The Gray One must be respected. There is iron in his words and he has earned the authority allowed a holy person. He does the work of a man here and keeps away the curses of the Man Nailed To A Tree. But this egg eater's behavior has become intolerable! We spare his life and what does he do? His lurks among us—listening at doors and windows trying to learn our speech. Even this we could tolerate. But this evening he committed a crime. He attempted to speak to the daughter of Standing Bear as if he were her equal! A stinking white wretch! Even if he were a born member of this tribe, such conduct would require permission and a proper chaperone. There would be the giving of gifts and talk of the proper time and place. Worse, his speaking forced me into an undignified and unseemly temper. Before my people, I beat him to the ground. This display has caused me to lose face with my soldiers and made me appear impulsive. I believe the gray one must now release this boy from your protection—and tell your spirits that such a transgression should allow a father satisfaction."

Prophet John listened carefully. He put his hands in his pockets and cast his eyes to the ground.

"This little boy is just another peddler—raised to be neighborly like any good American and ignorant of your ways. Satisfaction? If he speaks to your daughter again, I'll stake him out myself. But while the egg eater may be an innocent, chief, I'm not. I know the only reason to kill him now is to appear strong in front of all these young hotheads. Killing as a warrior is killing like the lion. Killing as a politician is killing like the weasel. The Gray One respects Standing Bear as the lion. It's with that respect that I ask you to spare the boy. If you do, I swear he'll be a light to your people. If you don't, I won't answer for the consequences."

Standing Bear fixed Prophet John with a stare. Then he grunted at the old scout, rose and left the lodge. McGarrigle looked after the chief for a moment and turned toward Julius. He knelt beside the boy and untied his bonds.

"Well, for right now you get to live, young Jules. Where and as what I can't say just yet. Be your poor luck to get hobbled or released into this wildness without a horse, but so far, so good. One thing, though—I told the chief that you would be a light to his people. If I was you, I'd get to work on that."

Julius hissed with the pain in his ribs as the prophet walked him from the lodge. Waiting at its entrance was Younger Sister, a toothless widow with whom McGarrigle had been keeping intermittent company. She carried a striped blanket and an earthen crock of what Julius took to be firewater. The gray man bowed toward the boy and, taking Younger Sister's arm, headed toward her poor *tipi*. Before long, all of the tribe had gone to their homes. Alone, Julius slumped to the ground in a haze of fear and relief.

"You look like hell, Jew boy. The chief tuned you up right good."

Julius looked up to see Lady-Jane standing over him. She sniffed hard into her throat and wrapped her blanket tighter.

"I knew your big mouth would get you in trouble. Just because your yap can talk like anyone, don't mean you should open it. You'd do well to take a lesson from us whores—we're natural versed in discretion. How would it be for business if Mrs. Jones knew that Mr. Jones liked his back walked on in suede boots—or if Mr. Smith's boss knew that Smith had a hankering to eat his mother's apple pie off my behind? No, we keep our mouths shut or starve. Your case, it's trap shut or die."

"I think I've learned that."

"Of course, that doesn't mean that Chased By Owls or one of his soldiers won't make you look like an accident. In case you haven't noticed, in this place, people die every day. You spoke to a princess like she was a human, instead of a little gift from above. Even *I* think they ought to kill you for that. So, from here on, I suggest you stay out of sight and prick your ears. You might even stay alive long enough to pick up their gibberish plain."

Julius rose and nodded but said nothing. Lady-Jane smiled.

"That's a start. I don't know why I bother to give you this advice. Maybe I'm honoring your uncle. Or maybe something tells me that if your white ass doesn't make it out of here, my red one won't either."

⊰◈⊱

Among the women of the village, it was one more scandal that the white whore still lived with her childhood name.

"Little Feather" was all right for an infant, but as adults, the Ponca were expected to take permanent names based on achievement or appearance. A girl who developed late might be called Bufferfly Suddenly Showing Wings, while one who laughed and cried with the lunar phases could be named Power Of The Moon. For a prostitute to go by the name of an innocent child seemed an insult to the entire custom. But then, who would wish to go through life as "Goes With Anyone" or "Plaything for Miners?" Clearly, she had been spoiled by the whites, becoming a creature of goose-down pillows and feather beds who awakened every morning to pain in her spine and limbs and then vomited at a breakfast of deer liver.

Through the work and filth, Lady-Jane kept a sharp eye out for a man. Yes, she was untouchable to every brave, but she knew sooner or later there would be someone, be he true love or meal ticket. Once he arrived, she would quit these savages as quickly as she had Omaha. It was a big world; and if she had to conquer it on her back again, so be it; only this time she would own both the equipment *and* the business. White or red, she would never again trust a man to hold her hand, much less her money.

Adrian Calhern had seen to that.

How simple it had been to kill him. Knowing his taste for the bizarre and degrading, it was the work of minutes to tempt him with a pink corset and tie him to the bed. When she lighted a large cigar and

121

put it in her mouth, the fool began to laugh, believing it another part of her role, a bit of fun to make their play more fulfilling. She smiled, remembering his expression when she pulled the mattress from under him and then used the cigar to ignite a hay bale beneath the springs. Lady-Jane jammed the cigar into his mouth and watched as the smoke rose through his appeals for life. The ministers at school had often said that vengeance was an empty action, a fruitless exercise that left its practitioners depleted and unfulfilled. Smelling him burn, she could not imagine how they had been so wrong. This revenge was deeply rewarding, the act of taking everything from the man who had taken everything from her. For the first time, she understood why her fellow Indians tortured those enemies who stole their lives and lands.

She had debated long and hard over mercy for the others; but in the end, she wrote only two letters of warning. Everyone else would have to take their chances in a city where fire, accidental or intended, killed people all the time.

The first of the notes had been to Eli Gershonson. Although he was unlikely to be at the Dime on any evening, Lady-Jane was taking no chances. She remembered how he had stood and bowed when she appeared for breakfast; how he brought her small trinkets from his journeys, not to impress her but to witness her delight. On mornings when she felt her humanity was gone and would never return, his simple talk over a few eggs had restored her to the living.

The other letter had been to Doris. Yes, she was the Dime's top girl, but the chef always treated everyone according to their conduct. The good and decent received smiles and jokes and the impolite smashed noses or a hock of saliva in their food. This philosophy even extended to town pariahs like Lil Wilson, the lowest whore at the lowest whorehouse in Omaha. Lady-Jane remembered how a year ago, she had come to the kitchen for coffee just before the beginning of her workday. There was a knock at the outside door and Doris had gone to answer it. When the blind girl began to stumble inside, the big Negro had gently taken her arm and seated her at the long table reserved for the restaurant staff. Lil grinned and laughed as the chef chattered like a plague of locusts, filling her in on all the latest gossip. The meal he prepared for her that day was exactly the same as that served to his richest customers: no inferior cuts, no wilted vegetables. Lady-Jane remembered a rare stirring in her heart as she watched Lil slowly eat the steak and potatoes, her smile that of a child, her sightless eyes radiating gratitude. If there was a heaven for the black man, Doris was bound for glory; but she would not be the one to send him on his way.

Lady-Jane smiled bitterly. In her past life, a few words from her could stop a gun duel or start a political campaign. She had personally prevented an additional tax on Omaha's taverns by offering herself to two of its alderman. But here, she was powerless: no one's daughter, no one's wife, not even anyone's slave.

If the gray man and the Jew boy elected to pray for their lives, she thought, they might never see a better time. After all, with a Christian, a Jew, and eight hundred Indians present, when would they again find this many gods in one place?

−◇−

By the final weeks of fall, Prophet John and Julius had managed to erect a makeshift shelter. They had built it a stick and leaf at a time, collecting the materials they needed only in the few brief moments they were not required to work. It stood apart from the colony proper, a rough lean-to bookended by large trees. Inside, its close quarters proved a boon; there would be times in the winter when only the body heat of one man prevented the frostbite of the other. After a while, the smell became comparable to that of the hut Julius had shared with the prophet, counting in the presence of Jim Riley's corpse. *My God,* he thought one night when the wind threatened to reduce their south wall to rubble. *Hovel Number Eight on the Des Moines River was the Plaza compared to this.*

Finding food was a daily struggle. As befitted his station, the prophet was allowed to keep his rifle, but had to make do with the limited amount of ammunition he already possessed. Julius was not permitted even a knife. McGarrigle showed his young friend how to lure rats and black-tailed prairie dogs from their holes and roast them on sticks. The rodents were hardly satisfying; hibernation had made them lean and their meat sparse and stringy. On the one occasion when they did manage to bring down an elk, the tribe's warriors waited until the animal was butchered and then selected the choicest parts. The captives were left only with the animal's back, bones, and lungs.

Starvation was staved off only by a weekly miracle.

One morning when they had been in the camp several months, Julius woke up and walked outside to relieve himself. On his way back to the lean-to, he noticed a white deerskin bag leaning against its entrance. He looked around carefully but saw nobody. He brought the bag inside and set it down beside his mat.

Inside were several pounds of buffalo jerky and several more of dried pintos and cherries; there was an earthen jug of goat's milk and enough flour and oil for a few days' worth of flatbread.

It took all of Julius's character not to plunge his hands into the bag and eat his fill—to stuff his mouth with the raw flour and crack his teeth on the beans. After all, the gray man was old—he had lived his life; would it be such a crime to keep this food for himself so that Julius could live his?

Prophet John wasn't happy to be awakened, but brightened considerably when the boy showed him the contents of the sack.

"Someone's interested in our survival," the old man said. "If we're not pigs, there's enough here to stretch out a week and more."

"Who do you suppose sent it?"

"Can't guess. But in the end, we've got to consider it comes from his lordship, himself."

"Standing Bear? He is sending us food?

McGarrigle smiled. "Well, it might not be his doing or even his idea—but there's nothin' what goes in the chief's camp that the chief doesn't know about. Whoever it is that's bringin' us these vittles is doin' it by his leave, whether that whoever knows it or not."

"But why should he care if I live? Phony or not, you're a shaman. I'm nobody."

"That's right, I'm a shaman—who told Bear that you would be a light to his people. You've seen how he speaks to you a little each day?"

"Yes."

"Normal circumstances, you'd be beneath his notice. The only time he might talk to you is to let you know you was doomed. But he's not stupid, boy. He sees that in less than fifty days in this camp, you're yakkin' like you was born in a *wikiup*. He keeps me alive because he's afraid some god he's never heard of might make his life even worse. Your case, he figures you're maybe an investment."

The food continued to arrive each week, always in the leather bag, the contents more or less the same. The prophet made bread from the flour and oil, and soup from the jerky and beans. The portions were small, but together with what the pair could beg or kill, they sustained a hungry life. Upon the arrival of every new package, McGarrigle would seek out Standing Bear and thank him for his largesse; the chief would routinely disavow any knowledge of the favor.

On the night of the fifth delivery, Julius awoke to a deep growl outside the lean-to, followed by a series of yips and cries. At first, he thought it was one of the camp dogs, although he couldn't imagine what would bring them out of the warm *tipis* into the Nebraska winter.

Then he heard words in Ponca; a woman's words. He sprang from his mat into the bright moonlight.

The wolf was the largest he had ever seen and all black; in its jaws was the white leather bag. On the bag's opposite end was a young woman holding on hard to its beaded straps. Her face was bright in the light reflected by the snow, eyes wide with defiance as she cursed the beast. The wolf tried twice to get behind her, but the woman whirled and remained facing it, her grip on the tearing satchel loosened by blood on her fingers.

Julius ran inside the lean-to and picked up the oak cudgel he used for clubbing rabbits. Barefoot in the snow, he charged the wolf, bashing it on the nose. The animal yelped high. Feinting to his left, Julius brought the club down again, hitting a dark ear. With a whimper, the wolf dropped the bag but stood its ground. The boy raised the cudgel over his head once more and hissed like a timber snake. The wolf cocked its head and looked puzzled for a moment, then turned tail and loped through a huge, white drift. Julius watched as it emerged on the other side and vanished into the shadows of the Ponca tents.

"You are hurt," Julius said.

"It's barely a wound. My hand has been scratched by brother wolf's paw."

"Please. Come inside so that we may see to this."

The woman betrayed nothing. No gratitude, no pain or fear. She nodded and followed Julius into the small, mean shelter.

The woman wrinkled her nose; the stench was horrible, the noise worse.

"How did you ever hear me through this?" she asked.

For the first time that night, Julius realized that he had again committed the crime of speaking to the daughter of Standing Bear. In his head, he heard the anger of the chief and the good advice of Lady-Jane; but to clam up now seemed the ultimate in disrespect.

He only hoped that if he was caught, he could plead outburst by emergency.

"I am used to the gray one's snoring. It has become like the call of an owl at night—just a part of darkness and sleep. I suppose I would hear anything unfamiliar over it if it was loud enough. I suppose the wolf was loud enough."

Julius picked up a leather bladder near the fire.

"I know this place is a disgrace," he said, "but this contains our clean water—what we drink and wash with. I also have a cloth to dress your wound. It is clean as well. Will Prairie Flower allow me to help her? No one in camp need ever know."

Prairie Flower looked down and nodded. Julius took a white cloth from a nearby pile, dipped it inside the bladder and handed it to her. She opened her left hand and washed the blood from her palm.

"You speak our language well," she said.

"Not so well. Not yet. But I am listening."

"We have never seen a white who could speak so well so fast."

"It is some sort of gift I was given. I am not proud of it. It simply happens. The gray man says that blessings are good only until they become curses."

Prairie Flower laughed. Julius realized that the natural expression of her face was a smile.

"My father says the same thing. 'Don't be proud, Flower. Such things as god has given freely may, in the end, cost you dearly.' He has no end of such parables. But it has taught me to approach all as equals. In my position, pride can be an ugly thing, something earned by birth, not work."

Her laugh cut the cold like silver chimes. *This face,* Julius thought, *is that of an Indian. The same race, even the same tribe—but it is the opposite of Lady-Jane's. There are no 'Indian bones' here—no chiseled cheeks and sharp planes. It is round and smooth, the almond eyes merry servants of her grin. She glows in the firelight—like a happy moon.*

Prairie Flower picked up the bag and inspected it for damage.

"It looks like brother wolf will have to find his own dinner today. All that I packed is here. I wish it could be more. But winter strains the stores of all of us. I hope the egg eater will remain quiet about this. Ponca politics are complicated enough. Chased By Owls will make my father's life hell if it's known that his daughter is bringing food to the heathen."

"Standing Bear knows of this?"

She grinned and rose but did not answer. She slung the empty bag over her shoulder and made for the doorway. Julius gently placed his hand on her shoulder and then realized what he had done. She turned back toward him, her serene face betraying no sign that his touch was an insult.

"I wonder if, amid all her other generosity, Prairie Flower might grant me one more favor?"

"If I can."

"In the months that I have been here, no one has called me by name. It has been '*egg eater*, fetch the firewood,' and '*boy*, curry my horse.' Even the gray man calls me by a thousand nicknames. I beg that, if Prairie Flower should ever have cause to speak to me again, that she use my name—my real name."

Prairie Flower laughed again. "This is a small task compared with slipping past guards and fighting off hungry wolves. If I can pronounce it, I shall be honored to call you by your Christian name."

He smiled slightly. This was no time to correct a princess on religion and nomenclature.

"Julius," he said.

"Julius," she repeated with a grin.

She took the punctured leather sack and, with a slight bow, disappeared into the snow.

She would return seven days hence—no longer leaving the food outside the lean-to, but entering and spending a few moments with Julius as the prophet slept. Each time, she would spend a few minutes more—bringing him news and helping him to better speak her language. As the spring neared, they spoke longer and longer, some nights until the sun peeked through the cracks in the hut. At every greeting and every leaving, she would take his hands in hers and speak his name.

❖

For all her eighteen years, the life of Lady-Jane Little Feather had been an exemplar of plains law. Here, a man was what he made of himself; a woman was what a man said she was.

If any fool required proof of this, he needed only to follow the progress of young Mr. Julius Meyer: Jew among animists, white among red, slave among warriors.

All through the winter, Lady-Jane had viewed him with disgust and fascination. She had seen him shiver in the cold and fight the dogs for scraps; she had watched as he and the gray man built the hovel of branches and leaves; she had even heard him sob like a child after being spat upon by a warrior who ordered that he pack his pipe and cook his food, the humiliating labor of a woman.

Her labor.

Still, the Jew boy managed to gain favor—not for how quickly he retrieved a meat knife or how long he could hold up the beam of a lodge—but for the sorcery of his ears and the glibness of his tongue.

Lady-Jane had been born to the Ponca and arrived at the village more than a month before him. Yet, with spring now nearly in sight, her imprecise pronunciation still brought ridicule from her "sisters" in the tribe. There had been no such derision for the Jew boy. At first, he dared not speak at all, accepting his orders as wordlessly as the horses he brushed or the curs he boiled.

But then as if by witchcraft, he began to talk.

All who heard were amazed. Full sentences poured from the boy's mouth, accompanied by the fluid gestures that were as much a part of Ponca as its idioms and phrases. Yes, he still had to beg for his food, but now he did so with perfect grammatical structure. There was even a rumor that the egg eater had dared to tell a funny story to Chased By Owls himself; the gossips claimed that the tall brave practically pissed himself with laughter and rewarded the boy with a piece of jerky large enough to keep him alive for a week.

On the day Julius Meyer was elevated from outcast to adviser, the snows had piled nearly to the top of the lodges. That morning and afternoon had been like all others, filled with work; the hides the women had tanned in the fall now demanded transformation into goods. All day and evening, Lady-Jane sat on her small mat in the main lodge stitching a pair of moccasins. She nearly cried at the state of her hands. In a single winter they had mutated into horny claws nearly as hard as the bone needles they grasped to pierce the leather.

From her mat, Lady-Jane could see Standing Bear sitting motionless by the central fire, smoke curling about his head. He did not move when McGarrigle and his frightened young companion entered the lodge. With the wave of a finger, the chief bade them sit.

The gray man spoke first. His English was sprinkled with what she recognized as Ponca terms for "sky" or "god" or "buffalo," but he needn't have bothered. Though here only some ninety days, the boy beside him absorbed words with the speed of a mustang and translated it for the chief just as quickly.

"We ask again for freedom," Julius said for the old man. "It's been many days we've been held here. I've tried to be patient and I thank Standing Bear for the use of the woman and the ration of whiskey. But the spirits become angry when one of their conduits is mistreated. As one of them conduits, I ask that Standing Bear forgive me if I speak plain. Whatever befalls you and the Ponca now must be on your head. I regret to make such blunt threats."

Standing Bear passed the pipe to Prophet John. There was sadness in his amber eyes.

"You speak of anger among the spirits. But, how much more angry can the spirits get with Bear? Bluecoats pursue me everywhere. The spit of land we now live on is to be given to the dog-birthed Sioux. They want to move us to a place I fear does not have enough water to brew a cup of tea. Every day, Chased By Owls becomes more restless and his followers more impatient for blood. You should thank your Man Nailed To A Tree that I can still imagine that God is capable of bringing more curses down on me or I would relieve at least one of my headaches by allowing my young men to use your penises as sheaths for their knives."

Smoke and silence filled the room. The two men passed the pipe between them until Standing Bear broke the silence with a cough.

"It seems that two kinds of magic have come my way," the chief said. "First, there is the gray one's magic, of which I have seen little lately. Perhaps this is good: when he rolls about on the ground, the news is usually bad.

"But the egg eater's magic—*that* I now hear every day. Never has anyone seen a white learn our language in less time than the cornstalk grows. This is truly something not to be taken lightly—medicine which may prove an antidote to what poisons this tribe."

For the first time, the chief passed the pipe to Julius. The boy drew a few shallow puffs, wiped the stinging vapors from his eyes, and passed it back.

"So my decision is this. The gray one will intercede with the spirits and tell them that the Ponca are sick of moving and ask them to make the whites agree to let us stay in the Niobrara. When he has done this, he will be set free, providing he does not reveal our location to the bluecoats."

Prophet John did all he could not to smile. "And the egg eater?" he asked.

Standing Bear again passed the pipe to Julius. Although his words seemed meant for McGarrigle, his eyes were fixed upon the boy.

"You have seen how Half Horse translates for me. His skills being what they are, I have often worried that someday I would find I had declared war when in fact, I had only remarked upon the fineness of the weather. In view of this, I have decided to keep the boy here. He shall have his own lodge. He will learn our ways—riding, war, and the tenets of our faith. No one will threaten him because he will be my son, and when the time comes to parlay with the whites, my speaker."

The prophet nodded. "Will this be a permanent arrangement?"

Standing Bear continued to look straight at Julius.

"We all know that nothing but the earth is permanent. But if by this you ask if I am kidnapping this boy, no man can kidnap his own son. I only command that he stay here long enough to know my people and negotiate with your army. This will be a year, perhaps two. But even when he is gone, still shall I be his father, which will mean to the Indian everywhere that he is of Standing Bear. My allies will greet him with food and drink; and his enemies will be mine."

Julius looked toward Prophet John for any sign of rescue; but the gray man had adopted his "red face," the smooth and impassive mask of a chief.

"Well, it's not perfect," McGarrigle said, "but it'll do compared to death."

The chief stood. Standing Bear clasped hands with the prophet and then turned to Julius. The boy hesitated and then took the hard hand in his own.

As she watched the two whites leave the lodge, Lady-Jane seethed with fury. From this day forward the Jew boy would sit at the chief's right hand, privy to the secrets of a body whose mission was chartered during the first days of creation. Skin had not mattered, nor birth, nor work, nor beauty, nor courage. In the end, Julius Meyer had only needed to be one thing—a man—for his world to change in an instant; while she remained a white man's slut, destined to live what remained of her life in a bitter limbo between daughters and dogs.

13

EVER SINCE THE THIRD CURTAIN CALL, SEAMUS DOWIE HAD been praying to the Virgin.

So fierce had been the clomping of boots in the balconies that he had begun to fear for their structural integrity. Standing in the wings, he wrapped a rosary around his hands and tried bellowing the Lord's Prayer directly into the audience. It was no use. Our Father might well be in heaven, he thought, but if he wants to quiet this crowd, he'll have to come down here and bring Jesus, the fire brigade, and the cops.

Kissing the cross, Seamus jammed the beads into his vest pocket and walked behind the main flat toward a large oaken door. He plucked a candle from an array at its left, lighted it, and walked two hundred and two steps straight down. At the bottom of the stairs, he lighted the first of forty candles lining an enormous cellar and waited for his master.

On stage, Alexander made one final bow and, rising to his full height, pointed both fingers toward the audience as if firing pistols. Alternating hands, he began hurling playing cards through the air at an astounding rate of speed. Then, as the crowd cheered, he crossed the apron from right to left, propelling card after card into the house, two, three, four at a time. Some patrons caught them mid-air, others stooped to pluck them from the theatre's floor. Struggles broke out, even between ladies, and whoops and hollers filled the auditorium, the victors holding their mementos aloft in triumph.

On its face, each card displayed a color drawing of Alexander as the Knave of Hearts, complete with crown and halberd. The obverse read:

THE GREAT HERRMANN
Souvenir of his
ONE-THOUSANDTH and FINAL SOLD-OUT PERFORMANCE!
32 months! Most consecutive standing room
shows in world history!
ALL CROWNED HEADS OF EUROPE OUR GUESTS!
December 21st 1871
THANK YOU, BELOVED BRITAIN!
MERRY CHRISTMAS AND GOODBYE.

The diversion created by the souvenirs allowed Alexander to make his escape. He walked swiftly beneath the stage left flies and down a cramped corridor bedecked with the flowers of well-wishers. Without a word, he entered his dressing room, throwing down his gloves and hat. His dresser, a white-haired man named Armbrister, helped strip him of his sweat-soaked clothing and handed him a simple shirt and trousers, the braces already attached. Alex put them on in seconds, grabbed a lighted candle, and hurried from the room. He crossed to the rear of the stage and, calling down to the Irishman, began descending the stairs.

Seamus Dowie had hoped that on his night of greatest triumph, Alex might relax for an evening; celebrate with a glass or two or give employment to a high-priced girl; but his entreaties hadn't succeeded on the hundredth night, nor the two hundredth, nor the five hundredth. The thousandth night would be no different. For the boss, the performances had become a simple job of work, the cheers and applause a mere handshake for a job well done. Once his task was completed, Alexander would run to this rat-infested cavern to perfect the only thing about which he now seemed to care.

Seamus removed the dust cover from the latest configuration of the apparatus and awaited further instructions.

Alexander crossed his arms and stared at the trunk. He walked around it, banged on its lid and sighed. He lifted his eyes to heaven, lowered them to the floor, and murmured oaths in German and Yiddish.

In his mind, the trunk talked back.

Fill me with trap doors, festoon me with mirrors, use all your hard-learned wiles to misdirect the audience. Still I will defy you! Your silly trick depends on speed. Right now, your best escape has taken three minutes—but even if you cut that down to one, who will be amazed? If that big redheaded horse of yours gets out in forty seconds, so what? But by all means, continue! It will be a delight to laugh along with the audience as it whistles and boos and hollers, "fake!" Compars is right, Little Sasha! My secret is safe—at least from you—a boy ungrateful for an unmatched legacy.

"All right, Seamus, let's try it again."

For the next several hours the two men labored over different combinations. Dowie entered the bag first while Alexander stood atop the trunk: three minutes, five seconds. They reversed positions and loosened the trapdoor: two minutes, forty-two seconds. Alex examined the bag's escape panel: still too hard to locate in darkness. The trunk might as well have been laughing aloud.

By three in the morning, the two men had attempted the escape over forty times. Their best reading was two minutes, thirty seconds.

Seamus Dowie picked up his coat from a bench and whisked his hands across its fabric; dust flew in his face.

"Ya can fire me if ya like, Mister Alex," Seamus said, "but sacking or no, I'm all in. It's bad enough we sail for Brooklyn in two day's time without so much as a celebratory ale between us, but now there'll be no sleep until the boat, unless ya fancy the other assistants forgettin' half the equipment on Southampton dock."

"You're too big," Alexander said.

"Mr. Alex?"

"You're too big, Seamus. To give you the space we need to maneuver in the bag, we need to build a bigger trunk, which would clearly announce the whole thing as phony."

"Well, you've got apprentices aplenty would be happy as clams to let themselves be trussed up however ya like," Seamus said. "I t'ink both Billy Robinson and Jimmy Ring are sufficiently undernourished for the job."

Alexander spat on the floor. "Neither of them has the brains God gave a goose. It's all I can do now to keep them from spilling my secrets when in their cups. I'll probably get rid of both of them when we get to New York. I swear, either of them breathes one word of my methods, I'll turn them over to Ianucci and his boys for a lesson."

Seamus circled the trunk and lit the last of his cigarettes.

"As much as it pains me to say it, sir, you're gettin' more like the Herr Docktor every day."

Alexander's eyes opened wide. He grabbed a hammer from a workbench and raised it above his head.

"Aye, strike me if ya must, or force me to break ya in two as ya know I can; but it's true as a bride on her weddin' day. This here Substitution Trunk is all ya can t'ink of even as a country is lyin' at yer feet. Ya speak of Billy and Jimmy as if they's yer enemies—two boys as would gladly walk through fire for ya. Ya talk of employin' villainous eye-talians to torture 'em. Beware, sir. Much more of this and you'll become the first Great Herrmann, not the second: as grand as Compars himself—and just as mad."

The magician's lips curled back from his teeth and he raised the hammer higher. Then he slumped, stumbling toward a broken and dirty chair. The hammer slipped from his hand and clattered to the floor, the sound echoing and re-echoing through the vast cellar. He wiped his eyes.

"You are right as usual, my good friend. The face in the mirror looks more and more like my brother: fascinated by nothing but the job, loving no one but the audience. I can't sleep for thinking of this illusion. I forget my meals and am losing weight I can't afford."

Alexander rose from the chair. His blue trousers had become gray with coal ash and black with machine oil. He reached up to place a hand on his big assistant's shoulder.

"I forget that my mania can drive sanity from the minds of others— but now I've been sufficiently told off. And so, bucko, we shall brave the hectic days between now and Southampton and then, no more work! On the ship, we'll have oysters and champagne, count the dolphins as they glide through the sea, and, as the great Jehovah is my witness, I shall perform only such magic as might advance us with the ladies."

Seamus smiled at his young master. Alex nodded and turned toward the mocking trunk.

"Then, once back home, we'll break the secret. And the world will stare open-mouthed at our metamorphosis."

Alexander ran his hands along the top of the trunk. The leather felt rough and the brasses were cold on his fingers.

"To turn a lock one needs a key. We haven't found it because I've been looking in the wrong place. It's not with us. No, it's held by someone tiny and strong—small and agile enough to defeat our merciless stopwatch. We'll find her, Seamus. Somewhere in America, she's waiting."

14

·

As HIS WAGON APPROACHED M. MEYER & Co., ELI Gershonson felt good about all he had accomplished and optimistic that he might find his brother-in-law in an agreeable humor.

Ever since Julius had disappeared, Max had conducted all of his Indian trade through Eli. The peddler was used to dealing with the tribes and, over time, he had come to consider them his friends. In the past year, his missions had been especially fruitful. With the last of the hostile tribes defeated and their hunting and farming grounds restricted, they were happy to barter their works for manufactured goods and some hard currency.

So, if he had to tolerate a bitter and unpleasant Max, so be it. He had been corresponding with a woman in lower Manhattan, hoping she might eventually join him in Omaha. The larger his nest egg, the better chance he had of winning her. Max's sourness seemed a small tax to pay for a down payment on happiness.

Eli tied his mules to a hitching post and opened the wagon's side panel. Drawing a sharp breath, he removed two huge canvas sacks from its interior and carried them through the front door of the shop. Inside the bag were buffalo-hide shirts inscribed with fine art, hand-tooled moccasins, and silver and bone jewelry. He stumbled inside and plunked the bags down on the floor.

"That looks heavy, Gershonson," Max said in Yiddish. "When will you stop such *narrishkeit* and give up that *farcockter* wagon of yours?"

Eli smiled his salesman's smile. "And hello to you, cousin. I missed you, too."

"Never mind," Max said, lifting one of the bags and looking inside. "My brother is gone a year. He's never coming back. I need help that won't rob me in the new store. Who else can I trust but family? You think that girl on Houston Street is going to wait forever for you to make a few *shekels*?"

Eli grinned wider. "Max, I think you have the kind of trouble everyone needs. Is it my fault that you are such a success? It looks to me like you're fine without my help. I know you're trying to be charitable to a relative, but if I took any more money from your pocket, I would feel even more guilty. Besides, I wouldn't know how to sell settees or sofas or, *gottenyu*, a grand piano!"

Max's face turned red with irritation. He had heard this "poor relation" speech before. But the truth was that Max was in dire need of Eli's skills for his new furniture store further down on Farnum. Here, Omaha's quickly growing middle class could purchase all that was needed to make a prairie home a haven of practicality and refinement. Business was good, but he knew that with the affable

Gershonson serving his customers, the new shop could be twice as profitable.

"Max!"

He stared first left, then right, but saw no one he knew. The voice called again and he turned toward it, his eyes staring straight up the street past the blackened hole that had been the Nickel & Dime. In the middle distance, he saw a man break into a gallop. His horse was a paint—the kind of small, spotted mongrel favored by the tribes. He was dressed in fringed buckskins that were undecorated and seemed nearly new. His face and hands were as brown as a Pawnee's, and the mouth beneath his black mustache was set in a wide, white smile. At first, Max took him for a savage, but the man's dark head betrayed him as something other. Instead of falling straight to his shoulders, his hair exploded outward in a halo of ringlets, curls so thick and tight, they seemed immovable even in the wind.

The rider streaked past him at full speed, letting out the kind of cry cowboys made on Saturday nights; the pony whistled high and long as the curly-headed man reared him toward the sky. The cigar fell from Max's mouth as the rider jumped his mount onto the wooden boardwalk and made straight for the spot where he stood. Before the animal had fully stopped, the rider reined him in and leaped from the paint's back, bouncing to a landing directly in front of him. Max made to turn and run, but a strong hand pulled hard on his sleeve and spun him around.

"Max, it's me!"

Max squinted at the rider. The voice was that of his brother, but the boy he had known was a scrawny, graceless youth, shy and awkward in his movements. This was a full-grown man—broad at the shoulder and fluid in motion. Julius's face had always been clean-shaven and pale, a *yeshiva bocher* who saw much of the library but little of the sun. This face was tanned and broad, the mustache thick as a horse brush and drooping at the corners.

Max stepped back and looked the man up and down as if he were an order to be inspected and assessed in value: *Julius Meyer. Sibling. Former clerk and traveling salesman. Feared lost. Returned in good condition.*

"I said *kaddish* for you," Max said. "I sat *shiva*. But as you are not dead, I wonder if this was a sin."

Julius smiled. "If the almighty is all-knowing, I don't think he'll hold it against you."

"So. You're an Indian now?"

"I don't know. I think it must take a long time to become an Indian."

Max picked his burning cigar up from the cracked boardwalk and surveyed his brother one more time.

"That's an Indian's answer."

Without another word, Max turned and walked back into the store. Julius followed him to the back room where Eli Gershonson stood, taking inventory of the new trinkets, separating them by size, color, and kind.

"*Feter* Eli!"

The peddler looked up from his work. He studied the source of the greeting for a few seconds and then rushed from behind the table. Holding his arms wide, he embraced Julius with all his strength.

"Julius, God bless you," Eli said. "You're an Indian now?"

"He says he needs time," Max said.

For the next hour, Julius explained his disappearance: how he had escaped death; his period as a lowly outcast; his elevation to Speaker and his adoption by Standing Bear. He told his brother and uncle of learning to ride a horse and shoot a rifle. The Ponca, he told them, had their heroes and villains, their faithful and their hypocrites.

"In a way," he said, "they are very like us."

Max's head jerked up. "Like us? We gave the world the Torah. We taught the world what the law is and how a scholar or a statesman should behave. We even gave the Christians their God. *Like us?* It has been four thousand years since we were a band of *vilda chiyahs,* screaming on horses and fighting and killing; and even then we produced Maccabeus."

Julius frowned at his brother. "They are like us, Max, not because of their holy books or their learned men, but because they are unique— just as we have always been unique. They see their gods in everything they touch or hunt or eat and are mocked and killed for it just like we once were for having only one god.

"They have had their country taken, as Jerusalem was taken from us. If the Indian surrenders, they say he is craven—a coward with no stomach for battle. If he fights, he is a beast, said to drink the blood of his victims. Where have we heard that before?"

Max's face colored in rage. It could be explained that when one is forced to live among primitives, one has little choice but to adopt primitive dress. But to take the part of the savages against the white race was not only a shame before the gentiles; it was the kind of talk that could ruin his trade in a place where some still refused to buy even a cigarette from one who killed Christ.

"Politics can wait," he said. "We will make an appointment with Gaita immediately for a haircut and bath for you. While you are there, I shall arrange with Simmons to fit you for work clothing and you may borrow some of my things until he can make you a proper suit. I will advance you the money and you can repay me some each week from your wages."

Julius picked up a bauble and frowned. It was a necklace of claws, similar to the one favored by Standing Bear; except this one consisted of the claws of a cub, something the tribes would never have created until the whites came.

"I am sorry, dear brother," Julius said, "but I am not coming back. At least not yet."

Max's eyes opened wide. He was now certain that exposure to the world of the savages had made his brother as *messhugah* as they.

"I have been honored in a way you may not understand. A king has made me his son. Given me a name—*Boxkareshahashtaka*—it means 'curly-headed chief who speaks with single tongue.' He has asked me to use the gift God gave me to be his 'speaker'—his interpreter. For him I translate the Jewish peddlers, the German homesteaders, the French fur trappers. Soon, I'll meet with General Crook himself—and with any luck, I may help prevent the Ponca being driven from lands that have known them a thousand years."

"So?" Max said. "I should care about savages running through the woods praying to trees? You think the Army will stop hunting them because all of a sudden you're their mouthpiece?"

Julius' face darkened and he sat down on the table. His legs dangled a foot from the floor.

"Max, I have no illusions that the Indians will win their battle with the white man. Those left fighting are too few in number and too poorly armed to hold out much longer. In ten years, perhaps less, they will be conquered. But conquered is not the same as exterminated."

Max stubbed his cigar out on the shop floor.

"Conquered . . . exterminated . . . what difference does it make? You say the Jew is like the Indian. Persecuted and banished. Did anyone care when we were being killed? Pushed from country to country? Forced to convert or die?"

"Perhaps that's why you *should* care, Max. If you can kill all the Indians, you can also kill the Catholics, the Chinese, and the Jews. But what if we let them keep some land? What if we gave them a place to sell their art for what it is really worth? Then they could prosper as they never have. Everybody rich, everybody happy."

"I'll assume that includes me?"

Prophet John McGarrigle stood in the doorway. Judging by the film on his eyes, he was slightly the worse for firewater.

"Just the man I want to see," Julius said. "My brother and I were just discussing the new store we're going to build to sell the craft work of the Indians. For the place to work, I'll have to spend two or three weeks in the month with the tribes, so I'll need an inside man. We all know Eli here won't ever give up his wagon. That leaves you. I've never seen you drink when you're working and you'll know when the weather will affect the business. Besides, I figure all your bullshit will either fascinate the customers or bore them into buying."

The gray man hiked up his pants and spat onto the boardwalk.

"Thank you, young Jules. You always was complimentary."

"I try my best. I need you for this, John. The last thing I want to do is deal with the public. I'm not sure I'm civilized enough for that anymore. I've sort of gotten into the habit of thanking the spirits for the day and moving on. Fighting with some farmer over the price of a buffalo head could interfere with that serenity."

"From what I hear," the prophet said, "you're thankin' the spirits for more than the day. Be careful, young Jules. Indian or not, she's the boss's daughter."

"Please, John . . ."

"Don't 'please' me, boy. You got two eyes and two ears inside Ponca camp—I got a couple dozen. They tell me you been fraternizin' with the Prairie Flower. Voice Like A Drum says the conversations go on long past the point they're interestin'—and that you've come to him for love charms and ordered a courtin' flute. Says your practicin' hurts his ears."

"Just because you saved my life, does that entitle you to run it?"

"It does."

"Do you want the job or not? Ten dollars a week and found."

"Sold, young Jules—I just hope she's worth the in-laws."

With these last words, Julius walked past his apoplectic brother and out the door. The paint had stepped down from the wooden boards and now stood grazing on a pot of flowers in front of the McGreevy boardinghouse. A crowd of boys had gathered to look at the animal. It wasn't every day you saw an Indian pony close up.

"Hello, Lemuel," Julius said. "Still reading your books?"

Lemuel Norcross turned from inspecting the horse in time to see Julius leap into the saddle. The "Indian" kicked the pony in the side and the animal lashed out with its hind legs, barely missing the head of young Giorgio Gaita, the barber's eldest.

Julius whirled the pony and shouted back toward his brother and uncle.

"Figure to start building by June. The only good Indian isn't a dead Indian if he's filling your cash box, Max. Even you can understand that."

As the boys ran in all directions, Julius reared the paint, spun him around twice, and began to gallop hard out of town. As he reached the doors of Third Congregationalist, he stopped short and began to scream a series of short, strangled yips followed by a long wolf howl. Then he turned the horse once more to the west and was gone.

Max and Eli stared after Julius as he dissolved through the dust. Lemuel Norcross stood thrilled but puzzled. How did this Indian know his name? And when did the red man learn to curl his hair?

15

D URING CONSTRUCTION, THE CORNER OF FOURTEENTH AND
Farnam came to look like the camp of a particularly produc-
tive tribe.

Robes, drums, and jewelry hung from every column and rafter;
weapons and the bleached skulls of buffalo piled up beneath the windows. No sooner had the merchandise been nailed to walls or placed
on shelves than Eli Gershonson arrived with another wagonload. John
McGarrigle barked orders at the new employees as they sorted the
cargo and boxed it for pricing. Once a day, Max came by and placed a
value on each item, grumbling his disapproval in several tongues.

Less than three weeks later, the shop opened its doors to great
fanfare. Its windows were hung with red, white, and blue bunting,

and territorial flags waved from its roof. The shop's wares tumbled out onto the boardwalk and hung from the shop's great awning. Spotted Tail of the Brulé, Iron Bull of the Mountain Crow, and Pawnee Killer of the Arapaho were the guests of honor, each bringing a colorful retinue with them. Men and women, some on horseback, most on foot, banged on drums and chanted songs. The citizens of Omaha nodded in approval at the riot of feathers and jewels, and the volunteer firemen's brass band played patriotic songs as Governor William H. James cut the ceremonial ribbon.

Julius made a speech thanking his native friends. The *Daily Herald* quoted him as saying:

> I hope that my new emporium will educate the citizens of Omaha and all who visit here that the Indian is not a savage or a brute, but a human being who tends his garden, creates great art, and loves his children as they do.

As the public was admitted to the shop, each patron was handed a complimentary printed souvenir photograph. It depicted Julius and Pawnee Killer standing against a painted backdrop of plains and hills. Seated in front of them were Spotted Tail and Iron Bull, surrounded by imitation shrubs and wildflowers. In addition to the free photo, customers could also buy for twenty-five cents a version with two images, side by side, specifically designed for stereopticons. On the reverse was printed:

INDIAN WIGWAM

234 Farnam Street   OMAHA, NEB.

JULIUS MEYER

Box-Ka-Re-Sha-Hash-Ta-Ka   Indian Interpreter

Indian Trader and Dealer in American Indian Curiosities

Tomahawks, Bows and Arrows, Blankets, Pipes, Moccasins,
Garments, Beadwork, Shells, Antediluvian Fossils,
Petrifactions, &c.

SPECIMENS OF ALL WESTERN MINERALS

Photographs of Indians and Western Landscapes, Views of Omaha
Buffalo Robes, Beaver, Mink, Otter, Wolf and other kinds of Indian
dressed furs and skins.

Prophet John watched the hoopla from the train depot across the street. Looking at the number of chiefs present, he wondered how many horses this day had cost the boss. Only young Jules could have managed to persuade Indians who were often at each other's throats to appear together to open a business. Still, no Ponca was here to support their Speaker. Had Standing Bear held out for more horses? Or had the chief simply decided that no matter how good Julius's intentions, it was beneath his dignity to play the performing seal?

The prophet's reverie was broken by the high, strangled sound of a whistle. As one, the people on the platform stepped closer to the tracks and began to wave and a great locomotive came into view. As its huge wheels seized to a halt, a cloud of soot blackened the raised handkerchiefs of the ladies. Prophet John pulled a red bandanna from his back pocket, sneezed into it, and made for the rear of the train.

He walked down the line and thought of how times had changed since the locomotives pulled basic freight and exhausted, miserable passengers. With railroad executives and eastern millionaires now regularly visiting the West, private railroad cars were a common sight in Omaha. Some sported gold accents, others purpose-built nurseries or glass ceilings. He had even visited one car that included its own chapel, complete with holy-water font and Stations of the Cross.

But never had he seen the like of this.

It was painted in red and green with a solid brass roof polished to a mirror finish. Delicate white pinstripes separated its windows and surrounded its doors. Above each of these was an arch in stained glass, its workmanship fine enough for any cathedral; but rather than illustrate the wonders of the bible, these windows depicted miracles of a different sort: a hand fanning a deck of cards; a magic wand spewing lightning; a smiling, mustachioed devil. A copperplate sign flew above the car's rear observation deck. It took the prophet four tries to sound out its name:

PRESTIDIGITATOR

John stopped at the end of the car. Through its frosted glass door, he could see urgent movements. Before long, a huge young man with close-cropped red hair and a fine dark suit emerged. He carried large suitcases in each hand. The color of their leather was nearly impossible to discern, so covered with labels was each one: LONDON, ST. PETERSBURG, DUBROVNIK, DETROIT . . .

The redhead jumped down from the train and, smiling, bounded up to the prophet.

"You'd be Mr. John McGarrigle, then?"

"Is it that obvious?"

"Seamus Dowie. Great pleasure. The gov'nor ought to be out any minute."

"Have a pleasant journey from Chicago, did you?"

"Just fine, Mr. McGarrigle. But then, ol' Pressy here's got all the comforts a' home . . . if home is Versailles. We even saw a few Indians here and there."

"Well, if you're a friend of Jules, young Seamus, I daresay you'll see a few more."

As the men shook hands, a deep and impatient voice called out across the platform.

"Mr. Dowie!"

The two men turned around in time to see the owner of the voice descend from the observation deck. Outside of an Oglala painted for war, he was the most extraordinary-looking human the prophet had ever seen.

His long cape, his swallowtail coat, his striped trousers, even his beaver topper were purple. In contrast, his gloves, waistcoat, cravat, and spats were snow-white and patterned in a lotus paisley. He was about six feet tall and slender as a whippet with a pale, fine face and penetrating blue-gray eyes. His mustache was waxed into curlicues just above a beard as pointed as a pencil. If his clothing had been red and included a tail, John would have wondered if he was seeing the model for the stained-glass devil that decorated the *Prestidigitator*.

The purple man walked down the car's gangway, his cape flowing behind him. He strode up to the prophet, removed his right glove, and offered his hand.

"Mr. John McGarrigle," Seamus Dowie said, "allow me to introduce the Great Herrmann."

The prophet took the magician's hand. Alexander bowed slightly.

"So you are the famous Prophet John! My cousin tells me that, while I fool people into belief in magic, you possess the real thing."

"I wouldn't call it magic, exactly, professor. Just a little present from who knows where that does who knows what and comes and goes who knows when."

"I'll be most interested to hear all about it, sir," Alexander said. "Little enough real magic in the world today, and most of it bad. But now, let's away. I'm famished, and Julius tells me the best steak in the world awaits us at a place called The Big Cheese." With a grin, Alexander released the prophet's hand and the trio began down the platform toward Farnam Street.

They had nearly reached the hotel before John McGarrigle realized that his third, second, and fourth fingers were now decorated with ruby, diamond, and emerald rings.

⋖◈⋗

There was a time when Lady-Jane Little Feather would not have missed the appearance of a great magician.

For weeks before such an event, members of Omaha's "sporting" society would vie for her company. Politicians, salesmen, pimps, and regulators would send letters and telegrams begging her attendance. Some would be accompanied by gold pieces, others by cash in advance. Jewelry would be proffered, dresses—even horses.

On opening night, Lady-Jane would scandalize the respectable women of the city with both her presence and her attire. As the gaslights of the Academy of Music sputtered and blazed, she would emerge from a fine landau, the flaming red or milky pink of her gown's skirt preceding her. Layers of silk and lace would bunch behind her to form the largest and longest bustle in the crowd. Gasps would be audible at the plunge of her neckline and the bareness of her arms.

Once inside, Lady-Jane would be seated in a box beside her highest bidder. Throughout the great hall would be heard the sound of gloved hands slapping the shoulders—and sometimes the heads—of admiring husbands. She relished these occasions; they not only provided first-class entertainment but also paid more than her going rate without her having to "perform" herself. The whoremaster Calhern seldom accompanied her, busy as he was lining up the women, the drink and cocaine, and the odd boy or two for the party to follow.

From the Academy's stage, she had listened to the stories of Mr. Mark Twain as he performed selections from *The Celebrated Jumping*

Frog of Calaveras County and *The Innocents Abroad*. She had thrilled to the moving voice of Madame Adelina Patti singing *Lucia di Lammermoor* and *Salammbô*. Over the years, there had been countless jugglers and contortionists, singers, and dancers, even a group of Negro college students from Fisk University whose spirituals brought the audience to tears.

Had she still been the Red Rose of Omaha, nothing would have kept her from the performance of the man thought to be the greatest magician in the world.

Now, she could only hear the details second-hand.

"It was amazing," Julius said as they sat in her corner of Standing Bear's lodge. "He strolled across the stage carrying an ordinary walking stick. Then, he let go of it. Everyone expected it to fall, but instead it stood straight up and began to bang on the floor and hop back and forth. People applauded and laughed. And then he borrowed a gold watch from old man Bennett, the bank president."

Lady-Jane smiled. "One of my best clients."

"I'll bet. Anyway, his assistant, a huge red-haired fellow, brought out a big target with a hook in the center of the bulls-eye; then he reached behind his back and produced an enormous blunderbuss—it looked like something the pilgrims would use to hunt turkeys. He told the audience that he would load the watch into the gun and shoot it at the target so it hung on the hook. I was sitting near Bennett. He was sweating like a pig. But Alexander fired it, and it hung right up in the bulls-eye; and when he called the old man back onstage and gave him back his watch, he looked like he'd been reprieved of murder."

They shared a hearty laugh. "It must have been wonderful," she said. "I can almost see him . . . and all the beautiful ladies in their best and the men in their long coats . . ."

She looked down at her rough hands. Tears came to her eyes. "I used to be a tough whore. Man tried to take more than he'd contracted for,

I'd kick his ass down the Dime's back stairs. Now I tear up because a magician comes to Omaha and I miss it. I tell you, Julius, I've got to get out of here."

Julius patted her hand. "Tall order." he said. "Hiding here was the best way to keep the whites believing you were burned with the Dime. But since those posters went up . . ."

Her tears turned to bitter laughter. "They say I killed twenty people. A thousand dollars doesn't seem like much of a reward for that: fifty dollars a head as I figure it, and less if they count the burned and the crippled. But most of them was whores, so I guess it's a bargain. Hell, I used to make that off of one railroad boss back when I still looked human."

Julius smiled ruefully. "You're still beautiful," he said.

"When I go to the river to wash myself, I don't look at the water. But I can feel my skin. I can see my arms and hands. Another year here and my hide will only be fit to stretch across a drum. Another two, and I'll be a monster like the rest of them."

"I think you're looking more like your old self," Julius said. "That's a fine necklace you're wearing, and you look less thin than on my last visit."

Lady-Jane smiled again. "Well, a whore needs a patron. Chased By Owls meets me in secret so his thugs won't know he's fucking a white slut. And as brutal as he is in war is nothing compared to how he treats a turncoat in bed. At the Dime, it would have cost a client five hundred to do what he does to me for some trinkets and extra meat. Twice, during his fun, I've reached for his knife, but I guess I'm still enough of a professional to bear it; and anyway, I wasn't even sure who I meant to kill: him or myself."

The shriek of a dozen children penetrated the lodge, followed by the sound of moccasins running over ground and hooves pounding. Lady-Jane and Julius made for the entrance and stepped outside.

Everywhere, people were laughing and waving their fringes, quickly making their way toward the camp's south entrance.

What greeted their eyes seemed to come from another world.

The mounted contingent was led by the shaman who, it was said, shook and cried by the hands of the gods, the better to tell things to come. The gray man was dressed not in his usual filthy buckskins, but in the kind of clothing the whites wore on Sundays to worship their gods. His suit was blue with a white stripe, and his tie shone red like a darting fish. Beside him rode a huge man who was whiter than any white the Ponca had yet seen, his hair and the tiny spots on his face as red as the sumac flower. Behind the riders came two wagons driven by nervous-looking Chinese. They were dressed in native garb, but not the kind seen on Omaha's railroad coolies or laundry men. Their tunics were deep crimson and decorated with gold mandalas, and their black trousers bore embroidered dragons from waist to ankle. The reins and bridles of their horses flowed with silken streamers, and each wagon carried an array of large and small boxes, lacquered in red and gold.

But it was the figure at the rear that brought gasps from the Ponca.

He rode a horse as black as a raven, its hide interrupted by not so much as a star on its nose. His saddle was also black, fine-tooled with the twelve signs of the zodiac and the sun and moon smiling with the faces of men. Black, too, were his long coat and the cloak that spread across the horse's hindquarters. Beneath his tall hat, his face was pale and bearded, its top half obscured by smoked glasses that hid his eyes from view.

The bizarre entourage stopped at the village center and dismounted in time to see Standing Bear emerge from the medicine lodge. Julius hurried to join him.

The chief nodded to the three white men. "As always, John McGarrigle, you are welcome among the people. I trust the wiles by which you are known have helped you elude any soldier or other nuisance seeking to find us."

"No worry about that, Bear. The way I send dogs off scents, anybody looking for the Ponca should be somewheres in Kansas by now. And if they're extra special dumb, Connecticut."

Julius translated this as "yes."

Standing Bear turned to the other two visitors. "My Speaker tells me that you are interested in our ways and that you may be trusted among us. I also understand that the man in black is kin to One Tongue and that he produces miracles for money. He has told me that he will do as such for us in exchange for our hospitality. My Speaker says that your medicine is caused by neither god nor demon, but by practice and skill, as a man would ride a horse. And so, you too are welcome; and I shall look forward to your demonstration."

Alexander bowed and removed the smoked glasses. "It is indeed a great honor to be invited to your village, your majesty. From my cousin, I have heard of the ways of the Ponca. He has told me there is much the white man may learn from you. As to a demonstration—if you will permit me?"

Standing Bear nodded, and The Great Herrmann shot his cuffs in the air. Moving slowly, the man in black reached behind Bear's ear and produced a large ring. On either side of its blue diamond were tiny hunting bows in gold and, beneath them, platinum arrows. Alexander held the ring up for all to see and then, falling to one knee, offered it to his host.

There was a great silence throughout the tribe. Wives grabbed the arms of their husbands and children ran toward their mothers; Chased By Owls cursed and brought his hand to the hilt of his knife.

Standing Bear stared at Alexander, incredulous. This was indeed powerful, even dangerous medicine; but to refuse a gift from a guest would be the height of bad manners. Julius stood rigid, hardly breathing, wondering when his insane cousin might break the tension.

Finally, Alexander winked at Julius and spoke.

"My sainted mother told me never to go visiting empty-handed."

Julius translated. Even the children were silent as Standing Bear absorbed the information. Then his red, weathered face broke into a grin and exploded in laughter.

"Tell him," the chief said to Julius," that my mother said the same thing."

Julius did as instructed and soon the entire village was holding its bellies. Alexander rose as if he had been dubbed a knight and placed the ring on the chief's index finger, only to have it appear on his own a second later. He apologized profusely and replaced the ring, which again made its way to his hand. By the time he had repeated the trick twice more, Standing Bear was nearly helpless, tears of delight tracing the deep creases in his cheeks. Finally, Alexander bowed and backed away, leaving the ring with his host.

"If One Tongue says this is not witchcraft, then I will believe it and hope that before you leave us you will show me a little of how this is done. Now, I must leave you. We are preparing a feast and I must supervise. I thank you for the fine gift and hope that it will not disappear again before you leave."

Still laughing, Standing Bear walked off. Prophet John made his apologies and went in search of firewater. Seamus Dowie began directing the Chinese assistants, removing the boxes from the wagons and unpacking the crates of equipment.

"So, Julius," the magician said in German. "You have become an Indian. What next? A Hindu? Or perhaps a member of Parliament, complete with an accent from Eton."

"I assume you have a message for me, Alex. I suspect it is the same one I've heard before. I suggest you deliver it, so that we may move on to happier topics."

"Yes, I've said this to you before—because I've seen you *do* this before. In the old land, to the Poles, you spoke as a Pole, to the Germans like a German. When we first came into Philadelphia, you were not a Jew, but a Russian, remember? Now you perform your miracles on these poor savages. I am used to you becoming what you behold, but as fetching as those moccasins may be, isn't this going a bit far?"

"Interesting judgment, coming from a man got up like a magpie. And I suppose that the Great Herrmann chants the week's Torah portion at every show and refuses to perform on *shabbos*?"

"I may not, cousin, but I've never denied my origins. Last year, the Munich press was full of an incident in which I knocked down a theatre manager who, believing I was a pure Aryan, made unkind remarks about the stinginess of our co-religionists."

"I'm sure the yids of the world are grateful. Still, it may interest you to know that my brothers and sisters here know well what I am. And perhaps because they are even more despised than we, I have become more a Jew than ever. Except I'm not the frightened Jew of the *shtetl*, but the Jew that we learned about in school—unafraid like a *Maccabee*. As for the moccasins, well, they are fitting for the environment and I don't get horse shit on my nice white spats."

The Great Herrmann looked down past the blackness of his trousers to see that his silken shoe coverings had turned brown with manure and mud. Alexander looked at Julius, then back down at the spats.

"Your point is taken," Alex said.

Arm in arm, the cousins walked toward the lodge that had been prepared for Alexander and his retinue.

"I assume that you will be able to help me in my little performance tonight?" Alexander said. "I'll need an assistant who understands English, and you'll do until someone better comes along."

"If you think the distinguished Speaker of the Ponca is going to make a fool of himself before the tribe, you're mad. But there's a woman here—a quite pretty woman, too—who speaks fine English and understands a thing or two about performance."

"A woman? Will our audience be tolerant of that?

Julius shook his head. "These are Indians, Alex. They haven't survived in this harsh land a thousand years by being fools. They don't waste time debating whether or not it's proper in the Lord's eyes for a woman to assist a magician; *their* gods are too busy supplying buffalo and making the snow fall to concern themselves about such nonsense. Only whites are stupid and dirty-minded enough to believe that Jesus sits around worrying about the niceties of show business."

❖

That evening, the Great Herrmann made no accommodation to the primitive setting, but offered up every part of his act that could be performed with fire for footlights.

He blazed through a litany of card magic; cut off and restored the bird's head and floated the goldfish bowl. He burned Standing Bear's necklace and returned it to him intact. He even performed "the floating boy." For the *dénouement*, he produced gifts for the chief and his wives from his tall black hat: a Colt single-action revolver, a bolt of orange silk, knives for cutting and carving, and, finally, a box of fine panatelas.

Throughout the evening, Lady-Jane performed her role flawlessly.

Informed of her part in the evening's entertainment, she had hurried to her lodge. From beneath her mat, she retrieved a small cardboard box, broke the seal and opened it. Inside was a small bar of plain hand soap. She had earned it on her knees before a Dutch peddler, but tonight it would be worth the price. Placing it in the pocket of her skirt, she ran toward the Niobrara.

Having bathed, Lady-Jane combed and tied her hair into a tight *chignon*. She reached down beneath the mat again and retrieved the one decent dress she had brought with her when she fled the Dime. She had kept it as flat as possible to maintain a semblance of pressing and periodically exposed it to sun and wind, avoiding the ruin of mildew. It was simple, made of cotton and gingham, with enough piping and lace to appear respectable, and enough silk and whalebone to highlight the charms beneath.

Asked to display the magician's doves, she did it with gesture and style. Commanded to step inside a box, she obeyed with grace, sliding in and out of Alexander's apparatus with feline nimbleness. Even Seamus Dowie was forced to admit that her presence added an element heretofore unseen in any magic act; something only a woman could provide. That night, stepping and whirling through a world of illusion, the Red Rose of Omaha seduced the audience—every man, woman, and child—as easily as she had the richest cattle barons and scions of railroad fortune.

⊰◇⊱

For nearly a year, Half Horse had pondered the source of the power that had cost him so dearly.

Before the egg-eater boy's arrival, he had been Speaker: a position of honor within the council and of status among the people. As such, he had traveled to the white man's villages and taken part in the negotiation of treaties. Sitting at Standing Bear's side, he had translated complex land partitions and water rights with the Blue Coats and their chiefs. True, mistakes had been made in these deliberations, and the chief had sometimes chided him for his interpretations; but could this not be attributed to the white man's trickery and a wicked language with a dozen meanings for every word?

At first, Standing Bear had informed him that the young white would be his assistant, schooling him in the finer points of English and helping him with idioms and slang no Indian could be expected to know. But at the very next negotiation, Half Horse found himself sitting silent as a boulder as the boy interpreted, purposely speaking too fast for understanding. A few days later, Half Horse returned from a hunt and was told that a white man and woman were being interrogated in the chief's lodge; but when he attempted to fulfill his duty, he was detained at the door by two braves. When the terrified couple emerged, it was the boy, not he, who shouted instructions for mounting a horse while blindfolded and the warnings to never return.

Half Horse was not called upon to interpret on any day thereafter.

He knew it was unnatural for a man to come into another man's world and speak his language as if born to it. He suspected that only a bargain between a man and a demon could produce such abilities.

Half Horse consulted Voice Like A Drum, the medicine man, to see if such a demon could be flushed into the open.

"Sometimes," Voice Like A Drum said, "a man may be given a gift by the Unknown and no demon is involved at all."

"Yes," Half Horse said. "This would be a man like me—gifted by the Almighty in return for hard work."

Voice Like A Drum sat impassively, his head wreathed in smoke. "All of the people in our village know that Little Horn has big ears and can hear a butterfly from here to the Niobrara. It is also well known that Yellow Wolf has a large penis that makes his wife smile. Like these, gifts may come in different sizes and bring different results. And just as some people may have bigger penises than other people, there are others who may have more words than other people."

Half Horse left the meeting feeling vaguely insulted and still unconvinced. He remained certain that only a spirit could bestow such power, but he lacked the evidence that would condemn the boy and restore him to rank.

Then the Great Herrmann arrived in camp.

If ever a demon existed, it was this white man. His clothing, his demeanor, and the miracles he worked—could there be more proof that this was a spirit sent to do mischief? Surely, this was the black devil that gave One Tongue his extraordinary powers!

After the evening's performance, Half Horse once again conferred with Voice Like A Drum and explained his theory.

"I believe that the black one's power is derived from his hat," Half Horse said.

Voice Like A Drum sighed deeply.

"Hear me out, please! We all saw how like a devil he looked and that his hat never left his head except to work wonders. From this hat, he produced birds, cloths, a rabbit fit for eating, and a flour cake. Doesn't it stand to reason that the source of his power would sit close to the brain, ready to receive its commands?"

Voice Like A Drum took a pull on his pipe. "I agree with you that this white man looks odd, and that his hat is unique—but I do not believe that our chief would bring a demon into our midst. Standing Bear tells us that these are mere tricks achieved by patience, another gift of the Unknown—like the penis we talked about."

"I tire of hearing about the penis!" Half Horse said. "A big penis and the ability to make a boy float in air are not the same thing."

"Perhaps this is not something we were meant to know," Voice Like A Drum said. "Perhaps Half Horse should simply be content to be amazed like the rest of us."

All that day Half Horse thought about the hat. How it had brought forth animals, how cards had gone into it and emerged from behind ears. The only way to know if the hat was the source of One Tongue's power was to see if that power could transfer to him.

For this it would be necessary to have the hat.

When the camp was asleep, Half Horse put his knife between his teeth and crept inside One Tongue's lodge. The bright moon shone through the smoke opening and he could see the two men asleep on their palettes. At first, it was hard to determine which man was which: both were white with black mustaches and both slept on their sides, hiding half their faces.

Then in the shadows, Half Horse saw the hat.

It stood like a trophy upon a pile of neatly folded clothes. Without a sound, he made his way toward the center of the Lodge and transferred the knife to his hand. Two swift cuts to each neck and a second to grab the hat would be all that was needed. Yes, Standing Bear would be angry at first, but once the hat's powers were transported to him, he would have proof that the magician was a demon and the egg eater his familiar; and he would be installed once again as Speaker.

The first blow to his head knocked him sideways; the second caused the knife to drop from his hand. As Half Horse attempted to rise, a blunt object caught him in the chest. In the near-darkness, he could see the outline of a man, naked and crouched low to fight. Half Horse threw himself upon the figure, his hands reaching for his neck; but the shadow dissolved and caught him with a fist to the kidney, knocking the wind from his lungs. Coughing and spitting, Half Horse reached toward the spot where the knife had fallen, seized it, and aimed its blade at the pale blue eye of the devil who had cost him so much.

16

As Adelaide Scarcez made her way down Kensington High Street, small aches tortured every part of her body.

She had underestimated just how difficult this new dance would be. The *cancan* it was called—and it had only recently been imported from France. When she had first seen the dance mistress' demonstration, it looked easy enough—a lot of bouncing on one foot and ruffling of frilly skirts. But Adelaide soon learned that this *cancan* utilized an entirely different set of muscles than *Coppelia* or *Giselle*; and the yelping and screaming required of the performer left the throat sore and the head aching. The rehearsal had lasted three hours and Adelaide had been released just as most of proper London was beginning its afternoon tea.

At Wright's Lane, she stopped before a French café called Le Patisserie Moliere. The window was filled with cream cakes and tiny sandwiches of salmon mousse and cucumber. Farther back in the room, she could see tables of ladies laughing into their steaming cups and taking delicate bites of watercress and butter. How she would have loved to stop and enjoy the four o'clock ritual; but she was already late for her appointment, and the lone tuppence she carried in her beaded bag was hardly enough for some Earl Grey and milk.

Adelaide turned left onto Kensington Church Street and left again into Bedford Gardens. The small street was lined with linden trees and tall blocks of homes and flats, their façades a beautiful pastiche: here classical Greek, there Romanesque or Georgian, a gorgeous jumble of terra-cotta and brick that nevertheless formed a pleasing whole. She found number twelve and walked through its double doors. She gave her card to the concierge and, as he guided her through the corridor and up the stairs, she hoped he wouldn't hear the growling below her waist.

At the top of the steps, they were met by a maid; she was young and pretty and dressed in a uniform so spotless that Adelaide couldn't imagine that she had ever held so much as a clothing whisk.

"You'd be Miss Scarcez, then?

"Yes."

"Welcome, ma'am. My name is Glynis. The master will be with you in half a mo."

The maid walked Adelaide into a reception hall off the main sitting room and gestured toward a large upholstered chair.

"If you'd sit here for just a few seconds, he'll come greet you personally."

· The maid left the room. Adelaide sat down and surveyed the large apartment.

It was designed in the style currently *a la mode*, French Second Empire throughout. The large mantel was carved from white marble,

Corinthian columns adorning each side. Soaring above it was a black onyx mirror some ten feet tall and inlaid with gold. The chairs and settees were fashioned from dark ebony and upholstered in a deep scarlet. They sat on a room-sized Persian carpet custom-designed to match their bamboo and rose flower patterns. The windows were hung with red floor-to-ceiling curtains trimmed in black brocade and topped with ebony capitals.

"Ah, Miss Scarcez!"

Adelaide jumped from the chair, her purse dropping from her hands.

"Oh! Professor Herrmann! Forgive me, but you gave me quite a start."

The Great Herrmann smiled and took her hand. "It is I who should ask forgiveness. We magicians are a sneaky lot—and sometimes we appear when we should simply arrive. But please. Sit down."

Adelaide smiled weakly and picked up her purse from the floor. From deeper in the flat came the smell of something cooking. *It is after four*, she thought. *Perhaps he will offer me some tea and a biscuit? Or invite me to stay to dinner?*

She reached into the purse and removed a small envelope.

"I have my references, Professor . . ."

"Please, dear young lady. I would ask that you address me as Herr Docktor or Herr Docktor Herrmann. A silly affectation, but there it is."

"Oh. Oh, of course. As I said, here are my references . . ."

"Thank you, but that will be quite unnecessary."

Adelaide gave the magician a puzzled look. "But the note you sent round to the theatre this morning. I believe it said something about an offer of employment."

"Indeed it, did, Miss Scarcez—but had I not known all I needed to know about you already, I would not have sent the message."

"I don't understand."

"Well, for instance, I know that you were born to Belgian parents here in London and that their untimely demise has left you an orphan nearly bereft of means. I know also that you are a fine dancer, a favorite among the aficionados of the smaller ballet companies, and that you are especially renowned for your *Sylphide*. I sent my letter to the theatre at which you are currently rehearsing, which should make it obvious that I am aware of your current incarnation as an exemplar of that *avant garde* art form—the *cancan*, is it not? Up until now, I had only heard of your titian hair, your fair skin and green eyes—in short, your beauty. But upon meeting you, I see that my source, so correct about all else, was a victim of the usual English understatement."

Adelaide was chilled by the compliment. Her stomach turned over, its hunger replaced by unease. His grin put her in mind of the villains in *Le Corsaire*.

"Sir, you surprise me, and that is no easy task—a girl alone who has been through what I have does not shock readily. Even so, I must please ask who is this 'source' of yours who spies on me as if I were a Whitechapel cutpurse."

"Miss Scarcez, this too is unnecessary. I am by trade a conjurer, and I ask that you simply accept that I have obtained these details by magic. Please know that I mean you no harm and that by listening to my proposition you will benefit greatly. The position that I offer will pay full ten and six a week from the employer and an additional guinea from me. As you shall live in the home of your master, there will be full meals included and no more rent to pay on that hovel in the Edgeware Road. The job will likely end by next year and if you are prudent and frugal, you will return to the stage a woman of some means, able to pick and choose your roles and avoid the sordid entanglements that sometimes victimize a young woman of the theatre."

Adelaide's fear turned to anger at his arrogance. She rose from her seat.

"Sir, your 'magic' does not work on me. As you have seen fit to spy on me and degrade me in a most cruel manner, I bid you good day with the admonition that you are not a gentleman."

Adelaide turned and began to walk toward the door. Compars called after her without raising his voice.

"In that case, I shall need to report my failure to the Baronet Sir Godfrey de Morgan. He shall be most disappointed."

Adelaide froze in place. She could feel the chill move from her stomach to her shoulders and arms and turn to heat on her face. She whirled and faced Compars with burning eyes.

"Oh, come, come, Miss Scarcez! Such righteous anger bores me. Sir Godfrey needs relief from his gambling debts and I need a smart girl to do a job. I say we get on with the transaction and let everyone involved be better off."

Adelaide gripped her purse in both hands. She could hear the paper of the envelope crackle inside.

"I do not believe that Godfrey would have betrayed me to such a heartless man as you. Even if our association no longer exists, we were once in love."

"That's as may be, Miss Scarcez, but apparently the noble Godfrey prefers your betrayal—and his wife's money—to his own ruin. The upper classes are used to a certain amount of scandal as long as their correspondents are from their own ranks—but a *cancan* dancer? I am afraid his reputation would be unrecoverable. As for yourself, the Lord Mayor and his sheriff assure me that there are already several reasons to lock you away in Holloway Castle: adultery, debt, even prostitution if it comes to that. Of course, you will get daily meals there—and it is not inconceivable that your Godfrey might even visit you from time to time. But I believe the plan I propose will bring a far better resolution all around."

"Sir, I am at a loss; I have many times been accosted by men who merely sought the pleasure of my person. They have cajoled, they have flattered and even threatened. I have taken them as they came and even on occasion, submitted if I deemed it in my interest. But for a world-famous man to use a past love to blackmail a poor woman—can it be that such cruelty exists?"

Compars grinned. "I assure you, Miss Scarcez, it does."

Adelaide's shoulders sagged. She was accustomed to self-serving schemes and ulterior motives, but such honest and cheerful admission of wrongdoing was new to her and increased the horror of her defeat.

"Herr Docktor Herrmann, I am in your power for now. But that power does not prevent my saying that you are a foul and soulless bastard, due for a fine comeuppance—a blackguard whose resemblance to the devil is well earned. And all the magic in the world cannot change that."

Compars smiled in appreciation. "Dry eyes. Straight back. You are all I was told of and more. A girl of guile and courage—exactly what is needed for this mission."

The magician rose and opened the top drawer of an elaborate highboy. Inside was a stiff cardboard pouch emblazoned with his initials. He handed it to Adelaide.

"The information you will need is contained in this envelope— the nature of your assignment, the date of the interview with your 'employer,' and complete dossiers on both him and the woman he has brought with him from America. Study these well—and never forget that from this moment, you are working for me. I hope that our association will be mutually fruitful. Glynis will see you out."

Compars bowed, turned on his heel and left the sitting room.

The pouch was heavy in her hands. Steadying herself on the balustrade, Adelaide edged down the stairs. She bade the maid good evening at the door and then crossed the street into Bedford Gardens park. She found an iron bench and sat down, trembling slightly and wondering what kind of deeds would be necessary to save her from disgrace and prison.

Adelaide unsealed the envelope. The first thing she saw inside was a ten-pound note.

Five minutes later, she was inside Le Patisserie Moliere. Afternoon tea was over and she sat alone in the café. She feared that she had embarrassed the waiter with the sheer amount she had ordered: four finger sandwiches, a beef pasty, and both a *tart fine au pommes* and two napoleons.

As she drained her second cup of tea, Adelaide reached into the pouch and pulled out two documents. They were written on cream-yellow paper in the finest of calligraphic hands.

She looked at the name on the top of the first one—and realized that whatever deviltry the great magician had in store was reserved for someone close to him.

HERRMANN, it read. ALEXANDER.

17

BEFORE ALEXANDER'S ARRIVAL, STANDING BEAR HAD SPENT an hour before the tribe explaining that what they would see that night was not hell's medicine, but a mere exhibition, achieved through worldly means.

"Replace fear with amazement," he had told them, "and above all, do not attack the cousin of One Tongue as a sorcerer." To his relief, this preparation was successful. No one had fainted at the sight of a boy in midair; no brave had sought the magician's death for turning milk from white to red. Instead, the Ponca had laughed and applauded, and the feast that followed the performance had lasted long into the night.

Then a jealous fool had committed the ultimate crime against hospitality. The sun had not yet risen when Standing Bear faced Alexander in his lodge.

"It is a bad thing that has occurred here. One Tongue's kin came to us in peace, hoping only to delight us as he has delighted the world. Now I fear he will go forth and repeat to that world what the whites have always said of us—that we are savages, unfit to share the same land with civilized people. I only hope the Herrmann will see that among the many Ponca, there was only one whose heart was blackened by evil. His life is yours for the asking."

Julius translated for his cousin.

"I thank Standing Bear," Alexander said. "I am also grateful to One Tongue for the bravery that saved my life. It is only because he has become one of you, an Indian skilled in battle, that I am still alive. Apparently, a kick to the kidney works in all cultures. As far as thinking ill of your people, I was asleep through much of the attempt on my life—and so, my memories of the Ponca are not of this man who attacked me, but of the fine evening I spent among a welcoming people."

Standing Bear nodded and passed his pipe to the magician. Alexander took a long draw, then turned his gaze toward Half Horse, who sat in a far corner, filthy and bleeding.

"As to the life of this man, as is One Tongue, I am an egg eater. Like your own people, we are an old and proud race, often persecuted by larger tribes. Even so, our holy book, which our god gave us on a mountain, tells us not to kill—so I do not demand the life of this Half Horse. But there is something I would ask of the Ponca."

"We would be honored to grant any wish," Standing Bear said.

"The girl who aided me tonight—may I please ask her name?"

Standing Bear passed the pipe to Voice Like A Drum. "That one? She is called Little Feather. She is much trouble."

Alexander nodded and smiled. "And this Little Feather. She is married?"

Several of the tribe began to laugh. Standing Bear held his hand high for silence.

"No, she is not married, nor is she anyone's daughter. We can tell you no more, except that she is Ponca."

Alexander opened his palm and produced a Queen of Hearts. He idly tore it in four pieces and then crushed it between his palms. He opened his hands to reveal it fully restored and its colors reversed.

"If this Little Feather is amenable, I would ask that Standing Bear allow me to take her from the Ponca to become my helper. I promise that she will be well cared for and never want for meat nor drink. Everywhere she goes, she will be feted and celebrated as the partner of the Great Herrmann; and as a woman in a man's profession, I daresay, she will make history."

Julius was almost too astounded to translate his cousin's words.

"I am not refusing the Herrmann's request. This night, Little Feather performed in your presentation as she has never performed at anything else. But I think the Herrmann should know what he is getting. The women here report that she is shiftless, and that her primary work is avoiding work. She is often defiant and ill tempered, although this could be put this down to her being deprived of the calming effects of the marriage bed. It is even said that she murdered a man in Omaha city. A bad man, yes, but murder is still murder. We would not be good hosts if we did not inform you of these things."

Alexander picked up a stone from the ground and tossed it in the air three times. On the third toss, it disappeared.

"Standing Bear's concern is much appreciated; but these are small things when considering the assets she would bring to my presentation. Her English is good. Obviously, she is intelligent and learns quickly and she is small of stature and slight of build, *exactly* the right size for my apparatus. She also possesses a special quality that I believe will increase the attendance of my audience—especially the men."

Standing Bear turned to Voice Like A Drum and asked his opinion. The medicine man looked down at his hands.

"It does no one any good for the woman to stay here," he said. "No self-respecting brave will risk his seed with her and thus, she is sour and miserable. This infects the women around her and they become demanding. She has no skill at any of the tasks here, and for her to continue with her old one, we would have to return her to her enemies. I say let the black one have her and let *his* magic hide her from the white law. Perhaps then she will be content; but in any case, she's off our hands."

Standing Bear sat still for a moment and then gestured to a young boy standing by the door. In moments, he returned with a sleepy Lady-Jane.

"The black one here says that he approves of how you worked for him tonight. He says you have medicine that will aid him in his presentation. He likes that you are small. He asks that we allow you to leave the Ponca and assist him. You are not commanded to do this, but he asks it as compensation for Half Horse's attempt on his life—and we hope you will see it as a matter of Ponca honor."

Lady-Jane snapped awake.

Had this old Indian just said that she was free to leave this place? That instead of a life of toil and humiliation, she was to travel the world as the assistant to its greatest magician? Had he really told her that instead of pounding corn and curing hides, she would spend her days in hotel beds and her nights appearing and disappearing as thousands applauded? Could a life change this much this quickly?

Betraying no excitement, Lady-Jane looked demurely at the ground. She was silent for several moments, as if deliberating upon a decision that she would have gladly shouted from the housetops, had there been any. Finally, she looked up and into the eyes of the old man.

"For the honor of the Ponca, I will go."

Standing Bear received the pipe once again and nodded. "I only wish the verdict regarding the transgressor himself was this easy. The family of Half Horse is as old as the tribe itself, and to punish someone from such stock requires the help of his ancestors. As I meditated upon it, the faces of his dead father and grandfather came to me. Their souls were full of pain, yet they agreed with my decision. "

The chief gestured and Half Horse rose.

"Because the victim is white, we would not normally mete out death to the perpetrator and in any case, the black one does not wish his attacker dead. But the Herrmann is kin to One Tongue and an honored guest of the tribe. This makes the attack a very serious matter. Therefore, it is our ruling that Half Horse retain his life; but he must today gather his wives and children and leave here. And if, in the greater world, anyone should ask him the name of his tribe, he must not answer with our name. He is no longer Ponca."

For a moment, Half Horse seemed to buckle at the knees; then he straightened and bowed to the chief. He looked around the smoky room for a moment, his eyes a mixture of anger and examination, as if making a list of every man and woman who had ever wronged him. Then he strode through the flap of the lodge.

The moment he was out of sight, an agonized cry split the silence of the council.

Chased By Owls jumped up and walked to the very spot where the exile had been standing. He pointed at Julius to translate for him.

"I ask the egg eater to change my words for the black one. I do this not for his benefit, but because I wish the devil to hear in his own tongue that there are still those who defy his evil; and to tell him this—if Half Horse's fate is Standing Bear's justice, then our enemies need not fear. We are a little tribe ruled by soft old men, worthy only to be patronized like children and shuffled about like toys—even now, he negotiates with Crook to move us once again. For the sake of this white play-actor you would banish a warrior with fifty scalps on his lance? For the worthless life of this trickster you would humiliate a noble family? Never have I been so ashamed!"

Chased By Owls spit on the hard-packed ground. Behind him, his soldiers rose and glared at the chief and council.

"Long ago, the grandfather of Standing Bear found that he could not remain an Omaha and keep a good name. Back then he told the weaklings and traitors who ruled the nation that he would rather take his chances with the Unknown than be less than a man. I must do the same before the weaklings and traitors of *my* time. If Half Horse is exile, than Chased By Owls is exile."

The braves whooped and yelped at their leader's declaration. He turned toward them and raised his fists.

"From this day, let Bear and his council protect the women and children and chase the whites that murder us in cold blood—let them kill and be killed. We will do as the Dog Soldiers of the Cheyenne—seek a separate place where a warrior may be a man in his own land—where we need no longer bear the shame of being Ponca."

Julius's mouth was dry. He waited for a reply from Standing Bear, but the chief only continued to smoke, staring straight up at the tall brave.

Chased By Owls left the lodge followed by his men. Soon, the village was a maelstrom of noise and rush. Horses were packed, wives and children mounted for the journey. In the first light of morning, the tall brave gave the command to move.

Julius listened as the braves screamed in defiance, rearing their horses against the rising sun. He seemed to understand every sound, as if his powers of language could now translate even the most primitive screech or moan. In them, he heard the voices of countless others going back a hundred years. *We are glad to sacrifice*, they said, *for a place to be wild on this earth.*

And somewhere in the uproar, he thought he heard the voice of Standing Bear himself—younger and stronger, and happy to die.

18

I N EUROPE, JULIUS MEYER HAD BEEN SOMETHING OF A
musician. As a child, he was encouraged toward the violin and became
proficient by the age of seven. Not long before his mother died, his teacher
informed her that with the correct amount of rehearsal, young Julius
might take his place among Prussia's *artistes*. When he had first come to
Omaha, he would often join an informal group of musicians who sought
to make a cultured noise within the western wilderness. It wasn't anything
serious, just a small chamber group; but they played a passable Haydn
Kaiser and Julius received applause for his solos.

But the Ponca courting flute was different. Weeks of practice had
brought forth a series of notes played in the correct order but little
more.

How can something so simple, he asked himself, *be so hard to play?*

After all, it was only a cedar rod not more than sixteen inches long, hollowed out and punched with six holes. It featured the beak of a swan at one end and the head of an elk near the mouthpiece. Like all things the Ponca made, it was beautiful—intricately carved and decorated with leather strapping and eagle feathers.

Once he had attained some skill with its fingering, he had attempted to play some Bach. This brought much laughter from members of the tribe, who told him the notes were crowding each other like ten children after one apple. Embarrassed and frustrated, Julius sought the advice of married men whose playing had presumably melted the hearts of their mates. This only brought more laughter. *The song is already in the air,* the men would tell him. *When it finds the one meant to play it, the flute will pull it down.*

Forced to improvise, Julius spent hours in a stand of trees far from the village and away from the ears of Prairie Flower, who, he imagined, could summon only pity at the noises he managed.

Then, one day Voice Like A Drum stopped him as he was about to leave for a practice session.

"Your playing," Drum said. "It goes well?"

"My playing goes badly," Julius said. "I have mastered the fingering and the blowing technique. The sound comes out clear and strong. But I have heard others play the flute, and it has sent a shiver through me. When I play, there are no shivers, only an acid taste in my mouth and a sadness at the idea that I shall never be able to court in the proper manner."

Voice Like A Drum nodded and was silent for a moment.

"I mean no offense by this, but because you are white, you are worried about the quality of your performance. You concern yourself that your audience may not appreciate the music you make. This is not the purpose of this music. When you play the courting flute, you are not offering something, you are *asking* for something. So when he picks up the flute, One Tongue must say to himself, 'this is not music as made in the white concert halls. This music is a prayer offered up to god that I may have love and fulfill his plan.' Once you can do this, your music will be sweet and the one for whom you wait will begin to listen."

From that day, Julius began to play in ways he had never thought possible.

He allowed his heart to move his fingers. For his breath he used the sighs of longing. He put aside all of his training and let the flute speak for him, begging for all that he wanted, the music becoming yet another language to study and understand. Within a month, Julius asked Standing Bear for permission to play for his daughter.

"I understand the flute is fighting with you," the chief said.

"It was, but I think I have finally begun to wrestle a decent tune from it."

"Good," Standing Bear said. "I would not want Prairie Flower to have to endure more of what you put the village through before you decided to practice alone."

They met on the shady side of the Niobrara. As was customary, Prairie Flower's grandmother, Many Questions, followed them at a discreet distance. For weeks, she had stayed close to the girl, as if she were a lamb among wolves. On several occasions, Julius had attempted to engage the old woman in small talk—*isn't it a fine day—that is a lovely necklace you are wearing*—but had been met only with silence or nods and grunts. After a month of this, he considered it a victory if she looked up from the moccasins she was sewing.

"It is fine to see One Tongue out in daylight," Prairie Flower said. "People have been saying that he has cut himself off a little from the Ponca, spending many hours in some trees a good ride away, and that he only returns when the sun has gone behind the earth."

"This has been necessary," Julius said. "I have been practicing music."

"Oh? How interesting. I was not aware that a Speaker of such great reputation and ability had interest in anything other than meetings and treaties. I consider it a great compliment that the *Boxkareshahash-taka* visits with me as I do my washing. But if I am to complete this task, I am afraid I must ask him to follow me."

Her laughter was like warm rain. As he stumbled behind her, the grace of her movement caused a lightness in his head. Even encumbered by a big basket, she moved like water across the land, the white fringes of her dress the crests of tiny waves.

They reached the river's edge. As she set the basket down, Julius drank her in.

Her hair was dressed modestly, with only a few yellow beads and a sprig of white Liatris to offset its blackness. Her almond eyes were large and merry and would reduce by half when crowded out by her wide smile. Even engaged in a mundane chore, he saw in her the same confidence he had noted in the royals of Prussia on the days when their carriages plied the streets. She was a princess at work, but still a princess.

"I have a flute with me," he murmured.

Prairie Flower grinned mischievously. "What is that you say? I am sorry but I cannot hear you over the river."

"Oh. I said I have a flute with me."

"A flute? This is fine. I was not aware that One Tongue played the flute in addition to his other achievements."

"Yes," Julius said. "I have just learned."

Prairie Flower began to remove the clothes from her basket.

"I congratulate you. I wish that I could also play the flute, but it is forbidden for women. People say that only men may play it. They say there are reasons."

"Yes," Julius said. "There are reasons for playing the flute. I would like to play it now. But perhaps Prairie Flower is too busy working. Perhaps she would find music at this time distracting."

Prairie Flower looked at Julius, then at the flute. He knew that if she said she would rather not hear him play, she was rejecting his love, at least for today. She looked down modestly at her hands. Her pause was torture for him.

"For some people music is distracting," she said. "I have even heard that there are some people who do not like music at all. Imagine! We Ponca are the greatest singers and players in all the nations and yet there are those among us who do not respond to a sweet tune. I am not one of these. I believe in the flute and all the things people say it can do. Therefore, I would be honored if the Speaker would play the flute while I work."

Julius made to raise the flute, but succeeded only in dropping it in the grass. As he bent to retrieve it, he noticed Many Questions gesturing at him, her hands fluttering like birds, her eyes rolling up in exasperation. *Fool,* she seemed to be saying. *Get on with it.*

Julius put the flute to his lips. His mouth had become suddenly dry and his first notes were fitful squeaks. But soon, his heart engaged; and a song rang out over the rushing of the river. It was soft and mournful, filled with the yearning of every young man who had visited this spot to ask the *Wakanda* to relieve his loneliness.

Many Questions looked at the couple and smiled. Although his position in the tribe carried significant status, the little *Boxkareshahashtaka* was hardly her idea of a royal match. But as the old woman listened, she found herself softly humming to the flute's melody. It was new to her, yes, but weren't all courting songs composed of the same long, slow notes, the same quivering vibratos? Hadn't they already been written and were simply waiting to be captured?

The more notes the grandmother heard, the more she knew this was a fine song, a fated song. In it, she could hear the desire that her own husband, dead these long years, had once channeled into his flute, back when the Ponca still ruled the Niobrara and she was the age of this precious child.

As Julius played, Prairie Flower made as if to remove a shirt from her basket but stopped and placed it back inside. She turned from the river and toward him, sitting with her legs folded beneath her. As he played, he watched her breathe deeply of the soft air. She looked first at his fingers and then his face. Her shoulders began to move to the song's rhythm, but only as much as modesty allowed.

Then, suddenly chilled, she wrapped her arms around herself and closed her eyes.

19

I F THE PONCA WERE TO LEAVE BY SUNUP, THERE WAS MUCH TO DO.
The lodges had to be emptied and their contents deposited into Army wagons. The *tipis* needed to be folded and placed on sledges. The children had been assigned to water and then release the horses. No mount would make the trip to Oklahoma, the blue coats fearing that Indians mounted were Indians escaped.

Mid-morning, Julius made the mistake of stopping to play with Single Stick, a boy of about four years old. When he had stooped to pick up a sack of grain, the boy jumped on his back and insisted that he was now his horse and that he must take him into battle against the whites. Julius bucked and danced as Stick squealed with laughter. Soon children appeared from every corner of the village, insisting on their turn at riding the brave steed. When Julius complied, the little ones insisted on a second ride, even a third. When he finally pleaded fatigue and asked to be released, the children attacked him en masse, knocking him to the ground, hoping to be thrown in the air or tickled.

Then in an instant they scattered. When Julius looked up from the ground, he saw Standing Bear looming over him.

"There can be no doubt our chief has great power," Julius said. "I had to beg them to leave me to my work. All you did was appear."

"Play is fine for a child," Standing Bear said. "It is, after all, how they learn. But ours are not white children who sit and play with toys. Each of these knows their duty. At this moment they should be helping their mothers, fetching and carrying whatever we must bring with us."

"Standing Bear is right," Julius said. "Everyone here, even the littlest, knows his duty. And yet, you will not allow me to carry out the duty I owe to the Ponca."

Standing Bear put his fingers to his eyes and sighed, clearly tired of repeating the reasons for a decision he had made days ago.

"Only a white man would question his chief as you do. I have seen it in the towns—when a man filled with liquor will argue with a sheriff even when he knows he cannot win. I have seen it on the reservations—a soldier will tell his captain how ill-advised his order is. Seeing this, I have allowed you a certain latitude because questioning authority is in your blood. But I have said it and I will say it no more. You will not accompany the Ponca on the journey to the new home."

Julius's face darkened. He found himself wishing for the physical stature of Chased By Owls or the age and wisdom of Voice Like A Drum. He wondered if Standing Bear would cast him out if he were bigger or older, or if he had been born red.

"You have been more of a father to me than any man," Julius said. "From you I have learned what God wants from us. You have taught me about love and duty and how to avoid hatred. If I am fortunate, some day you may even give me your daughter. But now, you exclude me from what we both know will be our greatest hardship; as if my race deemed me insufficient in courage or stamina to endure what even those little ones surely will."

It was the argument One Tongue had been making for days. His patience exhausted, the chief's face twisted with an anger Julius had never seen.

"Enough! At this moment in my life, I can care little for the feelings of a boy I have spoiled. If you believe your assignment makes you less than one of us, that is unfortunate—but you are more of a white man than I ever suspected if you see only your own sacrifice among those of so many. I will tell you only once more. I do not need the *Boxkaresha-hashtaka* to walk and die! I need him to talk and reason—to go to the government and plead our case—to tell them no matter how far they force us to walk, we are of the Niobrara and it is to the Niobrara that we must return. But more than this, I need him to make the white money appear—to produce the paper and gold the Ponca will need if we are to survive even one winter. And if the Speaker will not do these things, then Standing Bear needs him for nothing."

"So while the Ponca walk through want and danger you think that my place is in my shop in Omaha, standing behind a counter, selling trinkets?"

Standing Bear's eyes blazed. He pounded his fist on the bed of an empty wagon.

"Perhaps we are still quaint to you. The 'noble savages' that your politicians and do-gooders love to speak of. But the Ponca live in the real world. And just like all in that world, it is white money that comes between us and death. You say I am your father. If this is true, then obey me, and believe that where I tell you to go is the best position from which to do battle."

Julius looked out over the village. It was half what it had been yesterday. In a few more hours it would be half that, and by the morning it would be gone.

"The books of the egg eaters say that once we were many tribes, holding dominion over the world we knew. We were like the Sioux—numerous and powerful, making war and conquering enemies.

"But one day, our God became angry and our people became lost. He condemned us to wander the world until we could stand face to face with a brother of our tribe and not know him."

Julius turned back toward the chief. His cheeks were wet.

"Sometimes I imagine the Ponca are the tribe that was lost to me all that time ago—my people returned from wandering. With the Ponca I have known God as never before. For this blessing, I can never thank Standing Bear—but I can obey him."

Standing Bear placed a hand on Julius' shoulder and smiled. He turned quickly on his heel and walked back into the frenzy of leaving.

Julius ran to the north side of the camp. Beside her lodge, he found Prairie Flower wrapping the hide of a *tipi* around its wooden poles.

"Your father will not budge," Julius said. "He insists that I can do more good for us in the white world."

Prairie Flower looked up at Julius. The sadness in his eyes was mixed with anger.

"My father speaks the truth, of course," she said. "If you were still only some white boy, clever with words, he would not care if you stayed or went. But he is telling you that you are truly one of us now—and that as one of us, you must sacrifice."

"So while Prairie Flower freezes in the snow and bakes in the sun, I am to sell crafts at the Wigwam? While soldiers herd you like sheep, I am to talk and talk with men of my race, always wondering which pocket the railroad keeps them in, or how much Ponca grass their cattle will soon be eating? You and I have never embraced, never even touched. Now who knows if we ever will?"

Prairie Flower turned away from Julius. She knelt again to work. "I have much to do. These *tipis* will not wrap themselves, nor will the white world wait while you argue with me over a fate you have already accepted."

In her words, Julius heard a thousand years of Indian survival and ten thousand years of the wisdom of women. Yes, it enraged him to think that she could remain practical even as his soul broke in two before her eyes; but he also knew that his anger could never advance his cause in the face of her fierce serenity.

"I apologize for my selfishness," Julius said, "and I would ask Prairie Flower to stand once more so that she and I might take our leave."

Prairie Flower stood and faced him. "People say that if the betrothed are to embrace, it should be within the privacy of the courting blanket. Anything else would be unseemly—and followed by much talk and scandal."

"Yes," Julius said, "people say this."

"But look around you, beloved. Perhaps the people are too involved with their preparations to pay attention to a single man and woman. It is also possible that in the coming journey many hardships will make people forget a single breach of tradition."

"Perhaps."

She paused for a moment and then, as gently as a breeze, put her arms around Julius and pressed her cheek to his breast. He laid his chin on the top of her head and held her tightly.

They heard nothing of the panic surrounding them, nothing of the noise and rush. The sound and rhythm of their courting returned to them and they rocked back and forth in tears. Prairie Flower took his hands in hers and, bringing them to her cheek, quietly sang the remembered melody his flute had seized from the air.

⊰◇⊱

That night, Julius had a dream.

Haunted figures trudged forward in misery by the thousands; Jews dressed in the manner of the old world. Above them, soldiers on horseback shouted orders in all of the languages of Europe, but for some reason the Jews could not understand them.

The overseers lashed out with bullwhips and the handles of axes, barking their instructions in Hebrew and Yiddish to no effect. When the Jews talked amongst themselves, it was in the language of the Ponca. They asked for water and begged for meat and mercy; they invoked high officials and produced letters attesting to their status. But the grunted gibberish served only to enrage the soldiers. They began to dismount and pull infants from the arms of mothers. The officers laughed as children were thrown to the ground to be trampled under the hooves of horses or carried off by starving dogs.

Then, through a haze of dust and blood, Julius saw Prairie Flower.

She walked at the head of the sad procession, dressed in the rags of a white woman, a tarnished *Magen David* around her neck. Her long raven hair had been shaved near to baldness. Pale and hungry, she stared straight ahead as if numb, ignoring the horror and chaos.

In Ponca, English, Yiddish, and Hebrew he called to her; in French, German, Russian, and Polish he shouted her name. But the girl could understand nothing he said—even when he screamed in languages no ear had heard before.

20

THE HOUSE OF ROTHAKER DRILLED THE WORD INTO EVERY salesman: into every designer and draughtsman, every patternmaker and office boy.

Confidentiality. Confidentiality is the watchword of our business!

"No producer wants his competitor to know what his actors will be wearing opening night," Harold B. Rothaker would tell his employees. "I want every sketch of every suit and every gown locked up in the flat files at night. If we need to bring a dress pattern or a cloth swatch to a client, I want you to think of them like state secrets. And if you like to talk, don't work here."

Given this penchant for secrecy, it was no surprise that Mr. Rothaker was delighted by the pigeon.

At first, the entire transaction had seemed exactly like others that took place on his doorstep dozens of times a day. A messenger rang the bell, his pageboy answered, he notified his master, and the master read the note. This one said:

My Dear Mr. Rothaker,

Can you come to my home tomorrow, 2pm?

I have a major project which I believe only your skill can complete to my satisfaction.

I have made inquiries about your business. Your clients extol you as the very soul of discretion. But in this case, I beg that you seal your lips as if they held the battle plans for Antietam.

Your immediate reply is requested. My address is at the bottom of this letter. The boy will do the rest.

Sincerely,
Anonymous

Rothaker looked up from the note to the small bamboo cage the messenger held in his hand. Inside, burping and cooing, was an ordinary pigeon—rust and white and iridescent green at the neck. The typical winged garbage scow of New York.

"It's our latest service, sir," the messenger said. "Those needin' speed and info on the quiet say it beats all else. I tie a note to her leg with just your answer—*yes* or *no*. Even if somebody shot her out of the air, they'd never get much out of that. Then, I let her go and she flies hell-bent for our coop in Brooklyn. Once she lands, another boy takes your message to the sendin' party. He'll have his answer in two hours. Less, maybe."

Rothaker grinned at such ingenuity. He wrote "yes" on the note and watched as the messenger slipped it into a tiny iron cylinder. He tied it to the bird's leg and bussed her on the head.

"Fly good, Mollie," he said.

He tossed the bird into the air. Rothaker watched as she flew straight up and then took a hard right turn in midair.

"This is what we're doing," the boy said, "until everyone gets the telegraph at home."

Early the next day, Rothaker took a brougham to his *atelier* on Canal Street to collect the twin sisters Hannah and Ruby Eisenstein. They drove to the Fulton dock and boarded the Old Ferry to its corresponding landing in Brooklyn. From there, they took a hansom to a great brownstone on the Heights. Rothaker pulled the bell. Presently, a liveried butler answered the door.

"If youse'll please make yaselves cumftible in the parla," the butler said, "the praffessa'll be witch youse shawtly."

As soon as the servant had gone, Rothaker bade his assistants be seated and began to inspect the premises. He had always found this the best method of determining the worth of the client he was dealing with. There was nothing like furniture and carpets to calculate ability to pay.

The parlor did not disappoint. Its furnishings were clearly of the highest quality, their woods rare and hand-carved, their upholstery covered in silks and damask. The oriental rugs had been woven in Pakistan and China, and the paintings on the walls would have graced the Metropolitan. But what best indicated the wealth of the house was the portrait of a spade-bearded man above the mantle. Its wild brushstrokes and moody *chiaroscuro* clearly marked it as the work of Eakins of Philadelphia, currently society's most fashionable painter.

"The picture is of my brother, although there are some who believe it looks less like him than me."

Rothaker turned from the portrait in time to see its double entering the room. He was dressed in fencing clothes and still perspiring from his latest lesson.

"I hope the ferry was on time for you," he said. "They say that when the bridge is finished, we shall no longer be at the mercy of the river."

"Yes, sir," Rothaker said. "We passed right by it on our way across. I must say it is a most impressive structure."

The bearded man frowned. "We Brooklynites have put up with its congestion and noise going on seven years. If it ever is finished, I wonder if the promised convenience will be worth the headaches it's already cost us. But this small talk has led us to forget our manners! Might I become acquainted with these lovely ladies?"

"Forgive me, sir. Permit me to introduce my two assistants: Miss Hannah Eisenstein and her mirror image, Miss Ruby. They are respectively my finest draper and patternmaker. May I assure you that in their expertise they are as alike as they are in face and form."

"I am of course, charmed," the bearded man said, bowing. "I am also relieved they understand that to maintain complete anonymity in this transaction, I must refrain from introducing myself."

Rothaker sighed. "I am afraid, sir, that such a famed personage requires no introduction. I recognize you. And judging from their reactions, I fear this is true for the Misses Eisenstein, as well."

The young women smiled and nodded, obviously excited by the identity of their client.

"How could anyone fail to recognize the conjurer who has amazed half the world? But I also have a more intimate reason for knowing your identity. Tell me, the black Prince Albert coat with the beaver collar, is it still used in your act?"

"Every night," Alexander said. "I would be lost without it."

"My late father fashioned that garment for your brother Compars nearly twenty-five years ago. I assisted him as he personally sewed in every hidden pocket and secret compartment. So you see, sir, your family's association with the House of Rothaker precedes even your entry into our industry. I sincerely hope that this will inspire further confidence in us."

"I suppose I expected nothing less, Mr. Rothaker. Anonymity, I am afraid, goes out the window when notoriety walks through the door. But today, it is not my own privacy that concerns me. It is that of the person you have actually come here to dress. Please, this way."

Rothaker and the twins picked up their cases and followed Alexander through a long hallway that opened out into a large ballroom. Near the tall north windows sat a young woman clad only in cotton underclothes. She was small, little over five feet, but so perfectly formed that her size was not a factor in her beauty. As the women walked closer, they noted the girl's extraordinary skin. It was the color of copper and roses and, except for a certain roughness of the hands, so fine and smooth it appeared to have no pores. Her splendid head seemed sculpted from a single block, the cheekbones in perfect proportion to the almond eyes that in turn were in flawless harmony with the broad forehead and delicate nose. A small gasp betrayed Hannah's astonishment. She had spent most of her young life draping the most beautiful actresses of the stage, and she prided herself on knowing the female figure better than even the most promiscuous lothario or the oldest doctor. How could it be that the most proportionate body she had yet seen belonged to a red Indian?

"Again, I apologize for the lack of introduction," Alex said, "but it is imperative that my plans for this young lady never leave this house. When the public finally does meet her, they must think that she is the most exotic creature God has made, and that the exquisite costumes you will create for her are little more than the traditional clothing of her native land."

Rothaker appeared confused. "Of course, Professor Herrmann, we are only too happy to provide anything you wish. But please understand that we cannot prepare these items quickly, as such costumes require the finest buffalo leathers and eagle feathers, which must be imported from the West . . ."

"I am afraid you misunderstand," Alex said. "You speak as if I wanted you to dress her as some savage. Oh, no, Mr. Rothaker! I said I wanted her in the traditional dress of her native land—and her native land is Arabia."

"Arabia? Pardon me, sir—I've hardly been out of Manhattan in my poor life, but from the pictures I've seen in the illustrated magazines, this lovely lady . . ."

". . . is *Arabian*, Rothaker! A caliph's daughter, no less! A princess of the blood born, she was rescued from a harem by yours truly on one of the many journeys I've made to the mysterious East! That is what I will tell the world, Mr. Rothaker; and *that* is what you and the charming twins here must *show* that world! Isn't that correct, your highness?"

The young woman smiled, first at Alexander, then at Rothaker and the sisters.

"In-doob-a-dib-ly, Professor."

"There. You see? It's all settled. From this moment on, the House of Rothaker will have the great honor of dressing she who has escaped the clutches of the Sultan of Oman and learned the secrets of vanishing from the Grand Vizier of Bur Safajah! So, I suggest we get to work. If anyone can pull this one off, Harold old boy, I'm guessing it's you."

⊰◇⊱

Lady-Jane lay in the half-light, enveloped in pleasure.

She had heard about this "glow" from other women. It had been mentioned by the prostitutes at the Nickel & Dime from time to time; she had even been able to catch a few words about it from the women in the Ponca camp. It was something that apparently occurred during the sex act: a kind of rush in the blood followed by a warmth, or a feeling of well-being or security or some goddamn thing.

Lady-Jane didn't buy it. She had likely fucked ten times as many men as either the whores of the Dime or the wives of the Ponca; and she had never experienced any such feeling. Ever since Adrian Calhern had turned her out and taught her the moans and shrieks and the best things to tell the customer, she had carried out his orders to the letter. *Get them done quick*, he would say. *Once they get a look at you, they're halfway to finished, anyways. There's more behind them and time is money.* Not counting those who "finished" before their pants were off, two minutes constituted the average session—five was a veritable eternity.

With Alexander, it was different.

For her, the Great Herrmann was indeed magic. He did things with her no one ever had, exploring her like a strange valley or devouring her like a sumptuous meal. He would spend an hour pleasing her before even beginning the final consummation; and then he would stay within her for as long as she pleased, only breaking his spell when she begged him to stop or sought his satisfaction. Completed, he would hold her in his arms, her silent head against his breast, and speak of her charm and beauty. And through it all, he would kiss her, a skill he had needed to teach her in detail. Though Lady-Jane had been instructed in all of the basics of the courtesan's art, rarely had she put her lips to any man's and never as a professional. Such intimacy cost extra and few patrons seemed disposed to pay for the privilege.

Perhaps, she thought, this was love. It *did* seem very like the stories in the ladies' novels and the lyrics of songs she had heard. They all used words like *warm* and *tingle* and *shiver*. But as she watched Alexander sleep, she put such questions aside, concentrating instead on the funny bend in his black beard and the rising and falling of his chest.

Then she wept. And when she finally fell asleep, she dreamt of a land where she felt this way all the time, every day, according to her command as ruler of the kingdom called Arabia: the land of Princess Noor-Al-Haya, whose name means light of life.

21

SHIVERING OVER THE HUSK OF HER MEDICINE MAN, PRAIRIE
Flower wondered if the Ponca weren't suffering retribution for
all the times her father had cursed his ancestors.

Trudging toward Oklahoma, all of nature seemed allayed against
the tribe. The weather had been cruel; the white government, charged
with supplying the journey, had produced little in the way of food or
medicines. The promised salt beef and bison jerky had disappeared
in a few days; the guaranteed flour had never arrived, and so they ate
milled corn fouled by rats.

Colonel Nelson A. Miles had been assigned to guide the tribe from
the Niobrara to the Quapaw reservation. Seeing the meager state of
the supply wagons, he became livid, firing off telegram after telegram

to reservation agents and the Bureau of Indian Affairs. When he did finally receive a response, it was not from one of the officers to whom he appealed, but from a bureaucrat of whom he had never heard.

OUR QUARTERMASTERS FIND SUPPLIES FOR PONCA RESET-
TLEMENT SUFFICIENT BUT WILL ATTEMPT TO AUGMENT
IF POSSIBLE. YOU ARE ORDERED TO QUESTION YOUR MEN
AS TO LIKELY THEFT OF SUPPLIES ALREADY RENDERED.
YOUR REQUEST TO DELAY DEPARTURE UNTIL ARRIVAL OF
ADDITIONAL FOODSTUFFS ETC IS DENIED. FRATERNIZA-
TION ORDER ALSO PRECLUDES ANY DISTRIBUTION OF
TROOP FOODSTUFFS TO ENEMY COMBATANTS ON PAIN
OF COURT MARTIAL.

COL. F. X. HIGGINS

The first order was harsh enough. It had caused him to question good men as if they were criminals; but the second was far more cruel. As the trip became harder, he had been forced to turn away women and children begging for a bit of his meat or rice. For the first time, he blessed the flasks of whiskey his men kept hidden in their gun cases or secreted in their pockets. Without it, he knew many of his troops would not have had the courage to ignore the sick and starving before their eyes.

But now, even if the soldiers had been allowed such charity, they would not have been able to give it; Miles had ordered his men to ride at least a quarter of a mile away and upwind from the Ponca.

"It's the smallpox," he told the troops, "and it does not discriminate. It will kill a white man as soon as an Indian and if we get what we deserve, sooner. All personnel are ordered to wear their bandanas over their noses and mouths—no exceptions. Because believe me, gentlemen, when you see the death the pox brings with it, you will take the revolver before you become its victim."

Prairie Flower was now a witness to that death.

Over a week's time, she had watched as Voice Like A Drum sickened. It had begun with a simple cough, a guttural rattle deep in the chest. But soon the cough brought up black blood, and the old man began to hemorrhage from his eyes and nose. In the past few days, more and more blood had begun to pool beneath his skin until it turned his face and arms blue-black. She could almost feel the heat rise from him as he burned with fever. As she laid a cool rag across his cheek, she heard his murmured prayers and incantations. He spoke to the spirits of land and air, of earth and fire, even to the *Wakanda* itself.

She wanted to run, to hide. But, Standing Bear had made his wishes clear: no member of his family would falter—and he gave no permission to be exhausted or terrified. With the medicine man dying, the chief's son, Bear Shield, was placed in charge of the tribe's spiritual needs. He saw to it that the dead were buried with due ceremony; he said the warrior prayers and redistributed the rations. Prairie Flower was assigned to nursing duty and what Colonel Miles would have called the "maintenance of morale." "You have a good smile," Standing Bear had told her. "Your teeth are white and even and all where they should be. This will be a comfort to the dying."

And so, she went about her duties with a constant grin. There were times this made her feel like an idiot; but then she would detect someone trying to smile back at her through a face filled with pustules and a throat constricted by bile.

But now, she wondered how long she could continue.

Earlier that day, she had gone to the river to wash blood from rags and bury diseased clothing. She had seen her reflection in the water and remembered the days when her brother would tease her for the roundness of her cheeks and breasts and the womanly strip of fat about her middle. These had disappeared, replaced by the kind of sharp-cut planes she had always envied in women like Little Feather gifted with "Indian bones." The thin girl in the water seemed a stranger.

"My friend looks very bad."

Prairie Flower turned from Voice Like A Drum to see Standing Bear framed in the tipi's entry.

"He is close to death, Father. I have smiled at him all day, but it has not helped him. He bleeds from everywhere."

Standing Bear leaned toward Voice Like A Drum. The shaman's eyes were open. The whites were dark red.

"How much longer will he suffer like this?"

"This is hard to say, Father. He may remain like this another day or two days. This has been how it was with the others."

The chief nodded, resting his fingers on the handle of his knife.

"Daughter, I wish you to take a short refreshment period. It is nearly midday and you have attended my friend through the night. Go to our *tipi* and sleep, and return when the sun has gone down."

"But Father, Voice Like A Drum . . ."

"I wish that you rest. Does this little walk through the wilderness change that a daughter should obey her father?"

Prairie Flower rose from the muddy ground. She gently placed her hand on Standing Bear's shoulder and made for their tipi. Inside, she lay down on a pallet made filthy with travel. *I will rest for a moment,* she thought, *only a moment.*

When she awoke, the sun was low over the ridges. She jumped up, wrapped a shawl around herself, and ran through the village. When she reached the tent of Voice Like A Drum, she found her father still there and the medicine man motionless, peace across his face.

"He is dead, daughter. It happened in an instant. Such is the mercy for which we all might hope and in which we all must believe."

Prairie Flower looked down at the old man. She had gotten used to his blood: seeing it new and fresh, caked and old. But she had never before seen the stain which now spread across his breast, forming a neat circle beneath his tunic. Silently, she turned to her father, her face a mixture of sympathy and accusation.

"We shall speak no more of this," Standing Bear said. "I will call your brother to dress his body and I will speak over him. You will gather all well enough to honor him—and then we will return him to the earth."

She nodded and left the *tipi*. She spoke to Bear Shield and informed all of the shaman's family members. His wife and youngest son began to keen and wail at the news; his two daughters, one of whom had been born only the day before Prairie Flower, were too weak even to cry.

Night had fallen. In the distance, she could see the yellow fires of the soldiers, their white faces reflected in the light. The camp had fallen silent except for the wails of the dying. As she walked away from the tent in which Voice Like A Drum lay, she came upon young Wind Whistler and his new wife, Shadow Moon. As they greeted her, she remembered her father's order to present a cheerful face. She raised her hand to the couple, grinning widely. The smile froze on her face and she fell to the ground.

22

PRINCESS NOOR-AL-HAYA STOOD IN THE WINGS OF THE
Astor Place Opera House. She bit her knuckle as she watched
Mr. John McTammany stride confidently across the stage.

If only she were so sure of herself.

But then, she was only a woman; what McTammany was about to
present to the audience was a miracle.

"Ladies and gentlemen, I thank you," said McTammany in his Scots
burr. "I am fair grateful to you for coming to see my invention. I believe
that part of your interest is that, alone among all such inventions, my
instrument derives its beautiful tones from a mere roll of paper, such
as you might find at your butcher's."

GERALD KOLPAN

McTammany unrolled a continuous sheet of plain white bond and threw the end of it into the audience. The ladies in the front row tittered as it landed in their laps.

"But unlike the paper of that noble man, observe! My roll is shot through with these tiny oblong holes. Each roll represents a single song painstakingly encoded within these perforations."

McTammany reached toward a black lacquered box that sat atop a grand piano. He slid open a double door in the box to reveal one of the rolls already inside. Producing a large brass crank with an oak handle, he inserted it into the piano's side and gave it several quick revolutions. Then he let the crank loose.

The mechanism whirred for a moment and the first notes of Beethoven's Piano Sonata Number 14—the *Moonlight*—began to fill the auditorium. The audience burst into cheers and applause, amazed by the piano's seeming ability to play itself.

Princess Noor frowned. She and her partner were on next, and she wondered how much enthusiasm the crowd would have left. Being careful to not disturb her meticulously dressed hair, she pulled the collar of her robe close around her neck. Shivering, she walked to Alexander's dressing room and leaned against the door.

"That Scotchman and his piano are really tickling the audience."

Alexander said nothing. He had dipped his fingers into a small tin of black wax and was busily applying it to his mustache.

"I'm scared enough," she said. "The last thing I need is for some Scotchman with a shiny gadget to make us look like pikers."

Alexander twisted the wax through the tip of his beard and buried his fingers in a jar of cold cream. He wiped the cream and the blackness from his hands with a small towel.

"I understand your anxiety, my love," he said. "This is, after all, your *debut*. But please remember that you are now the protégé of the Great Herrmann. In all the years I've been performing, there has never been an act I was afraid to follow and there's never been one with the courage to follow me. And now, with the addition of your royal self, I daresay we'll be lucky to find anyone in the show business who'll have the courage to appear with us at all, let alone precede us onstage."

"That's easy for you to say, Alex. You've done this a thousand times. But now you're adding something new, and I'm it. Lady-Jane may be a tough bitch, but I don't mind telling you Princess Noor is fit to swoon. What if my appearance is unwelcome? What if my costumes are too much for these rubes?"

Alexander rose from his chair and put his arms around her. Then he untied her robe and let it fall to the floor.

She was a vision from the Old Testament or perhaps the Arabian Nights. Her dark shoulders and arms were bare to the elbow, her forearms encased in blue transparent silk, onyx bracelets at her wrists. Circling her throat was a silver and gold choker and a dozen delicate necklaces in a hundred colors. A bodice of blue and gold brocade decorated each breast with the wing of a dove; from this, jeweled fringes reached nearly to her waist, barely touching a wide blue belt jingling with rows of Turkish coins. The ensemble concluded with pantaloons of the sheerest silk, gathered at the ankle and set in gold cuffs. Her feet were bare.

"You are too much for *me*," Alexander said. "The sight of you inflames me to the point that all *I* worry about is the patrons noticing my . . . *excitement*. I fully expect you will have a similar effect upon the gentlemen in the house. Yes, your artistry will raise eyebrows, especially amongst the more proper old dragons. Good. May they enjoy their apoplexy while you educate them about the culture of your homeland."

"My homeland? That's a laugh. Most of my homeland is right now being shit on by some settler's goat."

Alexander held up his hand. "No, your homeland is the place of sands and pyramids, of Isis and Osiris. Let's not forget the name of the game, shall we?"

A man with a dirty collar and a derby hat knocked on the door.

"Two minutes, Professor."

Alexander let the princess go. "Of one thing I am certain. You shall cause a sensation of one kind or another but a sensation nonetheless. Don't forget your cue music. You dance into the light when the cymbal crashes. Not before." He kissed her and then hurried from the dressing room and through the backstage corridors.

As he took the stage, Princess Noor could hear the near-deafening applause. For what seemed an eternity, Alexander presented his usual litany of tricks: the Artist's Dream; the Cocoon Dance; the Coin from a Biscuit.

These old standbys completed, Alex walked to the edge of the footlights.

"Thank you so very much for your generosity, ladies and gentlemen. Every year I perform throughout the civilized world. But I believe in all sincerity that the New York audience is truly second to none!"

Like trained seals, the crowd clapped and stamped their feet.

"And because you are such a fine audience, I would now like to introduce a personage special and unique: a figure from the mysterious east, born in the very shadow of the Great Pyramid of Cheops. Although she may appear as a quite ordinary—albeit exceedingly beautiful—girl, she has in fact, seen and heard things that no woman in history can claim. Once the daughter of a king, she was a poor slave when your humble servant found and rescued her. Now, I bring her to you in all her exotic beauty—this ruler of the Nile, this Empress of Invisibility! Ladies and gentlemen, look at Noor! The Princess-Al-Haya!"

A flash of fire and smoke filled the proscenium. Cymbals crashed like waves on a shore. At first, the shape at the corner of the stage looked like a small tornado of blackened dust: but with its emergence into the light it became a dervish of lighted spots and silken veils. As it grew nearer to center stage, the audience could now see the perfect figure of a woman within a whirling cloth. In another explosion of sparks and flame, she crossed her hands above her head, her fingers striking brass castanets, and bowed nearly to the floor.

Then she began to dance.

She moved like a cobra being charmed; her shoulders shook, her belly rolled, and her feet arched nearly double. She slithered across the floor and somersaulted from apron to footlight. As her music proceeded, the orchestra increased its percussion, her hips swaying on every beat. From the center of her body, a tiny point of light glinted with scarlet fire. Finally, she sprang up—and with a playful pull, unknotted the tie of the great magician.

"Jezebel!"

Up until that moment, Mrs. Lucy Ware Hayes had been too dumbfounded to breathe, let alone speak. But as the fingers of Princess Noor-Al-Haya deftly loosened the black cravat, she found her voice.

"Harlot!"

Now, other women in the audience began to rise from their seats and join her in a chorus of incensed morality, emboldened by the outrage of the First Lady of the United States.

❦

GERALD KOLPAN

From the *New York World*
Late City Edition
March 12, 1879

MAGIC SHOW SCANDALIZES AUDIENCE, FIRST LADY!

"GREAT HERRMANN" BRINGS FEMALE ASSISTANT TO
STAGE OF ASTOR PLACE OPERA HOUSE, SHOCKS MRS. HAYES
Women in Audience Leave in Droves—
Find Costumes "Obscene"
POLICE CALLED TO QUELL NEAR-RIOT!
Mrs. Hayes Calls Performance of "Princess Noor" Disgusting

The Astor Place Opera House, normally a bastion of societal propriety and decorum, was the scene of a near-riot last night as the Great Herrmann, arguably the most famous and innovative magician of this age, presented his new program to the public.

According to witnesses, the row begin about fifteen minutes into the presentation, when Professor Herrmann introduced what the police are calling the first female magic assistant ever seen in New York or, apparently, the country.

The attractive young woman, who goes by the name "Princess Noor-Al-Haya," appeared dressed in costumes that many members of the audience deemed far too provocative for public viewing. According to Chief Constable H. B. Qualen of the Sixth Police District, the lady arrived onstage doing the sort of spinning dance associated with the women of the mysterious East.

"What we were told was, the female came out whirling like a dervish," the Constable said. "She was attired not in a gown or even a dress, but trousers of the type a man would wear: sort of sheer pantaloons with a vest, and her shoulders were bare to the world."

208

But the element that seemed to contribute most to the fracas was a small area of exposed brown skin between these "pantaloons" and a fringed, jewel-encrusted bodice. Many in the audience began to jeer when they realized that the red object glistening on the princess's stomach was a ruby that had apparently been inserted into her navel.

"It was simply disgusting," said Mrs. Rutherford B. Hayes, wife of the president, there for the first night's performance. "Never could I have imagined such a flagrant display of public nudity. There were children in the audience! I cannot see why such a brilliant *artiste* as Professor Herrmann should deem such filth necessary to his continued success."

Only a few minutes into the princess's appearance, many of the ladies, including Mrs. Hayes, began leaving the theatre, which necessitated the accompanying exit of their husbands. Some shouted "shame" at the dusky performer, and one woman reportedly threw a fox fur coat onto the stage exhorting the girl to "cover yourself." A Mrs. P. Stanley Stratton of Tuxedo Park fainted and had to be revived by her coachman.

Not everyone, however, was so offended. Many of the denizens of the third gallery, mostly men, could be heard whooping and applauding when the princess appeared. Police took several drunkards to jail.

The *World* has learned that a discussion was then held between Professor Herrmann and Constable Qualen. Once order was restored, the show was allowed to continue. Those who remained mostly praised the performance of the swarthy beauty.

"It was amazing," said Mr. Daniel P. Sorrell of New Rochelle, a druggist. "She danced beautifully. She really seemed to disappear at times, and I thought her costumes were fetching."

According to the show's program, Princess Noor, as she was often referred to from the stage, is the daughter of the three hundredth

Grand Caliph of Egypt. Several years ago, whilst studying the principles of invisibility with the Grand Vizier of Bur Safajah, she was kidnapped by the Sultan of Oman, and held as a member of his harem, which includes over one thousand wives. Professor Herrmann, in Oman to study with one of that country's mystic seers, rescued her from this terrible fate by a feat of champion swordsmanship against great odds. The famed mountebank offered to return her to her father in Egypt, but the girl, with the Caliph's permission and accompanied by the royal chaperone, opted to remain with the Great Herrmann in gratitude for her dramatic liberation. Thus, she has become the first female assistant to a stage magician.

"There is absolutely nothing off-color about Her Highness or my act," Professor Herrmann said in a statement to the press. "The princess simply appears in the beautiful and colorful costumes of her native land. Does her raiment contain somewhat less material than those of her sisters here? Undoubtedly. And does the combination of her exotic clothing and exquisite face and figure have the potential to shall we say, quicken the pulse? For any man with blood in his veins, yes! But all planet Earth knows that Herrmann is a name long associated only with wholesome family entertainment. In this spirit, we present our program not only as the finest magic show in all the world, but as an educational experience exposing . . . if that is the word . . . the wonders of that world. Princess Noor-Al-Haya is, I believe, one of those wonders."

It is possible that if such bodily exposure continues, Professor Herrmann will have to pay a fine. Princess Noor herself made no statement as, according to theater manager O. E. Thomason, she speaks no English.

The great magician says he will follow his New York stop with a national tour and engagements in Europe at the earliest opportunity. Performances continue tonight and through Saturday next. As of last night, the entire run is sold out.

23

COLONEL NELSON A. MILES WAS DRUNK, A CONDITION WITH which he had no prior experience.

The men of Omaha could have given him lessons. Most of them could consume a high percentage of their weight in beer and spirits and go about their business with confidence. And while the town's saloons boasted of serving the best cuts or having the comeliest dance-hall girls or the most skilled prostitutes, in Omaha this made little difference. A man drank closest to where his thirst struck him—or nearest the spot where he woke in the morning.

This alcoholic culture notwithstanding, no one had ever seen Nelson Miles in the town's bars, not even for a friendly whiskey. Until this evening, his had always been a steady hand: dependable in battle and formal in bearing and conversation. When he arrived at the Big Cheese around six, Horgan, the bartender, noted that Miles looked pale. The colonel started on beer but switched to whiskey around two hours in. Twice, he attempted to straighten up and leave, but the room had not cooperated, spinning both times like a dust devil and reuniting him with his chair. Now it was nearing ten; Miles rested his arms on the table and buried his head within them as if mourning a lost love. When he heard a kindly voice speak to him, he was unsure if it was coming from inside his head or out.

"Hello, Nelson," the voice said. "If my life depended on predictin' someone's future, I'd choose yours. Tomorrow morning you'll have a head like a medicine ball."

The colonel looked up to see John McGarrigle dressed in "store" clothing. Miles raised his eyes from his arms. The dim light of the oil lamps stabbed them.

"Go away, old man."

"Sure, sure, I'll get away and glad to," Prophet John said. "Now that I'm a respected member of the business community, I need to be particular about who I'm seen with."

Several tables burst into laughter. Horgan pounded the bar and coughed. "Shit," said Vic Mitchell, the whoremaster of the Silk Purse, drawing the word out and separating it into two syllables. The voices cut through the colonel's brain like a steam drill.

"Drinkin's like any other activity you'd like to become good at," McGarrigle said. "It takes years of practice. Look, young Julius is here. Isn't that right, Julius? Shouldn't a man know what he's doin' before he does it?"

Julius Meyer ignored the prophet. He placed his hand gently on Miles's wrist; though he was drunk, his pulse was racing.

"Anyway, Colonel, we know why you're here," McGarrigle said. "By now, the whole town's heard tell of it. I reckon the best we can hope for is that it's not as bad as they say."

Miles looked up from his folded arms. There were tears in his eyes.

"Whatever you may have heard, John McGarrigle, I can assure you it is worse."

Julius took his hand from Miles's arm and sat facing him.

"Worse than what we've heard is hell," Julius said.

"Yes, hell, Mr. Meyer—and I was there. Not as a sinner but as a demon charged with torturing wretched souls. Only in this hell, Mr. Meyer, the demon's work is unjustified because the damned are not guilty but innocent—their only sin being red."

Miles reached for his half-full glass and drained it.

"Come now, sir," Julius said. "Whatever happened out there, you had your orders."

"Oh, yes, our orders were clear. The Poncas were to be relocated and there was to be no more delay about it. Indian Affairs said we had already dithered with them too much. The Sioux may be all but defeated, they said, but there are a million of them in their nations. That many people with guns and arrows can make a lot of trouble—the Dakotas and Brulé demanded that we remove this thorn from their sides.

"And so we went. But when we gathered to escort the tribe from the Niobrara, I tell you, I wondered how any nation, white or red, could be threatened by so few people. My God, with all of their chiefs and their slaves and half-breeds, they numbered less than eight hundred—that's fewer souls than at Kearney—probably fewer than the Chinese in Omaha.

"Like a fool, I assumed that this detail would be as others had been. When we've had to move Fox or Omaha, the government had always provided the necessaries: dried meat, salt pork, and the like. There was always clothing and blankets and wood for the fires. But from the first, it was obvious there were too few supply wagons. The food contained in the hogsheads amounted to less than a half-pound a day per person—and our blessed government in its wisdom saw fit to provide only a single blanket for every two Indians."

The glass slipped from Miles's hand and shattered on the floor. The colonel seemed not to hear it.

"We started out sixteen April. None of the Poncas had horses, for fear they would escape, and so they trekked on foot. When we crossed the Niobrara, it was still frozen. Before long, the snow was marked by bloody footprints. Further south, it began to rain—rained as if Noah would return and gather the beasts. We were lucky to make ten miles a day. My men at least, had their warm underclothes and oilcloth coats. But there was no such protection for the Indians. They were hip-deep in water and mud, the women trying to hold their infants above the muck. Corporal Hedges, an old campaigner with fifty Indian lives to his credit, burst into tears at the sight. Three children died on that one day alone.

"With a turn in the weather, thunderstorms and tornadoes came. I saw once-brave Ponca men holding their hands before their faces as if they could stave off the lightning. *Tipis* shredded like paper. Horses and men were thrown a quarter-mile. One of my lieutenants was separated from his rifle in mid-air; and when they both returned to earth, it triggered and shot him dead.

"By the time we reached the Quapaw reservation in Oklahoma, a third of the tribe was gone. They had died of the sick or their spirits had been killed, which for an Indian is the same as murder."

Miles looked about for a glass, and Prophet John offered his. The colonel poured another drink, trembling as he knocked it back.

"At Quapaw, the Poncas found there were no preparations made for their arrival. The land was only sand and rock. The food, the mill, the pledged threshers and reapers had either never been shipped or had been stolen by stronger tribes. What corn there was had burned to death in the fields. Half-naked people moved about mumbling to themselves. Bodies littered the ground awaiting burial—some gnawed by animals. On the day we rode in, the local Indian agent ran toward me. His eyes were wild, and he begged to know if we had brought some promised quinine. 'The malaria,' he shouted at me. 'The scrofula!' I had nothing for him."

Miles leaped up from the table. His legs crossed one another and he nearly fell to the floor.

"Steady, man," Julius said.

Miles leaned on an old oak chair. He removed his hat and gripped it in his hands as if to transfer his pain.

"In due course, we were relieved. As our detail rode away, my second lieutenant, a young man named Bateson, third in his class at West Point, made the mistake of turning his horse about for one final look at that hellhole. To that moment, he had been the model of decorum, never allowing his personal emotions to interfere with his duty. But at that final unspeakable sight, his eyes filled with tears. He hunched over the neck of his horse and vomited on the ground."

Miles reeled. Before he could fall, Julius and Prophet John took his arms and guided him back to his chair.

"Through it all, I marveled at the conduct of Standing Bear. He was like a stone carving: silent, straight, and strong, never complaining or demanding. What our generals could learn from him! When a child shivered in fright, he became its father. When an old woman perished in the dirt, he was her priest."

Miles placed his elbows on the table and put his hands over his eyes.

"His daughter, Prairie Flower, had been the same. As the hunger and diseases took her people, she saved those she could and comforted the rest. Newly orphaned children came to her—competing for the privilege of dying in her lap. If she cried, I never saw it. Perhaps she didn't have time. There was always another woman to console, another infant to pray over.

"Through even this, Standing Bear remained a rock. But on five June his daughter, that fine and brave young woman, died in his arms."

Julius's eyes opened wide. His mouth was suddenly dry as he gripped the rough edge of the table.

"As the people keened and wailed in despair, he came to me and asked in sign for a spade. I had to avert my eyes as he dug a hole in that awful place. He buried his daughter in the filth and mud, with only one of their little spirit purses to mark her grave. I could only hope he was consoled that she would rest in the land of her ancestors; we had traveled fifty days and were less than twenty miles from the village we had left."

Julius marveled that his body remained upright. It was as if he had been hollowed out—as if all the bone and muscle inside him had vanished and been replaced with a thin bile that poisoned his mouth and threatened to leak from his eyes and ears. Then, as clear as a spoken word, Julius heard the courting flute, crisp and piercing. Only now, all its sweetness was gone, replaced by the kind of squeaks and screeches made by a young man learning its secrets. Each bitter tone brought its own measure of grief, its own quantity of anger. Taking a single step, Julius found he was staggering nearly as badly as Miles himself. His legs seemed fashioned from yarrow stalks and he moved as if through water. No words came in any language he knew.

McGarrigle turned to Julius. He had seen that same stunned look many times: after scouting parties were attacked, after massacres of civilians. He had even possessed it himself on two occasions: when some renegade Oglala had killed the officers leading his party, and again when the Blue Coats took their revenge.

"What you need now, Colonel, is rest," the prophet said. "We'll take you to a doctor and then to my rooms. We'll write General

Crook. If need be, we'll pay him a visit. But for now, we need to get you horizontal."

Miles looked at the two men with a sad smile.

"If only this was the end of the horror," he said. "Two days ago, south of the Niobrara, Chased By Owls wiped out a Mormon settlement. The men and women dead, the children carried off. I fear that this vengeance is only the beginning, and that the heartlessness shown the Poncas will soon sacrifice more innocents of both races."

Miles reached into a pocket of his tunic and produced a crumpled scrap of paper.

"This arrived at my camp last night."

Miles handed it to Julius. At the top of the note was a small symbol of an animal seemingly cut in two, with only a head and forelegs: Half Horse. Near the bottom was another drawing: two birds with spread wings and enormous eyes: Chased By Owls.

In the center, between the two, scratched out and written several times until its spelling was correct, was a single word in English:

BURN

24

THE GREAT HERRMANN WAS MORE THAN SATISFIED.

There was no place in London—or the world, for that matter—that served a steak and kidney pie like Simpson's. When paired with their famous treacle sponge and some Earl Grey, it was a meal to turn a good American like himself into a Jack-waving Brit.

Touching his napkin to his lips, he rose from the table and picked up a large Gladstone bag. He paid his bill and strolled out onto the Strand. His belly strained against his waistband. *Many more meals like this,* he thought to himself, *and they'll tap me for Father Christmas.*

A few streets up, he turned into a narrow alley, puffing slightly. The occupant of the building for which he searched had written that he would know it by a rusted sign in the form of a horse's head, a leftover from its days as a stable.

He knocked on the door with his cane. A boy of about thirteen, grimy and starved-looking, answered and waved him inside. The floorboards moaned like abandoned souls. The wallpaper peeled from the plaster and, from behind it, he could hear the skittering of rats.

As he followed the boy into a dark passageway, a piercing cacophony assaulted his ears: mallets beating metal; saws churning through wood; a hammer on an anvil; men shouting and cursing. At the end of the hall, a creaking door opened and the gloom gave way to sunshine provided by a mammoth skylight cut into the stable ceiling. The Great Herrmann instantly felt at home, so much did the shop remind him of his own back in Brooklyn. Only here, everything—the equipment, the machines, and the men—was poorer.

At the center of the din stood a small and somewhat sad-eyed man; his clothing was the best amid a shabby lot, and even this was worn and threadbare. Along with a co-worker, he was leaning inside a green metal cabinet inset with a solid oak door and a lock of unique design. At first, the magician couldn't make out exactly what sort of apparatus might contain something deserving of so much attention; but at length, the two men exited the steel box and the object inside was revealed.

It was a toilet.

The emaciated boy leaned over and whispered in the man's ear. Without hesitation, he put down his wrench and signaled to the assembled workmen.

"Hi, there, hi! We'll be taking dinner a spot early today as I have business with this gentleman. As this could take some time, I ask that you do not return to your respective benches until the usual hour. And fear not. This additional leisure will not be deducted. Thank you."

The crew dispersed. The man hurriedly removed his gloves and goggles and placed them on the workbench beside him. He smiled nervously and offered his hand.

"I assume I have the pleasure of addressing the great Professor Compars Herrmann?"

"Just so," Compars said. "And I can only surmise that you are Mr. John Nevil Maskelyne."

The man blushed. "Yes, sir. And to be him today is a great privilege. To think that I, so early in my career, should be paid a visit from the finest conjurer of our age—sir, I am overwhelmed."

Compars smiled and bowed. "I too am pleased, Mr. Maskelyne. For many months, all of London's smaller playhouses have been abuzz with praise over your fine illusions. Acting upon these happy rumors and *incognito*, I personally visited the Marylebone in the Edgware Road this Wednesday evening past. Allow me to offer you my congratulations."

Maskelyne's eyes brightened. "Oh, sir! I said before that I am overwhelmed: now I must add to that, stunned! For the Great Herrmann himself to witness my poor little performance in that squalid shoebox . . ."

"From such shoeboxes are great careers begun," Compars said. "I myself spent many years in filthy egg crates all over Europe, perfecting my craft so that when it came time to perform before those not exhausted from work or besotted by drink, I was well prepared, as you will be very soon. But I am afraid my curiosity has gotten the better of me."

Compars pointed to the white porcelain commode.

"This object, while indispensable, is not exactly something I expected to find in a magician's *atelier*. At least not beside a workbench."

Maskelyne flushed with embarrassment, but soon broke into a broad grin. "I suppose in the interests of decency, I should have placed a drape over it. As you have been kind enough to note, I am, if one can call oneself such a thing in your presence, an illusionist. But I am also an inventor with several minor patents to my credit. If you will be so kind as to step closer, I will prove that what you see before you is far more than an ordinary convenience."

Maskelyne approached the contraption and closed the oaken door.

"Professor, if you will please approach the cabinet and attempt to reopen it."

Compars did as asked. The door would not budge.

"Very good," Maskelyne said. "Now, do you notice anything odd or different about the lock itself?"

Compars inspected in carefully. "It has no key entry. The handle is of a design that I have never seen, and the whole appears to be attached to a metal box on the door's reverse side."

"Excellent! Now if I may beg you to insert this royal penny into the slot and turn that little handle."

Compars dropped the coin in and turned the handle clockwise until it clicked, and the door swung open. For a moment, the magician stood perplexed.

Then he broke into laughter.

"I see what you are getting at here. Capital! Capital, Mr. Maskelyne. Yes, there's a fortune in this for every pub owner, restaurateur, and hotelier in Europe herself, surely, and the world, undoubtedly! The functions of the body held hostage for a penny! By God, it's brilliant. Please allow me to congratulate you again."

"Thank you. I can only hope that a bit of that good fortune finds its way to this poor inventor. Especially in the current circumstances."

Compars turned away from the cabinet and stepped closer to his host.

"Yes, the current circumstances. In fact, Mr. Maskelyne, it is those current circumstances that have brought me before you today."

The younger man smiled. "I'm afraid I don't understand."

"It's quite simple. For your apparatus here to succeed, you need the financial means to market it to the establishments for which it is designed: hotels, public houses, and the like. In turn, its success will allow you to bring your magic out of the smaller houses and into the finer theatres where it belongs."

Maskelyne's smile vanished. "This would seem to be common sense, sir. But with all due respect, I fail to see why my financial condition should interest you."

Compars shrugged. "Because, my dear Masklelyne, the sad truth is that you lack the capital to make all this work. In fact, my sources inform me that without a substantial infusion of money, you will likely be facing bankruptcy within a matter of weeks."

Maskelyne's eyes opened wide.

"You know, my boy, it is a fine thing to have money; it was money that motivated the source of my information to supply it to me. It was money that helped verify that information; and today, if you are as clever as you appear to be, it is money that will be the source of your salvation."

The younger man's face fell. "Professor Herrmann, I still do not understand how you can know this or why you believe it to be any of your business."

Compars smiled soothingly. "Relax, my friend. I understand you are embarrassed that I have uncovered your unhappy state. But please believe me when I say that it is no disgrace. At one time or another, all we poor players have been where you are. I have come here today with a proposition that will not only allow you to finance this marvelous invention, but will catapult you before the kinds of audiences you truly deserve and that deserve to see you."

"Really, Professor, this is too much."

"Come, come. Let us not play about-the-pea-patch. Just as I know about your ingenious toilet, I am also aware of the *other* invention you are working on here. And if I am not mistaken, it should be located behind that curtain."

Compars pointed to a shimmering purple cloth loosely stretched between two metal stanchions.

Maskelyne's hands began to quiver in rage.

"So is this what the Great Herrmann has been reduced to? Buying off younger, more creative men so that he may claim the fruits of their labor as his own? Taking advantage of their poverty so that he may increase his fame at the expense of the advancement of our art? Sir, I am sick at heart."

"You misunderstand me," Compars said calmly. "Yes, as you say, I am here to 'buy off' your invention; but only for a prescribed time and not to be premiered in my act or any other. In fact, if a bargain can be reached, I will ask you to keep it here in your shop, even perfect it further. So long as it does not see the light of day."

"And suppose, Professor, there is nothing behind that curtain but dust and cobwebs?"

"Let's see, shall we?"

Before Maskelyne could stop him, Compars pulled the silk from the object. As the dust settled, he saw what he expected to see: a large trunk standing on a black plinth surrounded by machinery and tools. He turned to the younger man and grinned.

"I understand that you have gotten the substitution time down to forty seconds."

"Thirty," Maskelyne said, sounding defeated.

"Most excellent," Compars said. "At any rate, let us not waste more time—I have resources, you need them. I will buy the world rights to your substitution trunk, as I believe it is called. You may perfect it until the exchange of magician and assistant is a matter of two seconds, if you are able. You merely agree not to show it to the public for a period of ten years or the unlikely death of my brother."

"Your brother?"

"Yes. The more famous little Alex becomes, the more increasingly ungrateful. He has already attempted to change the elements of the infallible act I gave to him out of filial love and generosity. He adds pigeons! He enlarges boxes! He shamelessly rewrites a stage patter that captivated the world for twenty-five years. There are even critics who have had the temerity to suggest that he, an imitator, may be the greater of us two."

Compars tripped a hidden handle on the back of the trunk; its back panel opened noiselessly in less time than it took to register his surprise.

"He has long told me that a substitution trunk is possible. I have told him it is *not* possible. The public appearance of your apparatus would prove me wrong—and I cannot have that."

"And if I refuse?"

"That is your right, but first hear my terms. I will pay you ten thousand pounds sterling. I have this in notes, but should you prefer it in gold, that can be arranged. I will also pay an additional one thousand pounds toward the development of your penny-commode. Then, tomorrow, I shall visit the offices of Mr. Henry Irving, actor-manager. A few words from me, and you will soon be engaged at the Lyceum, a far higher class of house than the Marylebone, I'm sure you will agree. My personal endorsement will decorate every posting, handbill, and newspaper broadside. 'Amazing,' they will shout, 'stupendous!' From there, how well you succeed is up to you. But even if all your rabbits escape and every dove dies, you will be a very rich man."

Compars reached for the Gladstone bag and unlocked it. It was filled to the top with Bank of England currency.

"Eleven thousand quid. Right here, right now."

Maskelyne put his hand to his forehead. "All this. You would do all this simply to prove your brother wrong? To prove him wrong even if he is right?"

Compars's face darkened. His voice grew louder.

"This is about far more than mere pride, my dear Maskelyne. It is about the continuation of a tradition. After all, there may be two men called the Great Herrmann, but I believe posterity can tolerate only one legacy."

Compars closed the bag. "Think it over, dear boy. I am stopping at Durant's Hotel. I will be leaving England the day after tomorrow. I do hope that by then, we can reach an accommodation."

He smiled and bowed from the waist. Picking up the bag, he once again accompanied the starved boy through the fetid corridor and into the street.

Compars whistled for a cab. As he felt the heaviness of the bag, he mused that only the pride of the young could outweigh eleven thousand pounds sterling. A hansom stopped at the top of the street.

Before he could walk toward it, he heard footsteps behind him.

The Great Herrmann turned around to see John Nevil Maskelyne halfway up the alley, his right hand waving in the air.

25

Thomas Henry Tibbles was seething as he entered the stockade at Fort Omaha. Over the course of a lifetime, he had almost become used to anger as a natural state, the lot of a man who had battled to bring justice to an unjust world and frequently lost.

That battle had begun in 1856 in "Bleeding Kansas." By the age of fifteen, Tibbles was a guerrilla in the brigade of Jim Lane of Indiana, an abolitionist second in his zeal only to John Brown himself. Tibbles had been proud to wear the scarlet gaiters over his boots and to be christened one of Lane's "redlegs," a name that pro-slavery "border ruffians" soon learned to dread. The redlegs were experts in ambush, defeating their enemies before they could draw a single weapon. They stood their opponents before firing squads or hanged them from trees.

By the time two years had passed, Tibbles had killed more men before the Civil War than many would during it. "As Christ is my witness," he would say, "no bastard is going to kidnap a black man to Kansas and live to see him work."

Now as he walked through the prison corridor, he thought of the work yet to do. The negro had been saved, yes; but if the Army and the politicians and the Sioux could conspire to imprison a great Indian for his suffering, no American of any color was safe in his home, on his farm, or even in his church.

The turnkey inserted a long skeleton into the lock. "Two gentlemen to see you, chief," he said, as if the occupant could understand a word.

The door swung wide to admit the visitors. Standing Bear rose and embraced Julius Meyer.

"Father," Julius said, "I hope the blue coats are treating you well."

"As well as one man may treat another he has deprived of sun and sky."

Julius nodded and dropped a large canvas sack to the floor. "I have brought you food and medicine, Father. You must be strong when you face the judge. In this bag are fresh fruits and buffalo jerky. There is good bread baked by Mrs. Jo Ann McGreevy and provided by my uncle, Mr. Eli Gershonson, with his compliments."

Standing Bear looked into the bag but touched none of the items inside. "Please return those compliments to the fine lady and your good and generous uncle. Tell them Standing Bear will repay the debt."

Julius smiled and gestured toward his companion. "Allow me to introduce Mr. Thomas Henry Tibbles. He is the man who has been making the good newspaper writing that I have read to you in the past few days."

Tibbles bowed as if before the king of France. Standing Bear took the white man's hands in his own as Julius translated.

"You have the thanks of Standing Bear and all the Ponca," the chief said. "There is iron in the words you write."

Tibbles looked into the weathered face; could this really be the great chief of the Ponca? He looked more like one of the Indian beggars he saw outside the saloons. He was thin and shriveled, his speech often interrupted by a wet, hacking cough. His clothing was little more than a patchwork of buffalo leather held together with only enough rawhide to keep it from falling off his back. The necklace of bear claws, once the chief's trademark, was like a mouth with missing teeth.

"Standing Bear honors me with this audience. The Speaker has told me much of your travail. As editor of the *Daily Herald*, I am outraged that such a personage as yourself should be treated like a common criminal. Owing to the recent stories, many of our readers have begun to write the territorial governor and their representatives on your behalf. I believe this interview will go a long way toward building support for your cause."

Standing Bear bade his visitors sit. Tibbles reached into his breast pocket and retrieved a pencil and a leather-bound notebook.

"Now, sir, if you will simply tell what happened."

Standing Bear took his pipe from a low table and lit it. He passed it first to Tibbles and then to Julius.

"Over a hundred of your years ago, we came to the Niobrara. You cannot imagine what it was like to be an Indian there before the white man came! The game walked up to us and practically asked to be killed. Yes, there was bad weather and war. But it was a good life and nothing was defiled or wasted.

"When your people first arrived, we welcomed them. We traded with you and you brought us the gun. When I was a young man, the gun was my greatest friend. With it, I could shoot the buffalo quickly and with less pain for the animal. But then more whites came. These were different—impolite. They shot the buffalo for heads and horns and even killed them from trains. The animals melted away like the dream when I wake. But still the Ponca were peaceful. When the whites told us we must live by the plow, we agreed. After all, the *ground* could not melt away. Even the white man could not slaughter the ground.

"We gave up hunting. We gave up the *tipi* and built lodges and houses. We wanted to be like the white people who always have clothing and shelter and food to eat. We wanted our children to read and write. We would give up all it had meant to be an Indian if it meant we might have this. We kept our word.

"Then, your government told us there had been a mistake—and that we could no longer keep the ground of the Niobrara—that it was to be Sioux land. They said we had agreed to this. And so we marched many days in the wind and snow and rain and heat to the Quapaw reservation. When we got there, we found nothing—none of what the government had promised us. No mill for grain, no beasts to help us, the ground more rock than earth. Of this, you have already written.

"After a year, we were a third our number. The weather no good, the earth no good, the slow deaths came. One by one the children died, including my daughter Prairie Flower, beloved of One Tongue and betrothed to him. On his deathbed, my last son, Bear Shield, made me promise to bury him with our grandfathers. The last word from his lips was 'Niobrara.' I buried his body—promising that I would one day return for both my children.

"We planted the bodies of the others and left the hell in Oklahoma. We did not ask anyone's permission. Some of us rode, others walked. When we reached the Omaha reservation, our cousins welcomed us; but word had reached the great Sherman in Washington. He said we were rebellious and sent a party to arrest us. And now you find me here."

Tibbles nodded. He walked to the small, barred window and peered out.

"I do not doubt that Standing Bear speaks the truth—a truth I will print. When your trial begins, my little newspaper will put your story on the talking wire that speaks to bigger papers in bigger places. The whites will read these papers in Washington and New York and Philadelphia and Boston where the most righteous whites live—the same whites that freed the black men. They will believe you. They will make trouble for their chiefs to set Standing Bear free so that he may return home and bury his children where his ancestors lie."

Standing Bear inhaled some smoke and let it out slowly.

"To have the great Tibbles as an ally is indeed an advantage. But I fear it will take more than this for the Ponca to win in your court."

"What do you mean, Father?" Julius said.

"Lawyer Poppleton, the one who will speak for me, says that this trial will be about more than our right to sacred ground. Before anything else, Standing Bear must first prove to the judge that he is human."

"Surely you must misunderstand him, Father," Julius said. "You are standing here, a living man. Perhaps I should interpret with this Poppleton for you."

"The Omaha woman who says my words is the daughter of Chief Iron Eyes. She has attended your schools and dresses as your women do. She is born to our tongue and makes all clear to me. Through her, this Poppleton has told me that your law has never established that the Indian is a person—that there are many who say that our hearts are in the location of the white man's liver. There are books that write we are first cousins to the wolf. Some of your priests and shamans have claimed that we do not have souls—and without a soul, we cannot be people."

Tibbles' neck grew red. "Such bigotry makes the blood boil. Good! I will use this anger. I shall work day and night and enlist every right-thinking person in this country to help you prove your innocence and humanity."

The turnkey appeared at the door.

"Time, gentlemen."

Tibbles and the chief shook hands. As the door opened, the editor turned once more toward Standing Bear.

"Many righteous whites have written to my paper concerned about the rampage of Chased By Owls. In the past month, he has burned two settlements and attacked a train. These whites worry that his savagery will prejudice the judge against you, providing evidence that the red man is an animal unfit for the company of the civilized."

Standing Bear drew on his pipe but no smoke came. He laid it down on the bed.

"Chased By Owls is tortured by a memory that is not his. Somehow, this memory has migrated from an old warrior's brain to his own so that he does not see the time in which we live, but the free time before the whites. And so, he paints for war; hunts what little game remains; and takes the rest from those he kills. Inside himself, he knows our day is over and that he will be hunted down. But for him, it is only his vision that matters."

The two watched as the door clanged shut. Waving the turnkey off, Tibbles spoke through the bars.

"I will write in my paper that you condemn his acts—and that you hope that he will soon be brought to justice."

Standing Bear shook his head.

"You may write as you please—sometimes truth must be strangled for peace. But as my friend, I must tell you my heart. Your people have always called us 'wild' Indians. But soon we shall be civilized—farmers and herders—shadows of what we once were and paler shadows of the white man.

"But Chased By Owls will never be a shadow. He can only be alive as an Indian or dead as a spirit. When your people write their books about us, Standing Bear will be forgotten—a mere politician who valued life more than freedom. Chased By Owls will be a legend."

26

LEMUEL NORCROSS SAT IN THE THIRD ROW OF THE MAKESHIFT courtroom at Fort Omaha. *Standing Bear vs. Crook* was in its first day and the lawyers had begun their arguments.

Although he did not pretend to understand most of it, Lemuel listened closely to the government's case as laid out by the Omaha district attorney, the honorable Mr. Genio M. Lambertson.

"This entire exercise," Lambertson told the judge, "is outside the bounds of established law. The Indian has never been declared a human being or a citizen. And thus, *cadit quaestio,* is not a person nor a naturalized resident, and therefore has no standing to bring suit against General Crook or the United States."

The statement left Lemuel puzzled. Hadn't he played with them as a boy? Hadn't they laughed when they won at games and cried when they skinned their knees? When he and Little Pony and Talks As He Walks drank their first alcohol and fell down in the street, hadn't *their* mothers beaten them as hard as his own? And later on, when there was hell to be raised around the hidden stills and low-rent whorehouses, had the arresting lawmen asked *whose* hell it was? They had simply and unceremoniously thrown them all in the drunk tank—together.

Lemuel hoped that Mr. John Webster, attorney for the defense, would make more sense.

"The new fourteenth amendment to the constitution makes clear that he who is born in the United States is entitled to life, liberty, and property," Webster said. "This is not a dangerous horde of wild savages with which we deal. With the exception of one bloodthirsty hothead who will soon be brought to heel, the Ponca have seldom broken our laws nor caused their white neighbors to fear them. They have never favored the war axe and the longbow, but the hammer and plow. In this, they have become like the white farmers in this region and so I submit that they are, *ipso facto,* persons—and therefore entitled to the rights of said persons."

The torrent of words made Lemuel's head swim. *Ipso facto.* He wondered how the man on trial could possibly follow gibberish spoken in two languages, neither of them his.

Standing Bear offered no clues. Bolt upright and nearly immobile, the chief revealed nothing—not anger or confusion or indignation. As the hours wore on, he hardly acknowledged the presence of Webster or Mr. Andrew Poppleton, attorney for the Union Pacific, who was providing his services *pro bono*—two more words Lemuel didn't understand. The only time the chief even moved was to lean toward his interpreter, Miss Susette LaFlesche: a dark, tiny woman, plain of face and dressed in the humble manner of a minister's wife. Lemuel had read in the *Herald* that she was the daughter of the Omaha chief Joseph, known among the nations as Iron Eyes. Throughout the proceedings, she whispered to her client, translating testimony into the dialect that had been her mother's tongue. Lemuel was amazed this was even possible. *For the love of God*, he thought, *what is habeas corpus—and how do you say it in Ponca?*

Julius Meyer sat directly behind the defense table. Lemuel had read that during yesterday's pretrial motions, Webster had protested vigorously that the young man should be appointed interpreter for the chief, as he had long been what the Ponca called their "Speaker" and had represented Standing Bear in all treaties and negotiations over the past several years.

Lambertson strongly objected.

"Unlike Mr. Meyer," Lambertson said, "Miss LaFlesche is not a self-made savage known to live amongst primitives in wild lands, but a thoroughly civilized lady and a credit to her race. She was educated at a Presbyterian day school on her reservation and even attended the esteemed Institute for Young Ladies at Elizabeth, New Jersey. Unlike Mr. Meyer, a practitioner of the Hebrew faith and a known devotee of Indian animism, she worships the one true God and Savior. We also believe it an advantage to Mr. Standing Bear that a *real* Indian interpret for him, rather than have a white man— and a *European* in the bargain—attempt to convey the subtleties of American jurisprudence." After a short recess, the Honorable Elmer Scipio Dundy came down on the side of the government.

When Julius walked into court that morning, all the sketch artists reached for their pencils. The day before, he had worn a bespoke suit, tailored in New York, and fine English shoes. Now, such pretense was no longer necessary.

He was dressed in the full ceremonial regalia of the *Boxkaresha-hashtaka*, the esteemed Speaker of the Ponca. Beneath his beaver cap, his black hair corkscrewed in all directions. His shirt was of brown deerskin, its shoulders and arm seams draped in white fringe. The outside hems of his trousers were decorated with long red and yellow beads in patterns of wolves and eagles, as was the dagger on his belt. As he watched him take his seat, Lemuel thought that, but for the mustache and curls, Julius could have easily been a renegade on trial himself—and for worse crimes.

◆

The Big Cheese had never seen such business. The onslaught of reporters, politicians, and various brands of zealots required that tables meant for two now hold four and those meant for four, eight. By noon, men were three deep at the bar. By half-past, the clamor for service had become so great that the prostitutes upstairs were rousted from sleep and pressed into service as waitresses. Doris had even recruited two widow women and an old Pawnee beggar to handle the crowds. As much as it pained him, the chef had needed to pre-cook some of his beefsteaks, so high was the demand. He hadn't been able to determine if the chaos had been caused by the sheer number of new mouths to be fed, or the new gravy he had created for his trademark slabs of beef: meat drippings, dashes of Worcestershire, and pound after pound of butter.

"Mr. Julius?"

Julius Meyer looked up from his steak to see Lemuel Norcross, hat in hand. He barely recognized the boy. The lad who once bedeviled his brother had grown into a sturdy eighteen-year-old. Though nearly as short as Julius himself, he was wide at the shoulder and as slim-hipped as a girl. His face was round and full-cheeked with deep-set eyes and brown-blond hair as long as General Custer's.

"Hello, young Master Norcross," Julius said. "Have you eaten?"

"No, sir."

"Well, I hope you will do me and Mr. Thomas Tibbles here the great honor of joining us for lunch."

"Oh, I'm afraid I couldn't pay my way, sir."

"You misunderstand. I ask you to join our meal as my guest."

"Oh, I couldn't do that, sir."

Julius feigned annoyance. "As you may have heard, Master Norcross, I am a member of an old and revered race. My people have very specific ideas about what constitutes proper hospitality and even more specific ideas about insults to it. Among the greatest of these is the refusal to eat when offered food in good fellowship. And so, I ask you again: will you honor me by sharing meat with us?"

Lemuel looked around, embarrassed, and sat down.

Julius motioned to Lucy, normally a whore known for her oral skills. "Another, please," he said.

"Well, Master Norcross, now that you're quite the young man, what have you been doing with yourself? Still immersed in your stories?"

Lemuel tucked his napkin into his collar. "Yes, sir. I still very much like to read, although now I come into your brother's store, take a quick browse, and then buy what I want—a dollar's worth at a time sometimes. I've been cowboying out on Mr. William Beck's ranch; and pretty soon now I'll be able to strike out on my own and maybe have some of the fine times and adventures I've read about.

"You sure was lucky, Mr. Julius. When you was young and got captured, them Indians was still Indians. They wasn't all caught and dragged off and civilized. You was able to be their friend and be one a' them and talk for Standing Bear. People say you was even gonna marry his daughter . . ."

The flash in the Speaker's eyes stopped the boy dead.

"I wouldn't be so sure about the past," Julius said. "Especially one that's not your own. I can imagine my life sounds romantic to a devourer of fictions like yourself. But to be coldly honest, Master Norcross, if it weren't for the honor, I'd just as soon not have frozen and starved and lost the woman I loved."

The steaks arrived, huge and steaming and slathered with Doris's butter sauce. The potatoes accompanying them had been peeled of their skins, cut into slabs, baked, and then fried. Carrots in butter and salt and brown sugar gleamed by their side.

"All right, let's get to business," Julius said. "I believe you have something you wanted to ask me?"

"Yes, sir, if you don't mind. There's a lot about the trial I don't understand. All them foreign words—like *pro bone*."

Tibbles laughed quietly. "It's pro *bono*, son. And it's Latin for 'without payment.'"

"You mean that Mr. Poppleton is helping Standing Bear for free? That's a fine thing."

"A lot of people hereabouts seem to think so," Tibbles said. "The past three days, the Union Pacific and the do-gooders on the chief's side have been feting him from hotel to saloon to testimonial dinner. But to me, it seems only fair. The railroad and its goons and politicians have been stealing and destroying Indian villages and hunting grounds around here for the past ten years. Whole burial grounds and sacred altars are now nothing but track and tunnels. All accounts settled up, a free lawyer seems damn paltry compensation."

"I reckon," Lemuel said. "But they say its Standing Bear *versus* Crook. Someone said that means 'against.' The chief against the general."

"That's correct," Julius said.

"But if he's against him, why did General Crook jump up in court today to say that he thought Standing Bear is right? That he thinks

Standing Bear should go home and bury his son where his people are buried? The judge yelled at him and told him to sit down. I didn't even know that a judge was allowed to yell at a general! It don't seem like General Crook is against Standing Bear to me. It seems more like he's his friend and believes that he's a man—most like if he was white."

"There's the law and then there's decency, son," Tibbles said. "Too often, they don't have much truck with each other. Maybe after all these years of killing them—man, woman, and child, old Three Stars is fed to the teeth and come to Jesus. As far as being a man, Standing Bear look like a man to you?"

Lemuel lay his knife and fork beside his plate. "Except for the feathers and the gobbly-gook he talks, I'd say hell, yes."

"Well," Julius said, "we'll see if Judge Dundy agrees with you or the entire United States government."

Julius paid for the meal and the three men rose from the table. The waiter gave its surface a quick wipe and four journalists immediately occupied it. The largest of them, a hulking blond man with a red, bumpy face, remained standing. He tapped Julius on the shoulder.

"You're Meyer, right?"

"I'm Julius Meyer, yes."

"I'm Gondorf from the Hartford *Courant*."

Julius nodded. "Oldest paper in the country, I hear."

"That's right. They tell me you're a friend of that Indian."

"If by that you mean Standing Bear, you're right."

Gondorf reached into his pocket for a tablet and the stub of a pencil. "How about an interview? Maybe it'll help your friend."

"What do you want to know?"

"I hear you're a Jew."

"I've heard the same thing," Julius said.

"I also hear that you kept company with the chief's daughter. That right?"

Julius's eyes narrowed. He didn't answer.

Gondorf smiled. Julius saw that his two front teeth were missing and imagined this was probably the result of one too many coarse questions asked of the wrong subject.

"Aw, c'mon, Mr. Meyer. I want to tell the story about how a Jew boy from Europe comes to America, goes native, dresses up like a Ponker, opens up a store to peddle their gimcracks, and takes up with a squaw. Doesn't happen every day."

"No, I suppose it doesn't."

"So tell me. The squaw. What was her name? How'd she die?"

One of the other reporters rose and tried to lead Gondorf to his seat. "C'mon, Charlie," he said. "Sit down. You're drunk. Leave the guy alone before this ends up like New Orleans."

"The public has a right to know," Gondorf said, shrugging off his friend. "Don't you think they want to know how these Jews get in everywhere? The railroads, the banks. Shit, this one got himself in a squaw."

Julius sighed. "First of all, my friend, the term *squaw* is Algonquin. You'd have a lot more luck finding one of those back in Connecticut. Second, how the lady died isn't your business or the business of your readers. In fact, I don't think we have any business together. Good day."

The reporter put a giant hand on Julius' arm and squeezed.

"C'mon now, friend," Gondorf said, gripping Julius as if to break him. "No sense getting upset. I just want to know how a sawed-off hebe plays up to pappy so's he can pet the papoose, if you know what I mean."

Julius didn't reply. With his free hand he reached for the reporter's crotch and found his testicles. As he squeezed, Gondorf's breath deserted his lungs and he stopped speaking. Before he could retaliate, Julius pulled him down sharply until the big man's chin crashed into his curly head. As the reporter reeled, Julius leaped to the top of the table, scattering the dishes and glassware. He kicked high, smashing his moccasin into Gondorf's nose. Gushing from both nostrils, the reporter fell toward the floor, hit a chair on the way down, and finally came to rest in a pool of spilled beer.

Gondorf's fellow reporters sat frozen and amazed in their chairs. Julius leaped down from the table, his breath coming short, and turned toward them.

"Old Indian trick."

Lemuel Norcross stepped out of the way to let Julius pass. It was only then that he realized that the entire saloon had been watching the confrontation. As the Speaker walked through the double doors, the Big Cheese burst into cheers and applause. No one clapped louder than Gondorf's three companions.

The boy followed Julius out onto Farnam Street. He ran in front of him and put out his hand.

"You *got* 'im." Lemuel said, laughing. "You *dropped* that sombitch! It was over before he could raise his hand. My dad says Jews don't fight. He says they're too smart to. Maybe he should talk to that guy in there. *Damn*, Mr. Julius!"

Still panting, Julius stopped, whirled and grabbed Lemuel by the collar. His face was twisted in anger.

"I don't give a shit what your father thinks. And I don't want any of your compliments. All that happened in there is what's happened a million times: the white man picked on the wrong man and got what he had coming."

Terrified, Lemuel put his hand up in surrender. "But Mr. Julius, ain't you a white man?"

Julius brought the boy's face within an eyelash of his, then pushed him away. His eyes were ablaze.

"If I were a white man would I have spent three thousand years running for my life? If I were white, Master Norcross, would I have been banished from Palestine to Spain and Spain to Turkey and Minnesota to the Dakotas and the Niobrara to Oklahoma? If I were white, would my love be dead?"

Lemuel Norcross watched, fearful and thrilled, as Julius jumped to the saddle of a young pinto. As he took the reins, his beaded fringes flew and clicked.

"Give my apologies to Mr. Tibbles and tell him I will see him bright and early. And give some to yourself for the manhandling. I think this pony wants to run."

The horse's thick neck bent and he hissed and snorted as if infected by his rider's fury. Before the boy's eyes, Julius Meyer vanished. What remained seemed like Old Testament vengeance slipped into warrior buckskin: righteous enough to slay the wicked, wild enough to kill Blue Coat or Pharaoh.

27

BENEATH THE SHADOW OF A GREAT SHIP, PRINCESS
Noor-Al-Haya sat atop a large steamer trunk. As she smiled
at the assembled press and public, she smoothed the multiple skirts
of her purple silk dress.

Just below her, the Great Herrmann was busy entertaining the
crowd. He pulled shiny sixpences from the ears and noses of children.
He set a newspaper on fire and restored it to wholeness; and when
the ship's captain emerged from the gangway, Alexander shook hands
with him, exchanging their hats before the good master even had the
chance to utter a greeting.

Finally satisfied that the crowd of reporters and sketch artists was sufficient, the magician bowed to the throng and motioned for silence.

"Ladies and gentlemen, we are overwhelmed at your reception. We did not at all expect that you would honor our humble visit with such a welcome. I need not tell you of my emotions upon being back on the Southampton piers to begin our tour of England. It is through the generosity of the British public that I have attained whatever little reputation I possess, and for this I remain grateful. This time, however, I am especially gratified to be returning with the woman you have doubtless come here to meet: a personage some of your colleagues in America have referred to as the most exciting woman of the age— Princess Noor-Al-Haya, the lovely Pearl of the East."

Alexander turned toward the princess, doffed his purple hat, and bowed deeply. Passengers, passersby, and some of the reporters applauded. A few fellows near the rear of the crowd catcalled and whistled. Two women and a man stood off to the left. They bore identical signs that read:

BRITAIN HAS SIN ENOUGH!
GO HOME, PRINCESS NOOR!

Alexander bowed again, acknowledging the ovation.

"Thank you. Although she has never been to this lovely island before, I know that ere long, Princess Noor will come to love your people as I do, and I pray the public will return that love. At this time, we will be only too glad to answer all respectful questions. However, I must remind you that her highness, coming only recently from the Orient, speaks no English—so any questions for her should be addressed to me and I will translate through an ancient and time-honored system of signs used by the caliphate of her homeland for a thousand years! While you are scribbling in your notebooks, Mr. Seamus Dowie, that handsome redheaded fellow over there, will pass amongst you with a fine and dignified portrait of her highness, suitable for reproduction in any family publication. Now, who's first?"

A middle-aged woman raised her hand.

"The scent you wear is quite lovely," she said. "May I inform my lady readers of what it might be?"

Her male counterparts groaned. Here they had the opportunity to interview the most scandalous woman in America, a vixen who had appeared practically naked in the City of New York and had her shows shut down in Boston and Detroit, and all old Katie Farquhar wanted to talk about was how she covered the stench of her shame.

"Now, now, gentlemen," Alexander said. "We all have our jobs to do. Allow me to relay the question to her highness."

Alexander drew himself up to his full height, gave a sharp intake of breath, and exhaled slowly. Then he wiggled his nose, rotated both index fingers a half dozen times, pantomimed the spraying of an atomizer, and clapped his hands together twice. The princess smiled, nodded vigorously, jabbed two fingers in the air, and produced a small cut-glass bottle from her silver purse. Alexander pretended to read its label. "*Guerlain Eau de Cologne Impériale!*" he exclaimed, "not only a luscious fragrance, but the fine sponsor of our nightly program."

Several of the reporters burst out laughing. "How much to ask that one, Katie?" a burly man said. "Did they wire you a quid from the ship?" Miss Farquhar turned bright red.

Queried as to her opinion of the British men she met on the boat, Alex went through exactly the same manual ballet; only this time, he eliminated the atomizer, substituted a feigned hand through his hair and clapped only once. The princess smiled again, modestly looked toward her lap and made a snaky wave up and down with her fingers. "Handsome and elegant," came the translation, "a pity for me they are not proper Mohammedans."

"Princess . . ." began a man from the *Times*.

"The correct term is your highness," Alexander said.

"Forgive me, *your highness*. As your show begins here in London tomorrow night, how do you feel about the fact that, before even setting foot on the stage of the Egyptian, you have become a symbol of immorality throughout Britain? Pickets are here today and have already begun appearing in front of the theatre's doors. Does this not disturb you?"

Alexander nodded and began waving his arms, pounding his chest and swaying his hips. One of the reporters, unable to contain his laughter, was heard to say "can't he cluck like a chicken, then?" Princess Noor nodded back in understanding and proceeded to answer with more gestures including a short dance that had the gentlemen of the press rapt with attention.

"The princess says, 'this confuses me. In my country amid the palms and pyramids, the costumes I wear are traditional—a symbol of the beauty and fertility of woman. The dances I do celebrate this. As for the rest of my duties, they are to carry out the wishes of my master that he may successfully complete his wonderful miracles. I hope you will tell your readers that I hope to make friends with all the lovely people of your country and that everything I do is wholly innocent and suitable for children.'"

To Alex's delight, Skelton Knaggs, the oily little scandalmonger for the notorious daily *Packet*, waved for attention. Alexander had been hoping Knaggs would show, irresistibly drawn as he was to any story that exhibited even the slightest whiff of sex. Skelton could always be counted upon to ask a question others considered too rude to pose, but that invariably made the pages of their next editions.

"Royal highness," Knaggs began, "it is bandied about that the relationship between you and Professor Herrmann is more than professional. That your association is similar to that of man and wife but without benefit of clergy, as the Professor is rumored a Jew and you, as you have stated, are a Moslem. Please tell us that such a terrible rumor is untrue so that the *Packet* may lay all talk of such licentiousness to rest. Tell us instead that your love is pure."

The reporters whistled and applauded. Billings of the *Mail* clapped Knaggs on the back. Feigning the highest indignation, Alexander walked to within a foot of the shabby little man and raised his hands for silence.

"I need not offend the princess by translating such odious charges. These rumors are simply that. Cheap and disgraceful innuendo! Yes, I am in love—but it is the love of an affectionate father toward a devoted daughter. To suggest that there is anything unseemly between the Great Herrmann and a pure, unmarried woman, well, this is simply too much! I am sorry, gentlemen, but this interview is at an end!"

Alexander took the hand of the princess and helped her down from the trunk. The reporters began to shout questions at the pair, but Alex brandished his cane and refused to answer. With Seamus running interference, the pair made their way through the crowd toward a waiting barouche. Standing before it was a beautiful young woman, as delicate as the princess was bold, as pale as she was dark.

"Miss Adelaide Scarcez, then?" Alexander asked.

"Yes, Professor. I am Adelaide Scarcez."

"Well, for the love of God, get in the carriage. These ink-stained shits have gotten all they need from us. They can make up the rest."

They boarded the coach and drove out from the pier, the press still waving their notebooks. When they reached the Town Quay, Princess Noor spat out the side of the coach and heaved a disgusted sigh.

"For Christ's sake, Alex. When the hell do I learn English?"

Adelaide was amazed. Ever since the telegram had come affirming her engagement, she had kept up with all news and publicity about Professor Herrmann and his assistant. In every story and interview, he had spoken for her. Now, not only did she speak for herself, but did it in unaccented and colorful American.

"Please forgive the princess, Miss Scarcez. Having slept though this morning's breakfast, I'm afraid she is hungry—and when she is hungry she is apt to become irritable, poor lamb."

"I hope you won't think me rude," Adelaide said. "But, such an elaborate deception . . ."

"Rude? Not at all. You see, the princess is in reality what you over here call a 'red' Indian. On this continent, such a revelation would likely meet with little resistance. Indeed, she would probably be greeted as a new and exotic figure in entertainment. But in America, where, alas, much prejudice exists against our native brethren—and where most of our bread is buttered—it was necessary to create a new persona for her. Besides, this 'Egyptian princess' stuff has been a goldmine of publicity. Tell 'em it's something they shouldn't see and they'll crawl over glass to see it."

"That's right, Alex," Lady-Jane said, "talk about me like I'm not here."

"My dear, I wouldn't think to do such a thing. It's only that Miss Scarcez might want to hear our story without the usual pound of salt with which you flavor your language."

"He's quite the bullshitter, dearie. You mean salt like that, Alex? *Bullshitter*?"

"Just so," Alex said.

"Good. He doesn't ask for much, honey. Just to be worshipped as a god and a little smoked salmon on Sundays. Really, Alex, this mute business has me about at my limit. When can I order my own beer?"

"As far as that goes, your highness, never. You are a good Moslem girl—alcohol must never pass your lips. As to your language, while we are here, I have engaged the great Scots character actor, Sir Wilfred Brodie, to train you in crafting an authentic Arabian accent. Beginning tomorrow, he will appear daily at two, dressed in one of his celebrated disguises. I believe he described it as 'Wilkins the Bookseller.' You will take instruction from him until three. With all the wogs in this country, the last thing we need is for you to holler for a cab and some kaffir to cry out, 'She is not Arab! Allah will be avenged!' Once we board the ship back home, you can talk your lovely head off as long as you sound like the Grand Poobah of Whatsis."

"Piss," Princess Noor said, and sat back in a sulk.

"As to your duties, Miss Scarcez, they are simple. Your background in the dance will be used to aid the Princess in the preparation of her steps and the development of new routines. You will also supervise her wardrobe, take notes and letters, and serve as her chaperone. Under no circumstances are you to leave her side in public or allow her to venture abroad unescorted."

"In other words, ducky," the Princess said, "you're a spy."

Adelaide's stomach flipped over.

As the coach bumped along, Princess Noor sat with crossed arms and glared at the lovely new hire. If she had learned anything at all in the brothel, it was that men liked variety. They'd have an Irisher one night, a Negro the next, and the Red Rose of Omaha on payday. She had even heard about a man who had passed the afternoon with her, then spent the night at the Bucket of Blood in the arms of one Jenny Turpin, a girl with one leg and a wall eye. *Definitely trouble*, she thought. *Same size as me but all the rest is poles apart. Black eyes versus green; black hair versus red; red skin versus paper white; hot versus cool. All different from me. Far too different.*

When the barouche pulled into Blechynden station, Princess Noor stepped from it almost before it stopped and headed down the platform.

"Well, Miss Scarcez," Alexander said, "your duties have been described. I suggest you begin to carry them out."

Adelaide hesitated for a second and then leaped from the carriage. Walking quickly, she overtook the Princess, who had found a vendor near the London tracks and was already in the act of buying a roasted potato.

Adelaide was at a loss. Did she smile approvingly; or did she stand stone-faced like a sentinel charged with guarding a valuable property? Should she sign? She knew she couldn't speak.

Princess Noor-Al-Haya pulled tuppence from her purse and handed it the vendor. He thanked her and wrapped the potato in a page of newspaper. The princess took it in her glove and raised it to her mouth. Its steam temporarily obscuring the beautiful darkness of her face, she looked into the eyes of her chaperone and bit hard into the skin.

28

JULIUS MEYER HAD NEVER FELT SUCH FRUSTRATION.
The young Omaha woman who had been chosen as court interpreter was accurate in her translations; and she helped her client answer his questions quickly and accurately.

Yes, your honor, the Ponca had lived well on the Niobrara. No, the new territory had not been fit for plowing. Yes, my children had died of the disease that decimated one hundred fifty eight of us. It is true that my son and daughter had begged to be buried in the earth of our ancestors. Of course, I wish to live in harmony with the whites.

But where, he wondered, was the passion and intensity of Standing Bear, the depth of his emotion? When his voice rose in anger, the tone of Susette LaFlesche remained calm and even.

When his words lowered to a whisper, she delivered them loud and clear.

But emotion had not been absent in the voice of Andrew Poppleton, attorney for the defense.

On the final day of the trial, Poppleton's summation lasted three hours. He visited and revisited the legal points, arguing that the Dred Scott decision of 1857 had no bearing on the case, as the fourteenth amendment of the Constitution had rendered it moot. Under its protections, any American had the right to bring suit against any other—even such an esteemed personage as General George Crook and the government he represented. Only denying the Indian's humanity could keep him from such rights.

"I have believed it to be my duty," Poppleton told the judge, "to thank God that I was born under the shield and protection of this North American Republic—which has solved so many problems and which in God's time will solve so many more. But is it possible that this great government, dealing with this feeble remnant of a once-powerful nation, claims the right to place them in a condition which to them is worse than slaves, without a syllable of law? I don't believe that the courts will allow this—that they will agree to the proposition that these people are wild beasts."

The lawyer turned and pointed toward the chief. His voice rose in anger.

"This man not a human being? This man who wandered for sixty days through a strange country without guide or compass, aided by the sun and stars only, so that the bones and ashes of his kindred may be buried in the land of their birth? And if he is not a human being, then *what is he?* Are we to say that the Ethiopian, the Malay, the Chinaman, the Frenchman and every nationality upon the globe without regard for race, color, or creed, may come here and become a part of this great government, while the primitive inhabitants of this soil are *alone* barred from the right to become citizens? No! It is a libel upon all who have risked their lives to bring that gospel which Jesus Christ proclaimed to all the wide Earth, to say that this is not a man!"

Now shaking with rage, Poppleton thanked the court and took his seat. Standing Bear smiled and placed a hand on his shoulder.

Judge Dundy called for order.

"With the arguments presented, these legal proceedings are now at an end. However, the plaintiff wishes to make a final address to this court. It is highly irregular—and I imagine that this is the first time in our history that such a request has been made. But with the assent of the legal advisers on both sides, I have decided to grant it. Mr. Julius Meyer?"

Julius rose from his seat.

"As prearranged, Mr. Meyer, you will now interpret for the plaintiff."

Julius walked toward the plaintiff's table. Susette LaFlesche gracefully exchanged places with him, squeezing his hand as she passed him. Standing Bear now rose—his Speaker at his side—and raised his right hand before the court.

"This hand is not the color of yours, but if I pierce it, I shall feel pain. If you pierce your hand, you too, feel pain. The blood that flows from mine will be the same color as yours. I am a man! God made us both."

Standing Bear then turned from the judge to face the crowded courtroom. Julius's voice rose and fell with his.

"I have a vision. I seem to stand on the bank of a river. My wife and little girl are beside me. Before me, the river is wide and impassable—there are steep cliffs all around, the water is quickly rising. In desperation, I scan the cliffs and finally spot a rocky path to safety. I turn to my wife and child and shout that we are saved!

We will return to the Niobrara that pours down between the green islands where lie the graves of my fathers."

The chief slowly turned back toward the bench and stretched both arms toward the judge, Julius mimicking his every gesture.

"But a man bars our passage. If he says I cannot pass, I cannot. The long struggle will have been in vain. My wife and child and I will sink beneath the flood. I am weak and faint and sick. I can fight no more.

"You, your honor, are that man."

The courtroom remained silent for several minutes. Then the quiet was broken by the sound of men and women softly weeping. General Crook rose from his chair and straightened his tunic. Slowly, he walked toward Standing Bear. The general looked deep into the chief's amber eyes and took the red right hand in both of his. The eyes of both old warriors were full.

The crowd began to stomp and applaud; some left their seats and surrounded the two men, shaking their hands and clapping them on the back. The young boys at the rear of the courtroom cheered.

Judge Dundy ordered his bailiffs to restore order. When calm at last returned, he told the assembly that he would take the issue under advisement and render his decision in the coming days.

His gavel came down. Court was adjourned.

29

AS SHE SAT IN THE ORCHESTRA OF THE EGYPTIAN, ADELAIDE Scarcez felt a grudging respect. Compars Herrmann was nothing if not thorough.

The dossier he had provided to her contained all that a spy could want and more. Even as angry and conflicted as she was about her assignment, Adelaide marveled at the detail:

> *HERRMANN, ALEXANDER. Magician. Known throughout the world as THE GREAT HERRMANN, formerly as ALEXANDER THE GREAT. Born 10 February 1844, Bromberg (Bydgoszcz), Prussia. Youngest of sixteen children born to SAMUEL HERRMANN and ANNA*

(MEYER) HERRMANN. American citizenship, 1876. Successor to COMPARS HERRMANN (brother), known in America as CARL HERRMANN, also known internationally at THE GREAT HERRMANN. Born 23 July 1816, Karlsbad, Germany.

The file included height, weight, and personal habits, strengths, and weaknesses, even favorites of food and drink. Yes, *very* thorough. But when she turned to page one of the second dossier, Adelaide quickly went from impressed to uneasy.

Below the name SCARCEZ, ADELAIDE, she read a biography of herself every bit as detailed as that of Compars's own brother: her birthplace; her parentage; the professional engagements she had had as a dancer; her appetites ("occasionally dips snuff, large capacity for sweets"), and even a partial list of the lovers she had taken since leaving school:

1873: Truitt, John, Carriage Driver. 1874: C. Denham, animal keeper. 1874–1875: Harold E. Ponfritt, theatrical producer . . .

The devil deserved his due. Compars was as masterful a blackmailer as he was a conjurer, exerting the same effort to extortion that he applied to performance. For him, no detail was too small, no incident too private to be investigated and exploited.

And just as he did on the stage, he left nothing to chance. When she turned to page four she found the contract detailing the terms of her employment. It, too, left little to the imagination:

Miss Adelaide SCARCEZ will, under the terms of this indenture, carry out the following duties:

1. *She shall act as secretary to Mr. ALEXANDER HERRMANN. In such capacity, she will perform such*

tasks as expected of that office plus any additional and/or related work required by Mr. Herrmann.

2. *She shall observe all actions of Mr. Herrmann relating to his stage performances, most especially changes in his long-established and original act (see appendix) and the discussion or imminent performance of anything referred to as a SUBSTITUTION TRUNK, SUBSTITUTION BOX or any other device which may be construed as such.*

3. *She shall gather any and all information about the Herrmann staff, most especially the employee known as PRINCESS NOOR-AL-HAYA, including, if possible, name, birthplace, country of origin, criminal record, incriminating detail, and romantic history.*

4. *Under no circumstances will Miss Scarcez reveal her association with her true employer, his actual identity, his occupation, his motivation, or his relationship to Mr. Alexander Herrmann.*

Nowhere in the document was Compars named. The terms of employment referred only to the "Balaclava Corporation." Even if the document were to fall into the hands of the police, outside of accusations that would lead to her ruin and against which she had no defense, there would be no way to associate him with either the extortion or the espionage. After nearly a halfcentury of making fools of the world, Compars Herrmann was not about to make one of himself.

Adelaide returned the contract to her leather portfolio and looked up at the stage. Watching Alexander rehearse the Inexhaustible Bottle, she was awed at his dexterity and concentration. All morning she had wondered if, had its origins not been tainted, she might not actually enjoy this job. Like dance, magic was exhilarating, filled with mental and physical challenges and colorful characters backstage. Alexander himself was a charming and considerate boss; conceited like Compars, yes, but still capable of giving someone else credit for an idea or making a joke at his own expense.

And never had she seen any man so personally magnetic. At previews, the audience had consisted overwhelmingly of women: some with husbands and sweethearts, others with girlfriends or on club outings. At the conclusion of the show, his dressing room would always be crowded with female well-wishers. As he took their gloved hands in his, Adelaide could almost feel the radiance of their blushing faces. Yet their gentlemen seemed to take no offense. They shook his hand heartily, offering compliments and congratulations as if they were old lodge brothers.

As she watched from stage right, Alexander ran through his patter in a perfunctory manner, employing none of the usual pomp and grandiosity of an actual performance. Over the course of several minutes, he poured five different beverages from the same bottle: white sauterne, claret, port, scotch whiskey, and gin. Adelaide had seen him perform this trick dozens of times. But now, instead of simply putting down the bottle and motioning for the goblets to be cleared, he retrieved a silver hammer from a silk-draped stand and began to speak as if the empty hall were full to the third balcony.

"Now, my friends, I know that you are well and truly amazed that I have been able to produce five different delicious liquors from this one humble bottle! The kind gentleman from the audience (and here he indicated an imaginary participant) has already attested to their quality and, from the way he seems to be weaving a bit, their potency. However, to prove to you that this is indeed merely an ordinary bottle containing no secret pump or apparatus, I take the magic hammer and count. One! Two! Three!"

Holding the bottle by the neck, Alexander smashed it to bits. From its falling shards rose a white dove, fluttering in panic, a pink lace handkerchief tied about its neck. Alex elaborately feigned surprise.

"But what is this? Why, it is one of our little feathered friends from the Magic Hat! Nice little birdy! Nice little . . . but wait! Hullo! What can this be?"

With a flourish, Alex untied and removed the cloth from the dove and displayed it to the footlights.

"Why, it is a handkerchief! I daresay the very handkerchief lent to me by the lovely Miss Adelaide only moments ago."

Adelaide laughed as Alexander bowed to her.

"I wondered when I would get that back from you, Professor. This is going to be wonderful for the audience."

Alexander walked across the stage and draped the handkerchief over Adelaide's shoulder. He then reached behind her right ear, produced a gold sovereign, and pressed it into her hand.

"Wonderful? I hope so. New? Not really. I stole it from Robert-Houdin, who stole it from old John Henry Anderson. God only knows who he got it from—may his soul rest in peace. The only thing I added was the patter and the bit with the dove, which I believe works quite well, don't you think?"

"Indeed. I found myself quite amazed."

"*You* were amazed, Miss Adelaide? Imagine how the poor bird felt."

Her laughter was interrupted by a piercing scream from the left wing. It was followed by a firecracker chain of obscenities such as Adelaide had never heard from a female mouth. Blushing, she turned toward the sound in time to see Princess Noor-Al-Haya emerge from the backstage darkness.

She was dressed in the most beautiful of her harem costumes, its yellow gossamer and gold doubloons shining against the darkness of her skin. In her hand, she held another skein of cloth. It was of the same material and color. Adelaide could not help but be struck once again at the beauty of the Lady-Jane; the grace and determination of her stride, the high color brought to her lovely face by a fine Ponca temper.

"Look, Alex," the princess said. "Look! Look what they want me to wear!"

Princess Noor took the yellow swath in both hands, draping it over her shoulder and across her belly.

Alexander nodded. "I think it looks fetching."

"Fetching?" the princess cried. "It will be the ruin of me. This was my prettiest costume. *Now* look. See how it covers my middle, the part that the audience watches most closely. Look at how it destroys my line. How am I supposed to dance in this?"

The princess began to shimmer and shake. She slithered on the floor and rolled head first toward the footlights. Adelaide thought her even more magnificent in motion.

Alexander applauded.

"Excellent, your worship. Most excellent."

"It's *not* excellent, Alex. I can hardly move with this big rag around me. You've spent the past three weeks bullshitting the newspapers that the new emerald in my navel cost five thousand pounds. How is the audience going to feel when they can't even see it?"

"They'll get a glimpse, my darling. We'll make sure of that. As for the costume addition, well, I'm afraid it's the compromise I've had to make with the local police and politicians until all their bribes are distributed. So, until they are, you'll wear it and we'll go on. By next week, they'll all have their money and you can tread the boards wearing nothing but your god-given talent."

"I can't wear it," the princess shouted. "I won't!"

Adelaide watched as Alexander's eyes narrowed and his smile faded. When his face went dark like this, he looked enough like his brother to chill her blood.

"You can and you will," he said. "I have not come all the way from America to be a laughingstock."

"And if I still won't?"

"Then, as much as it would pain me, I should have no choice but to send you back to Nebraska—in steerage—where I am sure many of the patrons from your previous career await you. We shall have to get by with your understudy, more's the pity."

"Understudy?" the princess shouted, her eyes becoming large. "There's no understudy for me."

Alexander turned slowly downstage and looked directly at his newest employee.

"*Her?*" Lady-Jane shrieked. "That little orange-headed nothing? You're joking."

"My dearest, I am as serious as a mortgage in arrears. Miss Scarcez has been with us all throughout the rehearsals for the show. She is, like you, small and lithe. The night we danced the gavotte at the Grosvenor Hotel, she proved to me that she has excellent timing and rhythm. The rest is simply a matter of wig, costume, and enough makeup to cover. *Voilà!* Al-*Haya!*"

Adelaide blushed redder than the princess herself.

"Oh, no. Please. Please, Professor. I could never . . . I could never take the place of . . ."

Adelaide turned toward Lady-Jane. The princess's face was twisted in fury and she began to shred the huge sash with her long red nails.

"Princess," Adelaide said. "You cannot imagine that I could ever hope to equal you in any way."

"You're damn right you couldn't. Alex, tell her she couldn't."

"My dear, you are as irreplaceable as the Hope Diamond. Your movements are informed by a thousand years on the primitive plains and your eroticism could never be approached by our Miss Scarcez, who, being unmarried, I'm sure has little knowledge of such things. But we have contracts to honor and a public to entertain. It may be *cliché,* but the show must go on."

"You bastard. I'll expose you! What would happen to the Great Herrmann if the world found out that his great Egyptian discovery was an Indian whore from Omaha?"

"That is your prerogative," he said. "But your contract of employment indicates that should you reveal any of my trade secrets, you will be subject to prosecution, including fine or imprisonment or both. And, as it happens, my love, *you* are a trade secret. I hope you have saved the fine salary I have been paying you because, believe me, it will take all of it and then some to defend such a suit—and it would injure me greatly to have to visit you in the slammer."

Princess Noor seemed primed to explode. She looked from Alexander to Adelaide and back again, trying to decide which of the two she hated more. Choosing the magician, she reached up to scratch at his eyes. Alex took her by both wrists and held her easily, laughing at her struggle. She spit in his face and tried to knee him in the groin, but he skillfully avoided her maneuvers. Then, as Adelaide looked on in astonishment, he wrestled her through the wings to the door of his great dressing room and slammed it behind them. Adelaide stood alone on the quiet, empty stage, looking into the blackness beyond the enormous red curtains.

From beyond the dressing-room door she heard the princess's voice cut through the still theatre. She ranted at Alexander, her language laced with new oaths and expletives.

And then, as if a dial had been turned, there was silence. What she heard next was unmistakable.

It began as low moans, soft and guttural, punctuated here and there by a gasp or a strangled sigh. Then it escalated to muted whimpers and high shrieks of satisfaction. Adelaide colored with embarrassment. Even if Alexander and the princess seemed not to care, this was not something she was meant to hear.

Still, she found herself inching across the stage, moving closer to the source of the sound.

How long had it been since she had made such loving noise; since she had ebbed and flowed against the sinew of a man? Listening now to the pleasures of another, it felt as if years had passed. Wiping her brow, she leaned against the proscenium wall straining to hear every breath, every cry, all she had missed since Compars had claimed her life. In each murmer, she could hear the princess surrender.

When the passion subsided, Adelaide hurried to the place she had stood when the couple made their exit. She now knew what drove Princess Noor and her magician; and in that moment, divined how to feed the obsession of Compars Herrmann without revealing a single important truth.

Adelaide would report to him, yes; she would outline in painstaking detail all of the trivial changes that to him would seem monumental: the Inexhaustible Bottle and its more recent outrage, The Dove from the Glass; the switching of the Floating Boy from the right to the left of the stage. She would report to him every variation in the hokum and chatter, every movement of a footlight or curtain, every repainting of a box or cylinder.

And she would impart every fact concerning the mysterious princess—her wardrobe, her temper, her knowledge of his legacy—but more than this, she would speak to him of sex. In lurid detail, she would regale him with tales to equal the Arabian Nights—stories of an Eastern temptress who each night bewitched his brother, body and soul. She would tell all—except the single fact with which he could do the most mischief—that Princess Noor-Al-Haya was a redskin prostitute wanted in a mass murder.

He would devour it like red meat; and while he did, she would gain the time needed to free herself from his snare. Time to think and plan. Time to set a trap of her own.

30

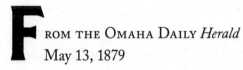ROM THE OMAHA DAILY *Herald*
May 13, 1879

STANDING BEAR'S VICTORY
Judge Dundy Issues Order Releasing the Ponca Indians.
A DECISION FAR REACHING IN ITS EFFECTS
There is no Law for Using the Military to
Force Indians from one Place to Another.
An Indian has Some Rights Which the Courts Will Protect.

In an historic decision sure to have far-reaching effects throughout the
land, United States District Court Judge Elmer S. Dundy has ruled

that the Ponca Indian chief Standing Bear, on trial for deserting from a reservation where he had been forced to move, can legally sue for redress in court and that the United States has no jurisdiction over his whereabouts.

As part of his finding, the judge ruled that the American Indian, heretofore seen as an alien member of a foreign race, is in fact, a person under the constitution.

In his remarks Judge Dundy wrote:

> "An Indian is a person within the meaning of the habeas corpus act, and as such is entitled to sue out a writ of Habeas corpus in the federal court, when it is shown that the petitioner is deprived of liberty under color of authority of the United States, or is in custody of an officer in violation of the constitution, or a law of the United States, or in violation of a treaty made in pursuance thereof."

The decision protects the red man from search, seizure and arrest unless the Indian in question is suspected of a crime. The judge went on to say that the Indian, though not yet legally a citizen, may not be moved from place to place by the government unless that Indian is found to be in violation of the law. "The right of expatriation," the judge wrote, "is a natural, inherent and inalienable right and extends to the Indians as well as the more fortunate white race." He also stated that the Indian, like all who are born on U.S. soil, has the right to "life, liberty and the pursuit of happiness."

During the three-day trial, supporters from the worlds of politics, academia and religion came from everywhere to support the beleaguered chief. Members of the press arrived from as far away as France and Germany. Many attending the trial agreed that it was the chief's tragic story of the so-called "Trail of Tears,"—a forced march during which three of his children died—as well as his dignity, that won the day for his cause.

Speaking through his court interpreter, the chief recounted how his dying son pleaded to be returned to the region of the upper Niobrara and be buried among his ancestors. Could any man in the court that day, he asked, refuse such a request? Holding up his weathered hand before the packed courtroom, Standing Bear made a plea for universal brotherhood and understanding, stating that although his hand was not the same color as that of the judge, it was made by the same God.

"This decision is not only gratifying, but it shows that our system of laws works for all, even the most wretched and despised," said Mr. John Webster, former Omaha mayor and an attorney for the Ponca chief. "It is a victory not only for my client, but for the American legal system and all oppressed peoples."

Asked for his reaction to the verdict, Standing Bear spoke through the voice of Mr. Julius Meyer, his great friend and longtime interpreter. "For a hundred years or more, the white men have been driving us about. They are shrewd, sharp and know how to cheat. But since I have been here, I have found them different. They have all treated me very kindly. Hitherto, when we have been wronged we went to war. To assert our rights and avenge our wrongs we took up the tomahawk. We had no law to punish those who did wrong, so we went to kill. You have gone into the court for us and I find our wrongs can be righted there. Now I have no more use for the tomahawk. I have found a better way."

Having found that the United States had no authority to hold the chief and his fellow Indians, Judge Dundy ordered the Ponca dissenters discharged from custody.

District Attorney G.M. Lambertson, speaking for the prosecution, expressed surprise and disappointment at the decision.

"We will seek redress upon appeal," he said. "While Mr. Standing Bear may be a good Indian, there are many of his brothers who still live in a state of barbarism. One need only mention the bloodthirsty beast called Chased By Owls—who yesterday attempted to ambush a hunting party made up of railroad executives and captains of industry, the cream of our society. It was only the quick action of their guards and scouts that spared their lives, costing, I am afraid, some of their own."

Asked what Standing Bear's further plans were, Mr. Meyer, a respected Jew businessman and expert in Indian affairs, told the *Herald*, "the Ponca have achieved a victory but they are still starving and miserable. We plan to travel to the East where the great abolitionist, Mr. Wendell Phillips, has arranged for Standing Bear to lecture and raise money from sympathetic whites. From there, I will travel to England where my cousin, Mr. Alexander Herrmann, has promised to introduce us to others who believe in the red man's freedom and will back up that belief in pounds sterling."

31

T HE GREAT HERRMANN STOOD AT THE BOTTOM OF THE
gangway of the *Berengaria*. It had taken some time for the giant
ship to dock, but he hadn't minded the wait. It had been thrilling to
watch the little tugboats push and pull the great vessel into place.
Periodically, supporters approached to report how much they enjoyed
his work and asked him to sign their ticket books or passport pages.

Adelaide Scarcez had enjoyed the time, too. The trip down from
London had been an unexpected pleasure, uninterrupted as it was by
the officious interventions of Seamus Dowie or the unnerving unpre-
dictability of Princess Noor. Liberated from performances or rehearsal,
Adelaide had her first chance to observe Alexander in ordinary circumstances, released from the grandeur and conceit required of his

role as World's Greatest Magician. She had felt unexpected warmth for him as he gazed through their compartment's window, pointing out a species of tree or a quaint farmhouse. After they had enjoyed a lovely breakfast in the parlor car, Alex had amused some children, cranky and exhausted with travel, with some sleight-of-hand. He produced shillings from their ears, made sugar cubes disappear, turned salt into pepper and water into wine. Adelaide found herself as charmed as the small ones by his performance, a little show presented with a patience and modesty she had never before seen.

"I suppose it will not be difficult to spot your cousin."

"I think not. Just look for the little Jew dressed in buckskin leading a retinue of red Indians similarly attired. I imagine there won't be more than four or five other parties like that on this ship."

As Adelaide grinned at the joke, the passengers began to disembark, first class leading. Their travel clothes were of the finest: rich velvet suits and dresses on the women, bespoke gabardines on the men. The children who accompanied them were no less turned out: the girls in creamy bonnets and summer crinolines, the boys in dark knickers with wide straw hats or white sailor suits trimmed in gold. Experienced seafarers, they smiled and waved to the family or servants who had come to collect them.

The passenger behind them could not have been more different.

Instead of the stark solids and clean whites of his predecessors, his costume vibrated with color—blue and yellow beads and tawny skins adorned with the art and history of the plains. When the small mustachioed man finally gained the foot of the long bridge, he took the hands of Alexander in his and kissed him on both cheeks.

"So, what should I call you?" Alex said. "Surely a warrior of your standing can no longer be addressed simply as Julius. So, what is it? Big Yiddish? Chief Makes Much Matzoh?"

Julius laughed. "Witty as ever. My friends have a different name for me, but you couldn't pronounce it; not that you would when you can make up your own. Alex, you look fine."

"As do you, O Mighty Morning Minyan. But please allow me to introduce my secretary, without whom I would surely have forgotten what day you were arriving. Miss Adelaide Scarcez, my cousin, Medicine Man Eats On Yom Kippur, better known as Mr. Julius Meyer."

Adelaide held out her hand. "How do you do, Mr. Meyer. The Professor has told me so much about you."

"It's my great pleasure, Miss Scarcez. You are as bright and pretty as Alex's letters have painted you—actually, more so. He has often written that without you, he would disappear into one of his own hats."

Adelaide flushed and smiled. "You are most kind."

"But *professor*? Really Alex, I believe you become more like Compars every day. What's next? *Herr Docktor*?"

"No, cousin, I think I'll leave that one to dear brother. He'll need it in retirement. One gets so many ailments at his age. Is his lordship here?"

"I'm afraid not. Lacking the Meyer-Herrmann blood, Standing Bear thinks it is beneath him to earn his keep as a performing seal. Still, he assures me that he will happily spend any funds we might raise through the perversion of our dignity. Where's our Red Rose?"

"Her highness has remained at our apartments today. The press, which follows her every move, has been told that she has a touch of the neuralgia. But between you, me, and about a dozen deeply offended Egyptian gods, I'm keeping her under tighter wraps these days. It's getting more and more difficult to take her for an airing without she starts yapping, and *not* in Arabic. Last week an Iranian or an Iraqi or some such filthy wog ran up to her and started jabbering in god-knows-what. Our Lady-Jane told him to, and I quote, "go fuck yourself." Luckily he didn't understand English any better than he spoke it, and so she remains unexposed except onstage, but that's hardly a matter of language."

"So I've heard," Julius said. "I was glad to receive your wire. Apparently our appointments are all arranged."

"The best venues holding the best people with only the best of intentions," Alex said. "I have told them that yours is a worthy cause. I have also scared most of them shitless by intimating most subtly that should they decline to donate, the forces of darkness both white and Indian would be most displeased."

Their laughter was interrupted by a commotion at the top of the gangway. Looking toward its guardrail, Adelaide could see two men in white carrying some sort of long object. As they made their way down, she saw it was a hospital gurney. Strapped to it was a man, his long gray beard resting upon the blanket that covered him. Directly behind them followed a ramrod-straight officer she assumed to be the ship's surgeon and, behind him, a young Indian. He was thin but with the kind of muscle that reminds one of bridge cables. When the gurney finally reached the dock, the man lying on it gestured for the Indian to halt; he lowered his hand slightly and then pointed it at Julius.

"I warned you," the man said, his voice the very sound of misery. "I told you this here trip would come to no good."

"Well, it would help if next time you got one of those tingles up your spine, you got it before we left America instead of at mid-ocean," Julius said, gesturing toward his companions. "My cousin Alexander. I believe you have met."

"Ahoy, Prophet," Alex said.

"And this is his charming secretary and indispensible *factotum*, Miss Adelaide Scarcez. Miss Scarcez, Mr. John Nathan McGarrigle and our young friend, Mr. Wind Whistler."

The young Indian nodded shyly in the lady's direction; Prophet John ignored her completely. "Young Jules, tell 'em to let me out of this thing. We're on dry land now."

Julius chuckled. "John, this is England. Nothing here can be described as dry; and I'm not about to overrule the doctor."

"What did he do this time?" Alex asked. "Take the wheel from the captain because his bones told him you were headed for an iceberg?"

"No," Julius said. "His crime was more an affront to common sense. We were all of us sick as dogs, but the prophet here somehow decided that straight bourbon whiskey was the best cure for motion sickness. It wasn't. Two hours later, it took me and Wind Whistler here to keep him from hurling himself over the side. By this morning, when everyone else had recovered, he was still so sick I nearly took a pistol to him myself."

"That's right, whippersnapper," Prophet John said, his lips twisted in disgust, "tell everyone. Shout my humiliation to the world. None of that changes the fact that I still say comin' here was a fool's errand."

Julius shook his head. "What say you, doctor? Will it be all right to release this young man, or will he try to steal the Crown Jewels?"

A minute later, John McGarrigle was released and on his feet. He glared at Julius, tipped his hat to Adelaide, and stomped off across the pier toward a sign picturing a large tankard.

"Perhaps he'll get lost," Alexander said.

Julius smiled. "I shouldn't worry. Prophet John can track a black cat through a coal mine. He should have no trouble finding us."

Alexander turned and whistled loudly through his teeth. At the sound, four matched grays headed in their direction drawing a large and elegant black landau. As it came to a stop, the magician invited the little party to board.

"You know, Adelaide," Alex said, "Southampton is where Julius and I left Europe for America when we were only boys. I fear much has changed since that day."

"I can well imagine," Adelaide said. "But then it seems natural that such a great port should alter over time. Don't you think so, Mr. Meyer?"

Julius was silent for a moment. The horse's hooves filled the silence in the coach.

"I believe Alexander doesn't speak only of Southampton, Miss Scarcez, but of our whole world. When I disembarked in Philadelphia all those years ago, I was only little Julius and he young *Sasha*. Today, I am *Mr.* Julius Meyer, Indian expert and Speaker of the Ponca whom the Indians call the *Boxkareshahashtaka*—the Curly Head, the Chief with One Tongue. And he? He is *Herr Professor, Mr.* Alexander Herrmann, the *Great* Herrmann, known everywhere as Master of the Mysterious and the World's Greatest Magician."

Julius paused and looked out the window to see the huge hulk of the *Berengaria* receding into the water.

"Yes, Miss Scarcez: for us, the world has certainly changed—if for no other reason than this promiscuous accumulation of names."

⬥

The little plainsman spurred his horse across the wet grassland. Its hooves made a sound almost like crashing cymbals as they pummeled the ground and water.

Screaming, the big palomino flew over a green hedgerow and landed. The rider bent low to its mane, relieved that the horse did not slip and fall onto the soaked field. It had been only an hour since the rain had gone; and while he worried about a firm footing, at least he didn't have to think about whether the sun was at his back and/or in his eyes. It was high noon.

The Indian, younger even than his adversary, rode a horse so red that from a few feet it looked composed of Jefferson County clay. He could feel the pony's feet slide beneath him as he made straight for his adversary. He reached back into his quiver and produced an eagle shaft painted in rings of blue and black. Holding the red tight with his legs, he notched the arrow into its bowstring, pulled back, and released. It missed the plainsman by inches.

The white man whipped the palomino into a zigzag pattern, hoping to avoid the next bolt. Putting his spurs to the palomino, he reached down and pulled a Sharps buffalo gun from its saddle scabbard. Now it was the Indian's turn to weave, knowing that at this range, one shot from the fifty-caliber rifle would explode his body. The plainsman cocked and shot. The report was like a cannon. The bullet whizzed past the pony's flank, close enough to split its tail.

Now the men were too close for shooting. The Indian rode straight for his enemy and leaped from the saddle. As he grabbed the white around the shoulders, his momentum sent both men tumbling from the palomino's back onto the sopping ground. In a moment, they were up, the Indian raising his tomahawk, the plainsman a Bowie knife. They circled each other, breathing heavily, hatred glaring from their eyes.

The white attacked first, tackling the Indian by the legs. The brave fell to the ground with a splash, but managed to raise his tomahawk, striking his enemy twice in the head. The plainsman stabbed down once, deep into the belly of the savage. The pair made feeble attempts to rise but it was no use. In a moment, their weapons lay useless on the ground and they were as still as the live oaks on the hillside.

Lady Caroline Carstairs screamed in panic, which gave permission to her female guests to give voice to their own horror. Directly beside her, the Baroness de Rochambeau fainted and was luckily caught by her husband before she could fall to the damp pavilion floor. The Duchess of Cornwall, known throughout Britain as its greatest lover of horses, had to be restrained in her effort to comfort the two now-riderless animals. Captain Richard Wilkinson-Barre, the Seventh Earl

Carroll, whom everyone assumed was made of sterner stuff, fell into a nearby chair and put his hands to his mouth, the better to contain his nausea.

Flushed and panting, Lady Caroline brought her fan to her face. She was used to scandal, yes: but what was a bit of financial chicanery or illicit sex compared to a double murder on her polo ground?

Just as the alarm threatened to engulf the entire gathering, the plainsman, dressed in a magnificent fringed jacket and trousers, scrambled to his feet and motioned for calm.

"My lords, ladies and gentlemen, what you have just witnessed symbolizes what for eighty years has been the state of relations between the white American and the Plains Indian. Conflict has been our milk and meat, death our father and mother. The result, as you have seen today, is tragedy on both sides: once-vital men lying dead by the hundreds and thousands, food for buzzards and fodder for further hatred and rage."

Julius Meyer turned on his heel and called to the young Indian in Ponca. He rose, standing tall and straight. The audience burst into relieved laughter and loud applause.

Julius once again held up his hands for silence.

"Permit me to introduce my fellow play-actor. To my left is Mr. Wind Whistler, esteemed horseman and decorated warrior of the Ponca tribe."

Whistler bowed awkwardly. The crowd clapped and shouted even louder. There were cries of "capital!" and "jolly good!"

"The exciting battle you have seen today," Julius said, "is not an event that occurs willy-nilly. Weeks of painstaking rehearsal have gone into every move made by my friend and myself and our no less courageous mounts. And while our little drama amply illustrates the terrible waste of life and treasure that American policies toward the Indian have caused, we also mean it to show you good lords, ladies, and gentlemen that hard work and cooperation between the white and red races, such as went into creating our display, can produce a quite astounding result—and that the two peoples can, even in the face of a poisoned history, live together upon the land that God made for all his children.

"It is in this spirit that we have come to England. No people have known the blessings of freedom more fully than the British. There can also be little doubt that there are no people on earth more fair-minded and honorable than the sons and daughters of John Bull. With this in mind, my cousin and your friend, Professor Alexander Herrmann, suggested that we journey here and seek your help so that you, who represent the finest of society, will aid us in our fight for legal redress and support us in our struggle to feed and clothe those tribes our government has cheated and abandoned."

The two men bowed again. They entered the wooden pavillion and were met with hearty handshakes and cries of "well done." Lady Caroline offered her hand to Julius. He brought his lips within an inch of her glove.

"Mr. Meyer, I suppose I should be very cross with you. You gave me and my guests the most terrible fright."

"I apologize, Lady Caroline," Julius said. "But we felt it necessary to make our point in a most dramatic way and deemed that this was exactly the kind of presentation required."

"Don't be concerned, Mr. Meyer. Your little pantomime was the most thrilling thing that's happened around here since Lord Carstairs discovered a new brand of gin. As Alexander may have told you, I welcome anything that will relieve the monotony of this country exis- tence. So I suppose I should be grateful to find that a certain amount of theatricality runs in your family."

"I am afraid I must plead guilty to that trait, ma'am. I have often been criticized for it in my home country. But I believe that people learn better when they are not bored—and if a bit of showing off can be put to work for a good cause, well, no one is harmed and many may be helped. But I was so hoping to meet Lord Carstairs today. He is well, I hope?"

Lady Caroline sighed. "His Lordship sends his regrets. He was apparently informed this morning that a single grouse still survived somewhere on the property and has taken his gun and gone in search of it. Generally, he isn't enthused by anything that doesn't involve the killing of small creatures or insults to butlers and groomsmen."

Lady Caroline took Julius's arm and presented him to the various guests. As usual, his tongue amazed. How was it that this wild little ruffian could speak perfect French to the French and textbook German to the Germans? Where did he learn his courtly ways and impeccable manners? And how, by the end of the night, did he manage to walk away from the gathering with pledges totaling more than ten thousand pounds? Perhaps there was something to the rumor that beneath the buckskin and beads beat the heart of a son of Abraham; and after all, weren't they all like magnets when it came to money?

⬥

Seamus Dowie did his best to hold his cup in the proper manner, but tea had never been his drink.

Even back in Ireland, where his mother seemed to brew it by the gallon, he had never taken a shine to the stuff and only drank it when he was sick or when forced to by the presence of company. The tiny sandwiches it came with were even more problematic. Between his huge, thick fingers, they seemed the size of a pencil eraser; and when he bit into one, it was difficult to not wolf what little was there. To him, they didn't seem like actual food, just fluffy little clouds of vinegar and salt and slices of things thin enough to taste like nothing.

Princess Noor-Al-Haya had a different attitude.

For her, a private booth in a fine hotel was heaven with food. Here, dressed in one of her newest frocks, the tedious work and everyday death of Nebraska seemed even farther away than it was in miles. The little sandwiches and cakes were delicate and delicious, as subtle as grilled elk was gross. Best of all, with the curtains drawn around the booth, she could speak in a language of which she was supposed to be ignorant, the waiters having been rewarded for their discretion in advance.

"Are ya enjoyin' that teacake there, yer highness?"

Noor raised her eyes from the morsel in her fingers, dabbed her mouth, and swallowed.

"We're alone, Seamus," she said. "When we're alone, it's Lady-Jane."

Lady-Jane. As regal as the name sounded, to him, it was impossible. At the very least, using such a name was disrespectful to the efforts of his master.

For months, he had watched as Professor Herrmann worked on her every aspect, transforming her from a harlot and savage into a consort fit for a prince. If she slouched, he made her walk about with a book on her head. If she swore, he replaced her oaths with the proper expressions for a woman of her station so that "shit" became "oh, bother" and "fuck a duck" transformed into "dear me." *Lady-Jane?* No. She was a princess to him now, and fit to be addressed only as such.

"I'm sorry, ma'am," Seamus said. "It's just that I haven't been alone with ya often enough to get used to either name."

Lady-Jane laughed. "Not *enough?* More like constantly. Hardly a day goes by these days that Alex doesn't figure a way to throw us together. *Seamus, take the princess for her fitting. Seamus, the princess looks a bit peaked. Tomorrow, you'll take her riding in the park. You know, Seamus, I can't make it to dinner on Wednesday, so will you accompany her highness to Sherry's? There's a good fellow.* Well, he doesn't fool me at all, Irish. If there's one thing a whore can do, it's smell pussy."

Dowie was shocked by her words but also aroused by her earthiness. The refined setting combined with the salt of her tongue excited him perhaps even more than the times he had seen her backstage struggling with a costume or veil, naked and perfect.

"Then ya believe there's another woman?"

"Probably more than one. Normally, I wouldn't give a damn. I've learned enough about men to know that they'll go to a lot of corners to find what they're looking for. Take that stuck-up tart, Caroline Carstairs. I only had to shake her hand to know she was Alex's twist. But she's no threat. Her family is broke—what they call 'land-poor' over here—and her whole clan butters their bread from the tub of that addled old cock she married. She's not going anywhere. If she has some fun with Alex, well, that's all it is.

But Miss Adelaide—she's another story. "

Seamus's heart leapt up and he felt a shiver through his limbs.

"Do ya believe the master's in love wit' her?"

Her laugh went right through him. "I'm not sure the Great Herrmann can love anyone after he's done with himself. No, it's her that's in love with him. He's got her bamboozled, hypnotized. Or maybe she just gets hot because he's mine. Plenty of girls like that in the world."

Seamus felt an ache in his back teeth. "Well, I imagine he's got great gratitude to ya, miss. You bein' in the act has brought in bigger flocks than we've ever had. A decent man might think to stay away from another woman in thanks for that."

Noor laughed again. "That's the way you *would* think, good Catholic boy. No, I can smell her all over him: that soft perfume and dancer's sweat. When he's talking to reporters, when he's tinkering with his tricks, even when he takes me at night, I can smell her."

Seamus felt his face go red. It was not only her nearness that tortured him but the casual sensuality with which she spoke of her rival's scent.

"What will you do?" he asked her.

Princess Noor placed her hands on the table and leaned forward. Her face became soft—soft as it was whenever Alexander entered a room. He was astonished. She was giving that softness to him.

"Whatever it is, I can't do it alone," she said. "Alex is far too clever. I must have help. Will you help me?"

Her right hand slipped into his, gripping it gently. Her left reached beneath the table, brushed aside the white damask, and took hold of him. His eyes went wide with shock. How could any woman be so brazen and so beautiful? He felt his mouth slowly open.

"Alex trusts you more than anyone on earth," she said, her eyes liquid. "But you are also *my* friend. Ever since I've been with Alex you've done everything for me. Driven me everywhere, run my errands, made sure I was safe and warm. I've never really rewarded you for that. Maybe I'm too hard a slut to be grateful."

Her gaze held him like a mouse before a cobra. His throat closed and his scalp felt pierced by needles. Under the table her grip tightened and he could feel her begin a gentle slide.

"You know I can never give up Alex. I love him. I need his money and his name. But oh, my lovely Irish, there is no reason I can't love you, too—if that is what I need to do. Will you help me do what I need to do?"

His eyes closed and his neck bowed. She released her hand from his and brought it to his chin. Gently, she lifted his head and her eyes pierced him.

"Will you help me do what I need to do?"

Seamus sighed. He closed his eyes and nodded. Lady-Jane shook him by the chin and made him meet her eyes again.

"Yes," he said. "Yes."

The princess released him and returned her hand to the table. Embarrassed, he tried to look away but she gripped his chin hard between finger and thumb and pulled his face back toward her.

"Will you help me do what I need to do?"

"Yes."

"Again."

"Yes. Yes."

She motioned for the waiter and paid the bill. They rose and left the restaurant. When they arrived back at the apartments, they were empty, as she knew they would be. Alex and Adelaide were gone. Not even the servants were present.

His bed was narrow but it served. He didn't need to tell her he had little experience of women. His clumsiness spoke to that. He even believed her when she told him that kissing was old-fashioned and unnecessary. She was gentle with him, tender. His needs became hers. In the days and weeks ahead, she would transform him from virgin to lover—and from lover to slave.

⌦◈⌫

Her head upon his chest, Adelaide Scarcez inhaled Alexander Herrmann.

As he slept, she pulled the clean, warm sheets up high, enjoying the identity of each scent.

Soap—plain lye and tallow, nothing fancy.

Mustache wax—essence of bees, rose water, the bergamot of Earl Grey tea, thyme, lampblack.

Cologne—flowers, bay laurel, ginger, lemon and an alcohol like fine gin.

Beneath all this lay his own smell: something akin to a fresh piecrust—salt and yeast and then all of the odors of her body so recently melded with his. Her nose read him as male and female, man and animal, mortal and immortal.

Given his reputation, Adelaide should not have been surprised to find herself in his bed; Alex was well known to women throughout Britain and the continent. Some were noble like Lady Caroline, slumming in the show business or curious to see if his magic extended beyond the stage. Others were mere members of the chorus or audience or aspiring actresses encouraged by agents or ambitious mothers. As his primary companion, Princess Noor had put a stop to most of these liaisons and Alex seemed less chagrined than relieved. After all, for an artist, time spent with the ladies was time unspent on improving the act; and the princess seemed more than prepared to meet his romantic needs for both quality and quantity.

Adelaide had never intended to compete with this female throng, nor had she intended to supplant the tough little Indian who had already staked her claim. In the end, it seemed an accident, a coincidence—born not of her need for love, but his for grace and motion. As Alex would later say, he fell in love with her "feet first."

It was late afternoon at the Egyptian, ten days before opening night. The assistants had all left. The crew had gone to dinner and the princess had gone back to their apartments to rest. Alexander visited the box office to ask about the previous night's receipts and then walked back through the house to retrieve his coat from the dressing room.

He walked through the double doors of the auditorium. It was deserted and silent, except for a faint knocking sound from backstage, smooth and rhythmic. Sensing something amiss, he stepped behind a large marble pillar at the end of the parquet circle.

From the left hand wings, he saw a small, lithe figure emerge *en pointe*. She was in street dress save for her shoes, which she had cast off by the footlights. Barefoot, the woman whirled across the stage in a series of perfect *pirouettes*. She spun in and out of the shadows like a wraith, seeming to appear and disappear like one of his illusions. During a high leap, her tight *chignon* came undone, allowing the red hair to trace her motion. At center stage she stopped without so much as a wobble and flew into a textbook *arabesque*, her right leg firmly planted on the boards, her left extended behind her until she formed a perfect "T." Slowly she lifted the leg higher until she was bent like a seesaw. Raising her arms in a supple arc, she snapped herself straight and descended into a *grande plié.*

Hidden behind the pillar, Alexander watched as she inhabited every part of the stage, her movements quick and precise: an ideal *pas de poisson*, a flawless *Grand rond de jambe,* and a *tours en l'air* the like of which he had seen executed only by a man. Then her motion became too swift for him to separate its parts and he simply absorbed her—a ferocious spirit combining both Muse and Fury.

From that afternoon, Alex kept a daily appointment with the pillar.

She didn't always appear. There were days when he would wait as long as an hour before quitting his post. Sometimes she would only perform a dreamy series of steps lasting a few minutes, other times she would whirl and lash, stepping high, bending low, whipping her head in ways no proper dancer would condone.

The dances changed him toward her. As she became more alluring to him, more enchanted, he became more tender. He asked her to please call him by his given name. He tripped over words in her presence and became more tongue-tied the closer she was. When he sent the princess her weekly bouquet, he now included an arrangement for Adelaide as well; smaller but somehow more beautiful.

I will not encourage this, she thought. *I will not place myself between Alexander and Princess Noor and Compars. On that path there is no light— and no love between a spy and an infidel will make it brighter. I am the agent of a foreign power.*

And so she contented herself with the watching stranger.

From the beginning, she had sensed his presence in the theatre. Part of her wanted to run to the wings in embarrassment, but another part was overjoyed to be admired. At some moments, above her own breathing, she swore she could hear his, strung out in long sighs or coming short as before climax. She would deliberately tease him: moving slowly and sinuously or dying like the swan; then she would unleash the demon: a red and white whirlwind spending itself against a greater storm.

The night before his first performance, Alexander had not expected to see her. Adelaide had not appeared the afternoon before, and the stage was now crowded with the apparatus necessary to perform his act: tables and chairs, a mummy case, bottles and small props, and palms for decoration. Still, he felt compelled to revisit the pillar. For five, ten, fifteen minutes he waited, trying to control his breathing.

Then he heard a rustle at stage left—and she appeared from the dark.

Her face was painted like a hieroglyph: the lips a red-orange slash, the eyes lined with strokes of black that shaped them into almonds. The flaming hair was dressed in beads, and she wore a short vest of green silk and gold coins. She coiled and uncoiled like a fakir's cobra and then vanished behind the mummy case. When she reemerged, he could see her bare belly, as white as Noor's was brown, twisting even as she whirled behind a curtain. Jumping into the light, she leaped to center stage, raised her foot above her head, and caught it in her fist—more brazen in this one action than women whose bodies he had known naked and deep.

She saw him come down the aisle but did not stop. It was through a haze of pleasure that she met him amid all that had brought him triumph. When he picked her up, she seemed light even to herself; and when he lay her down on the boards, she appeared to him delicate enough to break. She begged him to do as he wished and asked only that his eyes never leave hers; and they did not—until the moment they closed on their own.

Now as she watched him sleep, she counted again the reasons she should not be here: her betrayal, Princess Noor, the possible exposure of all they had worked for, Compars's threats of disgrace and prison.

She listened to his breathing a while, then rose up on her elbow and looked into his face. The right side of the carefully waxed mustache was bent and pointed straight into the air.

Adelaide smiled and gently placed her head back on his chest. From now until they returned to the world, she would be content to breathe him in; and if an end should come to her joy, she would endure it as she had since a girl. Her life had always been different from happiness.

32

J OHN NEVIL MASKELYNE HAD NEVER KNOWN SUCH PUBLICITY.
In the short time he had been producing his new product, it had
become both a practical sensation and the object of controversy.

The *Times* had opined in an editorial:

> The well-known magician, Mr. John N. Maskelyne, has pro-
> duced what can actually be called a miracle. Far better than a
> mere rabbit from a hat, Mr. Maskelyne has given Londoners
> a sanitary and convenient source of relief for only a penny.
> Unlike some, we see no reason why this enterprising young
> man should not profit from such an excellent idea—especially
> when those not in possession of the wherewithal to utilize

his invention will likely take their ease where they always have: in our parks and on our streets.

The *Telegraph*, however, had a different opinion:

Mr. Maskelyne's contraption is designed to extract payment from the most basic of human functions. What next, we wonder? A tariff on the breathing of air? A tax on the drinking of water? The penny toilet is only the latest manifestation of a British business culture in thrall to profit and choked with greed. Have we really become so avaricious that we would now deny a working-man his moment of evacuation until he has first searched his pockets for the penny once reserved to buy his children's bread?

As with most public disputes, the attention the various opinions gave to the contrivance only brought it more success. With each pub and restaurant sharing in the *largesse*, Maskelyne had needed to add a second shift and double his number of workers to meet demand. One hotel had ordered ten of the machines, asking if the wooden door of the kiosk could be painted in a pleasing Mediterranean tableau "for the aesthetic appreciation of the ladies."

So great was the shop's din that Adelaide Scarcez found it necessary to place her hands over her ears. Everywhere she looked, there was activity: men pouring steel into molds; boys seated at workbenches filing excess metal from plates and bolts; machinists cutting and calibrating tiny gears. In the center of it all stood a small, thin man in shirtsleeves, calling to this man and that. He seemed to Adelaide less a manager than a sort of policeman charged with the direction of traffic. Unable to attract his attention through the noise, Adelaide waved continuously until he caught sight of her.

Nodding vigorously, the slight man motioned her to join him in a large room off the main shop. It was far quieter and virtually deserted, but much work took place here as well. Scattered about the worktables and pinned to the walls were drawings large and small, mostly depicting large stage illusions. Some were new variations on old tricks, others she had never seen before. All around the floor sat large constructions covered by blankets and tarpaulins.

"Good afternoon," the slight man said with a courtly bow. "I am John Nevil Maskelyne. I believe I have the pleasure of addressing Miss Scarcez."

"I am Adelaide Scarcez."

"A pleasure, Miss Scarcez. I hope you won't mind meeting in the intimacy of my private laboratory, but I hardly think the business you have here today is worth the destruction of your hearing."

"Thank you, Mr. Maskelyne. Your thoughtfulness is much appreciated. How do you and your men stand it?"

"We manage. Cotton balls. Gin. But I suspect that you will want me to take you to Professor Herrmann now, Miss Scarcez."

"Yes, Mr. Maskelyne. For better or worse, it is he with whom I have my appointment."

Maskelyne looked like a man about to introduce a bird to a cat. "I shall take you to him, then. But please know that if Professor Herrmann should attempt anything inappropriate toward you, you need only to cry out and help will come immediately. I am sorry if any friendship you feel for him causes you to be offended by this offer, but it is made solely for your protection."

Adelaide smiled. "Be of good cheer, Mr. Maskelyne. Your willingness to offer me your protection only shows that you are well familiar with the character of our mutual friend. But rest assured, Herr Docktor's interest in me is purely professional—as I fear it is in you as well."

"Such mischievous tongues," a deep voice said, "and from such charming young people."

Compars Herrmann emerged from a side door. He was as erect as ever, as arrogant in stride and manner. But in the month since Adelaide had seen him, he seemed to have changed in a way that moved her from disdain to horror. There was now a droop to his eyes; they seemed more wrinkled beneath, the red of the lower rim exposed below the eyeball. The lips had taken on a kind of voluptuousness, a thickness and redness like those of a stage vampire. Yet his entire being seemed to radiate with a new happiness. Before, when she had met with him, he had seemed evil only by necessity. Now she feared he had made wickedness a choice, a joy in which to revel.

"Miss Scarcez, you are looking wonderfully well. Apparently the world of intrigue agrees with you."

"Herr Docktor, I imagine you have summoned me not to offer compliments, but to report on the activities of your brother."

Compars took several steps toward her. His *eau de cologne* smelled of sweetness and decay, like a rotting orange.

"You see, Maskelyne, how she treats her benefactor? Here I try to help her as I have helped you and what do I get from the two of you? Sour faces! I have never understood how the mere act of driving a hard bargain should cause such resentment. We are all adults here. Why can we not be friends?"

"I am thoroughly prepared to report to you everything you have requested," Adelaide said. "I believe this is the nature of the bargain we have made, and I will uphold my end of it."

Compars reached into his coat and retrieved a leather cigar case. He offered it to Maskelyne, who refused, and then plucked a long cheroot from its interior.

"Please forgive me, Maskelyne. I do not like to order a man about in his own house; but as the nature of the communication between

Miss Scarcez and me is of a most private nature, I must request that you withdraw."

Maskelyne looked at Adelaide. "I will do so only if Miss Scarcez gives me leave. Otherwise, I refuse to leave her alone with a bounder whom I would put nothing past. And know this, Professor: I will take my ruin gladly if it means preserving this woman's honor."

Compars's face was at first impassive; then he broke in to peals of laughter.

"I applaud you for your gallantry, young Jack. It is a fine thing to see that chivalry still exists in this benighted age. But please be assured that no harm will come to Miss Scarcez. I am well cared for in the areas which seem to concern you, being a member of a few exclusive gentlemen's clubs both here and on the Continent. Let me also add that there are several young ladies with whom I have made similar arrangements as with Miss Adelaide, only instead of quid and shillings, the nature of their payment serves to, shall we say, meet my *romantic* needs. Perhaps I might introduce you to several of them, as some of their agreements stipulate the occasional entertainment of my friends."

Adelaide shivered in disgust. "Please, Mr. Maskelyne. Have no concern for my safety. I have taken care of myself since age twelve. And if for any reason the Professor decides to break his pledge, I shall not hesitate to call upon you and your men."

Maskelyne stared at Compars, who grinned back at him. He noticed that since their last meeting, a tooth had rotted out of the magician's mouth.

"I shall be alert," he said. He bowed to Adelaide and withdrew.

Compars looked after him. "Fine young fellow, that Jack. All that racket outside is his penny toilet in production. It's already on its way to making him a wealthy man. Couldn't have done it without me. But here, Miss Scarcez! Why not marry him? He is attractive and gallant and as inventive a young magician as you will ever see. I daresay on occasion his tricks have even made me envious. And because I have brought you two together I would be only too glad to personally arrange the wedding breakfast if you would permit me the honor."

Adelaide suppressed her queasiness. "Thank you," she said. "Shall I deliver my report now?"

"By all means."

Adelaide reached into her leather portfolio and removed a matching notebook. For the next half-hour, she related information she had "learned" about Alexander. Most listeners would have found them small and trivial, but Compars was enraptured at every tiny change and detail: how his brother had not only added the Inexhaustible Bottle to the act, but changed the trick by the addition of the dove; how Alex had begun to ad-lib during the Floating Boy, making remarks individual to each audience volunteer. And then there was the incorporation of more modern music, even the commissioning of several new pieces from the young Mr. Edward Elgar, a church organist with little training but a fine harmonious ear. Attention to such trifles also allowed her to omit the most salient facts: that Princess Noor-Al-Haya was in reality a plains Indian; that his brother had once again resumed work on the substitution trunk; and that she and Alexander had made profoundly moving love only a few moments before she began preparing herself for this interview.

Throughout the recitation, she made constant but subtle comparisons between Alexander and Compars, always placing the elder brother in the brighter light. In the show business, she had encountered enough egotists to know when to use flattery against vanity; and it seemed to work on no one so well as the Great Herrmann.

When she closed her notebook, Compars smiled and slapped his palms together in polite applause.

"Excellent. Really, Miss Scarcez, I congratulate myself for choosing you for this mission. There are any number of girls who have pasts that they would wish to hide; but you are the one in all the world for this job. And since I have taken you so very much into my confidence, I feel that now you should know the next phase of my plan."

Compars snapped his fingers and from behind one of the tarpaulins, two assistants emerged. One was short and swarthy and wore a blue turban wrapped in the manner of the *Sufi*. The other was taller, Aryan by look, and bore the kind of facial scar obtained during duels at Heidelberg. Without a word, the two men removed the large cloth from its position, revealing an oversized but otherwise ordinary steamer trunk.

Compars motioned to his men. "Proceed."

Swiftly, the shorter man opened the trunk and stepped inside as the taller pulled a gigantic Royal Mail bag up and over him. The scarred man closed the bag with a leather strap, secured it with a thick padlock, and snapped the top of the trunk closed. Compars stepped forward and handed the Aryan a series of smaller padlocks. He placed them in slots around the lid and keyed each one closed; then he leaped atop the trunk. Compars rolled a large silk screen in front of both man and trunk, concealing all from view.

"It is inventions like this that are the reason I say you should seriously consider matrimony with young Maskelyne. Though I now own it, it is his creation and a tribute to his genius. I had originally bought the trick to hide it—to conceal it so that my brother would never know that such an apparatus was possible."

Compars strode from one side of the silk to the other, flaring his arms in his best theatrical manner. He ran his hand down the screen's surface as if caressing a longed-for lover with whom he had finally been reunited.

"But I have changed my mind! In a few weeks' time, the good Lord willing, Mr. Maskelyne's invention shall become the centerpiece of a great new act: the primary attraction in the triumphant return to the stage of the *true* Great Herrmann. As you will soon see, it is every-thing my little *Sasha* ever dreamed of."

Adelaide's eyes grew wide as the realization of what she was witnessing crept over her. Behind the curtain, she could hear bangs and rustles.

"Are you ready back there?" Compars called out.

"*Jawohl*, Herr Docktor."

"*Sehr gut*," Compars cried. "*Eins. Zwei. DREI!*"

The magician lunged forward and pulled the big silk away. Standing atop the trunk, his turban slightly askew, was the little man who had been locked in the bag. He leaped to the floor, unkeyed the locks, and sprang the trunk's top. From inside, the big bag rose like a comi-cally animated prop. The little man jumped onto a short stool behind the trunk and opened the mailbag's lock. As the bag dropped down, Adelaide could see a figure emerge.

It was the man with the scar.

Compars applauded again. "*Ausgezeichnet, meine Herren*. Obviously, we need to make it quicker, and I admit that Samir and Gerhardt have less than optimal stage presence; but when it is ready and my old assistant comes from the States to perform it with me, it shall be perfection. The original Substitution Trunk of the *original* Great Herrmann."

Compars gestured to the two assistants to cover the trunk.

"It will likely be less than a month until my first performance and only a few weeks before the handbills appear on every post and wall in London. Tell me, did the illusion amaze you?"

Adelaide's head was on fire. Her mouth was dry and her eyes began to tear with hatred; but she knew that if ever there was a moment to flatter a bastard, this was the one.

"It was the kind of thrill that one expects from the Herr Doctor."

Smiling, Compars bowed and then walked to the door. He picked up a wrench from a workbench and banged on the jamb. In moments, John Maskelyne and three of his men rushed through the laboratory door. One of them clutched a hammer.

"My dear Jack, my business with Miss Scarcez is concluded. I ask that you now escort her back through that rat's maze you call your headquarters, as I am sure it would take a better magician than I to find the way. But before you leave, allow me to comment upon what a handsome couple you make. I have already informed Miss Adelaide that you should propose to her. But alas—who can tell young people anything these days?"

John Nevil flushed bright red. Adelaide bowed stiffly to Compars and together, she and Maskelyne turned and walked back to the clamorous shop, through the twisting corridors and into the sun of early June.

"Miss Scarcez," said Maskelyne, "did he show you my illusion?"

"Yes, Mr. Maskelyne, he did."

"I had always hoped that I would make a great success of it. But now, it seems that success will be enjoyed by another man."

Adelaide smiled into his troubled face. "If my humble opinion soothes you at all, Mr. Maskelyne, I found your creation most astounding—the finest piece of magic I have ever seen. But now I must urge you to take heart. We may yet find a way to foil the plans of this parasite that has eaten into our lives."

"I fear that is impossible. As one does to the Devil, I owe my soul to Compars Herrmann—and I imagine that he holds you in his grasp as well—and God only knows how many others."

Adelaide took Maskelyne's hands in hers. "Still, there may be hope," she said. "I plan to reach into my arsenal and retrieve an old weapon. I just hope that I'll recognize it, as it has been a long time since I've used it."

The young magician looked into her green eyes. Regardless of being the suggestion of a villain, the idea of a marriage proposal suddenly began to make sense to him.

"I beg you to take no rash action, Miss Adelaide. He has told me time and again that if he should so much as suffer the sting of a bumblebee, his solicitors will ruin me and anyone else who crosses him."

Adelaide held his hand tighter. "Please don't worry, my new friend. I only fantasize about murder, I do not contemplate it. Still this weapon lies at my disposal; and if I am to aid the one I love as well as a man as fine as yourself, then use it I shall."

"But what is this amazing weapon?" Maskelyne asked.

Adelaide let his hands go and hailed a passing hansom.

"The truth, John Nevil," she said, waving good-bye. "The truth."

33

B Y THE TIME HE HAD BOARDED THE *Berengaria* FOR England, Prophet John McGarrigle was convinced that joining Julius Meyer on his trip across the sea was a mistake.

It was of course, his own fault. He had argued with the boy for hours to be allowed to go. *I deserve this, you little bastard. I've spent the past year strangled in a collar and tie makin' money for you and that whoremaster brother of yours. Anybody else'd been in charge, they'd have robbed you blind as a mole. Besides, you need a top hand, a man to see things through, so to speak. Listen, if I can't make this little visit, guess I'll quit—take my earnings and retire to the Cheese.*

The voyage had been a nightmare, and the prediction of disaster that visited him mid-ocean made it worse. The prophet was tasked with little to do besides ride herd on the seasick and homesick Indians. The food was inedible, they complained—too spicy or too bland; the beds were too soft; the whole country smelled of spoiled fruit and horse excrement; they couldn't see the sky through all the fog. McGarrigle spoke enough Ponca to tell them to shut up and act like men and that they would soon be back on the big boat bound for home. This only caused them to weep and wail at the prospect of another twelve days of nausea. To mollify them, he stated that while one could get sick on the way *to* England, it was impossible to become ill on the way *back*. The Indians were incredulous. They may have respected the gray man as a shaman, but such status did not diminish his reputation as a liar.

London's crippling expense was another bother. Yes, the whiskey was better here, especially what they called "malts" from Scotland and Ireland; but each shot cost the American equivalent of a half-dollar. At such prices, the prophet soon came to realize why so many Britishers drank beer. He found the women pricey, too. Any prostitute without visible sores cost anywhere from two crowns to a pound: prices that would have kept him in bed three days with Polly Ranstead or No Nipple Nancy.

Deprived of honest work and recreation, he begged Alexander for work.

"I'll sweep up," he said. "I'll clean the toilets with my tongue. Just give me something to do." With Julius vouching for his honesty, Alexander had the prophet sign the usual confidentiality agreement making him "a member of the Great Herrmann Company (U.S.) subject to all confidences required under copyright law of the United States, United Kingdom and any such jurisdictions in which the EMPLOYER might find employment for said company."

"How's your hearing?" Alex asked.

"Wait a second," John said, "what's that sound?"

"Sound? I don't hear anything," Alex said.

"Well, I do. Guess it's better than yours."

Amused, Alexander informed the gray man that he was now the troupe's designated "acoustician," a job that consisted of roaming the house, searching for aural dead spots. If he couldn't hear the stage patter clearly, the prophet would yell "louder, young Alex!" After the first day, the job was essentially completed; but as the week went on, McGarrigle continued to wend his way through the seats in search of any location that might be a problem, eventually finding some obscure portion of the theatre in which to fall asleep.

A week before opening, John had actually found one problem area near the top of the first balcony. Duly informing Alexander of the difficulty, he settled into a seat and nodded off. By the time the scream awakened him, the theatre lights had dimmed and the rehearsal was over. He stood up and hurried down the aisle. From the balcony's edge, he could see two figures on the stage. Rubbing his eyes, he ascertained that they were both female: one was dark, the other lighter. They seemed evenly matched in height and weight.

The dark woman took the redhead by the bodice and hurled her hard into the side of the proscenium. Prophet John tried hard to make sense of the shouting, but soon remembered that he was in one of the dead spots he had found days before. He moved to the balcony's left, hoping to catch the words being said. Just before he gained the end of the row, he heard the dull thud of a body hurled to the floor. The dark one's words became clear as day.

"Fucking slut!"

The dark one straddled her enemy, grabbing her by the linen of her shirtwaist. Then she leaned in, placing her face close enough to the redhead to kiss her.

"I should bash you—scar you with these nails—but then Alex would know who messed up his whore and it would go hard with me. But know this. He's made me dance like a puppet and shut up like a mute. He's told the world I'm a wog and heathen—the enemy of every decent woman alive. I've lived with it, taken it all. Do you think that after all that, I would let a little fire cunt take him from me?"

Princess Noor let go of Adelaide's shirt and moved both hands up to either side of her face. She seized her hair and raising her head, bashed her head into the boards.

"You like that, little whore? Eh? Bruise to the back of the head don't show, eh? What Alex can't see won't hurt him, eh?"

Noor crashed Adelaide to the floor once again.

"I should kill you right now; but I'll give you one chance. Never see him again. Leave here now and never come back and I'll let you live. But show your face here to so much as catch the show, and you are a dead woman. Understand me?"

Adelaide could only moan. Furious, Noor again yanked the pale face toward her own.

"*Do you understand me?*"

Adelaide murmured something McGarrigle couldn't make out. Breathing heavily, the Princess released her, rose, and stomped from the stage. Prophet John made to cry for help but thought better of it. From what he knew of Lady-Jane Little Feather, a witness could enrage her toward a move that might end her rival's life. The gray man ran through the balcony and down a flight of back steps. When he reached the stage, he wondered if he shouldn't have sought help after all. Adelaide Scarcez couldn't have looked more dead if he had called out the Marines.

⬥

Julius Meyer looked down at the beautiful face crossed with pain. The pillow of the *chaise-longue* was stained with blood.

"I found her this way," John said. "Dressing room was closest, so I carried her in here. She's out, but breathin.'"

"And you say Lady-Jane did this?"

"Sure as you're a Jew. I tell you, I'm a man full-growed, and I wouldn't want to tangle up with that lynx."

For nearly an hour, Julius patted Adelaide's face with water. When at last her green eyes opened, she began to scream, struggling against Julius's hands as if her enemy still sat atop her chest.

"I'll go! I'll leave and never return!"

Julius held her arms and tried to calm her. "Please don't be afraid, Miss Adelaide. Princess Noor is gone. I am strong and here to help. No harm will come to you, I promise."

Adelaide appeared not to hear him. She pounded on his chest and arms and bellowed into his ear. It took all of his strength and help from the prophet to hold her fast. Then, with a sound like all air being drained from her lungs, she went limp against his shoulder. When she could breathe again, she burst into long, shaking sobs.

"Oh, Mr. Meyer," she cried, "I must go away. If I stay here even one more hour, the princess. . . ."

Julius held her tight. "Please, Miss Adelaide. You must trust me. You must tell me why she attacked you."

"Kill me. She says she will kill me."

"We have sent for the doctor," Julius said. "You must allow him to examine you when he arrives. You seem to have retained your faculties, but a concussion must be avoided at all costs."

Adelaide looked stricken. "My head throbs, Mr. Meyer, but I need no treatment. What I need is a way *out*. A way back to my former life—to that squalid but safe existence where I wasn't threatened by my love's paramour or his even more deranged brother."

"His brother? Compars? What has that devil said to you?"

It took some coaxing, even some threats, but soon the entire mad tale poured from Adelaide: the summons to meet with the old magician; the bullying and blackmail; her bogus employment; and the unexpected loss of her heart to Alexander, which had brought her to the terror of this time and place.

Absorbing her anguish, Julius wished he were more of an Indian— or at least as much of an Indian as "Princess Noor." If he gave Lady-Jane what she deserved, *she* would now be the one weeping in terror; if he paid Compars what he had earned for his cruelty, the world would soon wonder how such a famous man could vanish so suddenly and permanently.

"Miss Adelaide, I know you are frightened. And if your good woman's instincts say you have reason to be, they are likely correct. I beg you to listen to those instincts. The princess has killed before and, if she feels sufficiently wronged, will kill again."

Adelaide's eyes filled again with pain.

"Then what hope can there be for me?"

"There is an old saying. Knowledge is power. Now that we know what we fight, Mr. McGarrigle and I will protect you. You may have no fear of that."

"But even if you succeed at saving my life, Compars Herrmann says he will have me put me in jail; that I will be outcast, disgraced."

"We will defeat both the princess and the conjurer. But you must put yourself entirely in my hands."

Adelaide nodded and broke down again.

The doctor arrived, cleaned and dressed Adelaide's wound, and declared her injured but fit. He admonished her to rest and immediately report to him any incidence of double vision. Julius placed a ten-pound note in his hand, and he bade them both a good afternoon.

"Can we trust him?" Adelaide asked.

Julius smiled. "The good Doctor Ware is a physician, but also a creature of the theatre. He sees men's faces scratched by women not their wives, women's bellies swelled by men not their husbands, and wounds made by actors unanxious to be revealed as sodomites. No, even more than surgery or analgesic, the doctor's stock in trade is discretion; a single violation of that, and he is, as we Hebrews say, *michulah*: out of business."

Adelaide's hands were shaking. "You must understand that I had planned on confessing everything to Alex after next week's *debut*. He has been so busy and nervous that I didn't want to burden him until the opening was past. The princess says that if I so much as appear in the building, I will be destroyed. But how can I simply vanish without telling him of the deceit into which I was forced—not tell him that amid the lies, my love was the one truth?"

Julius took the trembling hands in his. "I cannot predict what my cousin's reaction will be—but tonight you shall go to Alexander and do as you planned—tell him all you have told me. Then you will vanish, but only from the sight of Princess Noor. And I guarantee you that the moment Alexander's show begins, you will not only be alive but indispensible."

34

NELSON A. MILES GRIPPED THE REINS AND HELD THE WHITE flag above his head. Bridge had always been his game; but with the bluff he would need today, he wished it had been poker.

He knew he was outnumbered. His scouts had returned late that morning to report the grim numbers; the renegades could easily overwhelm him. Miles thanked God Chased By Owls had not discovered this weakness; otherwise the tall brave would never have accepted his offer of a parley. Riding across the flat plain, the colonel rehearsed his words. This enemy was no fool. If he betrayed even the slightest sign of compromise, the smallest hint of fear, he would be annihilated.

That Chased By Owls could have so many fighters would have been unthinkable even a year ago. He had begun his terror with perhaps twenty troops, not a few of them boys and old men. His early raids had been bloody but practical, the killing confined to the amount necessary to take the supplies his party needed. A sack of flour might cost one life—a beef cow, two or three.

But as he continued his attacks, renegades from every corner of the territory had rushed to join him, eager to serve the warrior who defied the whites. Members of tribes that had been enemies a hundred years formed uneasy alliances in pursuit of plunder and vengeance. Chased By Owls welcomed all into his band, commanding the hated Pawnee as well as the friendly Omaha. For the warriors, it meant food and pride and the spoils of victory. For the chief, it meant the death of the invaders who had turned the Indian into a diseased mendicant beholden to his enemies for the bread in his mouth.

Then came the incident at Bradley.

As he rode toward the meeting point Miles recalled the first time he had seen the settlement. It had been little more than a collection of tents and lean-tos, struggling against an autumn wind and echoing with the sound of hammers on nails. By his second visit, Bradley had begun to show the signs of a proper town. The tents were giving way to houses. The shops had put up signs, and a primitive newspaper had begun circulation. Franklin Stoves arrived from Chicago, and women kept peddlers busy haggling over a yard of gingham or the weight of a stockpot. The citizens had even voted to build a school and advertised in Baltimore for a teacher. The young woman who accepted the position would forever be grateful that her wedding delayed her arrival.

Then, two days ago, Miles paid his third visit to Bradley.

Even the day after the incident, the smoke was overpowering. Every tent and building lay ruined, consumed by the fires Chased By Owls now employed as his primary weapon. The soldiers coughed and pulled their bandannas tight; their horses' hooves crunched over a carpet of fine black ash. Children as young as two were discovered alive in storm cellars; others crouched frozen in grief over the bodies of their dead parents. Miles's new adjutant spurred his horse and deserted when he came upon a woman hanging halfway out her kitchen window, her crowning glory stripped from her skull.

Now, Miles rode out alone toward a depression in the plain—the agreed-upon place of meeting. He stood there perhaps an hour, then he saw four riders approaching.

Their flesh and their horses were a riot of color and pattern. One man appeared to be Pawnee, his hair cut in the "roach" style—shaved on the sides and full on the top—the opposite of a scalping. The porcupine quill beadwork on the breastplates of two of the men indicated that they might be Winnebago, although trade among the renegades had probably rendered any uniqueness of costume moot. In this army, the Ponca wore the jewelry of the Lakota; and the Lakota carried the shields of the Otoe.

Still, there was no mistaking the man at the center.

He sat tall. His clothing was covered with the tiny figures of his enemies. His face was painted blue around the eyes and nose and stark white below. Around his head he wore an explosion of eagle feathers, not set in the formal manner of the war bonnet, but stuck into a mass that made his head appear as large as a buffalo's. His lips were stained blood-red. Even carrying a flag of truce, he looked like death come calling.

Leaving two of his companions, he bade one follow him. Together they galloped to the spot where Miles stood waiting.

"This is Big Both Ways," he said. "He will say my words for me."

Miles looked amused. "I thought Half Horse spoke for Chased By Owls."

The tall brave smiled back. "I wished to be understood."

The colonel shook his head and laughed. "A wise policy."

"Apache Killer has aged much since our last meeting. Perhaps war no longer sits well with him—or maybe he is not getting enough attention from a woman. A man is like a horse, you know. If he is not ridden well and often, he pulls up lame."

"Chased By Owls is remarkably the same," Miles said. "He looks very much as he did the day I drove him across the Dismal River."

Chased By Owls grinned. "I remember that battle. For instance, I recall that after that night, there were far fewer bluecoats than had awoken that morning. As to my vigor, I am nourished by the good food so generously provided by your soldiers and settlers and heartened by the sight of their blood on my land and their hair on my lance."

Miles looked into the death-mask face. Moving slowly, he reached into a leather pouch and produced a document bearing the seal of the United States Senate.

"I have been sent today not to kill Chased By Owls or his men, but as a messenger of the president. He wishes to make a trade with Chased By Owls that he hopes will bring peace to both our peoples. I am charged to tell you the terms of this accommodation. Will Chased By Owls listen?"

"Apache Killer has his orders and I am a general. It would be against all rules of this parley not to allow him to carry them out. Only, my friend, please don't read them. It grows cold and there are only so many hours in a day."

"Very well," Miles said. "I shall summarize. As of the signing of this document, the government of the United States provides Chief Chased By Owls an amnesty for him and all of his men. The bounty placed upon your heads will be removed. The death sentences called for over previous infractions will be lifted. In return, you and your followers will surrender any and all weapons, down to the last tomahawk. You will then be granted safe passage under the protection of the United

States Army to the Quapaw reservation in the Oklahoma territory. There, you will join other tribes and work the land. Land and tools will be provided and all hostilities will cease."

Chased By Owls rested his flag across the pommel of his saddle. "Is that all the paper says?"

Miles nodded.

"I appreciate that Apache Killer has come with this treaty. I know that in the course of killing many Indians he has become sympathetic to us. But like Chased By Owls, Apache Killer is a soldier. To do his duty he must have pride in his army and honor in his life. So tell me—what would he do if strangers came to his house and told him that it was now their house? What would he do if these strangers told him that he could stay on—but only as a slave in the cellar or a dog in the backyard? Would Apache Killer say yes to such a bargain, or would he take up his fine sword and hack the strangers in two?"

"To fight is a fine thing," Miles said. "But Chased By Owls cannot fight alone and forever. Whether he or I like it, the whites will keep coming. More soldiers will come with them. Chased By Owls will watch his brave men die and in the end will die himself."

"Better a corpse that killed a hundred whites than a farmer. Better dead than to hear your storytellers say that every Indian lay down and offered his ass to the white man. A thousand years from now, Chased By Owls wants there to be at least one good answer for the child who asks, *did none of them fight back?*"

Miles leaned forward in his saddle.

"When Standing Bear was on trial there were those among the whites who used you as a demon to terrify their fellows. They said that your chief must be sent to prison lest he go renegade as well—and that your bloodlust is the true nature of the Indian."

The tall brave's smile exploded into laughter.

"Chased By Owls thanks Apache Killer for his compliment. I *am* a demon. I have worked night and day to become one. As for Standing Bear, he may as well be a white man; only one of you could be so craven, so attached to this temporary earth. So I say let a white be tried in a white court. The judgment that awaits him in the next world will be far worse than anything you devils could impose in this one."

Miles raised his flag above his head and clutched the reins of his horse. "I will inform my superiors of your refusal," he said. "I will tell them Chased By Owls would rather die than live to see his children grown. This will, of course, make up their minds for them. They will hunt you down—you and every man who offers you allegiance."

Chased By Owls's smile disappeared.

"Good! Tell them we welcome death—theirs as well as our own. Tell them we wish to meet the *Wakanda* as soon as possible and are happy to send them to the Man Nailed To A Tree. Tell them that they will see more fire from me on Earth than there is in their bible's hell. And tell them I am waiting. Tell them that!"

The tall brave and his interpreter spurred their ponies in a wide circle and galloped hard back toward their camp, screaming. Miles looked after them until they disappeared into a copse of stunted trees, then turned his horse around and rode for his men. Tonight he would call retreat and they would try to make Kearney before they were overwhelmed.

In his mind, Nelson Miles saw the valley that had once cradled the settlement of Bradley. He could not see the town or camp that lay beneath the rise, only an angry red glow rising from it. As he dug his spurs into his mount, the picture multiplied in his brain until an entire civilization was ablaze in a fire of hatred. He kicked the mare again and again, but it was no use. Tonight, it seemed his horse could run a million miles and never reach home.

35

I SADOR HAMERSCHMIDT FIRST ARRIVED IN LONDON IN September of 1835. He carried one pound and ten shillings, a tourist visa, and the dream to be an artist—something impossible back in Tarnopol, the provincial capital of the region known as Galicia in Austria-Hungary.

He spent those first days trudging the city's Jewish quarter, going door to door asking for work. *Employ me, landsman,* he had begged. *I will stoke fires, black boots, pluck chickens, deliver any and all things.* Some of the merchants were sympathetic, but had nothing for him; even more instantly banished the boy from their shops. Galicians were seen among many of their co-religionists as little better than gypsies—fools and knaves not to but trusted. *Go away,* they screamed. *There is no place here for a thieving Galicianer! We left to get away from you! Go back and steal horses!*

Isador's first weeks in London were spent sleeping in the doorways of the East End and resorting to the behavior of which the *Litvaks* and *Polacks* and *Daytchers* had accused him. He stole enough to eat: an apple, a bottle of milk from a doorstep, a loaf of bread delivered too early to a restaurant.

Without work, he wandered. Every day he would rise from wherever he had slept and explore the strange new city. The new sights took his mind off his hunger and gave him visions of the pictures he would paint someday; besides, it was now November, and the long walks kept him warm.

One sunny afternoon, Isador wandered into the Bloomsbury district, a wealthier section of town than any he had yet seen. Ladies and gentlemen of the neighborhood floated past him in their high hats and parasols. As he made his way down Guilford Street, he stayed close to the walls of buildings, hoping to become a less visible target for the police.

At Southampton Row, he crossed to Russell Square. As he turned toward a series of low benches, he saw a knot of people pointing and smiling at something beyond his vision. He walked around to the far left of the crowd and looked down at the pavement.

He was amazed by what he saw.

A small, neatly dressed man in a dull topper and checked trousers lay on his hands and knees, a thick piece of chalk in his hand. Beneath him was a huge drawing of a race track: crowds in the stands, touts taking bets, proud thoroughbreds galloping toward the finish line. As Isador watched, the little artist busily filled in the sky, creating a cloudless block of blue. The onlookers nodded and shouted their approval at his work, suggesting he add some yellow to a jockey's silks or red to the petals of a rose. At the top corner of the big creation sat a small leather box with the words "much obliged" written on it. As Isador looked on, members of the public dropped pennies into the box, sometimes two or even three at a time.

The next day, he returned to Bloomsbury with ten pieces of colored chalk he had bought for tuppence and a cardboard box rescued from a rubbish heap. He did not know what the words meant, but he wrote "much obliged" upon it. Finding a spot in the Conduit Fields near the Foundling Hospital, he began a drawing of a farm. By lunchtime, there was a barn, a windmill, and dozens of animals and birds. He managed to attract a small crowd and went back to his doorway that night with near eleven shillings. The next day, he drew a country fair—and a larger crowd—and fifteen shillings; the day after that, a joyous wedding party with bride, groom, vicar and a dozen attendants. This time, he earned eighteen shillings. Within a week, Isador had earned more than four pounds, rented a room, and bought a suit of clothes in keeping with his rising station.

His drawings drew regular spectators, but soon Isador began to notice that one patron returned nearly every day. The man was bearded and well dressed, wearing a bright silver waistcoat with a gold fob and a hat of the finest American beaver. The stranger watched his progress intently and then left after depositing thruppence in his box. Isador wanted to ask the man about his interest and generosity, but the words he had learned in English amounted to little more than "yes," "no," "thank you," and "tea."

After about a month, the man finally approached him.

"*Landsman?*" he said. "*Redstu Yiddish?*"

Isador grinned. "*Yo. Ich redn Yiddish.*"

The stranger smiled back. "*Gut!* I am very happy that we can speak together."

"But how did you know I was a Jew?" Isador asked.

"You mumble as you work," the man said. "And anyway, one *Galicianer* can always recognize another. I must tell you that your chalk drawings are the finest of any I have seen in London. I am especially impressed with your excellent lettering and calligraphy. The inscription you created for Westminster Abbey is a fair copy of the original. This is truly a rare skill—one worth far more than a sidewalk art monger can bring in. How'd you like to make some real money by your talent?"

Thus began Isador Hamerschmidt's illustrious career as Britain's greatest forger.

The stranger, whose name was Kristol, brought the young man to a large loft in Soho, where other young men sat at tables elbow to elbow, copying documents: wills; contracts; estate records; property settlements and indentures of all kinds in a dozen languages. After a short training period, Isador quickly distinguished himself as one of the operation's finest. By the time he had been in the business a year, he had successfully falsified a royal land grant, a certificate of medical graduation, and a page from a "medieval" Hebrew Bible that sold at auction for a thousand pounds. He was also able to create for himself the Resident Alien visa and work papers that allowed him to remain in the kingdom of Victoria.

At night after work, Isador attended English and elocution lessons. On Sundays, he received instructions in etiquette from a Madame Mayakovsky, who specialized in helping immigrants learn the manners and mores of their new land.

Within two years, his accent had been trained away; within three, he had taken on the good British name of Ivor Hammersmith and opened an exclusive shop in Knightsbridge, offering rare prints and drawings on the first floor and the finest in false documents on the second. For nearly thirty years, he served both constituencies with distinction. He married the daughter of a prominent surgeon named Barrymore in a ceremony at St. Paul's (his forged baptismal certificate was a wedding gift from Kristol), and both of his sons attended Cambridge, where one read mathematics, the other law.

Now, on a fine day in September, the bell above the shop door rang, and a young sales clerk rose to meet the customer. The man was tall and bearded, dressed all in dark blue and carrying a leather portfolio. As had been prearranged, the clerk led him through a cluttered back office filled with prints large and small. When they came to an ornate oak door, the clerk opened it, bowed, and announced the visitor.

"Mr. Alexander Herrmann, sir."

Smiling, Ivor Hammersmith rose to greet his new patron. Over the past three decades, the *artiste* had gone from a gaunt refugee to a man of substance, carrying just enough excess to inspire confidence in his success. His suit was of a rich, heavy gabardine, and a pair of golden pince-nez hung from a chain about his neck.

"This is indeed an honor, Professor Herrmann," Hammersmith said. "I have lost count of the number of times I have enjoyed the marvelous phenomena that you so effortlessly create. In fact, I daresay I am even old enough to have seen your brother before you. Pray be seated."

"Thank you," Alexander said. "I must also compliment you on the excellent business you have built here. I have ordered many a fine print from Hammersmith for my homes in America. My guests often remark upon them with appreciation and, I am delighted to say, a little jealousy."

Hammersmith chuckled. "That is a reaction we always appreciate." He reached into the center drawer of his desk and pulled out a large writing tablet.

"And now, what wonders can Hammersmith & Company work for the great magician today?"

Alexander leaned forward in his chair. "I am in rather urgent need of a passport."

"I see. For yourself, or someone else?"

"No, in this case, for a young lady who came into this country as one person and must, of necessity, leave as another."

"I understand. Would you be so kind as to provide me with the name by which the lady now goes?"

"I am afraid the spelling may prove both unusual and difficult," Alexander said, "but she is currently known as Her Royal Highness Princess Noor-Al-Haya."

Hammersmith's pen came to a dead stop above the cream-colored paper.

"Of course. Who has not heard of the exotic princess? Then am I to understand that your celebrated assistant wishes something by which she may travel incognito?"

Alex's face darkened. "Unfortunately, my dear Hammersmith, her highness's wishes have little to do with this request. I have deemed it essential that she return to the United States under her original identity; and for this she will need a document the quality of which only you can provide."

"You flatter me, sir," Hammersmith said, "but to redocument such a—forgive me—notorious personage is a delicate thing, involving considerable risk to Hammersmith. At this point in her career, Professor, I cannot imagine there will be a single policeman or ship's official who will not recognize the woman who has caused such a scandal in our city."

"Her disguise is my lookout, sir. You yourself have already attested to my capabilities of illusion. Rest assured that there will be no loose ends there. All I need from you is the paper. Cost is, of course, no object."

Frowning, Hammersmith rose from behind his desk and placed his hands behind his back. "As much as I would like to grant your request, Professor, I am afraid that materials of the kind you ask would not be available at any cost for such a high-profile individual. Normally, I would not shrink from the assignment—but with so much publicity surrounding the lady—"

Alexander interrupted. "You know, Hammersmith, this may surprise you, but it seems my grandmother knew your grandmother."

Hammersmith fell silent, his face ashen. He walked back to his desk and sat down heavily. He knew exactly what the magician meant and what it meant for him.

"Yes, good Isador, back in the old land! The rumor is they might even have been related, which could make you and me cousins, eh? As a relation, perhaps I could call on you and your good wife. How amazed she would be to hear your story! But perhaps you would prefer that we carry on this conversation in Yiddish, *nu?*"

"No, no, Professor Herrmann. I understand your implication. What exactly is it you want of me?"

Alexander reached into the portfolio and produced a sheaf of papers.

"Everything you need to know about Princess Noor can be found in this document: her age, approximate date of birth, her address in Nebraska—"

"I'm sorry, Professor, did you say Nebraska?"

"Yes," Alexander said. "This new passport will be the means by which we return the princess to her original identity of Miss Lady-Jane Little Feather, Ponca maiden. And if all goes as I so fervently hope, it will also return her to a life of tending fires, pounding maize, and spreading brains on hides."

⊰◇⊱

In the rough milieu in which he had grown, it had sometimes been necessary to defend himself. But Julius Meyer had never been predisposed to violence. So it disturbed him to find that he was deriving considerable satisfaction from backhanding the face of Compars Herrmann.

As his fingers found the magician's mustache, he felt a surge of joy that, to his embarrassment, felt almost sensual. Hitting the professor again, he realized that such behavior could not continue. Compars was far on the high side of sixty; it was simply unfair that someone of his own age and vigor should take advantage of a man so many years his senior.

Still, Julius told himself, he certainly seems in fine fettle. His figure still trim, his beard still black, one could easily take him for a man much younger—say forty or forty-five.

Julius hit him again.

The blow caused Compars to fall back against his desk. Julius took him by his vest and pushed him toward a chair. Compars pinched his nose to staunch the bleeding and looked up at his tormentor.

"So," he said, "it's murder, then."

The three words disgusted Julius, spoken as they were with both superiority and self-pity. He smacked Compars on the top of his head as one might an errant schoolboy and threw him onto the chair's embroidered cushion.

"Sit down and shut up. There will be no murder. At least not today—although I imagine there are offenses you've committed that require it. No, you're here to listen, and listen you will."

Julius pulled a chair from beneath a damask-covered side table and turned it to face him. He straddled its seat and looked straight at Compars.

"Cousin," he said, "we know everything."

Compars took a fine silk handkerchief from his now-scarlet waistcoat and put it to his face. His nose ran with blood and mucus.

"In my young life," Julius said, "I have seen many examples of cruelty. Indians left to starve because their camps blocked a railroad; whites staked out on anthills or buried alive up to their necks and left for coyotes. These were vicious, yes—acts of terror meant to horrify and caution the enemy. Perhaps they will someday be justified in history as acts of war. But when that fine young woman came to me and told me of your treatment of her, I knew then the difference between terror and evil—the kind of evil that can never be justified. The kind that laughs at the plight of its victims and takes pleasure in their despair."

Compars pulled the red cloth from his face.

"Adelaide Scarcez is a whore," he said, "and all whores are liars."

Julius put his hands over his eyes and hoped for restraint. It was bad enough that he had had to cold-cock the butler on his way upstairs. But today it seemed his discipline was deserting him for the pleasures of vengeance.

Julius grabbed Compars by both ears and pulled him out of the chair, bringing his head within an inch of his own. The old man moaned.

"I said you were here to listen, Herr Docktor. Miss Adelaide has told Alexander of all your misdeeds: her coercion, your extortion of poor Maskelyne, and your plan to reveal his substitution trunk to the public as your own. The message I bring from your brother is this: if any scandal touches Miss Adelaide—if there is so much as a notice in the papers that her petticoat was showing—it will take a better magician than you to reunite your torso with your head. Further, as of this second you will discontinue any contact with the good Jack Maskelyne; and the funds you have invested in his new invention are herewith to be considered a gift."

Julius pulled Compars's ears forward for an instant and then thrust him back into the chair.

"Blackmail? You are dead. Treachery? Dead. Retaliation—especially against Miss Scarcez? Well, as my good friend John McGarrigle would say, dead *aplenty*."

Through his fear and pain, Compars managed to smile. The whiteness of his teeth beneath the blood brought Julius a pang of nausea
the likes of which he had not experienced since the crossing of the
Berengaria.

"How like my little brother this is," he said. "I savage his little
girlfriend and throw his life into chaos; yet if I am such a demon, why
does he not have the courage to finish me off? Or is it his errand boy
that lacks what is required?"

Julius sighed, his hatred giving way to a bitter pity.

"You have caused considerable heartache, Professor; but since no
one is dead, neither are you. But from this day I suggest you consider
yourself the favorite subject of the *malakh-ha-maves*: if you remember
your bible . . ."

"Yes," said Compars, "the Angel of Death."

"Very good," Julius said.

Julius pulled a water pitcher from the side table with his right hand.
With his left, he pulled away its embroidered cloth, sending pictures
and mementos clattering to the floor. He poured some of the water
over his bloody hands and wiped them clean. Without another word,
he turned to leave.

"One moment, cousin."

Julius turned back to face Compars. For the first time, he noticed
the tooth on the magician's lapel.

"You have made your limits on my freedom quite clear. But you have
not said whether ten days from now I may open my new show—neither
have you stated if that act may contain the trick so long beloved of my
dear Alexander. I assume this, too, is forbidden by you and *Sasha* and
of course, the Angel of Death."

Julius threw the tablecloth on the carpet.

"I did not mention it because it is not a condition of your staying
alive. You found the substitution trunk before Alex did and bought

it before he could. Thus has it always been among magicians—buy, borrow, copy, and steal—a long tradition of the roguish and reprehensible. So go ahead, Great Herrmann: the show must go on—and luck before damnation."

Julius dropped the pitcher to the floor. It shattered to every corner of the room. He walked to the door and then turned once more toward Compars.

"But know this. What Alexander is preparing will render your efforts futile. It will be the most spectacular illusion of the age. It will render you hack and ordinary and wipe you off the theatrical pages. That is, if he lives through it."

36

BILLY ROBINSON WAS LATE FOR WORK. HE HAD MET a pretty girl in Hyde Park and she had remarked upon his black hair and almond-shaped eyes. It had taken the boy nearly ten minutes to ascertain that the innocent-looking blond was a prostitute looking for a mark. By then, he was past his appointed time.

As he bounded up the steps of the Egyptian, he saw the posters for the upcoming performance. They covered every wall and window of the theatre and stood upright on the pavements. His heart sank. The boss was going through with it after all.

SATURDAY EVENING, OCTOBER 6, 1883. OPENING NIGHT! 8 PM!

EGYPTIAN HALL

Piccadilly at Jermyn Street

BENEFIT OF THE GREAT

PROFESSOR ALEXANDER HERRMANN

THE WORLD'S GREATEST MAGICIAN!

PERFORMER BEFORE PRESIDENTS,

KINGS AND QUEENS, THE CZAR AND CZARINA OF THE RUSSIAS, ETC.,

WHO NOW OFFERS THE PUBLIC HIS GREATEST ILLUSION!

THE ONE AND ONLY ORIGINAL TO HIM AND SINGULAR

BULLET CATCH FIRING SQUAD!

THE MOST DANGEROUS ILLUSION OF ALL TIME!

SIX SHARPSHOOTERS

ALL ARMED WITH MUZZLE-LOADING RIFLES

WILL AIM AND FIRE AT THE GREAT HERRMANN

WHO WILL THEN ATTEMPT TO CATCH

THEIR MUSKET BALLS IN HIS MOUTH AND

DISPLAY THEM UPON A SILVER PLATTER!

OVER 50 MAGICIANS HAVE DIED

DURING THE PERFORMANCE OF THIS DEADLY TRICK. THEY FACED

ONLY A SINGLE GUN. THE GREAT HERRMANN WILL FACE SIX!

DUE TO THE EXTREME PERIL

THE BULLET CATCH FIRING SQUAD WILL BE PERFORMED ONLY

ONCE—ON THIS EVENING!

FOR THE PROTECTION OF THE LADIES, THE MANAGEMENT WILL

PROVIDE AMPLE TIME TO EXIT THE AUDITORIUM BEFORE THE

FIRING SQUAD BEGINS. A LICENSED AND QUALIFIED DOCTOR

AND NURSE WILL BE ON THE PREMISES SHOULD THERE BE ANY

UNEXPECTED INCIDENTS OF FAINTING OR HYSTERIA.

NO ONE WILL BE ADMITTED ONCE THE CURTAIN HAS GONE UP!

Damn thing's bad luck, he thought, running through the lobby and into the theatre. *Even the boss himself said so. Now he wants to try it with six guns.*

Billy clattered down a flight of stairs and into the men's lounge. He opened a door marked PRIVATE and quietly stepped into a makeshift workshop beneath the stage. Dropping his coat and hat onto a battered chair, he sat down at his workbench, hoping to appear as if he had been there since his appointed hour.

Looking across the room, Billy saw Alexander hunched over a set of old wooden molds, dark protective goggles over his eyes. Beside him sat an iron pot hissing over a gas flame. Periodically, he would dip a tiny ladle into the pot and then pour a steaming gray liquid into each mold. The air smelled of burnt sugar.

"Mr. Robinson, come here."

Now I'm for it, Billy thought. It wasn't the first time he had been caught tardy in the past few months. He only hoped that the professor would be good enough to provide him with his ship passage back to Hell's Kitchen.

"Mr. Robinson, please stir that solution, would you? It wouldn't do for it to harden before we wish it to."

Billy sighed in relief. He took the ladle and dipped it into the pot. The liquid popped and bubbled.

"Might I ask, sir, exactly what we are doing today?"

Alexander smiled. "No questions, no answers. No answers, no learning. What we are doing here today Bill, is manufacturing ammunition."

"Ammunition, sir?"

"Exactly. Watch."

Alexander put the ladle down on the bench. He reached for one of the wooden molds and opened it.

Inside were eighteen nearly perfect musket balls. Their texture was exact, as was their color and even the slight pitting and surface variations one noted in a piece of shot. Alexander picked up a small box with a picture of a tall brick structure on it. It read: SPARKS SHOT TOWER • PHILADELPHIA, PA. He reached inside, removed a ball, and placed it side by side with the one he had just created.

"Well, Bill?"

"They're identical, boss. But why make your own shot when you've already bought a box?"

The magician took up the two balls and held them on either side of his head.

"This one," Alex said, turning to his right, "is Mr. Sparks's ball—made in a big tower where they drop molten lead from the top to the bottom where it lands in a water bath, producing what you see here. Up to a few hundred yards, this little fellow can make one considerably dead."

Alex now turned to his left. "This one is mine. It is the same shape and approximately the same weight as its brother. But . . ."

Alex took the musket ball, popped it in his mouth, chewed, and swallowed.

"Here, try one."

Billy took one of the balls and, ascertaining that he had the correct one, placed it on his tongue.

"Lovely flavor," Alex said. "Now, what does the magician always ask an audience member to do for this trick?"

"Well, the first thing is, they write their initials on the ball."

"Excellent! Only on opening night, I shall ask *six* members of our audience to mark a half dozen of Mr. Sparks's fine Philadelphia musket balls. Using misdirection, the *true* bullets will then be hidden within my mouth. These sweet little creations will then be loaded into the muskets, and with a great roll of drums and business with blindfolds, fired directly at my head. *Bang!* The moment the powder in the rifles explodes, my little candies will vaporize harmlessly. Once the din subsides, and the ladies who have fainted are cleared away, one by one I will spit the balls secreted in my mouth onto the promised silver tray. The patrons will then each positively identify their individual initials and *voilà*—applause followed by money."

"But that seems so simple, boss."

"That's as may be, Billy. But we're still dealing with firearms here. The slightest bit of carelessness and I could easily join the others who have fallen victim to this illusion. And now if you will be so kind as to return to work—we have much to do between now and the big night. It would also suit me well if from now on you wouldn't set your own hours."

Billy gulped and his stomach flipped over. He bowed and returned to his bench.

Alexander walked across the dirty floor and stopped at the old table that served as his desk. At its center was a handbill, yellow with bold red type.

THE TRIUMPHANT RETURN OF THE ONE,

THE ONLY AND THE ORIGINAL

GREAT HERRMANN!

(PROFESSOR CARL HERRMANN)

WHO, AFTER SEVERAL YEARS IN RETIREMENT, IS BACK TO AMUSE AND

AMAZE YOUNG AND OLD ALIKE IN HIS GREAT NEW SHOW AT THE

OPERA COMIQUE

EASTERN STRAND AT HOLYWELL STREET,

SATURDAY EVENING, OCTOBER 6, 8 PM

Professor Herrmann is not to be confused with his younger

brother, Alexander, currently appearing at the Egyptian Theatre.

ALEXANDER HERRMANN IS A MERE IMITATOR
HAVING LEARNED HIS ENTIRE ART FROM HIS ESTEEMED
PREDECESSOR!
ON THIS NIGHT AND ALL SUBSEQUENT NIGHTS PROFESSOR
HERRMANN WILL INTRODUCE THE GREATEST MAGICAL
MARVEL EVER SEEN BY MAN. HIS OWN CREATION,
THE SUBSTITUTION TRUNK
*Never before seen in Britain or anywhere else on the globe. Opening
night will see its World Premiere. All those in attendance will consider
themselves fortunate indeed to have witnessed magic history!*
SPLENDID NEW SCENERY! MAGNIFICENT WARDROBE!
ALL TICKETS TO ALEXANDER HERRMANN'S PERFORMANCE
WILL BE HONORED HERE. FIRST COME, FIRST SERVED.
HUZZAH!

Alexander smiled. In a way, such bold words were a relief. At last, he and Compars would be going head to head in the same city on the same night. The next morning's papers would decide the winner.

He put the handbill back on the table and picked up the passport he had ordered from Hammersmith. Old Isador had lived up to his reputation. He doubted if anyone in customs or the Foreign Service could distinguish this document from the genuine article; its cover and paper were identical to that used by the United States; and every typeface, stamp, and official signature was exact.

Alex put the passport in a gray envelope, scrawled a message on a slip of paper, folded it, and whistled for his page.

"You are to take this to Mr. Julius Meyer at Brown's Hotel. If he is not in, you will wait for him. If he doesn't show up until tomorrow, you will wait for him. You are to put this envelope in his hand and bid him read this note. He will understand."

The page, a small red-faced Scot of about twelve, nodded and took the papers. When he reached the street, he unfolded the note. It read:

HERE IS THE PAPER. YOU TAKE THE PRIZE.

❖

From the London *Pall Mall Gazette*
1 October 1883

MAGICIAN'S ASSISTANT KIDNAPPED
Woman who scandalized two continents vanishes!
Police believe Arab caliph has recaptured famous beauty for harem!
FAMOUS MAGICIAN HERRMANN REPORTED CRESTFALLEN!

The woman known to the theatre-going public as Princess Noor-Al-Haya has been reported kidnapped said her friend and employer, the world-famous magician known as the Great Herrmann.

The incident is reported to have occurred yesterday night or morning at the apartments shared by Professor Alexander Herrmann, the princess, her chaperone, Miss Adelaide Scarcez, and Mr. Seamus Dowie, Herrmann's assistant.

According to Police Inspector Lestrade, around midnight, three Eastern-appearing men, wearing the traditional dress of their native lands, abducted the young woman from her bed. An unwrapped turban was found at the scene, indicating that the young woman put up a struggle.

"She fought right enough," the inspector said. "By the time the Professor and Miss Scarcez were awakened, one of the suspects' turbans was lying on the carpet. Mr. Herrmann says he tried to free her from the grasp of one of the wogs, but was overpowered—knocked on the head by a gun or sap or some such."

Dr. Stephan C. Ware, a well-known physician to the theatrical community, was brought in to examine the injured magician and declared him fit and needing no time in hospital.

Prof. Herrmann believes that Princess Noor was taken by agents of the Grand Sultan of Oman. Early last year, the famed magician effected a daring rescue of the exotic beauty from the Sultan's harem, where she was said to be one of over 300 women designated as "wives" of the heathen king. Since that fateful day, the loyal girl has refused to leave Prof. Herrmann's side, becoming his assistant in his magic performances.

"She was the Sultan's favorite," the crestfallen Professor said. "I am not surprised that he should try to recapture her in this way. It is my clumsiness, my lack of vigilance, that has allowed this to happen."

Prof. Herrmann created a considerable scandal in New York City when he first introduced Princess Noor to the public on May 11. Appearing in the clothing of her native land, which often consisted of little more than transparent silks and gold coins, she inspired protests by religious groups and was denounced by politicians. A similar reaction greeted her in London.

Perhaps owing to the controversy, performances both here and in America were consistently sold out. Herrmann and Princess Noor were slated to open a new show beginning Monday.

"With only six days until our premire, my managers have advised me to cancel the date," Prof. Herrmann told the press. "But the princess would not have countenanced such an action. She was a professional—what we in the show business call a 'trouper'—and she would insist that the show go on. The police are scouring every dock and boat slip and I myself have engaged a veritable army of private detectives to find her. And so, I promise the public two things: first, if Princess Noor-Al-Haya is anywhere in Britain, she shall be found! Second, all ticket-buying patrons to my exhibition may be assured of my best efforts and will be provided with new and bigger thrills as always, at popular prices."

37

WHEN THE YOUNG WOMAN AWOKE IN HER STATEROOM, SHE knew that Princess Noor-Al-Haya was dead.

Her first indication was the room itself. It was not the kind of accommodation the princess would ever tolerate: the bed was narrow, its blanket brown and coarse; the walls had been given only the barest whitewash and were stained with grime. There was only one small porthole, and the furnishings consisted of the bed, a plain nightstand with pitcher and basin, and a single iron chair.

Although groggy from whatever drug she had been given, her skin still possessed enough memory to realize it was encased in animal hide. Staggering to her feet, she stumbled to the mirror above the dressing table.

Looking back at her was Lady-Jane Little Feather.

This was not the Lady-Jane who had been the Red Rose of Omaha; it was not even the apprentice prostitute receiving fifty cents or a dollar for her two minutes' work. This was the Lady-Jane she most hated and feared.

The face was devoid of paint. A band of unadorned leather encircled her head. Her clothing was stitched from the kinds of skins reserved for a family's least favored daughter. This was the woman harbored by the Ponca, the Lady-Jane of hard work and want.

Turning from the mirror, she looked out the porthole and saw the docks of Southampton. She ran to the door and began to pound on it. In seconds, Wind Whistler opened the door. Lady-Jane flung herself upon him, scratching and biting and cursing him in two languages.

"Don't blame me," Wind Whistler said, fending off a slap. "I'm just here to guard you. If Little Feather feels the need to complain, I suggest you speak with One Tongue. It was he that put me here."

"Then get him, Shit Whistle."

"I have been instructed to wait until one of the white-coated slaves comes by and then send him for anything needed. I will do this if Little Feather will stop shouting and calling me names and hitting me."

Lady-Jane didn't reply. Panting, she walked to the edge of the bed and sat down. Wind Whistler nodded and returned to the corridor, locking the door behind him. A few moments later, she could hear him speak haltingly:

"Fetch . . . Mister . . . Jool-is . . . My-er." Wind Whistler needed to repeat the phrase several times, but at last he stopped and she heard the sound of footsteps in the hall.

When Julius Meyer entered the room, he was dressed in a new suit. The sight of his gold watch fob and bowler hat only made Lady-Jane angrier. She spat on the floor.

"So. I see you've gone back to being a Jew."

"And you've gone back to being an Indian."

Lady-Jane laughed bitterly. "You think you can hold me on this goddamn boat? Wait until Alex hears of this."

"He has heard of it, Lady-Jane. I'm afraid it was his idea."

"You're full of shit, Julius. He loves me. I've made him more famous than he's ever been. I went through everything for him, shared his bed, kept my mouth shut."

Julius crossed the floor and sat down in the iron chair.

"And now that's over," he said. "Your passage has been booked and paid for, your passport, which I assure you is in order, is in the possession of the prophet for safekeeping. As far as the dock officials know, you're a red girl leaving this country unconscious; another Indian who couldn't hold her liquor."

Lady-Jane leaped upon Julius. She tried to bite his face, to scratch out both his eyes. He took hold of her wrists and held her fast until she stopped struggling and then deposited her back on to the narrow bed.

"I'm sorry, Lady-Jane. It's not exactly with relish that we do this. Believe me when I tell you that Alex saw you as a valuable member of his troupe and was truly grateful for all you did. He was thoroughly prepared to keep you in his act, to exalt your talents, to make you rich. But then you attacked Adelaide."

"That lying whore. No one saw me do anything."

"Oh, but someone did—and that witness told Alex everything. He wept when he saw the blood caked in her hair, the bruises across her body; and when he asked me if I thought you could tolerate the presence of another woman in his life, I had no choice but to tell him about your past; and how you had dealt with others you had come to hate."

Lady-Jane's eyes began to fill with hot tears. "You have no proof."

"I have the word of the great and good Eli Gershonson. Just as he had *your* word in the letter you wrote, warning him. If you had not escaped to the Ponca after the Nickel & Dime fire, you would have long been hanged by now. Not that I blame you for barbecuing that pig, Calhern. You should have put an apple in his mouth. But to destroy all those girls . . ."

"A few less white whores, Julius—an inconvenience for Swain and his partners, including your Jew miser brother. It took all of a week to replace them. Besides, I noticed that you were always too good to risk your holy circumcision on any of us. Why should you care?"

"It doesn't matter, Lady-Jane," Julius said. "You're going home."

Lady-Jane threw her hands over her eyes. She would be damned if she would let this little bastard see her cry.

"Home to squat in horseshit? Home to watch a bunch of savages begging white trash to show them which is the business end of a plow?"

Julius shifted in the chair. He took a silver case from his jacket pocket and offered her a small cigar. She spat at him again.

"A substantial sum of money has been wired to my bank in Omaha," Julius said. "It's the equivalent of the salary you would have made in the next two years plus a bonus. If you live wisely, or perhaps open your own business, you'll be comfortable the rest of your days."

Lady-Jane removed her hands from her face; her eyes were dry.

"You white bastards make me laugh. First, you drag me to your school. Then you turn me out before I'm grown enough to bleed regular. You hoodwink the world about who I am and get rich off the lie. You think you can put a few dollars aside for the whore and that's all it'll take to buy her off—that she'll jump for fucking joy at your generosity! Well, I don't care about the money. Don't you understand? He loves me."

"Lady-Jane . . ."

"He *loves* me."

Julius stood up. "I'm afraid there's nothing more to say. I need to stay here and raise more money. You and Wind Whistler and the prophet sail in another hour."

Lady-Jane whirled. She seized the pitcher from the nightstand and hurled it at Julius. He ducked down and saw it shatter against the rough pine wainscoting.

"Bring Alex here," Lady-Jane shouted. "When he finds out what you've done, he'll put you in jail. He won't stand for this. He can't open the show without me."

Julius sighed. He could not bring himself to tell her of Alexander's cold rage when he was informed of the assault: or to tell her that her lover's first suggestion was to have her transported to Whitechapel and murdered as a streetwalker. When Julius told him he could be no part of such a scheme, Alex suggested sending her back to Nebraska penniless, to finish her days in her old profession or as the wife of some red farmer. It was only after Julius told Alex that he would not help him unless she was provided sufficient funds to live in dignity that the current solution was reached.

"I suppose it's up to you if you want to spend the next hour screaming and throwing yourself against walls," Julius said, "but this stateroom is far down in steerage—where cries and moans are hardly unusual. The crew has been warned that you are likely to become hysterical—to holler and carry on—and to pay you no attention."

Lady-Jane sprung at Julius, again swiping at him with her nails, her feet trying to find his groin. She spat at him over and over, covering his nose and eyes. Wiping his face, he found her saliva mixed with his own tears. He turned and quickly left the room, locking the door from outside.

In the corridor, he collapsed against the wall, exhausted. From inside the stateroom, he could hear Lady-Jane shriek in vain, shouting out her hatred of him and her love for Alexander. "You can't do this," she pleaded, "you *can't.*

"*I was a princess.*"

As he continued toward the stairs, Julius marveled at how quickly her cries faded, swallowed up by the clattering sounds of the main galley and the dull roars of the engine room.

Still, he wondered what sympathies might be raised from anyone who passed a room so filled with fury, seeming to contain its own storm at sea.

38

FOR THE LONDONERS WHO SOUGHT OUT THE GREAT HERRMANN to amaze them, nothing matched the pomp and majesty of his grand entrances. At every performance, the orchestra began with a stirring trumpet voluntary, heralding his arrival. Following this, anything could happen.

At one show he entered dressed as an Eastern potentate, a monkey on each shoulder and flanked by two snarling tigers; at another he emerged from a coffin in a black leotard decorated with bones of phosphorus paint, so that he looked for all the world like a skeleton come to life. Many still spoke of the famous evening he rode down the center aisle astride a baby elephant, followed by a fully armed contingent of Khyber Rifles.

But how, many wondered, could the Great Herrmann possibly take the stage tonight—only days after the disappearance of his notorious assistant?

Not a person in the theatre could have been unaware of her abduction; newspaper hawkers had arrived early that evening, descending upon the Egyptian and shouting their headlines at the incoming patrons.

Times here! Princess Noor still missing!

Get your *Telegraph*! No clues in the disappearance of magician's girl!

Evening Standard here! Magician's assistant feared dead!

Ever since she had vanished the week before, all of London's papers had speculated upon what the Great Herrmann would do without his illustrious auxiliary. Opinions varied widely. The *Herald*, for example, had insisted that the professor would continue to dazzle audiences exactly as he had before the advent of Princess Noor, while the *Gazette* maintained that it was curiosity about the renowned exotic that had been the key to the magician's current popularity. "Without her," its critic said, "he is just another conjuror, certainly inferior to his brother Carl, whose new show is premiering the very same night at the Opera Comique."

In the event, it took Alexander less than five minutes to make the audience forget her completely.

As the lights went down, there was no blare of trumpets, no trademark fanfare. Dressed in a black velvet suit with britches and white stockings, Alexander appeared without introduction or musical accompaniment, the only sound the wild applause of the audience. Walking slowly to center stage, he acknowledged their enthusiasm and, his hand over his heart, bowed humbly.

"My lords, ladies and gentlemen . . . my friends. I cannot possibly express my gratitude to you for the support I have received since the terrible kidnapping of my helper and protégé. Ever since her taking on the last night of November, I have been deluged with letters and telegrams from both heads of state and little schoolchildren. You, the people of this great country, have offered me, an outsider, succor and hope during a time in which it has been impossible—even for a magician of my powers—to make such heartache disappear. But now . . ."

Alexander looked toward the orchestra. They began to softly play the sensuous, whirling notes of Princess Noor's theme, a tune well known to the many repeat members of the audience. As the notes rose and fell, smoke began to billow from an opening at the center of the stage and the hall was soon filled with the aroma of sandalwood incense.

". . . it is my happy duty, my dear friends, to tell you that Princess Noor-Al-Haya—the Pearl of the East and Gem of the Nile—has been found!"

Alexander turned to his left and indicated the swirling mist. As he pointed toward the smoke, a light suddenly shone through it.

At first, the audience could discern nothing; but then ragged outlines began to appear, dark against the brilliance: first a hand, followed by an arm or a leg and finally a long sweep of wild hair. The orchestra played louder and faster, cymbals crashing, drums beating.

At last, a figure broke through, its golden tunic of coins shimmering in the footlights. The dark, strong limbs shone through the transparent sheen of her silks. The long, black hair whipped up and down. At the *ting-ting* sound of her finger cymbals, the audience rose to its feet, stomping and applauding as the music ended. On the last beat she stopped center stage and froze, feet arched, hands and head raised high.

The applause became a roar. Men shouted, women screamed and waved lace handkerchiefs. After what seemed an hour, Alexander raised his hands for silence.

"Thank you so very much, my dear, dear friends. I am sure that you are both relieved and amazed at this appearance. But please allow me to remind you that ours is a performance of magic—that all may not be exactly as it seems—so pray permit me to read to you this letter."

Alexander raised an arm and from nowhere, a piece of yellow paper appeared in his hand.

"'Dear Professor Herrmann. I much appreciate your rescue of my daughter from my enemies. But I cannot allow you to continue to employ her. According to our faith, this is unseemly. By the time you receive this, my agents will have restored her safely to the bosom of her family. I am certain you understand that I do this drastic thing only out of a father's love. Still, I thank you. You protected my child. May Allah protect you.' And it is signed His Royal Highness Daoud Ali, Third Caliph of Egypt.'"

There was near dead silence in the audience and then a murmur of confusion began to arise. How could this be? The orchestra struck up the princess's music once more and the beautiful figure began dancing again.

"So! I know what you all must be wondering: if Princess Noor-Al-Haya is safe with her father in Arabia, then how can she also be on the stage of Egyptian Hall, dancing for you as only she can? Not even at a performance by the Great Herrmann could a woman be in two places at once. Or could she?"

From the misty rear of the stage, an elaborate Moroccan tent floated forward and came to rest. Its walls were purest white with tent ropes of gold brocade, and its roof was red and yellow silk. Princess Noor continued to revolve and twist, dancing twice around the magician; and then, with the kick of a heel, gliding upstage.

"In fact, my friends, the presence of the princess here tonight is less in the nature of an appearance and more of a tribute—a fond farewell to a beloved colleague who added much to the legend of the Great Herrmann. Her bold, exotic beauty captured the hearts of two continents. Unique! Irreplaceable! But now . . ."

The princess danced into the great tent, disappearing from sight.

". . . with the princess's enthusiastic permission, I now present *another* great lady of illusion. Though British by birth, she was years in a convent school in Italy, where she spent her formative years in prayer and contemplation. Some time ago, her simple, hardworking parents died in the great train accident at Luton and she had not a soul in the world to care for her. Luckily, her mother had once served as my governess and her father my parents' footman. They left her in my care in the hope that she would perhaps become my cook or maid or even take on holy orders. But no, my friends—she was made for something higher!"

The audience gasped to see a figure in purple and gold descend toward the stage from the top of the proscenium. She hung suspended in mid-air, her red hair flying as if blown by a hurricane. Her head tilted slightly to the right, her hands clasped as if in prayer, she might have been a *Madonna* straight from a canvas by Giotto or del Sarto. As she continued her descent, two gigantic hoops inched toward her from both sides of the stage, each passing over her body, proving no wires held her aloft. As the music swelled, the young woman spread her arms wide as if blessing the audience.

When at last she reached the floor, she was enveloped from head to toe in a cool blue flame. Amid the fire, she disappeared, only to emerge from a huge pagoda-shaped box at stage right. Now she was dressed in a gown of purest white, a black choker at her throat, her arms encased in sheer silk. She twirled about twice, not with the abandon of an Arabian princess but the grace and élan of a prima ballerina.

"My lords, ladies and gentlemen: I take the greatest of pleasure in introducing to you a young lady who is sure to ignite the imagination and quicken the heart with her beauty and daring! She has worked like a Trojan since the very hour of her predecessor's disappearance, all so that she might please you in some small way. Judging by the wonders you have all just witnessed, I believe that she will."

The beautiful redhead bowed to the audience. They rose as one person, clapping and stomping even longer and louder than they had for the "princess." Alexander crossed to where she stood and took her hand.

"My lords, ladies and gentlemen—please join me in greeting Adelaide—Queen of Magic!"

She curtsied this time—and as she rose, doves as white as her dress flew from her hands. The men in the top balcony whistled and threw their hats at the stage. Women wept onto their pearls.

The remainder of the show went off perfectly.

Adelaide performed all of Noor's duties to the letter. She carried Alexander's cards and props, was beheaded, sawed in half, burned alive, and, in a new illusion entitled "After the Ball," vanished while standing before a huge mirror. In performance, she was everything her predecessor was not. Where the princess had been brazen and provocative, Adelaide was fluid and angelic; if Princess Noor-Al-Haya had been the she-devil of magic, Adelaide Scarcez was its angel.

High above the stage in the left flies, Julius Meyer smiled bitterly. He had made all of these lies possible.

He had kidnapped Lady-Jane. He had ordered her drugged and imprisoned. Of course, there was no doubt this was required; with the Red Rose loose in England, it was likely they would all be dead in short order. By now she was in the center of the ocean, screaming in her little room. There she would remain until Prophet John and Wind Whistler made sight of land. Then they would drug her again, douse her with alcohol, and get her past customs—exactly the same way they they had smuggled her aboard.

Yes, it had all been necessary; but as Julius looked down to see his cousin dazzle his admirers, he wondered just how much of his crime had been committed in the service of love and chivalry, and how much for the benefit of the World's Greatest Magician. He heard himself curse in a dozen languages.

The bulk of the act complete, Alexander walked to the apron of the stage, bowed, and once again begged for quiet.

"My good friends, I cannot tell you what this evening has meant to me. To find that the princess, so dear to me, is safe! To present to you a matchless new performer in the person of Adelaide, Queen of Magic! And to hear your enjoyment and appreciation of our work, I am overwhelmed."

Alexander shot his cuffs in the air and produced a gilt-edged hand-kerchief as big as a tablecloth. He feigned tears and comically blew his nose in the enormous tissue. The audience laughed and clapped.

"But, magnanimous as you are, I also know that you have come here tonight to witness something never attempted before: a variation on the most deadly and dangerous of all illusions—a trick that, using only *one* bullet, has caused the unfortunate deaths of nearly fifty of my esteemed colleagues. Gentlemen?"

Alexander gestured stage left, and six men in military uniforms marched onto the stage. Each one carried a gleaming musket.

Julius watched as Alexander introduced the firing squad, extolling each man's qualifications: this shooting medal, that military honor. He leaned against the iron balustrade as the magician called six members of the audience onstage and had each of them mark a musket ball with their initials.

Then, something else caught his eye.

In the backstage half-light, he saw a dark figure dressed in a monk's robe and a facemask of inky black—the uniform of his cousin's back-stage assistants. At first, this seemed a normal function of the show. In the past hour, other black-garbed helpers had come and gone, aiding with various illusions. But at this moment, all of them—five young men now dressed in tie and tails—were assisting the audience members in the marking of their bullets.

In a flash, Julius realized that there should *be* no sixth man; and then saw that that man was not alone.

In his grasp was another dark figure. Across his mouth was a cloth to keep him silent, and girding his wrists were a pair of Alexander's

Central Arkansas Library System

Checked Out Items 7/12/2016 14:18
XXXXXXXXXX3181

Item Title	Due Date
37653012581016	8/9/2016
To kill a mockingbird [CD recording] / by Harper Lee.	
37653018206840	8/9/2016
Magic words / Gerald Kolpan.	
37653019338725	8/9/2016
Doctor Sleep : a novel / Stephen King.	

Thank you for visiting the library!

handcuffs. Beneath the gag, Julius could see the slash of a pointed black beard, and above it, clear blue eyes opened wide in panic. Without a sound, the black-robed man pushed his victim against the metal post used for the "Donkey's Tail" illusion. Producing a length of rope from beneath his robe, the dark man proceeded to bind his prisoner to the stake. Now only the backdrop curtain stood between him and the muskets' line of fire.

Julius leaned further forward until nearly half his body was over the iron railing. Then he nearly fell to the stage with the shock of recognition.

The man bound so securely was Compars Herrmann.

His mission completed, the black-robed figure vanished into the darkness backstage. Julius shouted for help, but the music of the orchestra and the laughter and applause of the audience drowned his voice. He looked to the stage and saw that Alexander was instructing his marksmen to load their guns.

As if shot from a cannon, Julius ran along the slender catwalk toward a cluster of thick ropes. He pulled on one and it came away in his hands, falling beneath the backstage eaves. He tugged on another and was met by the strong resistance of a sandbag at its end.

Desperate now, he yanked the third rope and felt it hold fast, its knot attached to a large curtain flap above him. He clambered to the top of the railing, gave the rope one more pull and launched himself at his target.

He flew into the darkness, the hemp knots hard against his hands. He crossed his legs around the rope for speed and then splayed them wide to brace his landing. His heels against the boards were like pistol shots, and caused a nervous titter to go up in the audience. Letting go of the rope, Julius raced at Compars and felt for the handcuffs, hoping that the black-robed man had not secured them around the post.

He had.

GERALD KOLPAN

On stage, Alexander dismissed the audience participants, admonishing them to return to their seats for the sake of their safety.

"And now, my lords, ladies and gentlemen, these fine shootists will aim their muskets straight at your humble servant. I shall then attempt to catch all six musket balls in my mouth and present them to you on this fine English sterling platter. If all goes as planned, you shall have been witnesses to the most death-defying feat in the history of the dark arts; if they don't, you will nonetheless have seen another historic event, the like of which, I daresay, occurs only once."

Alexander turned toward the marksmen.

"Firing squad!" he shouted. "Are you ready?"

The men raised the muskets to their shoulders.

Behind the curtain, Julius pushed on the metal stake with all his strength, hoping to break the floorboards where its bolts had been attached. Through the gag, he could hear Compars moans of fear. Both of them knew that if the sixth assistant had placed him here, in the line of fire, then at least one or two—or perhaps even all of Alexander's sugar bullets had been replaced by the genuine article.

"Aim!"

Julius now pushed against Compars, adding the magician's weight to his own. With a strong shove, he heard a floorboard crack as one of the bolts gave way. He pushed again and the metal groaned, sending a second bolt skittering across the stage floor.

"Fire!"

The Great Herrmann puffed out his chest and stood stock-still. The cries and shouts of the ladies in the audience rose like a wave, and half the audience covered their ears. The sharp report of the six muskets was earsplitting. The stage of Egyptian Hall turned a smoky blue as their powder exploded.

39

T HE LONGER BILLY ROBINSON WORKED FOR ALEXANDER
Herrmann, the more he was convinced the boss controlled
forces other than the natural.

As one of his assistants, Billy knew how all the illusions worked.
Some were highly complex, others deceptively simple; but it was
Alexander's ability to manipulate the physical world around him—
its accepted truths and perceptions of reality—that truly amazed
the boy. If the Great Herrmann said an Indian was an Arabian, the
world believed him. If he pronounced a girl whose parents still lived
an orphan, his truth prevailed.

But Billy still had trouble working out why the events of the previous evening had not become the scandal of London and the nation.

Treachery had gone undetected and murder narrowly averted; it was just the sort of thing reporters lived on.

And yet the morning's papers carried no news of the debacle save for the surprising information that Compars had failed to appear for his performance. For the past week, the press had made much of the competition between the two siblings and how each had promised the public a trick so astounding that stage magic, if not all the show business, would forever be altered. With Compars a no-show, a firestorm of criticism and scorn was unleashed on the elder Herrmann. Fellow magicians gathered in Hyde Park to denounce him, and there was a stampede for refunds at the Comique's box office.

Alexander meanwhile basked in the glow of splendid reviews, the writers describing the details of a show that had seemingly gone off without a hitch.

Billy Robinson knew better.

On the night in question he had been standing backstage left, getting ready to move a large box for Alexander's *denouement*—a trifle with doves and cards—his *adieu* to the audience—when he saw Alexander's cousin, Mr. Julius Meyer, take off from the catwalk railing.

For a moment, Billy thought the action almost comic: the dapper American, in full tie and tails, his shining topper still on his head, taking a flyer by rope. By the time the boy could gather his thoughts, Julius was struggling with someone or something just left of center stage. Billy stepped forward to offer what aid he could. Julius hissed at him as loudly as he dared.

"Push with me, Mr. Robinson! Push!"

Out in the house, the orchestra swelled to a pinnacle of suspense; Billy heard Alexander's instructions to the firing squad.

"Ready . . . aim . . ."

At the word "fire," Billy and Julius crumpled to the floor. The boy could hear the muskets fire and smell the clouds of smoke pouring from their locks. There was a sharp crack as a lead ball tore through the curtain and the airspace where Compars had been. The patrons went silent and the orchestra stopped playing. Then, one by one, Alexander spat the musket balls onto the silver platter. With the appearance of each ball, the applause rose, until the audience reached a frenzy. Behind the curtain the three men lay prone on the boards, panting from exertion and shock; it wasn't until the Great Herrmann invited the volunteers back on stage to identify their bullets that they scrambled further into the backstage darkness.

Exhausted, the three leaned against the wall by the chorus dressing room. Julius removed the victim's gag. At first, he thought that Alexander himself had somehow managed to rush backstage, so much did the man look like the boss. But as he drew nearer, he saw that this man was older; and in his eyes was an expression of panic he could never imagine in Alexander.

"Back to your knitting, boyo."

Seamus Dowie appeared from the gloom and placed a huge paw on Billy's chest. "This here's a business of adults. You go on about your own. And Billy boy—if ya so much as whisper a word about what happened here to friend or foe, you'll find yerself with no tongue, jugglin' for dimes in Times Square."

Billy nodded and returned to his station just in time for the final trifle. He opened a cage filled with white doves and handed them off to a runner in black, who passed them through the curtain. Onstage, the birds appeared to emerge from packs of cards secreted about the magician's coat. As they flew into the audience, Alexander bowed, pleaded with the Almighty to bless his audience, and bade them good night.

In the gloom beneath the stage, Compars Herrmann smiled bitterly at his brother.

"Well, *Sasha*, I see you've brought the Angel of Death with you."

Julius frowned. Once Compars had realized he wasn't dead, it had taken him no time to return to his former arrogance.

"Our cousin saved your worthless hide tonight," Alexander said. "And if by chance you think this is my doing, you've underestimated me. I am the man who successfully disappeared the most notorious woman in civilization and gained the love of a spy you planted. Believe me, brother, if I wanted you dead, you'd be dead."

Compars slumped in his chair. "Well, whoever did this to me may as well have killed me off. I failed my audience—promised them the spectacular and then turned up missing. From tonight, I am finished. My congratulations."

Julius' face flushed red. "Deceit, treachery, theft, blackmail and now—my god—self-pity. I imagine we shall never discover the identity of your attacker, cousin, as it would take the remainder of our lives simply to sift through the suspects."

Alexander paced in front of one of the long workbenches. He picked up a small wrench and shifted it from hand to hand.

"But I shall save you, brother. I shall provide you with an alibi for your absence that your public will not only accept, but will lionize you as a hero and a patriot—and in return, you will accede to my terms."

"Don't fool yourself, Alex. I neither need nor want your help."

"Oh, but you do. Of course, whoever wants you dead, that is your lookout. Personally, your life means little to me, as mine is much easier without it. But as long as you *are* alive, I need you working and out of mischief. I have seen what you get up to when 'retired.' So you shall do as I instruct, or tomorrow the world will learn how the 'the original' Great Herrmann got kidnapped like a rube and set up for a musket ball by a cabal of jealous husbands and a brother magician from whom he stole his latest illusion."

"Jack Maskelyne would never agree to such a fiction."

"I think Jack will jump at the chance to screw you and get his invention back. But even if he doesn't take it, there is enough hatred among your fellow wizards to recruit a dozen magicians to make the claim. As for the husbands, that's a matter of spreading around a few pounds. By the time the flies are done feeding on this pile of horseshit, you won't be able to get booked in Bournemouth for a split week."

Compars rose from the chair. He raised his fist above his shoulder and brought it down hard on a drill bench.

"I created you," he screamed at Alexander. "I gave you everything."

Alexander stood still and said nothing.

Compars brought both fists down on the table, harder this time. His eyes filled with tears of rage and frustration. The interior of his mouth tasted of iron. Swallowing hard, he straightened his back and faced his brother.

"The terms," he said.

"You are never to return to the United States. That will be my territory, except for once a year when I shall play the Egyptian—a venue that will be forever off limits to you. You are to apologize to Miss Adelaide Scarcez and render to her the sum of ten thousand pounds. And you will return all rights to the Substitution Trunk to our good Maskelyne and relinquish all profitable interest in his remarkable toilet. What you tell the audience is a 'Substitution Trunk' is your problem. I'm sure you'll come up with something."

"I'm sure. Anything else?"

"This is not a demand, but I do suggest that you invest in a bodyguard—preferably one big and strong and who goes armed."

"And my—what shall we call it—rehabilitation?"

"Fear not, *Herr Docktor*," Alexander said. "Within a fortnight you shall be completely exonerated and more publicly worshipped than ever before. It will of course, require your total and complete cooperation with my plans, beginning with a visit to one of our co-religionists. A remarkable fellow, really; an *artiste* with an eye for art and a hand for forgery."

From the *Daily Mail*
18 October, 1883

MAGICIAN'S ABSENCE EXPLAINED!
PROFESSOR HERRMANN ON SECRET MISSION FOR
THE GOVERNMENTS OF BRITAIN, AMERICA
AMAZING DOCUMENTS FOUND!
HERRMANN EXONERATED!
"I AM NOT A HERO," SAYS WORLD-FAMOUS WIZARD

A major scandal was laid to rest yesterday when magician Carl Herrmann, known throughout the world as the Great Herrmann, revealed the circumstances behind his absence from an opening night performance here in London on October the 6th.

On that evening, there was much consternation on the part of the public when Professor Herrmann failed to appear at the Opera Comique. For weeks preceding the opening, the magico had vowed to reveal a spectacular new illusion called the "Substitution Trunk." After he had gone missing from the stage, there was much criticism of Prof. Herrmann in the press.

"I had to make the choice to do my civic duty or disappoint the British public," Prof. Herrmann told reporters. "As much as it pained me to be unable to entertain my supporters, I knew that the governments of two nations were relying on me to bring a positive conclusion to a delicate affair, and I had faith that in the end all would be put right."

Some of the details of Prof. Herrmann's mission are confidential under the Official Secrets Act; but the magician was permitted to tell the *Mail* that his duties involved a meeting between a foreign spy and a member of Her Majesty's government and the quick switching of one document for another. "They thought of me because of my experience," Prof. Herrmann remarked. "I have been a practicing magician forty years and such a substitution is for me, a trifle."

Professor Herrmann produced a copy of the document, cleared by authorities. It appeared to be a Crown grant, dated 1686. The signature and seal of King James II showed the indenture to be genuine. When asked by a reporter just why the grant was so important, Professor Herrmann said that he was not allowed to divulge the details of his mission. "Let us just say that the current location of this slip of paper will not be viewed favorably by Wilhelm and his fellow Hohenzollerns in Germany."

Joining the esteemed conjuror was his younger brother and successor, Alexander, who also performs magic as the Great Herrmann. Much publicity had surrounded the fact that the brothers were both opening their magic acts at different theatres on the same night and both offering dramatic new tricks. The younger Herrmann stated that the entire affair had been devised simply to generate publicity and that, far from being rivals, he and Carl were in fact the best of friends.

"For any performer to do what my brother did—come when his country called him at the expense of great ridicule to himself, well, it only speaks of his magnanimous personality and laudable patriotism."

To this, his brother answered, "I am not a hero. I only did what any other loyal, self-sacrificing citizen of England or America would have done."

Professor Herrmann said that his performance has now been rescheduled for Saturday, November 10. Anyone holding a ticket from the original show would be admitted. Alexander Herrmann added that any patron bringing a punched ticket from his brother's show to the Egyptian Hall would also be admitted to one of his performances at half charge.

As is usual in cases involving matters of national security, the Home Office refused to comment on the adventure, and a confidential source within the Gladstone government disavowed any knowledge of the affair.

40

CHASED BY OWLS LOOKED INTO THE DISTANCE AND LIKED HIS position. He was far enough away from the new train spur to avoid federal entanglements, but close enough for his visitor to unload her horse at the railhead and ride out to meet him.

By the location of the sun, he estimated she was on time. The day was not especially hot, but she appeared on the horizon through shimmering air. It did not surprise him that she was dressed in the manner of a white woman; but she rode like an Indian, full on, chin up and hatless. As she came nearer, he noted a second horse behind the first, laden down with cases and packages. Even from a hundred yards, he could see the white foam sweat from both.

Calmly, he took the reins of his pony and walked toward the woman.

"You will kill your horses if you continue to abuse them in this manner," Chased By Owls said. "You beg to rejoin the Indian world, and yet you treat your animals in a way that only a white could."

She smiled at the tall brave. "I had hoped to begin our new association without pretense," she said. "Chased By Owls has no interest in how much of an Indian I am or how I uphold the traditions of the Ponca or the Pawnee or any other of the pathetic man-women that once ruled this plain. He knows only that my return brings the money he needs to buy guns and that once in his *tipi*, I will perform acts for him that no woman—wife or concubine—would ever agree to."

"I see civilization has left Little Feather unchanged," Chased By Owls said. "One would think all that time in England and New York would have produced someone more understated, especially when speaking to a chief from whom she asks a new life."

Lady-Jane spat into the high grass. "Take my word, you were not my first choice. But as soon as my brothel in Manhattan began to show signs of success, the local madams conspired against me, telling all the wealthiest customers that my girls carried a kind of syphilis that only Indians get—one that would shrivel a white penis in a week. I couldn't return to Omaha. There, I'm considered not just a whore but a murderess as well. And so, my love, I come back to you—with a pocketbook that will keep you in Henrys and Winchesters, and an ass that can still provide enough pleasure to make you call the gods by name."

"Little Feather is blunt. But then she was always blunt and greedy. I expect for these treasures she will want certain things in return."

"Chased By Owls expects correctly," Lady-Jane said. "All that shit work that I was forced into the last time I lived among you? No dice. My hands have almost returned to the point where they could belong to a woman—and I will not risk their destruction tanning hides and hauling water while you and your cronies sit in *tipis* and smoke."

"This might not sit well with the other women," he said.

"Chased By Owls can make any excuse he wants. I'm lazy, I'm sick—he can even tell the truth if it comes to that. His women are his problem."

The tall brave nodded. "Anything else?"

"Yes. When the whites come—and we both know they will—I demand a fine rifle and a good horse. I refuse to be denied the chance to kill as many as I can. I care as little for my life now as Chased By Owls cares for his—and I have scores to settle that require payment in blood."

⋘◈⋙

Given the terrain, Lieutenant Randall Fix should not have been surprised at his situation. Before the contingent had left Fort Kearney, General Nelson Miles had warned every man.

"The country we go to is at the far northwest of the territory," Miles told his troops. "Chadron is a nightmare of forest, river, gully, and hiding-place. It is filled with what are called draws—little valleys like deep bowls. The enemy shall be perched at the top of these draws, waiting for us to explore the bottoms so that they may rain down their arrows and bullets. I tell you now; get trapped in one of those draws and my best advice is to get right with God."

Fix had listened in fear. Two days before, the renegades had sacked the Chadron settlement, taking every morsel of its food and ravaging the population. All the men had been killed. Women had been raped, as had children, male and female. There was even a story of a pregnant woman being cut open and her infant nailed to a tree and used as a target; such outrages could not go unavenged.

Now, from the top of a ridge, Fix looked down and realized just how difficult it would be to avoid death. Despite the warnings, the realities of combat had caused the soldiers to chase the savages into the pines and cottonwoods. Once inside, the Indians melted into the green, invisible until their rifles exploded from the trees. Men fell screaming to the forest floor; dead and alive, their hair was taken.

Pretending retreat, the renegades lured the soldiers down into the draws. Fix saw Private First Class Harold Murphy, his horse dead beneath him, raise his arms above his head as if could stop a hail of arrows with his fists. Howling in terror, his forearms and shoulders penetrated by long shafts, Murphy lowered his limbs. A tomahawk flew through the air and decapitated him. Already wounded, Corporal S. J. Bunch, whom Fix knew to be a fine and brave man, charged up the far side of a draw, firing at the renegades. He was cut nearly in two by gunfire. Randall watched as a Pawnee plucked Bunch's blue Stetson from his head and placed it on his own. Fix knew then that Miles's strategy was pure attrition: to break through the enemy's defenses over the bodies of his own men.

As his troops fell around him, Fix galloped down the ridge. "Skirt the high hills!" he called out. "Do not follow the savages. Anywhere they lead us will bring death! Bring them out! Fight them here!"

Below the White River, ground troops formed thick phalanxes. At the first sign of the Indians, they fired as one. Braves and horses tumbled to the ground. Some rose with axes and rifles and were quickly cut down, others simply offered themselves in prayer, dying with their gods on their lips. When the field was still, a dozen men ran toward the bodies, knives held high. Fix galloped forward in a fury, placing himself between the soldiers and the dead.

"No scalps, curse you!" he shouted. "Take even one and by God, if these Indians don't kill you I'll hang you right here."

The battle raged on, hour after hour. Cannon disintegrated trees; arrows bit necks of horses and men. The Chadron and Bordeaux creeks, filled with blood and bodies red and white, choked the Niobrara.

Exhausted and covered in gore, Fix slumped on his horse, his lips kissing the red-gold mane; his sword felt like a hundredweight in his hand. Staring at the ground, he wondered how great this victory would seem to the widow of Sergeant Ezra Petty, who lay just below his horse's left leg, Paiute knives through both eyes.

Fix wiped away tears. When his eyes cleared, he could make out General Miles in the middle distance, his sword raised, his horse rearing up against a mounted brave.

The Indian was tough and sinewy, colored ghostly white with a mask of black above his nose and crooked yellow patterns on each cheek. He wore a full bonnet of eagle feathers that reached nearly to the ground and was screaming loud and high.

Chased By Owls charged at Miles, his knife parallel to his body. He sliced into the general's blue coat, turning the sleeve purple. His terrified horse baying and whistling, Miles pivoted to the left, bringing his sword down hard on his enemy's wrist. Fix saw the red hand fly up into the air, the fingers seeming still to move. Chased By Owls' arm became a cannon of blood, spurting red at Miles—face, medals, and coat.

Chased By Owls took the reins in his teeth. His remaining hand reached down for a tomahawk and, with a bellow of rage, he hurled it at Miles. The general ducked his head and pulled his mount sharply to the right. The horse's neck burst as the tomahawk found a vein. Shrieking, it fell to earth, landing on the leg of the general, trapping him in the snow. Miles reached below his twisted body to find his revolver. His wrist now a geyser, the tall brave dismounted and pulled his lance from his saddle. Staggering closer to the trapped bluecoat, he raised it high above his head.

Miles's blast knocked the Indian off his feet. Fix later said it was as if someone has suspended him by wires. The general shot a second time. To the lieutenant, the big Army Colt sounded louder than the Gatling cannon shooting through the culverts.

Chased By Owls called out to the Wakanda and flung the lance with all he had left. He was dead before it landed.

Fix saw the lance strike the frozen ground. He rode toward the wounded General, hoping to reach him before the enemy.

His way was blocked by a demon.

It rode straight for him, ululating like a damned soul. Its horse was painted the red of a cardinal and smeared with green and red lines. Its face was half blue and half gray, and its lips were a deep blue-black. From every part of its clothing flew long fringes bleached white as snow. In one small hand, it carried a feathered stone axe, in the other a Henry rifle.

Saints preserve us, Fix murmured to himself, *it's a woman.*

The apparition threw the axe directly at his head. She missed by inches, but the action gave her time to raise the Henry to her shoulder. She cocked the handle and fired. The first shot whizzed by his head; the second grazed his shoulder. At the sight of his blood she grinned through the black lips, and to his astonishment, cursed him in perfect English.

"Son of a bitch! How's that? The next one'll lay you on the ground!"

She retreated a short distance, turned and fired again. The shell ricocheted off his metal stirrup.

"Ma'am!" Fix cried out. "The army is not engaged to fight women. I beg of you—retire so that neither of us is hurt further."

"You're the only one hurt, whoremaster. Besides, since when does a bluecoat care if he kills a woman? Except this time . . ."

She fired again.

". . . ladies first."

Her next shot went wild. Fix galloped hard to the left, convinced now that, male or female, the creature intended to destroy him. He rushed forward and grabbed the barrel of her rifle, pulling it from her hands. With a scream of rage, she produced a long knife and tried in vain to slash him. Turning his horse at her again, he ran straight in, closed his fist and struck the woman in the face. Her nose crushed to her face and ran red.

"White bastard!" she cried.

At the sight of his pistols, the woman whirled her horse and made for the trees. Fix hesitated for a moment. She was defeated, retreating. Would it do any good now to leave one more body in the valleys of Chadron?

He watched as she galloped into the distance. Amid the cacophony of gunfire he did not hear the single shot, nor could he have told who fired it or from where it came. What he saw was the she-devil falling from her horse, a mass of white buckskin and scattered fringe tumbling against the green of the pines.

41

ALEXANDER HERRMANN HELD A GLASS ABOVE HIS HEAD. HE toasted the bride, his cousin, his assistant, and himself. He toasted the people of London and the good mayor of New York City who had, only an hour before, bound him in holy matrimony. With each salutation, Julius Meyer offered health in a different language: *santé; l'chayim; prosit; skol; salud!* People throughout Delmonico's great dining room heard his joyful voice and joined him in his tributes.

"I believe," Alexander said, "that if it were submitted to the rigors of the scientific method, there would be incontrovertible proof that I am, at this moment, the happiest man in the city of New York."

"Hear, hear!" shouted Seamus Dowie, who had exchanged his champagne for a pint of black stout.

Julius held up a hand for attention. "Should I perhaps walk out to the street and accost the first scientist I see? I understand they may be recognized by thick spectacles and backs stooped from much study."

"Yes, that would be an excellent idea," Alex said. "The moment you find one, we'll give him a drink and give him a gander at the former Miss Scarcez here. *You, sir*, he will say, *must be the happiest man in all of New York*. Run and fetch him now, Julius—and bring that mayor back here, too. I expect he would fancy a good lunch, wot?"

Adelaide blushed. "Please, Alex. I should think you've embarrassed that poor man enough already. Pulling a roll of bills from his beard!"

"And why not? He's only a poor public official—and graft isn't what it used to be. Besides, my dove, he took it in stride. Laughed as hard as anyone else in the chamber, even the reporters. Still, I do hope I will have enough money for this party. When at last we got a moment alone, he asked me to slip the roll into his jacket."

Adelaide straightened in her chair. "He didn't!"

"He did—and *then* he asked if I could spare twenty ducats to the next show *gratis*. He apparently has five children and a wife plus some dozen favors to repay."

Seamus pounded the table, making the silver chime; Adelaide demurely placed her hand over her mouth and her shoulders shook. But Julius had been a serious boy who grew to be a serious man; the kind of laugh that takes one's breath and brings a sore stomach was not something Alexander had ever associated with his cousin. As he watched Julius laugh, Alex felt like one of those explorers who sight a rare bird; an occasion to be treasured all the more for its scarcity. When the rest of the patrons had gone and the waiters began preparing their tables for dinner, the quartet was still there, laughing and ordering wine.

"I owe youse two," Seamus said, rising and raising his glass to Alex. "I owe ya, boss, for your long employment and entrustin' me with the secrets of yer trade. It's not everyone would take in a poor ignorant from Armagh and make him keeper of the keys. I can only hope there's been sufficient givin' along with what I've took."

The Irishman now turned to Julius. As he toasted him, a small splash of black beer washed over the rim of his glass. A mist covered his eyes.

"And *you*, sir—well, I owe ya in ways I can only hope to repay as time marches—and I promise ya I will, though it take every day I've got."

Finally, with the light dimming outside, Julius looked at his watch and nodded to Alex. The magician took the check, frowned at the price, signed it, and called their bus-girl over.

"Young lady," he said. "Your service and that of your colleagues has been stellar. But I am not so sure about the kitchen. There are ingredients in the food that I am afraid should not have been there."

The girl, Scots and no older than fourteen, blushed bright red.

"Ingredients, sir? I am afraid I do not understand."

"Well, even offhand—there was this beneath Mr. Dowie's dessert dome."

Alexander removed the silver cover from Seamus's untouched plate. Inside was a large slice of cherry cobbler. The magician produced a long spoon and dug into the fragrant, bleeding pile.

"Voilà!"

From within the purple fruit, Alexander extracted a ring. It was a diamond approximately two karats in weight, set in a mounting of yellow gold. Adelaide checked her finger to make sure her engagement band was still there.

"Well, well, miss," Alex said. "This *is* quite the scandal. What would have happened if my friend Mr. Dowie here had bitten into this piece of jewelry instead of those tasty berries? Perhaps you or someone in your kitchen is missing a bauble now, hmmm?"

The waitress looked frightened. "No one in our restaurant has such a costly ring, sir. I would have seen it."

Adelaide put her hand on the girl's thin arm. "Enough, Alex! You're torturing the poor child. Allow me to apologize, my dear. My new husband enjoys playing tricks on people. Well, he'll think twice before he plays another one."

Adelaide reached toward Alexander, plucked the ring from the spoon, and pressed it in the palm of the waitress.

"For you, my dear. And may you wear it well. Come, Alex."

Alexander protested, but his new wife took him by the sleeve of his coat. Seamus Dowie howled; and if it was true that the Great Herrmann had never seen Julius Meyer truly laugh, now would have been a good time to look at him.

⋘◇⋙

The Pennsylvania Station was crowded. Even though the snow had thickened outside, the crush of passengers made the station hot and close; it smelled of hair oil and wet wool.

"You can still change your mind, you know," Alexander said to Julius as they stood with Adelaide at the station gate. "I can think of a million things you could do here in New York, even if you don't want to work for me."

"Thank you, cousin," Julius said, clapping his hand on Alexander's shoulder, "but I've been away from home too long."

"Home! *Omaha?* What kind of home is it where you are surrounded by *meshugenah goyim* with guns? *Gutenu*, Julius! What do you need it for? Prophet John is trustworthy—he can run your business. Stay here and get to know your own kind again. We might even scare up a bride for *you* someday."

361

Julius shook his head. "No, Alex. I don't belong here. My real *landsmen* are back in Nebraska and being treated worse every day, even worse than we were in the old country. The few advocates they have are poor devils like Crook, who only knows their greatness from killing them most of his life. Maybe I can do better. At least I can give them a voice. As for a bride, I don't think so. The woman I love is, shall we say, out of reach. Besides, you're in no position to recommend the institution. It's four in the afternoon—and you've only been hitched up since ten. I suppose now you'll finally show the world that Substitution Trunk?"

Alexander shook his head. "No, dear Julius, I think not. Yes, it exists thanks to the brilliance of Mr. John Nevil Maskelyne. As he is making money hand over fist with his toilet, he is more than willing to lease it to me—exclusive, of course. But alas, it is not my invention and therefore no longer my dream. I understand he is currently negotiating to sell it to a young man—a rabbi's boy out on Coney Island, name of Erich Weiss."

"Never heard of him."

"Calls himself Whodoonoo or something like that."

The big door of the gate slid open. A fat conductor appeared and began to announce the stops.

Adelaide put her arms around Julius and pressed her wet eyes to his coat.

"You will give our love to John McGarrigle. And you will promise to be careful. They say there is death a thousand times in your West."

Julius shrugged. "There was once. But I think before long the horseless carriages and flying machines I read about will replace the pony and the eagles and hawks. The white man has learned to eat the rattlesnakes. Harder to die in such a place."

Julius gave Adelaide one more embrace and then took the hands of his cousin. Alexander kissed Julius on both cheeks and stepped back.

"Do you remember the day we first came to America?" he asked.

"The *Balaclava*, Alex."

"It was sometimes all I could do not to throw you overboard. Every day you made a mockery of your gift—fooling this one, tricking that one—seeking revenge from strangers because the gentiles had so hurt you and all our people. I saw you humiliate them by becoming them, watched you deny who you were."

Julius looked over at Adelaide. She had begun to weep.

"But you were changed by America. I don't know, maybe you didn't want to become your brother, perhaps it was Prairie Flower or even old McGarrigle. But as an Indian you have become the best Jew I have ever known. Go to your people, *kleiner* Julius. Help them as no one helped us—and maybe our God and theirs will bless you both."

"Chicago Special! Board!"

Alexander reached behind Julius' ear. He pulled his hand back quickly, closed it into a fist, then opened it to reveal a silver dollar crowned by an Indian's head.

Julius picked up his carpetbag, turned and headed toward the platform. Alexander noticed that the bag was the same one his cousin had carried on the *Balaclava*. Framed by the entrance, Julius turned and waved. Adelaide and Alexander returned his farewell. They kept looking after him until all the passengers passed through the arch and the gate clanged shut.

⬦

The little house was more than two weeks into construction. Normally, framing a place so small would have taken about half that time, but the white foremen assigned to the job quickly discovered that the Ponca way of looking at progress tended to extend established deadlines.

It wasn't that they were lazy. Far from it. It was only that the idea of appointed times and strict rules was alien to them. In their world, when a lodge or *tipi* needed building, it went up as needed, the various construction chores dictated by who happened to be present. The white tools also were strange: the hammers and saws, the screwdrivers and steel nails. It was days before the Indians were convinced these little iron animals wouldn't bite them at the first opportunity.

Through a warren of just-felled trees, Standing Bear sat on a large stump, his head wreathed in smoke. He had never been an impressive man. He lacked the height and ferocity of Chased By Owls or the weighty authority of Voice Like A Drum. But now, Thomas Henry Tibbles thought him smaller still—as shrunken in body as he had become in influence. The white buckskins swam on his arms; and the great necklace of claws appeared almost comical on such an aged brave.

Standing Bear greeted Tibbles with a nod of his head.

"The Speaker. Has he arrived?"

"I received a cable from him when I was in Omaha last night," Tibbles said. "He should be here soon. He asked that I tell Standing Bear that all of the rites regarding his mission had been carried out correctly and with great respect."

The chief frowned. "That is good."

"It looks like it is going to be a fine house for you," Tibbles said, gesturing toward the structure.

Standing Bear was silent for a long time. The wreath of smoke around him dissipated and he tapped his pipe on the side of the stump.

"I have often said that I would like to have what the white man has. To live in a house such as he has, with a pump for water and a fireplace for warmth—to have my children and my people learn his language and know the many things that he knows. You have written these words in your newspaper, and the other newspapers have also carried these words. And now it seems I will get my wish."

"That is fine," Tibbles said.

"It is. But it is a white wish. To have a white wish come true is only fine when it is no longer possible to be an Indian. I may keep my buckskins and my Indian face. I may pray to the gods that have helped and protected me throughout my life. But while I live in my fine white house, where will those gods live? Where are their houses? They lived in flowers and in elk and buffalo. But if there are no flowers, there can be no flower spirit. And if there are no buffalo, there can be no buffalo spirit. I suppose now I will need some new gods. Maybe a spirit of the fireplace or one that provides for a kitchen table. Or perhaps such functions can be assigned to the Man Nailed To A Tree. They tell me he hears all prayers."

"Perhaps Standing Bear will discover that with peace, there will be a way to return to the old ways."

Standing Bear smiled. "We have seen what your people do to those who prefer the old ways. When my great friend Three Stars failed to find Geronimo, he was called back here. They sent General Miles— Apache Killer—to Arizona and Mexico to find him. He went and Geronimo surrendered. Apache Killer returned here to find Chased By Owls. Chased By Owls would not surrender. He said the Ponca had no word for surrender. I think now that word is written."

As Standing Bear and Tibbles gazed at the house, a brave working on the roof began to cheer and shout. Throwing down his hammer, he leapt to the ground and ran in the direction of the river. In seconds, all the Indians on the site joined him; they threw down saws and tossed tiles in the air. Soon, the frame was empty save for the two white foremen who stood bewildered inside its wooden skeleton.

Standing Bear and Tibbles followed the braves. When they reached the Niobrara, they saw what looked like a parade coming toward them.

At its center was a large truck-wagon drawn by four matched blacks, their breath visible in the crisp air. Holding the reins was a small man in buckskins smoking a white man's pipe, a red and white blanket wrapped around him. Next to him sat an older white man with long gray hair and a beard. On either side of the wagon rode braves armed with bows and rifles, *bandoleros* crisscrossing their chests in the Mexican style. All around them now, the workmen were celebrating, leaping and crying and shouting prayers. The small man pulled up on the team and saluted in greeting. Then he leaped from the seat into the arms of the chief.

"Father," he said, "it is good to be with you."

Standing Bear clapped Julius Meyer on the back and shook the hand of Prophet John. They both embraced Tibbles, who laughed in relief at the sight of them.

Standing Bear raised his hand and the entire party fell silent. The Indians bowed their heads. As Tibbles removed his broad-brimmed Stetson, the old chief jumped up onto the wagon and looked into its wide bed.

Its bottom was covered in plain gray blankets. Carefully placed atop them was an oblong shape, perhaps five feet from end to end. It was wrapped in a magnificent robe, tanned to a rich gray-brown and painted with six rows of mounted warriors. These were drawn in simple outlines—as if to better see their souls—and their horses were rendered in red and green and gold. The robe was bisected by four holy sun symbols: black and white concentric circles quartered by a yellow cross with a red bull's-eye dead center of each. Standing Bear ran his hands over the buffalo hide. Long ago, this robe had been his, a relic of a time when it was still possible to be an Indian.

Stiffly and slowly, he made his way down from the wagon. Tibbles thought he had aged ten years in the few seconds it took to inspect his daughter's corpse. Then he gestured toward a young boy.

"Bring the women."

The boy raced toward the large *tipi* that held Standing Bear's two remaining wives, their sisters and daughters and their few small children.

"I reckon we're about to have a funeral," the prophet said.

"Reckon?" Tibbles said. "I'd think that a great clairvoyant like you would know at least that much of the future."

The Prophet smiled. "No more visions for me, Tommy boy. I haven't had a decent visitation nor seizure since merry old England. Sure, I can still predict sun or clouds from a Sunday 'til the week's middle; but anything more momentous, well, no longer at your service. I suppose I needed the world I used to live in to have 'em. But in a world with no wonders, it's hard to be magic."

"You sound like the chief. He just told me pretty well the same thing."

McGarrigle nodded. "Well, maybe I'm more magic than I think, if I can see into the brain of ol' Ponca Kingy. Still, I've often said if it weren't for the honor, I'd just as soon not fall down, foam at the mouth, and shiver like Saint Vitus. It's a hell of a strain on a man. A hell of a strain."

"Did you two ever find Bear Shield?"

"We looked. Went straight to the spot where they planted him, but all we found was snow. The dirt 'round his pit had been rolled out smooth as grandma's piecrust. Figure they must have put him somewhere on a flood plain and the good ol' *Wakanda* decided he needed baptizin'—washed him clean away to where some fishes or beavers had him for supper. Either way, he's with the ancestors and little Flower—or at least he will be once we're done with her today."

"I heard Lady-Jane fought like a man at Chadron; dead, too."

"Only heard she was hit. Dead? Can't say. I know one thing for sure, though, Tommy boy. For the sake of anybody she calls an enemy, I hope so."

A contingent of men emerged from one of the work *tipis* dressed in the best they had. Carefully, they lifted Prairie Flower from the wagon box and bore her to a bare tree near a rise. The men danced and prayed, the women wept and keened. Watching the ceremony, Prophet John shook his head. He could remember when a funeral was an event—even among a tribe as small as the Ponca. The entire village would be present and honored guests from allied tribes would come bearing gifts for both the living and dead. Now there was only this handful to see the young spirit into the next world.

The men carrying Prairie Flower placed her among the branches of the little tree.

"My daughter, thanks be to god, has returned to the Niobrara," Standing Bear said. "She has been too long in strange earth. Therefore, she shall remain above ground for a time so that she may look out upon the trees and plains and the river and know that she is home with us. We pray today also for Bear Shield, whom god has decided to hide from us. I thank the *Wakanda* for all he has done and ask only that the price my children paid buys peace."

As always, Standing Bear gestured toward Julius when interpretation was needed; after all, the gray man and the three white supervisors had attended the rites and shown proper respect. It would have been impolite not to translate his words for them.

But Julius could only look at his father. Inside him, no words came. None in English; nor in Ponca or Dakota or Lakota; none in Yiddish or Russian or French or German; none in Polish or Spanish or Ukrainian. Standing Bear gestured again, but Julius only stared at the little tree embracing the body of his betrothed.

Then he saw the women. As they cried and moaned, they rocked back and forth, seeming to bow and bow again to the only power that could end their pain. Soon, Julius found that he too was bending at the waist, swaying and weeping. Perhaps it was only the chill of the day that caused him to pull his blanket up over his head; but if he could have seen himself, he would have marveled at how much he resembled the old men of Bromberg: the saints and zealots who bowed over and over, pulling at their beards and covering their eyes beneath the eastern wall of the great synagogue.

And then, as automatically as he had begun to *daven*, he chanted; the words seeming to be spoken in the only language he had ever learned.

Yis-ga-dal v'yis-ka-dash sh'mei ra-ba,
b'al-ma di-v'ra chi-ru-sei, v'yam-lich mal-chu-sei
b'chai-yei-chon uv'yo-mei-chon . . .

May his great Name be exalted and sanctified,
In the world He created as he willed.
May He give reign to His kingship,
In your lifetimes and in your days.

42

JULIUS MEYER LOOKED THROUGH THE OPEN WINDOW OF HIS second-floor apartment and took a deep and happy breath. He was sure he had never seen a more glorious day; but then he had always loved May in Omaha. The snow and cold had gone, but it remained cool enough to wear one of his hand-tailored suits.

He picked his bowler off its hook by the door and descended the narrow steps onto Twelfth Street. Outside, the sun was warm and the air bracing. The flower boxes in the windows were alive with crocus and star of Bethlehem.

Over forty years, Omaha had become a busy place, and Julius smiled at the bustle. The electric tramcars were filled with people en route to work and school. There were still plenty of horses about—Julius knew most of their names—but in the past year more and more of Mr. Ford's monstrosities had begun filling the streets. Many of his old friends were appalled. The machines threw up dust, they said, and frightened the milk from their cows. Besides, what use was a contraption that wouldn't run in the Nebraska muddy seasons? Julius viewed the motorcars in a somewhat different light. He was general agent for the Provident Life Assurance Society now; and anything that cost a man $850.00 was damn well worth insuring.

He turned at Farnam Street and walked through the doors of Max Meyer & Co. Unlike the city, the store had changed little in the years since its founding. It carried more merchandise—more exotic cigarettes and cigars, and now books as well as eastern magazines—but the display cases and shelves, the floorboards and signs were where they had always been.

Max himself had changed in that he was himself, only more so. Never a happy or talkative soul, he had become further withdrawn after the huge fire that destroyed his big department store in 1889. He was nearly wiped out in the Panic of '93, and when the ensuing depression shuttered the Indian Wigwam, the little cigar store was all he had left. The shop's receipts were insufficient to earn both brothers a living, so Julius had turned to the Provident. With his connections to all of the city's business and cultural elites and his status as a man of respect and reputation, he was soon writing more business than any other agent between Ohio and California.

Julius didn't expect a greeting from Max, and he was not disappointed; his brother looked up from his newspaper only long enough to ascertain that whoever had entered didn't intend to rob the place. Julius went to the cigar rack, picked out a ten-cent panatela, and brought it to the counter.

"Lovely day today, *mein brudder,*" Julius said. "You really should try to get outside."

Max grunted, took a dime from Julius, and dropped it in the cash box.

Knowing this was all the conversation he could expect, Julius saluted his brother with the cigar and turned to leave.

"*Kleiner,*" Max said in Yiddish, "this came for you this morning."

"Here? If they wanted to send me a letter, why didn't they just mail it to the office?"

"Business ain't so bad I'm already a fortune teller," Max said. "All I know is the little Stebbins kid ran in here and said a man gave him a dime he should deliver this. When I asked him *what* man, he just said 'big' and ran out."

Julius took the envelope. It was of standard, inexpensive business grade stock. The paper inside matched. It read:

May 8, 1909
Dear Mr. Julius Meyer,

> I am new to the state and will be engaged in some business here—cattle and sheep, mostly.
>
> I have been told that you are the man to see on all matters pertaining to business in Omaha and for that matter, all of Nebraska.
>
> My affairs will require not only your wise counsel, but a considerable investment on my part in life, health, livestock and vehicle insurance for myself, my family and my employees.
>
> It being a fine day, I ask that you meet me near the fountain in Hanscom Park at noontime. I sincerely hope that this rendezvous will produce results mutually beneficial.
>
> Very truly yours,
> I. M. Gael

"Well, this is welcome. I've been a little lazy of late. Perhaps my sloth is being rewarded."

"You used to work for me, remember?" Max said without humor. "If lazy was rewarded, you'd be president."

Julius walked out into the sunshine and checked his watch: 10:30—plenty of time for a late breakfast. He crossed the street to the building that had once been The Big Cheese; it was now the home of a spotless new Harvey House, one of many that the ambitious Fred Harvey Company was building across the West.

He walked inside. The head waitress, a ruddy-faced girl named Henrietta Johnson, greeted him warmly.

"Good morning, Mr. Julius. Such a fine day."

"A fine day, indeed, Miss Johnson. Gives a man an appetite."

"Well, hearty appetite then, sir. I can of course, seat you anywhere convenient, but I'm pleased to inform you that Mr. Eli has just this moment ordered, and I expect you might enjoy joining him."

"By all means. Thank you, Miss Johnson."

The young woman led him across the tastefully appointed dining room. At the sight of his nephew, Eli Gershonson rose. Henrietta took their drink orders, placing their coffee cups in different positions, and vanished into the kitchen.

"Such a nice girl," Eli said. "And such a classy place. Sure beats hell out of the old Cheese. Fights, whores. The food was good, but that place was a shithouse, a *surichah*."

"Food's good here, too, Eli."

"That's because they kept Doris on. Much more decorum here, though—he hasn't brained anyone with a skillet since they took over."

As if by magic, their drinks arrived: coffee for Julius, tea for Eli. The positions to which Henrietta had moved their cups had notified the "drink girl" as to their preferences.

"So nice," Eli said.

"Very efficient," said Julius.

Henrietta came back and took their orders. Julius took a celery stalk from the plate on the table and broke it in half.

"So, Eli, last week Max told me you're retiring. I almost fainted."

"Nobody needs a peddler anymore," Eli said. "Anything they want they can buy here in town—and if they can't, they order it from the Roebuck. You know that place Mick Rodney is building out by Mill Road?"

"I've seen it."

"Roebuck catalog—the whole thing. Doors, windows, floors, all sent to the railhead to be snapped together like a child's puzzle. Sometimes I think civilization is overrated. Old McGarrigle would have just shook his head. Which reminds me . . ."

Julius's face expressed pain. "Please, Uncle Eli, not this again."

"I'm just looking after you, lad. Just doing what the McGarrigle asked me to. So, are you keeping watch?"

"Eli, this is absurd. Prophet John is dead these nine years. And yet every time you see me you ask 'are you watching yourself,' 'are you keeping your eyes open?'"

"Julius, the old man had his last vision for you. Had that last big fit and died. Had it and said 'Watch hard for the salt bear,' and then crawled to where I stood and implored me to watch over you."

"Jesus Christ, Eli! It's nine years on! Besides, you may have noticed that the white man has done a pretty good job of wiping out every bear around here, black or brown. There's never been any grizzly and I'm pretty sure there's never been anything called a salt, either. Anyway, he was shaking and foaming and writhing worse than I'd ever seen him. I could hardly understand a word. To this day, I still think he said *sot*. That would make a lot more sense in this place."

"All right, all right. I'm just, *kana hora*, trying to carry out a dying man's last wish. So, please. Be careful."

Their breakfasts arrived, huge and piping hot. They ate in silence for a while, and then Eli smiled.

"You know, Julius, this is the very same table where I used to meet Lady-Jane Little Feather—she should rest in peace—for breakfast every morning I was in town. That was before the Nickel & Dime fire—before all those girls died and Mack Swain went crazy. It feels like it was before . . . everything."

"You were lucky she liked you," Julius said, biting into a biscuit. "I've seen what she could do to those she didn't."

"Oh, Julius, you don't remember. You don't remember how she looked coming down that stairway dressed in green or gold. But what's the use of talking? It's forty years ago. She's been dead a long time."

"Nobody's seen her dead, Eli. Only shot. When they rooted out the last of Chased By Owls's army she was never found. If she had been, they'd have hung her with the rest. But I guess she *must* have died that day at Chadron."

"And what makes you so sure, Julius?"

"Because it's eighteen years since Chadron and I'm still alive. And with Compars and Alexander both dead, no madwoman ever had better cause to kill a man than Lady-Jane did me."

⊰◇⊱

Unlike the stone and concrete waterspouts in most public places, the fountain in Hanscom Park looked as if God had created it, not man.

It sprang directly from the center of the park's man-made lake; a jet of water twenty feet high formed its center, with two smaller sprays at its base. It was a popular place for citizens to meet. On Saturdays, the shore near the fountain often saw people standing two deep—and Sundays after church it was the favored assignation point for the city's lovers.

But this was a Monday. Few would visit the park today, at least not until after the school bells rang. Waiting for Mr. Gael, Julius saw only a single dog walker heading toward the Woolworth Avenue gate.

Julius sat down on a bench. He looked at the fat geese that had just migrated down from Canada and watched as their ducking heads made ripples in the water. He followed the concentric rings as they widened out from the gray bodies, until they led his eyes to a tall figure emerging from behind the park's main pavilion.

He was thin, even gaunt, and walked slowly, dragging one leg. Beneath his black bowler, his hair was long; steel gray streaked with rust. His face was a pale, pure white, deeply lined and with a blaze of freckles across the nose and mouth. He had drinker's eyes: the green irises turned milky and the whites shot through with veins. Beneath them, the skin was stretched and baggy, long wrinkles radiating from their corners and down each cheek. Like the eyes, the nose was swollen and veined, but the fine lines here were blue, not red, and they flowed over bumps Prophet John always called "gin blossoms." His black suit hung on him like a funeral shroud.

Julius stood up and approached the stranger.

"Mr. Gael."

"Yes," said the man, his voice soft and with a lilt of Erin. "I am the man what wrote ya the note."

"Well, I am pleased to make your acquaintance," Julius said, "and I welcome you to Omaha."

Gael wheezed heavily and coughed into a handkerchief Julius could see was already stained with blood. "I am afraid, Mr. Meyer, that once ya've learned the nature of my business, ya may not be so willin' to greet me as ya suppose."

"I hope that will not be the case," Julius said. "If I may say so, it has always been my greatest pleasure to solve problems that seem insoluble, and I hope that I may do so for your family and your business."

Gael coughed once again into the handkerchief. Julius saw a blot of red explode from the thin man's mouth and spread across the white linen. Gael wiped the blood and saliva away and pocketed the cloth in his breast pocket. When his hand emerged again, it held a pistol.

"Thanks in great part to yerself, Julius Meyer, I have no family—no wife or children—no business or home or health. Because of ya and yer conspirators, I have had no love but a memory since the year of eighteen-eighty and three. So now, I come to collect upon the debt what you established when ya took from me my precious jewel."

Julius stared into the ravaged face. "I am sorry if you have found such misfortunes, Mr. Gael. But I cannot imagine how I could have any hand in them. I believe I would remember if I had seen you before. You are not the sort of figure one forgets."

For the first time, Gael smiled. His teeth were yellow-brown and narrowed at their tops; there were gaps and stumps across his gums.

"Have ya not, now? Well, perhaps ya might indulge me by takin' a closer look at the ruin what stands before ya. Imagine it without the consumption what eats away at its insides like a rat through grain— without the gray skin and diseased leg. Use yer fine imagination, Mr. Meyer! Broaden the shoulders from the hunched bumps ya see. Whiten the teeth and straighten the carriage. Then wash the sad gray from my head and replace it with hair red and thick as a nest a' cardinals. Do all that, Julius Meyer, and then speak the name of the wretch before yer eyes."

Julius' mind raced. He was tempted to do as this sick, sad man had asked if only to perceive the reason for his threat; but he had spent too much of his life defeating death to be distracted by an enemy's request. As he stared at the cadaverous face, he carefully calculated the distance between himself and Gael and the difference in their respective strengths. Perhaps a frontal assault might allow him to avoid a direct shot or, failing that, escape with a wound that would allow him to live. Perhaps a kick would dislodge the gun; or a handful of dust foil the accuracy of his enemy's aim.

Then, as if he were standing beside him, Julius could hear the warning of the dying John McGarrigle.

Beware, young Julius. Keep your wits about you. Watch hard for the salt bear.

"My God," Julius said in horror. "You are Seamus Dowie."

"The same," the gaunt man croaked.

The selt bear. Now, at last, the words made sense. Seamus Dowie, the Irishman—*the Celt*—once big and powerful as a grizzly.

"I see," said Julius. "And you have come to kill me."

Dowie limped forward. "And who with better right? If not for ya and yer cousin, I would today be a happy man—livin' the life what was meant for me and consort of a princess. Instead, I have wandered the world, drinkin' and starvin'—waitin' for whatever would take me to her in the life after. The Lord has seen fit to make that death slow and agonizin', but no matter. When my princess next sees me, I shall be as she knew me, straight and strong—not this pitiful creature spewin' gore."

"You confuse me, Seamus," Julius said. "You speak of Princess Noor, yet you knew she was an imposter, a fake—an Indian disguised as royalty for the pleasure of a mob."

"It was as a princess I knew her and as a princess I loved her," Dowie said. "And just as I'll appear to her as the boy she knew, so she'll be to me: an A-rab girl—flyin' her veils and chimin' her cymbals. If not, then, as the poet says, what's a heaven for?"

"My God. It was *you* that tied Compars Herrmann to that stake at the Egyptian—you who tried to kill him."

"Yes."

"But I don't understand. If you knew the princess was kidnapped and who took her, then surely you must have hated Alexander even more than me. It was the two of us who carried out the plot—why didn't you try to kill him or me for what we did? Why Compars?"

Seamus Dowie gave a bitter, brown smile. "One had nothin' ta do with the other. I took ol' Carl and set him up to be shot so as to ruin Alexander. I figured nothin' would do it like the killin' of his brother, his rival what he hated. I even had a diary forged and ready for the police. 'Today, I kill my brother,' and so on, written in Alexander's own style. Compars would be dead and unable to testify, your Alex would rot in prison for murder, and I'd be free and clear with the one I loved. Then you came along and rescued the old fool.

"As for me knowin' who was behind the princess's kidnappin',' ya overestimate my abilities. I only discovered your deception weeks later, drownin' my troubles in a waterfront bar. A sailor, deep in his cups, told me about the bound Indian girl aboard his ship, H.M.S. *Sofia*—and of the curly-haired little man what brought her aboard. Even such a rude boyo as me could suss out the rest. Straightaway, I went from there and tried to shoot Alexander, but the drink made me fail. Alex's connections at court—that whore, Lady Caroline fucking Carstairs—got the trial closed and kept it all out of the papers. Our Great Herrmann never even showed up—they trumped it up as an attempt on that wee shit, Billy Robinson—and I rotted twenty-five years in the Dartmoor where I picked up the little pixie what now devours me from the insides out."

"And then Alex cheated you again," Julius said. "A heart attack at fifty-two."

"Aye. So with him dead, I settled on yerself, bucko. I shoveled shit and bounced drunks in Dublin. I worked the hole on a smuggler in the Caribbean, all to earn me passage here. All to bring me face to face with the little Christ-killer what done me out of life."

The opening Julius had been looking for was a small one: only a slight shifting of the pistol to Dowie's right that put his body out of the line of fire. In that instant, Julius brought his boot up toward Seamus' groin. With surprising speed, Dowie pulled back and avoided the kick. Both feet back on the ground, Julius planted himself to deliver a left to his enemy's jaw but was stopped short by a pain above his heart. He fell to his knees, staring straight ahead. His chest was warm where the bullet had penetrated. He brought his hand before his face; his fingers were red.

Wheezing, Dowie stepped forward and crouched down, looking into Julius's dark eyes.

"You're dead, Julius Meyer, as dead as I am, though I'll walk a few more days. I don't know what next world awaits the Jew, but if it's Hell, I'll not greet ya there. What I done this day is righteous—and the righteous are permitted retribution without sin."

As if the gun weighed a thousand pounds, the gaunt figure raised it to the temple of Julius Meyer. In his mind, the Speaker prayed in a patchwork of Hebrew and Ponca. He asked all Israel to hear him and alerted the *Wakanda* of his coming.

Seamus Dowie cocked the pistol and fired.

43

WITH JULIUS MEYER DEAD ON THE GROUND, RYLAND Norcross did as he was instructed. He went in search of Dr. Henry Ball, heading first to the two taverns mentioned by Constable Palmer.

At Marty's, a dive on eleventh, the bartender said that he hadn't seen the physician since the previous Friday, but if Ryland should see him first, would he please tell him to come by and settle his tab. Brian O'Hair, the day manager of an only slighter nicer spot called The Smiling Irishman, said that the doc had been in around nine that morning for some hair of the dog, but that he hadn't seen him since he walked out an hour later.

Dr. Ball's office was only a few minutes' run from the Irishman, on the second floor of the drugstore building. Dashing inside and rounding the broken balustrade, Ryland took the steps two at a time and sprinted down the long hallway to the office. He knocked at the door and waited. A minute passed and he knocked again. From behind the frosted glass, he heard a single cough—not the dry, shallow bark of a cold sufferer, but a moist, reverberating hack built on the poisons of a lifetime.

"All right, all right," said a voice from behind the door, "I'm coming."

A shadow filled the glass and the door opened.

Dr. Henry Ball stood blinking in the doorway. He was a small man, not much over five feet, and he wore the thickest spectacles Ryland had ever seen. His hair, white at its roots, had been dyed so black that the small amount of light allowed to penetrate the office brought blue highlights to its strands. His suit was brown and rumpled and his cravat stained by food and red wine. One shoe was covered by a gray spat, one not. A heavy, acrid odor accompanied him into the hallway.

"Yes, yes. What is it you want, boy?"

"Constable Palmer wants you to come quick, Doctor Ball," Ryland said. "My dad, too. There's a man dead over near the Fountain and they want you to come see to him."

"Dead, eh? Dead how?"

"Well, he's been shot. Gun's in his hand. Constable thinks he done it to hisself."

"Himself," the doctor said.

"Beg pardon?" Ryland said.

"*Himself,* young man, not *hisself.* Did it to *himself.* I understand you are excited—but a possible crime against a citizen is no excuse for a definite one against our language."

"Sorry, sir."

"All right, boy. Come in."

Ryland ventured into the gloom. The odor he had first detected in the hallway became strong, almost overpowering. In the near-darkness, the boy started to notice small, yellow-green lights, some still, some moving. As his eyes adjusted he began to discern their source: cats—large and small, old and newborn, fat and thin, alive and dead.

"I fail to understand why you have called on me. I was of the impression that the county employed the esteemed Dr. Watkins for such investigations."

"Constable Palmer said to get you, sir."

"He did, eh? All right then, young fellow—just give me a moment to find my bag and take my medicine."

Doctor Ball searched through one of the piles that littered the space. Some were comprised primarily of clothing, others of objects: pots, glasses, syringes, and empty bottles. There was also a mound dedicated solely to household trash and garbage: everything from discarded newspapers to denuded chicken bones. An unmade cot in the corner made it clear that at some point in his practice, the doctor had made the office his home, as well as a sanctuary for felines as lost as he was.

"Ah, here we are! My medicine."

Ball reached toward a low table covered in ashtrays overflowing with the butts of cigarettes and cigars; toward its back stood a bottle of amber liquid with no label. Lemuel, Jr. immediately recognized it as firewater—the false whiskey illegally sold to the local Indians. Produced from grain alcohol and a few herbs for flavor and color, it was the harshest and cheapest beverage available on the plain, cheaper even than beer. His father had always told him that once a white man resorted to it, he had lost all self-respect and could expect a sordid death at any moment. Ball took the bottle, upended it, and took a long pull. The motion created a flurry of shorthairs in the room. Lemuel, Jr. could see them dance against the single shaft of light struggling between the windowsill and shade.

Replacing the bottle, the doctor put on his hat and retrieved a dried-out medical bag from a chair near the door.

"*Tempis fugit*, my boy," he said. "All in Omaha know the Ball motto: quick and friendly service—e'en for the dead."

Ball opened the door. Ryland bolted though it and down into the street. As he stood in the dust, gasping for air, he heard the sound of wet, coughing laughter descending the stairs behind him.

⤏◇⤎

Constable E. Seymour Palmer had never been inside the home of a Jew before; he hadn't needed to.

In general, Omaha's Hebrews didn't get into trouble: no drunken fights, no beating of wives, no children breaking windows. Most of the time, they kept to themselves; and when he did have an interaction with them, it was as victims, not perpetrators. In fact, Palmer always said that if all the people he had to police were Jews, he could put his feet up and shine his badge.

Still, the contents of Julius Meyer's apartment surprised him not at all. It was more Indian *tipi* than Jew temple; a fitting environment for a man who had spent forty years of his life helping the red man to make sense of the white. There were shelves filled with elaborate belts and moccasins, and glass-fronted cabinets displaying jewelry of many tribes. On the north wall, stretched out like a master painting, was a magnificent buffalo robe; on the south hung framed photographs of The Speaker himself, posing with the great chiefs of his day: Sitting Bull, Spotted Tail, Red Cloud, and at least a half dozen poses with Standing Bear. The place was neat and orderly, with hardly a speck of dust anywhere; and every object had been preserved as if for a museum.

Constable Palmer walked into the parlor. Seated at Julius's immaculately organized desk he could see a small figure silhouetted against a window. The man was stooped over in what could have been taken for either concentration or grief. Laid before him were a few of the papers the deceased had left behind.

"Good evening, Mr. Eli."

Eli Gershonson turned toward the voice and smiled to see the policeman.

"And a good evening to you, Constable. Is there anything I can do for you?"

"Well, I was told you were here. My family and I offer our sympathies about Mr. Julius—and in the present circumstances, I had hoped there was something I could do for you or the members of your congregation."

Eli stood and shook hands with Palmer. "No, thank you, Constable. I believe we have my nephew's affairs in hand, although it will be a job of work to sort through all these things. As you know, our beloved Julius had no wife or children. He named me executor, so I suppose it's up to me."

"No will?"

"Just a note telling me to dispose of everything as I see fit. His attorney informs me that he left no other documents behind."

"It's certainly a handsome collection of artifacts," Palmer said. "I suppose you could sell it at auction to benefit yourself or your temple."

Eli sighed. "Unfortunately, Constable, this stuff doesn't bring much anymore. I've been trying to sell it from my wagon and, mostly, there are no takers. I suppose it's seen as old-fashioned—something from a bygone era that doesn't fit in with telephones and typewriters. I suppose I'll sell some, try to return a few of the nicer pieces to Julius's Indian friends and make gifts of the rest. Maybe you would like something?"

Palmer blushed and shook his head. "I'm afraid a man in my position can't afford to take presents—appearance of impropriety. You understand."

Gershonson shook his head.

"Mr. Eli, I was wondering if there was anything you or Mr. Max or your people wished me to do from here."

"From here?" Eli said. "I'm not sure I'm following."

"Well, the way your nephew died—the two bullets in his body. That's one more than we usually find in a suicide. And the doctor who made the determination, I only used him because the county told me to. Not to cast aspersions, but I don't think if you or me had a choice, he'd be the doctor we'd go to. So I just thought that you might want me to take a bit of a look-see to find out if anything—what's the word—*untoward* occurred."

Eli nodded again and ran his hands over a huge headdress fashioned from the skull and horns of a bison.

"Constable Palmer, do you know why my nephew kept all these things?"

"I imagine that he felt a great affinity for them—having spent all those years as a friend of the Indian. Old-timers around here like to say there was a time when Julius Meyer was more of an Indian than Sitting Bull."

Eli laughed quietly. "That's probably true. He lived where they lived, ate what they ate, their enemies were his. At one time, he even was set to marry an Indian girl—very nice, from a good family. But all of that isn't why he held on to these things. No."

Eli opened one of the cabinets and removed a headband woven of gold and set with lapis lazuli. He arrayed it across his hand and held it up for Palmer to see.

"He kept them as a warning. To remind himself that if God turns his head at the wrong moment, an entire people can disappear. They can be killed in the thousands—their art and their ways taken from them and their children turned into slaves. Even those left alive can disappear, made invisible by shame and grief—forced to walk like ghosts among their own murderers. This is not only the world of the Indian, Constable—it is the kind of world we came from, Julius and Max and me. We came to America to keep from disappearing—and arrived just in time to watch it happen to someone else."

Gershonson crossed the room and sat back down in the chair beside the desk.

"Thank you very much, Constable—but my co-religionists have decided it is better that you do not investigate my nephew's death. Competent medical authority has determined that he took his own life—and the little handful of souls that make up our Temple has decided that is good enough. They also make much of the fact that Julius died yesterday and our custom dictates that he be buried by tomorrow. At least this is what they say."

Eli ran his palms across a letter in his nephew's hand and then turned his head to look directly in the lawman's eyes.

"But the truth is, they are afraid. They are worried that if they make too much noise or demand the justice that is due a *real* American, it will not be—what is the phrase?—'good for the Jews'—and that God will then turn his head as he did from the Indian and before they know it, two other men like ourselves will stand in a room filled with torahs and menorahs and prayer shawls and speak of how *they* disappeared and isn't it a shame."

Eli replaced the headband in the case and shut the glass door.

"No, Constable Palmer. We will bury our dead and say our prayers and leave you to keep the peace."

From the stairway, Gershonson and Palmer could hear a loud clatter—the sharp sound of boots bounding up the steps. As the noise reached the second floor, young Ryland Norcross appeared in the doorway, his face flushed red.

"Hello, Mr. Eli," the boy said. "I was told in the street that you was lookin' for me and that I was to come up here."

Eli raised his hand in greeting. "Yes, Ryland. The congregation and I wanted to thank you for all the help you provided the constable and the doctor on the day of my nephew's death. You were quick and brave—two things a man needs if he is to do well in a country like this."

Ryland turned more crimson. "It wasn't nothin,' Mr. Eli. I just did what my Pa told me. 'Sides, Mr. Julius was always real nice to me since I was little. All the kids thought a lot of him."

"Nevertheless," Eli said, "I am the executor of my nephew's estate—and as such I have been charged with the disposition of his property. I'd like you to look around here and pick out anything you like."

Ryland's eyes grew wide. "For true?"

"Yes," Eli said, "Anything you like. A buffalo head, a bow and arrows, a blanket, a war bonnet—anything."

Ryland looked at Eli and then at Constable Palmer. The policeman nodded as if to give his permission, and the boy began to silently rummage through the treasures: a Springfield rifle, its stock carved in Lakota symbols; a pair of moccasins beaded to form a butterfly; a yellowed necklace of long bear claws.

"If it's all right," the boy said, "I'll take that."

Eli pulled a key from his pocket, crouched down, and carefully unlocked the glass door of a low display case. From its second shelf, he removed a brown cedar rod about sixteen inches long, hollowed out and punched with six holes. At one end, it was curved like the beak of a swan—and near its mouthpiece was whittled the horned head of an elk. Perhaps among all the things in the home of Julius Meyer, it was the most beautiful—intricately carved and painted, and decorated with eagle feathers.

"What is it?" Ryland asked.

"They call it a courting flute," Eli said. "At one time the braves used to play it for their women. Julius used to sell quite a few of them when he had the store. It's really not much compared to a lot of things you could have, son. Are you sure it's what you want?"

"Yessir," Ryland said. "If it's all the same."

Eli Gershonson closed the glass door, stood, and handed the flute to the boy. Ryland's eyes lit like fires at the sight and feel of its fine sculpture. He smiled, thanked both men, and descended the staircase.

As he walked into the street, the sun was beginning to set. Shops were closing their doors all along Farnam, and men were entering the saloons. In the distance, he could hear the calls of mothers announcing supper and the happy excuses of children unwilling to give up the day.

Ryland Norcross put the flute to his lips and blew a lonely note into the wind.

EPILOGUE

JULIUS MEYER ACCOMPLISHED MUCH BETWEEN THE TIME HE became an Indian interpreter and his death. By 1896, Julius and Max (and their two additional brothers, Adolph and Moritz) established what became a virtual retail empire in Omaha, selling just about everything for the home from cigars and pianos to jewelry and furniture. During this time, Julius founded Omaha's first symphony orchestra and opera house and was one of the founders of the synagogue now known as Temple Israel. He is buried there. In addition to Standing Bear, Julius also counted other famed Indian chiefs among his friends. They included Sitting Bull, Swift Bear, Spotted Tail, and Red Cloud and he was the interpreter for many more. Julius was known to speak at least six Siouxan dialects and possibly more. He never married. Julius

Meyer was found with two bullets in him in Hanscom Park in Omaha on May 10, 1909. If he was indeed murdered, his killer has never been found or even searched for. To this day, his death is officially recorded as a suicide.

ALEXANDER HERRMANN was the most famous magician in America before Harry Houdini and was well known throughout the world. He still holds the English record for most consecutive sold-out nights by a single performer. His stage illusions and close-up magic were among the most innovative of their time. Alexander was also famous for his practical jokes. Once while dining with comedian Ben Nye, he produced a diamond ring from beneath a lettuce leaf. While Alex was laughing, Nye gave it to their waitress (the incident formed the basis for the story in this book in which Adelaide offers up the bauble). He lived in a fabulous mansion called Herrmann Manor in Whitestone Landing, Long Island and owned the yacht *Fra Diavolo*. In 1896, he died of a sudden heart attack in Great Valley, New York. He was fifty two. Alexander Herrmann rests at Woodlawn Cemetery in the Bronx. Although there is some evidence that Julius and Alexander were related (Alexander's mother's maiden name was in fact, Meyer), and the historical record shows that they knew each other (the performance and attempted murder of Alex at the Ponca camp is a true story), the idea that they were first cousins is purely conjecture on the author's part.

STANDING BEAR (Mah-chu-na-zha) continued to travel and lecture on Indian freedom, often sponsored by the great abolitionist Wendell Phillips. He was supported in his cause by other famous Americans of the time, including the poet Henry Wadsworth Longfellow. Today he is one of Nebraska's greatest heroes and has several places named for him in the state, including an elementary school in Omaha. His final days were spent with his surviving family on a small settlement near the Niobrara River. Standing Bear died there in 1908 at age seventy four. He is arguably the most politically important Indian in American history.

ADELAIDE SCARCEZ was born in London to Belgian parents and trained as a dancer. After meeting Alexander Herrmann at age twenty two, she moved to the United States and married him in a ceremony presided over by William Wickham, the mayor of New York. Adelaide assisted her husband in his act for over twenty years, from the time before their wedding until his untimely death. Initially aided by Alexander's nephew, Leon Herrmann, Adelaide became a famous and respected magician in her own right, continuing her husband's act and adding much new material of her own. "Adelaide, Queen of Magic" practiced her art until 1928. She disappeared for good in 1932, aged seventy nine.

COMPARS HERRMANN was considered the greatest magician of his time. He is largely credited for the Mephistophelean look of black goatee and devilish eyebrows associated with stage magicians and still copied by conjurors to this day. After turning over his magician's mantle to Alexander, Compars retired to Europe; but the panic of 1873 ruined him financially and he was forced to return to the stage, thus becoming a competitor to his much younger brother. In order to preserve their relationship, they divided the world, with Alexander taking the Americas and Compars, Europe. Compars Herrmann died in Karlsbad, Germany in 1887. While the two brothers had their differences, nothing in the Herrmann family history indicates Compars was anywhere near as evil as the villain of this book.

PRAIRIE FLOWER was one of many who died on the Ponca Trail of Tears. Her date of birth is unknown, but she was probably the eldest child of Standing Bear and his first wife, Gra-da-we, who died about the time the Civil War began. Her funeral was a rite of rare cooperation between Indians and whites. Hearing that she was near death, the people of Milford, Nebraska arranged for a Christian Burial. A Mrs. Borden washed her body and her husband, a local carpenter, built a coffin for her. Mrs. Mary Walsh sewed a new dress for Prairie Flower and Mennonite women brought flowers to decorate her grave. The cause of her death on June 5, 1877 was probably tuberculosis. Her resting place is unmarked today. Some accounts say that Prairie Flower was married to a brave named Shines White and was the mother of two children; others claim that "Shines White" was actually the name of her mother.

MAX MEYER continued to be an important businessman in Omaha and was well respected. He founded the Commercial Club (forerunner of the Omaha Chamber of Commerce) and was a principal of the Omaha Savings Bank. His businesses prospered until a fire destroyed his main store at 16th and Farnam Streets in 1889. He was wiped out in the depression of 1893 and spent his last years in New York City.

GENERAL NELSON MILES, after successfully defeating Geronimo in 1886, became the battle commander during the Lakota Ghost Dance uprising of 1890 and was largely responsible for the massacre of approximately three hundred Sioux at Wounded Knee. In 1895 he became Commanding General of the United States Army, a post he held throughout the Spanish-American War. Although he retired in 1903, he offered himself for service during World War I but was rejected because of his age. A Medal of Honor recipient, Nelson Miles died in Washington, D.C. in 1925 at the age of eighty five. He is buried in one of only two mausoleums at Arlington National Cemetery.

GENERAL GEORGE CROOK, after a long career fighting Indians, was ordered to the Arizona Territory to handle the rebellion of Geronimo, only to be replaced by his rival, Nelson Miles. After this campaign, President Grover Cleveland promoted him to major general and put him in charge of the Department of the West. In this role, Crook became an advocate for the tribes, taking their part in treaty disputes, land disagreements and policy decisions. In 1890, General Crook died of a heart attack in Chicago, aged sixty two. He too is buried in Arlington. Upon the general's death, the Oglala chief Red Cloud said "he, at least, never lied to us. His words gave us hope."

JOHN NEVIL MASKELYNE carried on with his magic and his inventions. He was also the author of *Sharps and Flats: A Complete Revelation of the Secrets of Cheating at Games of Chance and Skill.* Along with Houdini, Maskelyne was a member of the Magic Circle, a group that researched and exposed fake mediums and spiritualists. Maskelyne's son, Nevil, became a magician, as did his grandson, Jasper. Maskelyne died in 1917 at age seventy eight.

THOMAS HENRY TIBBLES was a champion of the Indian cause all his life. Tibbles witnessed and wrote about the Wounded Knee massacre and worked as a Washington, D.C. reporter at the end of the nineteenth century. He married Suzette LaFlesche (known as "Bright Eyes"), the Omaha woman who interpreted for Standing Bear at his trial. He eventually returned to Nebraska to edit the *Independent* newspaper and was the Populist Party Candidate for Vice President in the election of 1904. Tibbles died at eighty eight in 1928.

BILLY ROBINSON (William Ellsworth Robinson) went on to have a considerable magic career of his own. Beginning as "Robinson, the Man of Mystery," he eventually found his niche as the "Chinese" magician Chun Ling Soo. He was so careful about hiding his Caucasian identity that he never spoke on stage and used an interpreter when talking to reporters. He died in 1918 when, due to carelessness, he was fatally shot while performing the Bullet Catch. He was fifty seven.

Lady-Jane Little Feather, Prophet John McGarrigle, Chased By Owls, Eli Gershonson, Seamus Dowie, Doris, Ryland Norcross, Lemuel Norcross, Constable E. Seymour Palmer, Adrian Calhern, Dr. Henry Ball, Half Horse, Voice Like A Drum, and Isador Hamerschmidt are fictional characters.

ACKNOWLEDGMENTS

THERE ARE MANY PEOPLE WHO SUPPORT AN AUTHOR during the writing of a book. I am always amazed that through the long process, they continue to listen, care, and give sage advice even when they have far more important things to do.

As usual, my wife, Joan Weiner, was my rock. She calmly went about her business while a wild-eyed neurotic went mad in the next room, agonizing over each noun and adverb. She never offered a single helpful suggestion until she was asked to, and then her contributions were brilliant. I am lucky to have her love and counsel.

Our children, Kate (the anthropology doctoral candidate) and Ned (the fledgling screenwriter) Kolpan, to whom this book is dedicated, make me proud every day. They were also fine editors, slogging through the longer versions of the manuscript and doing it with a smile. Thanks to them, the book is better (and shorter).

As she did with my first novel, *Etta*, my agent, the amazing Katharine Cluverius, encouraged and supported me from the first page, and her edits were invaluable. Still, it seems that every time I write another book, Katharine has another baby. Last time it was the lovely Grace, this time the handsome Jonathan. I'd take some credit if it weren't for the esteemed Jerry Boak, educator, cookbook author, and Katharine's husband. I'm writing another one, kids. Get ready.

Katharine left the agent business in 2011, but left me in the capable hands of the dynamic Kate Lee. Thanks very much to her and everyone at ICM.

Like Katharine, Robin Rolewicz Duchnowski, who edited *Etta* at Ballantine, also has a baby every time I write a book. Except this time, she had *two* while also editing a book by Katie Couric! With all this, Robin took the time to look *Magic Words* over, only this time strictly as a friend. Many thanks.

At Pegasus Books, my editor, Maia Larson, made *Magic Words* a far better book than the one she bought. Also thanks to my visionary publisher, Claiborne Hancock, who believed in Julius and Alexander from his first look. Michael Fusco's jacket design exceeded all expectations, as did the lovely interior by Maria Fernandez. Jonathan Rubin of Studio Nine, Philadelphia took the author photo. Also, a tip of the red pencil goes to copy editor Philip Gaskill.

As always, web guru Jacob Smith of Dinkum, Inc. came to my rescue when a great website (and the advice on how to use it) was needed. Felix Widjaja carried out the beautiful design as he did on *Etta*.

Margie Smith and Todd Wall of Little Window Video shot the video interviews that appear on my author home page and across the

Internet. I've worked with them for over twenty years and they are as fine artists are they are true friends.

Five excellent books were key to my research for *Magic Words*: *Jews Among the Indians* by M.L. Marks; the indispensable *Illustrated History of Magic* by Milbourne Christopher; *The Plains Indians* by Colin F. Taylor; the fine Standing Bear biography *I Am A Man* by Joe Starita; and *The Magic Brothers*, a charming book about Compars and Alexander Herrmann by I. G. Edmonds.

Also invaluable were Mary Jo Miller, Linda Hein, and the staff at the Nebraska State Historical Society, who provided me with essential information on Julius Meyer. Much obliged also to Tanya Elder of the American Jewish Historical Society for digging up further articles and lore on Julius's life.

My old friend and *consigliere* Dr. Charles Hardy of West Chester University not only knew all about immigration to the Philadelphia Lazaretto, but also took me to see its remains. I rewarded him by naming a character in this book after him and then having the character slaughtered. Charlie was delighted.

Jennifer Pankoke and Stephany Thompson of the Willa Cather Foundation were generous with their time when I needed help identifying and authenticating photographs of Julius and the Indians. Gary Rosenberg, archivist at the Douglas County, Nebraska Historical Society unearthed the photograph of Julius Meyer and Standing Bear that serves as the frontispiece of this book. I'd been looking for it in vain for two years. He found it in five minutes.

The incredibly personable Barb McDaniel at the town office in Chadron, Nebraska, put me on to Tom Buecher, who runs the Ft. Robinson Museum. Tom gave me great details on the topography of Northwest Nebraska and what the Indian wars were like there; heartfelt thanks to both of them.

And now, ladies and gentlemen, some applause for Tom Ewing, historian *extraordinaire* of the Society of American Magicians, who gave me the lowdown about magic shows of the late 19th century.

This tall tale couldn't have been told without the help of the friends who gave the various drafts a peruse prior to publication: Pancho and Linda Carner; Ron Cohen and Lisa Moroz; Doreen Hardy; Beryl and Jeff Rosenstock; and Bruce Schimmel. A special thanks goes out to Denise Goren, who always reads my early efforts with the dedication of a book lover and the eye of a detective. *Magic Words* was written in loving memory of Denise's husband, Steven Waxman, who died just before I began this story. Steve was a great lawyer and an even greater friend.